MIRANDA MONTROSE

Happy Reading

Miranda Montrose

Kindred Embrace

Model: Mikey
Photographer: Eric Battershell Photography
Editing: Team at Red Quill Editing. LLC
Formatting and cover design: www.formatting4U.com

Acknowledgements

I would like to take this opportunity to say thank you to the readers that have begun their journey into the Kindred world with me. My main goal is to take you away from your normal day to day life and give you an escape.

I need to say a special thank you to my husband, Dale, for putting up with me and occasionally using him as my personal fact finder. He's faster than the web on certain topics. Thank you to my daughter Cheyanne for some of her insight and also, I'd like to say thank you to my personal trainer Stefano Sarge for at times giving me advice if a scene troubled me and help me through it besides being an awesome personal trainer. There's no one like you. Thank you to my fellow Valley Forge Romance Writers group for I would have been lost if not for your guidance, and to those that have beta read for me. Your input is invaluable.

Table of Contents

Chapter 1

Fates, this is sickening.

Steffan Lavelle held Raquel Dulcati close on the couch, kissing her temple as he pressed his head firmly against her's; inhaling the lemon- lavender scent of her hair. *Fates, she smelled good.* He desperately wanted to remember everything about her in this moment. He wanted to remember how her hair tickled his cheek, sitting next to her, the way she smelled, the sound of her heart beating in her chest, and her human warmth. In a few minutes, he'd erase anything she knew related to his species of Kindred. He'd however would remember everything they'd shared together. He had to send her away in order to keep her safe, but this was slowly killing him.

He'd began to view Raquel as a ray of sunshine in his lonely, dreary world of secrecy, and he relished every minute of it.

Until a day ago.

He'd taken Raquel out to the edge of the Lavelle property in Bayou Cane, Louisiana, and hadn't paid attention to how close they'd gotten to the property line. A chitterling screech forced him to glance up into the sky. They were being watched. A little more than a hundred yards away, Alpha Tavia had landed in her hawk form and shifted.

Raquel had stood her ground against the female's insults to Steffan regarding having a *human* on the Lavelle property. Tavia threatened Raquel's life, and once he told Roman everything, Roman gave him the choice of turning Raquel into a Halfling or erasing her memory and allowing her return to the human world.

He hated the Kindred Law.

If a human discovered the existence of Were-shifters, they were to be killed or have their memory instantly erased so they could be sent back to live out their natural lives, oblivious to his kind or be turned into a Halfling.

There were no choices in the matter. It's still unknown if the other Alpha had told any of the other Commission members about his relationship with a human.

The fear of losing her gripped him. He hadn't meant to fall in love with her.

He thought back to when he first met her. He'd been in his panther form and was coming back from hunting prey in the bayou when he heard the car pull up. His brother and Alpha, Roman Lavella had told him another human would be visiting his First Mate, Genevieve and Steffan was to give her curtesy. Genevieve was helping Raquel with her wedding. He hadn't had time to shift and changed so he hid in the embracing shadows of the bushes.

She had been trying to get a box of loose flowers out of the back of her white Jetta. It was stuck. Normally he would've stayed where he was but an urge to help her persisted. He snuck over to his Porche, willed the locks to disengage, shifted to his human form and put on the pair of jeans he kept in the car for such an occasion.

Raquel's beauty had struck him stupid and instead of asking her if he could lend a hand, he stared at her when she turned to face him. Her eyes were so blue he thought he was looking into a crystal pool and saw his own refelction. Finally, he managed to motion towards the box and when she nodded, he quickly grabbed it and easily pulled it out from the confining space of her car.

He made sure to stay away from her after he set the box down in the front sitting room of the house and it wasn't until he saw Alpha Genevieve and Raquel being kidnapped from the house by Alpha Dupree, that he tried to intervene. It still stunned him he leapt onto the hood of a speeding limosine to try and stop the bastard.

Steffan, along with Roman and Connor went to Dupree's house to rescue the females but in the malee, Raquel had sustained a head injury and Dupree had marked her but gouging his claws into her back. He'd ripped a portion of her skin from between her shoulder blades almost down to her waist.

He took a deep, steadying breath to quiet the memories and calm his racing heart. Her hair was clean and she'd been using the lemon-lavendar soap he'd given her.

He remembered how shocked everyone was because he'd voulunteered at night to change the dandages on her back. Genevieve wanted to take her to a hospital. Steffan explained to her the pard would treat her injuries and if she survived, then and only then would it be considered taking her to a hospital for treatment.

During the initial months Raquel recuperated, she'd remained unconscious and antibiotics along with the herbal remedies Ascenza used had barely brought the infection under control, but continued to rage on. Steffan was worried when she spiked a high fever.

Steffan made the decision to use a small amount of his enzyme to speed up recovery. Even though he understood the risk it would be to her.

If he gave her too much of the enzyme, she'd die. If he gave her too little and it stayed on the surface of her skin, it would close the wound and heal the damage that had been done. However, if he gave her enough of it, it would be able to enter her bloodstream causing a chemical reaction to start and she'd end up bearing a Mating Mark of blue and black curly-cues depicting she belonged to a Lavelle on her back—to him and thus would have to give her more of it in order to turn her into a Were-panther otherwise she'd be killed.

Alpha Roman and Cristoff had ripped into him for using his enzyme on Raquel. He hadn't given a damn as to what they thought. There was no way he was letting another human die on his watch.

Then a miracle happened. One day he opened one of the blinds in the bedroom she'd occupied. Her eyes fluttered as soon as the beam of sunshine illuminated her face. Her hair was fanned in a tousled mess across the pillow. Her voice croaked, and her eyes looked around, confusion warped in her expression on her face

Relief flooded Steffan and it took time for her to heal and in that time he let his guard down and fell for her.

Until Alpha Tavia's threat and then darkness graced his soul and the fear of Raquel being killed because she was a human, also brought back haunting images of how his former mate, Michelle, had been murdered. All because she had been human and the notification, he sent out to the Commission letting the powers that be know Michelle had been turned, didn't reach the Commission in time.

The taste of fear and helplessness triggered his panther to send Steffan messages about keeping Raquel safe, and protecting an innocent female; was overwhelming.

He'd be damned if anything happened to Raquel now. This was why she had to go back.

He pulled Raquel closer, as close as he could and rubbed her back with the palm of his hand. The pads of his fingers gently brushing over the raised edges of the scar through her thin shirt.

His heart sank.

Fates, how could he wipe her memory of five months' worth of information? Not just of his pard but of him as well. His stomach clenched at the monumental task.

No, he had to let her go. It was time. She'd be safer.

"I'm sorry, *bébé*. It has to be done. There's no other way."

Raquel winced and pulled slightly away from Steffan to look up at him, her bright, shimmering blue eyes pleading with him.

Steffan captured her small wrist and glanced down to study her delicate hands. He couldn't bear seeing the hurt reflected in those orbs.

Mindlessly he caressed over the tiny, pulsating vein with his thumb.

Fates, I wish there was another way. I feel like another part of me is dying.

Raquel murmured, "Will I be allowed to at least remember parts of you? Of us?" She caressed the side of his face, but he pulled away. He let go of her wrist, planted the palms of his hands on his lap, and swallowed.

"You'll know I am Genevieve's brother-in-law. That's all. I can't risk you remembering anything more. Anything we've shared over the past few months will be gone."

"So, the scar on my back you healed with your enzyme—"

"You won't remember how it was healed."

"Steffan, you've helped me heal, not just physically, and I've fallen for you."

This was *not* supposed to happen. How could *this* happen? *Why* did this have to happen?

His Were-panther pushed forward, and felt the sting of his eyes shifting.

"I'm not going to remember your eyes changing color from brown to blue, am I?"

"No. I'm sorry."

He sensed his panther sending him images of him transforming

4

so Raquel's small hands could roam all over his body, stroke his fur. His skin tingled with the urgent need to shift.

He drew in a calming breath. "*Bébé*, no. Once I erase the knowledge of the cell you and Genevieve were locked in, Alpha Dupree changing into a lion, my pard shifting, all of it, especially how Dupree gouged the middle of your back, you'll be much happier."

And a part of me is going to die because of it.

Steffan shuddered as cold air rushed down his bare back. He had forgotten he only had on jeans. This was how he had been dressed when he first met Raquel, and he figured it would help anchor the image of him when they first met.

Steffan turned in time to see his brother, Alpha Roman, and Roman's Mate, Alpha Genevieve, shift from their Were-panthers to humanoid form. Roman's eyes narrowed and flashed to gold, pinning Steffan to where he sat on the couch.

Oh yeah. Big bro was not happy Raquel was still here. She should have been gone hours ago; instead, Steffan had stalled as long as he could. He didn't want this day to end.

Steffan's temple ached, and he allowed Roman to mindlink with him.

"*I thought you were going to wipe her memories before we got back.*"

Annoyed, Steffan replied, "*I thought it would be wise to explain everything to her before I wiped her memories.*"

Roman stated out loud for everyone to hear, "If you won't, then I will."

Steffan grunted his frustration.

And there it was. *Roman's not happy she's still in the house, and now he thinks I can't do my job. I shouldn't expect anything less.*

"Mine Alpha, I said I will do it."

Raquel's sharp gasp was like a knife piercing his flesh.

Alpha Genevieve wriggled into a short black dress, sat next to Raquel, taking a hold of her hands.

Raquel pleaded, "Gena. Why? I'm happy here."

Genevieve wrapped her arms around Raquel.

"This isn't goodbye. You'll see me at work; we'll still get together and have our girls' night outs. The only thing you'll know is that you and Keith didn't get married, and you won't remember

5

anything related to the Kindred world. Raquel, it's for your safety as well as ours. I'm sorry. The other alternative is for you to be turned. You'll get used to—"

"No. I shouldn't have to be turned because I know about Kindred in general. I have a life, but I'd rather stay here with Steffan."

Steffan was looking at Raquel but observed Roman out of the corner of his eye. The muscle in his right cheek ticked, but his eyes had turned brown with gold rimming the irises. Roman drew in a long breath.

Steffan was unprepared to see Roman express frustration and Steffan shot through the mindlink, *"So this isn't easy for you either?"*

"No, Steff, it's not. Listen, I understand why you are hesitant to erase her memory, but it needs to be done. I would have done it had you not used your enzyme to heal her back. If I do it now though, there could be repercussions. Your enzyme is running through her blood She's imprinted on you."

Steffan quirked a brow.

"Seriously? Back when she was unconscious, you would've risked her dying from her infection?"

Roman's growl echoed through the mindlink. *"Damn it, Steffan, you know once a human receives the enzyme, they are automatically imprinted on that Kindred. I think you did it on purpose to keep her here!"* He jerked on a pair of trousers.

Steffan glanced back at Raquel. Perhaps his brother had a point, but all Steffan had been interested in was keeping her alive, and his gamble had paid off. Raquel's wound between her shoulder blades was closed, albeit with scar tissue, but she had healed nonetheless.

A small part of Steffan was angry enough to consider contacting a witch and have her resurrect the bastard Dupree just so he could kill him slowly. Dupree's claws had struck her, and to Steffan, it resembled some type of mark.

He couldn't protect his former Mate, Michelle, and the claw marks on Raquel's back were a reminder of his inability to protect her as well.

"You know, Mine Alpha, I could take her to a neutral territory."

Roman glowered. Steffan was just as pissed off and frustrated as his older brother was and he couldn't help himself and goad the male by using the formal Mine Alpha in his brother's presence.

"You'd be giving up your Beta status, any funding from the

6

House of Lavelle, and because you're still alive, there won't be anyone able to take my seat as Alpha, should anything happen to me. The House of Lavelle would cease to exist. No, I won't allow it."

Steffan growled low.

"Steff, I understand your frustration, but a Beta cannot freely go into a neutral territory without consequences. You know this. Besides, Cristoff would have to be voted into the Beta position from pard members, and that could take up to a year."

Raquel abruptly stood, her anger undulated off of her in waves and Steffan sighed. She paced around the room until she stopped in front of Roman. His brother stood a foot and a half taller than her but that didn't phase her.

"Fuck you, Roman; you're a jerk! I want to stay with Steffan! I don't understand why I need to lose what I know about all of you!"

Roman just stood there, eyes flashing with gold rims around the irises. A hint of fear wafted from Raquel to Steffan but he was proud of the way she stood her ground. He knew Roman would never harm her but Steffan went to her and pulled her back from him anyways.

Genevieve replied, "You won't lose the friendship, but parts of your relationship with us will change. It's going to be all right."

Raquel frowned; anger shone brightly upon her face as she turned to her best friend. "I don't agree. I should be able to continue my relationship with Steffan. You have no right to do any of this!" She growled. "It's my life!"

For a human, her growl was damn near sexy.

Roman sighed, shaking his head. "Look. This needs to be done. Your life is already in danger, and Alpha Tavia will make good on her threat. I'd hate to make her an enemy. Tavia has been known to force her weight around at Commission meetings, and I would have to kill you." Roman slowly came closer to Raquel, and Steffan fought the urge to beat the crap out of his older brother.

Fates, the instinct to protect Raquel had gotten stronger.

Steffan held up his hand to ward off his brother. "Roman—"

Raquel jerked away from everyone, pacing back and forth from the window to the opposite wall where the family crest hung above the French mahogany doors.

"I don't like it. I don't understand it, but then again"—Raquel sent Genevieve an accusing glare—"I thought I was your best friend."

"You are, hon."

"But it's glaringly evident I'm not one of you. I'm not going to be changed, no matter what. I'm human. So since *it* has to be done, do it and get it over with!"

Cristoff burst through the doorway. "Roman, Alpha Fievel is pulling up the driveway. Tavia went and—" Cristoff paused in shock once he noticed Raquel and pointed at her. "What's *she* doing here?"

Raquel rolled her eyes and clenched her fists at her side. "Oh for God's sake, Cristoff, go to hell!"

Cristoff gawked, his mouth opening and closing; words seemed to escape him.

Steffan snorted. *Kid brother speechless, that's a first.*

Roman quickly said, "Steffan, get to erasing Raquel's memory; you've run out of time. Cristoff, once Steffan is done with his task, help him take Raquel home."

"What are you going to do?"

Roman's level stare hit Steffan. "Genevieve and I will stall Alpha Fievel. Hopefully, with his age, he won't be able to smell Raquel's scent." Roman placed Genevieve's hand in the crook of his arm.

Genevieve smiled at Raquel. "I'll see you at work. Love you, Raquel."

Raquel chewed the inside of her cheek but only nodded at Genevieve as they left the office. Once the door was shut, Steffan sighed.

Fates, how he wished there was another way.

"So what do I do? Do I stand? Do I sit? Where do you want me?"

Cristoff coughed. "Well, I'll wait over by the bar. But hurry up. This is like watching water boil, and I have a poker game to get to."

Steffan rolled his eyes and motioned for Raquel. She stood her ground.

"Raquel, come to me. We don't have much time."

He deliberately wanted Raquel to come to him of her own free will. If she did, her mind would be easier to get into; if she didn't, and he went to her, then it would be painful, not just for her, but for him too.

A few seconds ticked by before she gave in. "I'm here. Now what?"

8

Thank the Fates she chose.

Steffan wrapped his arm around her waist, his palm splayed flat against her lower back, and drew her close. He knew every dip and sensual curve. The close proximity allowed him to monitor whether or not she was in pain. If all went smoothly, she would likely fall into a deep sleep, and he could sweep her into his arms to carry her out to the car.

"Is this necessary?" Raquel's voice softened, staring up at him.

"Yes. I want you to look into my eyes, take a deep breath, and let it out slowly." Steffan smiled when she did as instructed. "Listen closely to the quiet and the stillness of the room. The only sound you hear is my voice. Listen... listen... your body is getting heavy... the only thing you know is me... your heart is slowing... calming... that's it... release the tension on the next breath."

"Steffan—"

"Sh-sh-sh... no talking. Only *listen* to my voice and my breathing. I want you to breathe when I do. Let me guide you. Give me your trust and breathe."

The smell of the lavender and lemon soap she used tantalized him. The sun shone through the large bay window, illuminating her warm skin. Raquel looked up at him, the depth of her blue eyes drawing him in.

Steffan stilled. He'd always known she had a lot of spunk, and found it alluring. She was a brilliant female, and he admired her strength.

He had to admit, it took guts to stand up to Roman and call him a jerk and live to tell about it.

Raquel's brows drew downward.

She didn't have to say anything, and he didn't need to hear her say the words *what are you doing* to know she was getting impatient for this to be over and done with.

Steffan never thought he'd ever be in tune with another female ever again. He wanted to wait a little longer and explore the possibility of—.

I need to complete this before I go down a rabbit hole.

"Raquel, breathe with me."

He slowly inhaled, counted to ten, and then exhaled slowly until his lungs screamed for more air. He repeated this a few times until her body started to lean into his embrace, and he slipped into her mind with ease.

Time stood still for him.

The serenity he experienced when linking with Raquel's mind was like none other.

Time flew as he wiped and rewired memories together, and when Raquel sagged in his embrace, Steffan scooped her up into his arms.

Cristoff said, "'Bout damn time. For a moment, I thought you were having sex via mindlink." He flashed a wicked smile then drank the rest of the blueberry martini.

Steffan growled. "Remind me to kick your ass after we take her home."

Cristoff's snarky reply was thick. "Tsk, tsk, tsk. Don't tell me you like her."

Steffan ignored Cristoff. He didn't want to admit anything. As long as she returned to her human world, she would be safe.

"Let's get her back to her apartment."

The hardest part about letting her go? He'd never be able to forget what they shared—no matter how many centuries passed.

Chapter 2

Two months later

Raquel frowned at the back of her hand. A drop of red cranberry juice had splashed onto her skin, and it slowly followed along the vein to the side and clung to her skin for dear life. The drop stayed suspended for a few minutes before freefalling in slow motion into a small pool of juice on the counter.

A sudden wave of uncomfortable warmth enveloped her, along with the crisp image of a gray floor in a cement block room with cream-colored walls. She glanced up and noted bars, perpendicular to the floor, lined along one side. Just beyond the bars was a cement staircase leading up to the first floor. Something warm covered her hand. Looking down, she saw blood.

Her ears began to ring, and her head hurt like a bitch.

Raquel squeezed her eyes shut against the pain and prayed the headache wouldn't last long. When she opened them, her hand still was covered in blood. She blinked hard and fought the nausea until she was able to breathe. In a few seconds, the nausea abated and her vision miraculously cleared. She stared at the red cranberry juice.

The image of her in a cell and blood everywhere flickered for a time, interchanging with the Emergency Department's staff lounge, and then it was gone.

This is getting annoying.

Nervously, Raquel glanced around the breakroom in confusion. She still stood in front of the counter. Not in a cell with bars. But it had been so real. Every time she thought about the cell, her nose tingled like there was a damp, mildewy aroma. For some dumb reason she remembered she'd lost a shoe.

She viewed her feet. Two white shoes covered both.

Why is this happening to me? Did I see it in a movie on Netflix?
I must be losing my mind.

11

Or maybe it was time to switch to first shift. Working third meant she slept during the day, and with the new neighbors next to her apartment making a ruckus, she'd had very little sleep this past week.

An exterior spotlight illuminated the tree outside the window, drawing her attention. The branches swayed gently in the light breeze, calming the disorientation she felt. Some of the buds were already opened and formed the shape of a butterfly.

Raquel remembered there had been a Mopane tree outside the Airbnb she rented in Africa.

Africa. She loved Africa. The next time she traveled out of the country, she wasn't going to go alone. The safari took a lot of energy out of her, and she hadn't been able to shake the tiredness from her system. Unless it was a virus or something.

Even the trip didn't make much sense. *Why did I go alone? I was supposed to get married, and the trip was supposed to be our honeymoon. Keith and I broke up; I went anyway. The wedding was supposed to be in October and—* Raquel glanced at the budding greens again— *now it's spring? Good grief! I'm losing my mind.*

Raquel shook her head. She kept losing track of time, and it was so not like her.

A hand touched Raquel's shoulder, and she nearly jumped out of her skin.

Raquel quickly turned to see Genevieve and sucked in a relieved breath. God, the woman was a stealthy as a cat. When did she get here? Better yet, how did Genevieve know she was on break? They were working in different sections of the ED tonight. Raquel hadn't seen Gena since the start of her shift in the locker room. Come to think about it, Genevieve *always* managed to be around when things weren't going right. She'd been Raquel's saving grace since she'd returned to work.

She's always around... Raquel's stomach lodged itself in her throat. *Oh no. Is Gena keeping tabs on me? Is she reporting back to the charge nurse?*

Gena's probing stare was more curious than accusatory.

"Raquel? You're awfully jumpy tonight. Are you all right? You've been staring at your hand for five minutes."

"Y-yes. I'll be fine. I think I'm sleep deprived from the sixteen-hour flight home."

"That was over a week ago. I would've thought you'd be back to normal when you came on shift tonight."

Genevieve's warm smile barely met her eyes.

She is watching me.

Raquel hesitantly smiled back, poured the juice down the drain, and tossed the cup in the trash. She'd thought the sugar would help with the brain fog, but fresh brewed coffee would work better. *Especially if it'll keep me from making any more mistakes.*

"Gena, I'm glad to be back to work, and next time I decide to take a vacation for six weeks, remind me not to." She barked out a frustrated laugh. "Honestly, I'm having a hard time tonight. I haven't been sleeping too well. Nightmares have kept me awake most of the day—as well as my new neighbors."

Genevieve hugged her. "Do you need to talk about it?"

Raquel shrugged. "No. Not really. I mean, I feel like I'm having an out of body experience, and then I get a killer migraine." She sighed. "It's hard to explain."

She rubbed the side of her head, and out of the corner of her eye, Gena blanched. Okay, not the reaction she'd expected.

Genevieve chewed the corner of her lip. "Well, let me know if you need anything. You know you can talk to me about anything. 'Cept talking me into dying my hair purple again."

Raquel snorted. "I haven't seen your hair that color since nursing school. Yeah, that didn't turn out too well."

Genevieve was more like a sister to her, and she knew she could count on her anytime. But for some unknown reason, Genevieve was "there" every time something went wrong. And the notion bothered Raquel.

I'll talk to her about it later. No sense in ruining Gena's night too.

The door to the lounge swung open, and Dr. Jeffrey briefly popped his head in and yelled, "Look alive, ladies! We got incoming!" before darting back out.

So much for getting something to eat.

"Gena, how'd he know we were here? He never comes in here."

Genevieve chortled. "I think someone let it slip where the doughnuts were. Let's go, Raquel. Heaven forbid we take a break from the craziness."

13

Raquel ran out with Genevieve close behind. She didn't feel like getting written up when she'd just returned from vacation. Turning the corner, Raquel felt a hand yank on her bicep. She stopped to look back at Genevieve. "You should be more careful. You almost collided with the paramedic."

The paramedic guided the gurney through the doorway and Raquel felt queasy. She leaned against the doorjamb.

Raquel smiled at Gena. "I'm good. You go on."

Genevieve nodded and left Raquel standing in the doorway.

Raquel stared at the patient; half of her face and golden blonde hair were covered in blood, and the rich tang of copper hit her nose. The room got uncomfortably warm and started to do a tilt-a-whirl. Her hand shot out to grab onto the solid, metal frame of the doorjamb. Her stomach churned, threatening to bring up what little she had left in her stomach from the meal she had right before she left home to come to work.

The sight of blood never made me queasy before. Now I know I have a virus.

"The woman's name is Sue Allan, thirty-four, and she wasn't wearing a seatbelt. There was a pile-up on the off ramp. She's lucky to be alive. Her car turned into a plane, landing on its roof."

Raquel barely heard the rest of what the paramedic said. She was too fixated on the blood and watched as another nurse started an IV in the patient bay.

Blood streamed from the head wound.

That's a lot of blood.

Panic seized Raquel.

I should be doing something, but what?

Raquel's mind went blank. Then images flickered in front of her. The cell and bars floated; people turned into... *panthers.*

What the hell is happening to me?

Her heart pounded in her ears. The woman laid on the gurney, and fellow nurses worked on her. Raquel knew she should be doing something to help the others, but what? What was she supposed to do?

"Raquel! Get the blood bank on the horn; we're going to need more."

Who called my name?

A nurse removed the woman's torn, dirty sweater and tossed it in a heap near the hazardous waste bin. The ghost image of a lion painfully flashed in front of her. *What the hell?*

Raquel tried to dig her nails into the metal, praying the tilt-a-whirl would stop. *God help me!*

A nurse said, "Call a code. She's crashing!"

Dr. Jeffrey angrily shouted, "Raquel, stop standing there like a corpse!"

What do I do? I should know what to do. Why can't I remember?

Someone bumped into Raquel, and the room spun as she fumbled around to regain her balance. People in blue uniforms hurried about getting... things. But all she did was go over to the patient and stare at the blood.

"Raquel!" He yelled so loud and sharp it was as if he'd slapped her in the face to get her attention.

Reality took a nosedive. Ghost-like images flashed before her in rapid succession. One minute she was lying in her own blood in a cell. The next, she was watching Dr. Jeffrey straddle the woman's chest, hands clasped on top of each other and pumping with enough force that, if he wasn't careful, he'd fracture the woman's sternum. Another nurse intubated the woman, and alarms on machines cried out.

I know what he's doing; I know what all this stuff is. Shouldn't I be doing something?

"Raquel! Do your damn job! Ya know what? Get out of the damn way!" Dr. Jeffrey growled through clenched teeth.

The procedure he was doing was on the edge of her mind, but for the life of her she was drawing a blank. The harder she thought, the more the pressure built in the back of her head near her ear until something popped and protocols flooded her mind. Everything became crystal clear.

I'm at work! Dr. Jeffrey is doing CPR! I know what all this does!

She grabbed the crash cart, placed the gel on the paddles, and before she could hand them over, he snatched them out of her grip and jumped down off the gurney.

Dr. Jeffrey's ice-cold glare made Raquel's stomach churn. He hissed. "Clear!—*Misssss Dulcati!*" He placed the paddles on the woman's chest, and her body jerked from the jolt of electricity. "I

15

think your mind is still on vacation! Get your carcass moving, or *get out* of my damn workspace! Am I *clear,* or do you need a translator! Charge again! CLEAR!"

Raquel's face grew hot. She'd never been so embarrassed in her life.

She swallowed, choking down the urge to vomit all over his shoes. She'd never pissed off the head doc before. "No, I'm all right."

"We got a rhythm!" a nurse said.

Dr. Jeffrey replied, "Andy, I trust *you* to get this woman up to the OR."

Andy shouldered Raquel out of the way.

Raquel absentmindedly rubbed over the spot Andy knocked against her. It didn't hurt, but it magnified what she felt.

Ever since she had returned to work this week, it's been one disaster after another. Her second day back, she lost a patient. Literally. Instead of taking him to a regular room, she'd marked him down for ICU. On the third day back, she'd placed a cast on a patient who didn't need one. She'd waltzed right in, didn't read the chart, and proceeded to wrap the kid's arm in a pink cast. The cast should've gone to the kid in the next room. The man she sent to the maternity ward was the cherry on top. Now this accident victim had almost died because of her.

Surprisingly, she hadn't been suspended.

Out of the corner of her eye, Raquel caught Genevieve observing her. In fact, Gena was always somewhere within earshot, somewhere in Raquel's visual periphery, or simply stepping in and doing something for her.

Ice-cold fear ran down her spine. Gena had been running interference in each scenario. Her best friend was looking out for her.

Raquel sucked in a breath to keep her unshed tears at bay. Crying never solved anything.

"Okay, people, wrap it up."

Dr. Jeffrey turned his undivided attention to her. Raquel held her breath.

Oh God.

"A *word,* Miss Dulcati—*my* office." He ripped off the bloodied gloves. "As soon as you finish restocking the crash cart. And don't *forget* to sign off that you did restock it." He tossed the gloves into

16

the biohazard bin and made a beeline for his office past the round check-in desk.

Crap.

She ignored the glares of some of her co-workers and mechanically cleaned off the paddles, replaced meds, restocked the drawers, and placed the crash cart back against the wall.

Genevieve gripped her arm, stopping her cold. "Hey, Raquel? What's going on with you? Talk to me. Let me help you."

She hadn't even noticed Genevieve come up to her. Her emotional support to the rescue once again.

Raquel wanted to crawl into a hole to and hide for the rest of her life.

"Honestly, Gena, I have no clue. I thought I was going to lose my dinner when I saw the blood and, *oh my word*, I froze. My mind went blank. I'm acting like it's my first time here! I've never done anything like this, not since nursing school!" Choking panic welled up inside of her to the point she fought the urge to scream. "What's wrong with me?"

Raquel eased into Genevieve's hug.

"Hey, easy, Raquel. Deep breaths. Calm down."

Gena soothingly rubbed her back and accidently grazed over the scar in the middle of her back. The shock was instant, but it never lasted long.

"Sorry. I forgot about your back. It's horrible you were attacked by a lion, but I'm thankful the wound has healed and over time, you'll heal emotionally. You've had a lot of difficulty getting back into the swing of things. I'm sure things will smooth over."

"I hope you're right." Raquel drew in a deep, steadying breath. It helped somewhat to calm her nerves. "I can't afford to lose my job, and I owe you big time for helping me out since I came back. You shouldn't have to do this, but I owe you."

"You know I'm here for you. Always."

"Yeah, but I don't want to get you suspended along with me. I know it's coming. I'm sure Dr. Jeffrey will write me up for an audit, and I'll get suspended, and then it's goodbye job. Speaking of which, I better go talk to him before he comes after me."

"That's *not* going to happen. *Call me* and let me know what Dr. Jeffrey does."

Perplexed, Raquel searched Genevieve's face. She didn't expect Gena's daggered glare. Worry she expected, not anger.

What the hell was she angry about?

"Gena, I just wish I knew why I'm making all these mistakes."

"Do you think it's from the head trauma you got on your trip?" Genevieve's eyes turned from a heated glare to concern. "You said the last thing you remember was hitting your head on a rock when the lion pushed you out of the way to get at a guide."

"Yeah... and?"

"My point, Raquel, is you've had some head trauma. Any brain injury you've sustained would require therapy. Have you seen Dr. Okito?"

Raquel frowned. She hadn't thought about it. "Dr. Okito works first shift, and if I'm going to see a neuropsychologist, I'd rather see Dr. Slotkins, over in Baton Rouge. He's better from what I hear." She shook her head. "I'm fine, honestly. Everything else in my life is in order. I'm sleeping, except for the new neighbors. I'm eating. I don't black out, although I keep seeing people turn into animals. Not just any animals, panthers and lions, mainly."

Raquel did a double take when Genevieve's face went glacial white, and her eyes glowed emerald green. *Did Gena just growl?*

Genevieve tartly replied, "You better go see Doctor Jeffrey. I need to get back to work. I'll see you later."

Why is Gena upset?

Raquel, pasted on a smile, and walked to Dr. Jeffrey's office. Her heart pounded in her ears, and her throat constricted at the sight of the open door to his office. His door was always closed. Dr. Jeffrey ran his emergency department like a tight ship—and she was a loose rivet in the hull of the ship, threatening to sink the boat.

He waved her in and motioned for her to sit but kept his head down, filling out something in front of him.

Dismissal forms?

Raquel slowly sank into the avocado green chair. *If he is going to fire me, so be it. Something inside of me is broken, and I deserve whatever I get. But I will figure out what is broken and fix it. Damn it to hell, I worked hard to get here, and I will be back.*

She stared at the top of his head. His short layered blond hair reflected the overhead light. The waves looked soft.

18

Dr. Jeffrey paused and then scribbled his name on the bottom of the paper.

Unexpectedly, he rolled his shoulders, apparently to relieve the tension, and the thick muscles stretched his lab coat.

Why is he uncomfortable? I'm the one with my head on the chopping block.

A lot of women thought he looked like an angel when he'd first taken the position. The man was sexy enough and well put together. What would it be like to be with him in the sack?

She blinked. *Okay, where the hell did* that *come from?* Now she was fantasizing about having sex with her boss.

An unusual, intense heat gained momentum in her core and engulfed her body. She fanned her face with her hand. *This has to be menopause.* Cool and calm one minute and the next, she wanted to do the horizontal polka, with her on her back and strong virile man thrusting hard into her core. Raquel shuddered. This was the third hot flash fantasy she'd had since she returned from Africa.

He coughed, shoved himself back from his desk, and went over to the counter.

Is he blushing? His face was so red, it had spread to the tips of his ears. *I wonder what he's thinking about? Maybe it's been awhile since he had sex too.*

Dr. Jeffrey coughed and shook his head with a crooked smile and then poured a cup of coffee, dumped some sugar in, and dropped a dollop of cream into the cup. He handed the mug to her.

Surprised, she graciously took the mug. "Thank you, sir." *Sir? Where the hell did that come from? Did he ever go to Sanctuary of Desire?*

His eyes locked with hers, and she forced herself to look down and wrap her hands around the mug.

The heat comforted her in some strange way and helped to ground her mind. At least she wouldn't fidget under his scrutinizing stare.

Dr. Jeffrey coughed and cleared his throat and sat in the adjacent chair.

Slowly, she looked at his face.

"Please explain to me what the *hell* is going on with you?"

Raquel could not help but stare into his face. Dreamy eyes,

perfect symmetry. He lifted his mug to yummy, delectable lips before sipping the liquid.

Damn. Those lips looked good enough to nibble on.

He choked, cleared his throat with a rumble, and wiped his mouth with the back of his hand.

Get a grip, Raquel.

"You've been through a lot of personal things recently, which concerns me. Your focus and performance on your job since coming back to work have been less than the normal standard, I know you're capable of. I believe the injuries you've sustained are more extensive, and I'm recommending that you take a medical leave of absence. It will give you more time to fully recover and get your head together."

"Wait, Dr. Jeffrey, I can do better. I haven't been feeling well and—"

He held up his hand and quickly added. "Only for a few weeks, of course. With the errors I've seen and heard about, it's only a matter of time until the hospital ends up in a lawsuit, which will go on your record. You will lose your license, which would make getting a new job in any medical field difficult."

He wasn't firing her? "I don't know or understand what's happening to me. I'll work ten times harder than before. You'll see."

She shook her head. God, she was a mess.

"Unless I should quit."

Dr. Jeffrey took the mug from her hands and placed it on his desk. He surprised her when he took her hands in his, rubbing the top of her hands with his thumbs, circling in small even strokes. She found it soothing. Mesmerizing in a way.

He kept up the slow rhythm until her temples started to pound with a threatening migraine.

He slowly released his gentle grip, sat back in the chair, and sighed. Irritation and surprise marred his features.

"No one wants you to quit. Tell you what, start your leave of absence tonight. You look like you're about to pass out. You've gotten very pale within the last few seconds. I'll hold your position for you until you come back, and you'll be paid through short term disability."

She sat there, stunned. She thought for sure he would replace her. She had heard stories about what a hardhead he was, but he was being nice to her. He hadn't yelled like he had in the ED.

"What happens if I don't improve? What then?"

"Then there are other options you will be asked to consider. I can't have distracted staff in the ED. I think you're one of the brightest nurses I've worked with, one who's hit a rough patch in her life. But let's not go there right now. We'll cross that bridge *if* we come to it."

At least she hadn't lost her job. She didn't want to be out of work, but given the circumstances, what choice did she have?

***

Dr. Benjamin Jeffrey saw the myriad of emotions reflected in Raquel's blue eyes. She stared in disbelief and rubbed her temple with her free hand. He didn't have to read her mind to know what she was thinking. *This is for her own good.* He'd worked alongside humans for a long time, but Raquel's performance disappointed him.

A minute later, what he had just said hit home. Finally, Raquel understood what he was saying, and he inwardly cringed. He'd smelled her pain, her anger, her confusion, and felt the truth of the situation radiate off of her on the tips of his hair-like feathers at the base of his neck.

Raquel mechanically rose from the chair and left his office once the effect of him getting into her mind wore off.

Ben reflected on the phone conversation with Alpha Lavelle over a month ago. The male had briefly explained that Raquel would come back to work within a few weeks. He was fine with that. What he wasn't fine with was the Head Alpha didn't acknowledge the head trauma or the fact that Raquel knew how to project her mind to someone, as she had at the start of their meeting. *Unless* the Alpha Roman was unaware of it.

When she first came into his office and stood there, he slowly eased his mind into hers and caught her thoughts as she projected out to him.

Good grief, the sexual fantasies were nothing short of pornographic! Ben hoped to the Fates she could learn to control her ability.

As he probed further into the mind link, he sensed her discomfort, which quickly turned into pain. The body's first response to what it interpreted as an invasion was pain.

21

Humans generally didn't express they were in pain unless there was some psychic ability, and her mind rode back on the same frequency he transmitted. Most humans couldn't project as far as Kindred could, and Raquel was projecting back into his mind with the same ability as if she had been born of Kindred blood. No wonder she'd developed an immediate headache.

Through the mindlink, he saw fragmented memories. Areas of her mind were blacked out with what appeared to be shattered glass floating around edges of a frame. Her memory engrams looked like a broken, fragmented mirror. Those were likely the areas where her medical knowledge should have been. Memories had been wiped clean all right.

He recalled the first evening Genevieve came back to work. He'd smelled the scent of a panther in the ED. There were three tigers, a rhino, and a few hawks, not to mention approximately a dozen humans, so when Genevieve came up to him and announced she was back and ready to work, her scent had shocked him. Roman's Mating Mark on her neck shocked him further.

In comparison, on Raquel's first day back after her trip, he was confounded. He should've known better than to just assume she'd been turned. Instead, she'd smelled like she always had—a human. Whereas he'd expected her to have the scent of a panther—considering she'd been under the roof at Lavelle House for over five months. A record for any human.

According to Kindred Law, he should've alerted the Commission. However, Alpha Roman assured him Raquel's mind had been swept clean of any knowledge pertaining to Were-shifters. But since returning to work, she'd put others in jeopardy.

What else could I do? My hands are tied.

He sipped his coffee and leaned back in the leather chair in front of his desk. He barely heard the light knock on his door.

"Enter."

The door squeaked opened, and Genevieve, the First Mate to Alpha Lavelle, stood in his doorway.

"Mine Alpha, won't you come in? Please, have a seat."

The female seemed perplexed with a tinge of protectiveness, all rolled into one.

Ben chuckled as her cheeks flushed. "Still not used to being

22

called by the formal title?" He casually motioned to the leather chair beside him. He smiled over the rim of his cup. "What can I do for you?"

"No, I'm not, but I'm worried about Raquel."

"Mine Alpha—"

"Genevieve or Gena, if you will."

He chuckled and went to get her a cup of coffee. He handed the cup to her and caught a glimpse of the Mating Mark tattoo encircling her neck. It still stunned him Roman was mated.

"All right—Genevieve. I'll tell you what I told her. Raquel is on a paid medical leave of absence. She'll collect short-term disability until she feels better."

She hesitantly nodded and set the mug down on the desk, her hands nervously clasping and unclasping together. "For how long?"

"A few weeks."

Her thin brows shot up. Her shock like ice water to his senses.

"I got inside her mind to see for myself why she's been making all these damn mistakes. It's not like her. Well, when I did, I read a little bit, and then she blocked me, so I tried harder. Once I pushed through, I ended up in a dark room. I accidentally triggered a migraine. One, might I add, she's going to have for the rest of the night with how hard I pushed. Raquel's mind is missing some key memories. She won't be able to do her job until the fragments are fixed." He frowned. "Who did the wipe job on her mind?"

"I believe Steffan did. Why? Can't Roman fix it?"

Ben blinked in surprise.

"And I should also let you know Steffan used some of his enzyme to heal her."

Ben blinked again and scrubbed a hand over his face.

"If Steffan had as hard a time erasing her memories as I just did when trying to mindlink, then I suspect he might've wiped out fragments of her medical training to the point she won't be able to function properly in this type of environment. Since he did the wipe, her mind is going to be imprinted so that only he can fix what he erased. The fact he'd used his enzyme on her, a human, only complicates things more."

Genevieve crossed her legs and sipped her coffee. "Why'd this happen?"

23

Ben sighed in thought. "She's a human. No offense, Mine Alpha, eh, sorry, Genevieve. Human brain patterns run on a linear scale and should be easy to follow. Erasing human memories at times causes the brain pattern to become scattered in places. Think of a damaged CD or DVD. If the signal is interrupted by a scratch on the surface, the picture isn't clear, and it skips in places. That's what's happening to Raquel. The enzyme has encoded her engrams and will prevent any Kindred other than Steffan from fixing her memories. With her having sustained the head injury though, it complicates things. I'll have to contact Alpha Lavelle about this and see if he can get his Beta to do something to help her. If nothing can be done, then I'll have to find her a desk job, one where she's only taking information from patients, or fire her for incompetence."

Her eyes flashed, and her lips pressed firmly together as she swallowed the brew; waves of anger rolled off the female.

Raquel and Genevieve were like sisters, attached at the hip. If one was hurt, the other became the mother hen and watched over her until she was better. May the Fates tell Steffan to run like hell. Man, he wished he could be a fly on the wall.

"Don't worry about it. I'll talk to Steffan and Roman about what's been happening to her when I get home. Thank you, Dr. Jeffrey, for seeing me."

"My door is always open, Mine Al—" He sensed the wave of irritation. "Sorry, Genevieve. Old habits die hard when you are as old as me."

The intercom crackled to life. "Dr. Jeffrey to triage."

"Duty calls, Genevieve."

Chapter 3

Steffan kept to the shadows of the back part of the parking lot at Sanctuary of Desire. An old client had called him about his Shibari class he'd taught over a decade ago, just to ask questions and it took him offguard. It'd been a long time since he'd stepped foot inside the BDSM club. He'd tried once after Michelle's murder and felt nothing but crushing anxiety. But he had a hunch he'd find his mate's killer within the walls of the club and that hunch paid off. He had to tamp down the urge to shift into his Were-panther. Steffan and his brother Roman had hunted down the bastards and disposed of them.

After he found Michelle murdered and hung in the rigging in their bedroom, he'd lost all desire to practice and ended up in an anxiety attack. His brother had said it was some sort of post traumatic stress. Perhaps he had been right.

The phone call brought back some good memories this time so he thought he'd venture out and try again.

Baby steps. This was a baby step.

He stared at the front door, watching the comings and goings of patrons and wished the anxiety nestled in his stomach would dissipate. He didn't want to be recognized and questioned as to why he no longer taught Shibari at the club.

Anxiety crisscrossed all over his body, and he glanced down at his trembling hands and clenched them into fists and barked out a laugh. Muscle memory begged for him to go inside, choose a willing submissive, and pick up either the nylon or hemp rope and glide the strands over the palms of his hands until the rope became an extension of him. An extension that was alive.

A part of him missed binding wrists and ankles and encircling the female body with yards of rope. It was more artistry to him than a turn-on, and those who were willing to be bound for a few hours, he cherished.

Damn it to hell. He viewed the entrance to the club. Maybe this

25

was a bad idea. He figured over time he'd heal from the mental trauma of finding his murdered mate, and he wanted to go back to playing in the club, except he found it difficult to do so.

He'd met his mate in the club. Michelle was a human, so he made sure to take extra care. Once she volunteered and bound her with the rope, something inside of him wanted a more permanent bond and took a chance at being with a human. He was hooked and subsequently called only upon her to do the demonstrations with him.

That was a lifetime ago, and even though he'd avenged her murder, the hole in his heart left him feeling numb. It had been a mistake to fall for a human.

He'd never forgiven Roman for the circumstances surrounding Michelle's death, but he had learned to cope with the outcome.

It was a good thing Raquel was sent back to the human world. Out of sight. Out of mind. Out of danger. Raquel's face floated in front of him, and he swore he heard his panther moan. It had been a while since he last saw her and he was fine with that, even though he thought about her often.

Steffan felt the nudge from his Were-panther and glanced down into the side mirror of his bike. The sharp sting in his eyes was a no-brainer. His pupils were wide with a ring of blue around them.

Protect.

Raquel is protected, damn it! She's in her world. Let it be!

Steffan clenched his fists, fighting the urge to shift. A bead of sweat trickled uncomfortably down the middle of his back. He struggled to breathe.

He took a deep breath and exhaled slowly, refocusing on the front door.

The door opened, and a couple came out. In their wake, the wind picked up and his Kindred senses were assaulted by the smell of leather, Were-shifter and human sweat, and he heard the sound of the crack of a whip or two, followed by euphoric gasps that led into a series of moans before the door closed.

Fuck it. The past is the past, and if I'm ever going to move on from my dead Mate's ghost, I need to go inside. He shuddered and dismounted the Harley-Davidson Dyna Super Glide. He stood by the bike, a hand resting on the seat as he steadied his shaking legs.

Fates, what am I doing?

His palms began to sweat, and his heart pounded so hard inside his chest, his panther started to push through. With his anxiety spiking, it gave his Were-panther the signals that he was in danger and needed the beasts full onset of power to protect himself. Only thing though, there wasn't any danger.

Easy, boy. I smell a few humans in the parking lot.

Steffan dragged in the crisp air and leaned against the seat of his bike. He glanced back at the doorman. The sharp eyes of the Were-hawk guarding the entrance tracked him. The familiar pressure of a mindlink hummed against his temples.

"Sir, are you all right? From here you look whiter than a sheet."

Steffan forced a smile. *"Alex, I'll be fine. I just need to clear my head. Where's Pete?"*

"He took the night off. I drew the short straw, so I had to cover for him. Let me know if you need anything."

Steffan sighed once the link was closed off. This whole scenario was hard enough for him. He couldn't explain to someone new what his issue was when he had a hard time understanding it.

He shoved sweaty palms into the pockets of his leather coat. This wasn't going to work.

He perused his surroundings. A white car stopped in front of the entrance and let out a group of females. One looked familiar enough he did a double take to make sure he was seeing things right. He couldn't stop staring at the female's hair. Tight, warm-blonde curls bounced as she jogged up the steps and disappeared into the club.

Is that?

A ghostly image of Raquel's kinky curls fanned across a pillow formed in his mind. A breathy sigh of contentment had escaped her lips after he'd used his enzyme to heal her back. Her wound had knitted back together, but she was going to have a scar for the rest of her life.

The middle of his chest ached.

Raquel had gone back to her life two months ago, but he couldn't get her out of his mind. She had gotten under his skin. He shouldn't have insisted on taking the watch over her, but she'd soothed his inner panther. He also replayed her pain-filled glare when he erased her mind of the events surrounding her and Genevieve's abduction.

At least Raquel was safe. *I wonder what she's doing. Is she at work? I could call the ER and ask to speak with her.*

He scoffed. He should know better than to think about being with *any* human female. They were fragile creatures.

The familiar purr of Roman's '69 Camaro distracted Steffan, and he watched it turn into the parking lot. His brother parked in the front row reserved for Alphas.

Steffan closed his eyes, praying his brother didn't see him, and remained motionless to blend in better with the shadows. His ears picked up on his brother's voice on a call, and then Steffan watched his brother get out of the car, walk up the steps, and stop in front of Alex. The doorman had the gall to point Steffan out, and Roman turned to glance in Steffan's direction.

Oh crap, here he comes. So much for going unnoticed. I don't need Roman's counsel right now.

"Mine Alpha."

Steffan tried to keep the cockiness out of his voice, but he enjoyed goading Roman. Ever since Raquel had returned to her life, Steffan couldn't help but take little jabs at his older brother whenever the temptation arose.

Roman's jaw clenched, then he shrugged. For once, Roman wasn't going to argue with him about calling him by formal address.

"Steff, I'm surprised to see you here. It's been a while." Roman rubbed his hands together as if trying to figure out what to say next.

Awkward much.

"Yes, well. I'm here. Where's Genevieve?"

"She's coming from the hospital. She worked a shortened shift." Roman paused. "Is everything in order for the Mating Ceremony?"

"I've rented the eight-foot ceremonial drums from Thailand. They're coming into port the day before the ceremony. Connor has a semi lined up for delivery. I have the schematics for the Mating Ceremony; you should check your e-mail more often. Ascenza is figuring out the rest of the ceremony along with how to incorporate a human tradition using a Unity Candle."

As best as Steffan knew, the Unity Candle symbolized two halves of two families coming together as one and starting a new life together. Or something similar.

Roman nodded. "*Mon ange* did mention it to me. Anything else?

How about security? Make sure Josh and Kerry go over everyone's ID. I don't like surprises. Ramp up the security. I know there are those Kindred that don't think Genevieve is worth my time."

Steffan barely heard Roman. Images of Raquel kept flickering before him whenever he thought about safety measures.

Safety was the issue. If the ceremony was outside, should a rogue Mulatese Tenebrae attack, they would have easy access. Holding the ceremony indoors, like Steffan had recommended for the Alphas, doors would be closed and locked, and extra security details would be posted on the roof. Now he wished he had hired snipers.

Steffan growled in frustration. *I hope it rains a monsoon and forces everyone inside.*

"Wishful thinking, brother?"

Roman's smile was not amused, and he cocked a brow as if gauging Steffan's reaction. Steffan lowered his gaze in apology. He wanted his brother to be happy, and he was letting his thoughts and fears over his deceased Mate dictate his actions.

"Steff—security—let's focus."

"There will be enough security for the five hundred guests, and I have planned for the Commission members to sit near the center but close enough to the platform for them to bear witness. And speaking of the Commission... " Steffan took in his brother's suit. Roman never wore a suit to Sanctuary of Desire. "... did something happen at your meeting?"

Roman's half-lopsided smile was not reassuring.

"Care to hear what's been done about the rest of David Dupree's property? Despite it not being a whole lot."

Steffan inwardly braced himself. Judging by the flash of panther gold in Roman's eyes, it hadn't gone well. "Do tell. Any bloodshed at the Commission meeting?"

"Almost, but it's going to get interesting. Jerox and Fievel are now officially partners in the shipping industry. Speaking about shipping, that reminds me; the ceremonial drums and the stone altar are arriving the day before the ceremony, make sure delivery goes to Jerox's end of the docks. If it accidentally goes to Fievel's end, I'll never see it."

Steffan paused. "Hold up. What do you *mean* Jerox and Fievel? They're partners?"

"I just told you they're partners. Get your head out of the clouds and focus. You've been distracted lately. Anyway, they both wanted the shipping business down at the docks, so they ended up partners. Fievel wanted it so he could ship more business overseas. I think Jerox wanted Gia to have something of her own, since she'd refused a mating proposal. It's a means of starting her own business. She's still going to work for us for a time. It was interesting watching a Were-lion and a Were-lynx go at it as if they were fighting over a bone."

"I see." Steffan didn't want to get into the details of Fievel's business, knowing full well how deep the male was in the drug trade. Not just pharmaceuticals, but illegal too. "If, in fact, Jerox is handing over his fifty percent of the business to his daughter, is Gia aware of what Fievel's business is?"

Roman's eyes narrowed. "She might. I'm sure Jerox will have a string of guards around her."

"I don't trust Fievel. He was too close to our Sire."

"So noted." Roman glanced between the door to Sanctuary and Steffan. "You seem better. Are you heading inside? You and I could sit at the bar until Genevieve gets here."

Steffan hesitated, his heart starting to pound inside his chest, and drew in a quick breath to steady himself.

"No, thanks. Another time perhaps."

Roman's gaze softened. "You don't have to do this alone. Let's go inside. We can talk." Roman stretched his arm toward the club.

"Mine Alpha, I appreciate your support, but I'm not a charity case."

Roman's hardened stare sent chills up Steffan's spine.

"We're going to wait for Genevieve but not out here." His chin jutted in the direction of the door. "Inside. It's been a while since we last spoke. Tell me what you've been doing. I'm curious as to all the late hours you've put in town."

It was not a request.

Steffan took a step, and Roman stayed by his side, his stride even and matching Steffan's.

"I was working on selling my home. So far, there are no buyers but plenty of lookers."

Roman nodded. "I see. I wasn't one hundred percent sure if you were going to sell it or not. I know there are a lot of memories there for you. If you'd like, Cristoff or I can unload it for you. I know how hard this must be."

"Thank you for the help."

An ache blossomed in his chest. The house was supposed to have been a new beginning with his Mate, and now the house in the French Quarter of New Orleans sat empty. *Roman's right. I should hand it off to one of them.*

Steffan slowed his pace, and Roman gave him a cursory glance, but continued. "Let's head in, Steff."

Steffan followed Roman across the parking lot and up the steps and into the club. Steffan took a deep breath once the metal door clanged shut behind him.

The fear Steffan experienced in the parking lot dissipated, and his body came alive. The sights and sounds combined to result in a euphoric onslaught to his senses. His fingers tingled for the sensation of rope.

Fates, he missed this.

He closed his eyes tightly.

"Steff, are you all right?"

The concern in his brother's voice centered him, and the ache eased. Michelle might be gone, but he was still here—alive. He needed to move on and had hoped to do it with Raquel, but it wasn't meant to be.

He gave a single affirmative nod, took a deep breath, and opened his eyes to find Roman standing in front of him.

"This is still hard for me, but I'm all right."

Roman nodded. "It will get easier as time passes. Anyway, I'd thought you'd like to know Daleena asked about you. In fact, she *enquired* about you."

Steffan tried not to cringe.

"Why? Is she investigating me for some reason?"

Roman shrugged. "She's concerned for you, but if I didn't know any better, I'd say she was gunning for you. Daleena doesn't have a First Mate, and since she is Alpha of her cheetah clan, I believe she's looking at you." The corner of Roman's mouth twitched into an amused smile. "She mentioned something about finding a surrogate if you wanted cubs; because of the cubs resulting in being Mulatese Tenebrae— half cheetah, half black panther."

Steffan choked back the bile rising in his throat. He'd made the mistake of sleeping with her once—three months before meeting Michelle.

"She'll have to wait until hell freezes over." *Time to change the subject.* "Anyway, I'll make sure everything is set up for the Ceremony."

"Speaking of which, two of the Commission members aren't going to attend the Mating Ceremony."

Steffan frowned. "Isn't that an insult to the Head Alpha and punishable?"

"It is. But I don't care. They don't believe Genevieve is worthy of me. So, strike Alpha Tavia and Alpha Sanchez off our guest list."

The mention of Tavia's name was like claws on a chalkboard. Had it not been for that bitch, Raquel might be with him now. At least he wouldn't have to keep his eye on both of those females.

A menacing growl erupted deep within his chest, and Roman quirked a brow. The male didn't say anything, but he knew how much trouble Alpha Tavia could've been had Raquel not gone back to the human world.

"Why? Isn't Genevieve a good choice for you? You turned her, so there shouldn't be an issue."

"True, Steff, so very true. No, it's due to the fact she wasn't *born* a shifter. Those females don't consider her a Kindred since she wasn't born with the inner soul of the panther and it's only now developing with each shift Genevieve does. Plus I believe they had hoped to line their purses with House of Lavelle money as First Mate to me." Roman pointed his finger at Steffan. "Which is *why* Daleena is after you. Just saying."

It made perfect sense.

Genevieve waltzed up to Roman. He gripped the back of her neck, her body molding against Roman's, and his older brother transformed into a loving and protective male.

No one would doubt the possession.

Absentmindedly, Steffan rubbed the expanding ache in the center of his chest.

Roman frowned. Steffan followed Roman's acute, intense stare. Genevieve was trembling.

"Something happen?" Roman gazed down at her when she didn't answer right away.

Shakily, Genevieve said, "Sir, I need to talk to you."

Steffan sighed. He knew when he wasn't wanted. "I'll leave you two love birds alone and—"

"No." Genevieve whipped her head in Steffan's direction. Glowing emeralds hit Steffan, and his stomach contracted as if his Were-panther had perked up out of curiosity.

Okay, was she angry or upset? It was always hard to tell with females and their complex emotions.

Genevieve's emerald eyes pulsed. "Sir, allow him to stay; it concerns him too."

"What is it?"

Genevieve dragged in a breath. "It's Raquel. I think she's trying to remember... things."

Steffan certainly didn't miss the low menacing growl.

Fuck!

Roman's golden stare flashed, pinning Steffan. The Alpha dared him to look away. Roman forced open a mindlink.

"What happened?"

"Roman, I have no clue! I wiped her memories!"

What could be wrong? She was fine after he had finished deleting and rethreading her memories. He and Cristoff took her home. He carried her up to her apartment, placed her on her bed, and arranged her luggage as if she had just finished unpacking before lying down for a nap.

Genevieve cleared her throat. "Raquel's made a lot of mistakes at the hospital. Mistakes that shouldn't be happening, given her experience. She should know her job like the back of her hand and be able to do it practically blindfolded. But tonight, she almost killed a patient!"

A sinking sensation engulfed Steffan. He'd tried to warn Roman about erasing Raquel's memories. Damn Roman for wanting the female out from under the Lavelle roof.

He took a deep breath to say something, but a warning growl erupted from Roman.

Roman turned away from Steffan and leveled his gaze to Genevieve. "What about Dr. Jeffrey? I asked him to watch over her. He was supposed to inform me if there were any changes. Why didn't he? What went wrong?"

"Sir... " Anger dripped from her voice. "He tried to mindlink to see if he could figure out what was wrong. He found Raquel's mind resembled a darkened room with fragments like a broken mirror. Ben thinks Steffan might've gone too far with the memory wipe, and unless Steffan fixes it, he might have to assign her to permanent desk duty or fire her!" Genevieve punched Steffan in the chest. "Raquel was sent home tonight! What the hell did you do to my best friend?"

Roman grabbed her by the wrist, pulling her to him. "Easy, *mon ange*. Remember where you are. There are humans around."

Alpha Genevieve's anger was hot enough to singe Steffan's fur, and the muscle twitching in Roman's jaw told him that Roman probably planned on making a panther skin rug out of him.

Genevieve lowered her eyes but growled low. "My best friend is upset and thinks she's losing her mind!" She darted her gaze to Steffan. "Fix what you've done!"

It's entirely my fault. I put her in harm's way. Another female was going to be innocently exterminated, all thanks to me.

This was the last thing he wanted for Raquel.

Now Raquel was in danger—again.

But the question remained: Had he gone too far while wiping her memories? He'd watched her memories as she relived them and picked the ones needing to be erased. Some memories he found fascinating to watch. Raquel had grown up differently from him. She intrigued him.

Frustration welled up inside of him. This was a mess. Fuck the Commission Laws! If you date a human, long story short, you had better turn them into Kindred of your species. The laws needed some serious overhauling.

"This makes no sense, Mine Alpha! I went through her memories of the day she and Genevieve were abducted from the house, all the way up until they were rescued. She was mostly unconscious for some of the events, and I altered what she knew with new memories, which *you*, Mine Alpha, wrote down for me. Including the African safari. So don't either one of you put all the blame on me!"

"Steff, you gave her *your* enzyme. Raquel's mind is imprinted on you. It's safer for her if you do it, but you've let me down. Now I'll have to kill her. She's seen too much. I can't take the risk of her remembering."

Genevieve gasped and whirled out of Roman's embrace. "You will *not* kill her! If you so much as entertain any inclination of killing her, I'll see to it you're neutered!" She growled, baring her canines at him, then turned to Steffan getting in his face.

She grumbled, poking Steffan in the chest. "I want Steffan to fix this little problem *both* of you have created!"

Roman pulled her to his side, capturing her wrist, kissing the inside of the crease. "Fates, I love you. As you wish, *mon ange*. I'm interested in what your proposition is."

She thought for moment and then steadied her breath. "The day Raquel and I were on our way to the wedding site, she filled me in on some of the new procedures and protocols at the hospital. Considering I'd been at your house the whole time, I had no clue what she was talking about. I'm guessing when *Steffan* erased her mind, he erased the conversation we had concerning medicine and protocols. *Am I right*?"

She might be.

Part of wiping memory and transposing new ones was getting a clean slate to lay new ones down. In order to do that, it was necessary to go deep.

Memories were infinitely complex and involved all five senses for the brain to record the person's surroundings. Was it possible he had gone *too deep*? Erased not just the conversation itself but the resulting information Raquel processed from the conversation?

He hadn't known what they had been talking about. He only sensed Raquel's discontentment. He'd assumed the negative emotions she had fed him while he ghosted around in her mind were the same as the emotions stemming from the time period in the cell and getting kidnapped. If she had negative emotions while discussing anything going on at work, then yeah, it was possible he'd messed up.

Steffan nodded slowly. "It's possible, but I've been wiping memories from humans for centuries. I have no idea what went wrong."

Roman growled. "*Mon ange*, this is a situation we've never found ourselves in before. Steffan, you need to repair the damage you've done. Right now, *this* takes precedence."

Roman glanced at his watch. "You took her back to her apartment two months ago. It takes three months for the botched-up erase job you did to become permanent. Considering this month has just started, you're going to hand over anything for the Mating Ceremony to Ascenza and focus on finding and fixing Raquel's memories. If you don't do it soon, then she might as well look for another job. In the meantime, I'll contact a few doctors I know and see if they are looking for new staff to hire."

Genevieve gasped. "You want her to lose her job?" Her pitch rose almost a full octave in shock.

"It's only a precaution, *mon ange*. I should at least be able to provide her employment if this doesn't work out. It's the least I can do for her. If she doesn't get hired somewhere else, I'll make sure she somehow receives some type of a sizable inheritance from some deceased relative. Steffan, you might not need to completely unravel the thread you've woven. Only the part pertaining to any medical knowledge she may have been talking to Genevieve about."

Genevieve gaped at both of them. Steffan felt the weight of her worry, and his shoulders sagged.

"I'll fix this, Mine Alpha."

Genevieve gave Steffan a curt nod, but the subsonic, too low for humans to detect, growl told him not to fuck up again or he'd be dealing with her.

He hadn't meant to cause this much pain to anyone.

Determination to fix everything took root. "Is she still at the hospital?"

"Ummm... no." She chewed her lip. "She left before I did. She might've gone home to her apartment or headed downtown to the bakery. Sometimes, when she's stressed out like this, she'll grab a few fresh bagels after coming off third shift. The bakery opens at six, though, so she might still be at home. Raquel left work around two this morning."

Steffan shot out the door and ran to his bike. The night sky held an edge of pink. Sunrise. Time was not on his side. If his calculations were correct, he didn't have much time left to add a part of her memory back, and this day was only getting started.

36

Chapter 4

Raquel's head throbbed like someone had taken a jackhammer and decided to drill into her eye sockets. She'd thrown up immediately after getting home, and the pain momentarily abated. Now Raquel's mouth was desert dry, her stomach hurt from heaving, and the migraine started to gain momentum as she glanced up and noticed the sun intruding into her once-darkened living room.

She squinted hard to find the damn cord, her hand flopping around to feel for it along the side of the wall and yanked the room-darkening curtains shut.

"Okay, somewhat better at least." The throbbing behind her eyes diminished.

So. This is what roadkill feels like.

She sighed heavily.

When did my life turn upside down? What the hell happened to me?

Raquel's thoughts drifted back to her trip to Africa. All she remembered was the jeep slowing down because of a dead lioness in the road. *Off the road? Hell, I can't remember. I got out of the vehicle to take pictures.*

The lioness was dead. I wasn't in any danger if I got too close. What harm would it be?

Plenty.

God, my head hurts.

Raquel had been trying to take a selfie with her phone when something hard, big, and hairy suddenly knocked her to the ground. Sharp, agonizing pain had exploded as claws dug into her back. A second later, the lion released her. She'd scrambled in her panic to get away and hit her head on a rock. The guide had saved her life and killed the lion that attacked her. Or so she'd been told.

She'd definitely sustained a concussion and, depending on the severity of the injury, it might take a long time for her to fully recover. Weeks? Months? Years?

Do I need to consider rehab for the injury.

Raquel reflected on the events in the hospital leading up to her forced leave of absence: the blood, Dr. Jeffrey's protocols, and her missing medical knowledge. Well, not all of it was missing. For some dumb reason, she remembered how to do everything in the NICU but not the ED.

Dr. Jeffrey *might* be right about needing to replace her.

Hot tears trickled down Raquel's cheeks, and she punched a pillow next to her. God she was so angry. *Of all the stupid things to do. I'll need to look for a new job, but doing what exactly?*

Absentmindedly, Raquel fingered the delicate gold necklace she wore. It had been her Gramma's before inheriting it. She'd helped the older woman during the summers when school was out, and especially around the holidays. Gramma had been gone for five years now. She sure could use some good advice as to what to do.

The sun managed to sneak through the crack in the curtain, and in the dim lighting, she beheld her grandmother's smiling face peering out at her from a silver picture frame. *Miss you, Gramma.* The picture gave Raquel some comfort in times when she was most stressed.

One thing bothered Raquel. Why did she go halfway around the world alone and not with her fiancé, Keith? *When did I break up with him? Or did he break up with me?*

This doesn't feel right. Why can't I remember?

Once the pounding subsided, she pushed herself off the couch, headed into the kitchen, and stood at the sink, staring down at the few dirty dishes. Keith had promised her, after they were married, he would buy her a dishwasher as a wedding present.

At least washing some dishes would get her mind off things.

The faded red coffee mug sitting in the sink had been her Gramma's. It was one of the few things Raquel kept after she died.

She wrapped nimble fingers around the handle, picking it up. Immediately an uncomfortable heat enveloped her, making it hard to breathe. She snapped her eyes shut and took in gulps of air.

A ghosted image of her Gramma arguing with Gapa popped into her head. Gapa argued he'd taken on a second job, but Gramma found out he'd been cheating on her. The emotional toll of Gramma's pain hit Raquel so hard, she cried out; losing the image and opening her

38

eyes. The cup slipped out of Raquel's grasp, hit the bottom of the white porcelain sink, and broke into five large pieces.

The image had seemed so real, she really thought she'd been there but she remembered she'd been on a school field trip. She'd only stayed with Gramma and Gapa during the summer and that summer, when she walked through the kitchen door, Gramma had been sitting alone at the kitchen table. The house didn't have its usual smell of sugar cookies baking in the oven. And the only sound was the haunting tick-tock of the clock in the hall.

Gapa hadn't been outside, and he wasn't in the house or the barn.

She'd asked where Gapa was, and the only thing her grandmother said, "He's gone. It's okay, though. I knew he was gonna leave. Don' fret your pretty li'l head none 'bout it. How's about some mac'n'cheese tonight for supper? You git washed up."

The ghosts of the past disappeared. But what she'd said rang in Raquel's ears.

"I knew he was gonna leave."

Her grandmother *always* knew when things were going to happen before anyone else did.

Raquel had once asked Gramma how she knew or saw things happen.

Gram's replied, "Child, I see things no one else can. Past mostly, but the future is unpredictable. And I *knows* you can as well. You remember your uncle? I saw you hold something, and you told that cop exactly what your uncle had done with the bag full of money when he robbed Mr. Gougler's hardware store. I remember you told the cop exactly where to find the cash. You was born with a veil. It skipped your momma, though. There's power there." The old woman raised an arthritic finger and tapped the center of Raquel's forehead.

That's all in the past. I held the hammer he used to break the glass on the counter. I hadn't been there, and I saw Gramma and Gapa having an argument. That was... what? I was seven years old at the time.

The last time she'd had a vision about the past was when she was—*eight*? The visions stopped coming after she fell out of a tree and hit her head on the ground. She'd been out cold for a few minutes. The wind knocked right out of her.

Raquel never had another premonition or saw things from the past again.

Until now.

Perhaps hitting my head on the rock gave it back to me. Not exactly the gift I wanted.

The more she thought about the trip, the angrier she got, and Keith had all the answers; she did not. Genevieve had told her the break-up was nasty. *If it had been a nasty break-up, I should remember it. Keith knows.* She had to find him. It was Tuesday. Keith always bought fresh pastries for his law office on Tuesday. And it wasn't too far away from her apartment; Raquel could walk downtown.

She changed into clean clothes and grabbed her keys.

***

Steffan spotted Raquel's white Jetta in the parking lot of the apartment complex. He quickly glanced up to the second-floor windows of her apartment. The curtains were drawn.

Steffan released the throttle of his Harley, parked next to her car, and hurried over to the metal fire escape. He glanced around, making sure no one was watching, crouched low, and jumped straight up to the second landing before cautiously heading down to Raquel's apartment. He rapped the back of his knuckles on the door and waited.

"Raquel? You home? I'd thought I'd stop by."

Waiting seemed like an eternity. He guardedly looked to his left and right then leaned in, placing his ear close to the door. Nothing. Not a single sound of movement, only the sound from the television blaring in the background on the other side. Not good.

Steffan placed his hand over the tumblers for the lock and focused until he heard the lock pop and the door swung open. He stepped through and shut the door; his eyes adjusting to the darkness of the room.

"Raquel?" Silence met his ears. He inhaled sharply. Her scent was everywhere, and she'd been sick to her stomach.

If I heard someone breaking into my home, I'd meet whoever it was, and she should remember I'm Genevieve's brother-in-law.

40

In the living room, he'd found a lavender blanket in disarray on the couch and an empty bottle of over-the-counter pain meds on the coffee table. Frowning, he moved to her kitchen. The smell of vomit was stronger, and he glanced in the sink. It was empty except for a few pieces of a broken mug, but the odor came from there. She'd thrown up in the sink.

Bedroom? Since she was ill, she might've been sleeping and never heard me come in.

He ambled down the hall, his inner panther getting anxious the closer he got to the bedroom. It felt as though a noose had tightened around his throat, he started to shake all over, and his breathing became labored, his heart thudded against his chest.

The tidal wave of fear nearly knocked him over, and the white door to her bedroom shrank, moving farther and farther away from him. His eyes slammed shut, and courtesy of his Were-panther, a not-so-wonderful image appeared—Raquel in a coffin, holding a daylily. *No, not again!* The panther was scared he'd find Raquel as he'd found Michelle. No wonder the panther was persistent.

A wave of nausea hit Steffan so hard, he made a beeline for the bathroom, leaned over the bowl, and lost his breakfast.

Shaking and breathing hard, he attempted to soothe his panther. His blood pulsated in his ears, his mouth went dry, and the anxiety made him struggle against shifting into full panther mode as his skin tingled and ferociously itched. "I'm fine. I'll just open the door; you'll see. Easy."

The panther persisted, the fur starting to sprout all over.

"Nah-ah. Stay put. I am not letting you out here. Too many humans around in the other apartments, and you have a habit of roaring, so stand down."

After a few minutes, Steffan's labored breathing, which usually occurred during the change, subsided. The pain lessened, and he sighed in relief. He was as anxious as his cat to see Raquel, but shifting wouldn't help.

If anything happened to her, he'd never forgive himself.

Gut-wrenching fear fired off in every cell in his body, and he launched himself through the bedroom door.

Empty! The room is empty! He laughed.

His heart hammered against his chest.

She's not here! Praise the Fates!

From across the bed, he stared at his reflection in the closet door mirror. The gray-blue gaze of his panther stared back at him. The surface of his skin had stopped burning, but the panther's emotions raged in his mind: concern, fear, anger, and the persistent feeling of loss. He had lost so much over the past couple of years.

Steffan slowly sank down on the neatly made bed. The palms of his hands smoothed over the cool blue star adorning the quilt, bringing a sense of calm to his chaotic mind.

He inhaled. Her scent mingled with the perfume she used, branded into his memory, quieting his were-panther.

Raquel's not here. Her car's in the lot, so she must be down at the bakery. I need to find her and fix the problem I created.

Chapter 5

Maximo's jaw cracked loudly as he phased out from the partial shift, he had held for over the past five hours. Coming out of a partial shift, even if it's only the face was quite painful the longer he held onto it. *Fuck, that hurt.* The pain resonated, but he endured the discomfort.

His panther wasn't happy about the disguise; however, the one advantage was it allowed him to move freely among humans, and as long as he kept his distance from other shifters and stayed downwind, no one recognized him. Except for those he wanted to know.

His scent would give him away immediately. It wouldn't do any good to have someone go back to Roman and reveal he was actually alive, then all of his plans for taking over the Southern Commission Council would be for nothing. The other Commissions in America would soon follow suit. Especially when the Head Alpha of the Northern Commission was killed. He would control the North and the South, and because the other Commissions were smaller, a power play would topple them, and Maximo would be the sole governing entity. Stavslaka poured himself a drink and eyed Maximo as his shifting stopped. "Feeling better?"

Maximo cautiously observed Alpha Stavslaka where he sat across from him in the back of the limo. It wasn't that he didn't trust the male, but he wasn't one hundred percent sure where the male's loyalties lay. Right now, he had to rely on the male's connections. "*Da.* Thank you for your hospitality." Maximo loosened his tie. "I've just came back from gathering my things from Dupree's office down at the docks. Since there's been a change of hands, will it affect our business? I still need to maintain a low profile and the *funds* to conduct... business."

Alpha Stavslaka shook his head and poured Stolichnaya Elit into a glass and handed it to him.

"*Nyet.* It won't. Dupree's holdings and buildings were split up between Fievel and Jerox. I doubt Jerox will even check on the shipments himself. If he does, then whoever he sends will be discreetly taken care of. Now, the new shipment of potential employees will be arriving Wednesday of next week. A few will be... *detained* for your inspection. As per our usual agreement."

He swallowed the alcohol, and the warmth spread in his gullet.

Stavslaka was one of the few who brought in illegal Were-shifters. The shifters were required to be fully shifted into whatever animal form they were. The forged paperwork reflected the proper documentation for animal transfers for zoos, circuses, or any outfit legally able to house wild animals.

Once the merchandise was here, they were given fake identification of human American citizenship and their choice of jobs. It just so happened this current *shipment of merchandise* also had a few prostitutes on board.

Stavslaka was cunningly discreet, but he often played both sides.

"Distrusting me already?" The Were-fox smiled crookedly.

Maximo slowly returned Stavslaka's smile, baring the tip of one canine. The other, jagged from where it had been broken off a century ago, pushed into his lower lip. "Alpha Stavslaka... I don't trust anyone."

This had nothing to do with trust, only a means to an end should the services be needed.

Stavslaka tsked. "I'd assumed we were past this. Considering I've been supplying you with females—you know the ones I'm talking about, don't you? The ones turning up *dead*. Really, you should get a different hobby."

Maximo viewed Siber through the window. His back was facing the door. Ever the watchful guard. One tap on the glass and Siber would be in the cabin of the limo and taking Alpha Stavslaka's life, should Maximo require it.

"I do have a hobby. Getting rid of Alphas that don't suit my needs. It's quite exhilarating. So far, most of my plan has been moving along accordingly. Except for my oldest cub, Roman." He growled in irritation.

He hated the fact he had to wait to kill the male.

"So noted, but some will swear allegiance to you once this is all over. But I agree with Lars. He is right about keeping the Head Alpha alive. For now, at least. There would be too much suspicion should the male wind up dead." Stavslaka casually pointed to Siber. "Your *guard* can join us."

44

"The bastard is fine where he is. He's been fed and watered."

Stavslaka scoffed. "The male only works for you because you pay him." The hard gleam in his eye shone brightly, and his words were sharp. "I'm surprised the rogues are willing to work with you, considering how little you think of them as an actual society. Just so we are clear, I'm doing *this* for the *Mulatese Tenebrae*! Some can pass as human and get regular jobs, while others can't hide their markings." Stavslaka's cheeks flushed from anger. Red eyes glowed, the menacing predator coming to the surface. "My brother was killed by *humans* because they didn't have the safety of the European Commission, and the ones here in America want nothing to do with them unless they need to get their hands dirty."

Maximo kept his mouth shut and poured himself another drink, swirling the clear liquid in the tumbler. "Next Wednesday then, I will be there. And before you start spouting more words on the Mulatese Tenebrae—don't. If they live up to their bargain, I will see they are on the council once it's renamed. But they'll answer to *me*."

Hopefully that'll shut the bastard up.

Mulatese Tenebrae were disposable.

"Until Wednesday. I need to get back to the club and make preparations." Alpha Stavslaka gave a curt nod before getting out of the limo and disappearing into his own limo parked a few feet away.

A second later, the door opened, and Siber plopped down in the seat across from Maximo. Maximo ground his molars at the disturbance. The long orange and black hair hung loosely to his shoulders, and amber tiger eyes stared out from his tawny complexion. The eyes though stared coldly back at him, the pupil slits unnervingly narrow.

He waited as Siber's hands palmed his knees but the male was tense sitting from across him.

"What?" Five minutes. Was that too much to ask in order to rest his face? He had one more place to go and needed the time to relax his muscles so he could hold another partial shift for a lengthy amount of time.

"When will the vote be cast?" Siber purred out his annoyance.

"What do you mean?" Perhaps if he acted innocent, the male would shut up.

The muscle in Siber's right cheek ticked. "You know damn well what I'm talking about, you French bastard. Have Lars tell his brother

45

Fievel to cast a vote to reappoint the Mulatese Tenebrae to the Commission. If Fievel brings it up, he will most certainly be backed by Roman's vote. It will cause the rest to follow due to the respect Fievel holds. Sheep follow a shepherd, and Roman has proven himself over time since he filled your old Head Alpha position."

So, the bastard thought this meeting was to regain their seat on the Commission. How interesting.

"We'll see. Stay close while I'm in town."

Siber answered with a growl, but Maximo didn't bother to respond to the male's little temper tantrum. He glanced at Siber's sharp, protruding canines. A thick vein popped out on his forehead and made the faint tiger stripe ripple. The male's claws dug into his palms as he clenched his fists tight, drawing blood. If Maximo hadn't known any better, he'd think the male was fighting to shift but everyone knew that mixed bloods can't shift because their souls can't make up their mind which animal to bring forth.

Too bad Maximo needed Siber and his followers at this time; otherwise, he'd kill the bastard now. Maximo ached for a good fight.

"Are you through, Siber? I have work to do."

Maximo smirked when Siber didn't reply, exited the limo, and headed in the direction of an old business associate.

Time to collect on a debt.

***

Siber trailed Maximo from the rooftops because he couldn't shift into a human form and follow on the ground. Up here, at least, he was safe, and the aerial view allowed him a far better vantage point. Too bad the money had come through to his account. Now he'd have to do his job. If it were up to him, he'd let the cocksucker suffer any consequences the Fates dished out.

One thing was certain, Lars had noticed Maximo's handiwork. Siber believed Maximo's ruthlessness was the reason why Lars had funded Maximo's death and enabled him to rise again like a Phoenix in the future. But to what extent?

Siber knew this couldn't go on forever. The knowledge of what he'd signed on for ate at him like a parasite while he waited for the day he could sink his claws into Maximo's throat and rip it out.

But Siber had made his bed. Now he had to lie in it.

Siber jumped across to the next rooftop. The loose gravel crunched under the soles of his boots as he landed.

"Where are you going?" he muttered.

Maximo hesitated in front of a small tavern, his reflection quivering. Siber did a double take once he realized Maximo had shifted back to his real face. The male entered the coffee shop, flipped the sign around to *Closed,* and headed over to the counter.

What the hell? Not someone the male pretended to be, not an illusion of a famous celebrity like he'd seen the male do, but his *actual* face.

Siber knew who owned the coffee shop. One of the Betas from the Commission, if memory served him right. This particular Beta's hands were immersed in some shady dealings in Nicaragua, and he'd previously worked for Maximo. Maximo was collecting on a favor. It explained *why* the bastard was here.

He jumped over to the coffee shop and found an air vent on top of the roof. The aroma of coffee beans and food, as well as the voices of the owners, wafted up to him.

This is bad.

Siber glanced around. If some shit was about to go down, he'd need some sort of leverage for the future. And ever since he'd struck up a bargain and decided to work for Maximo, he'd kept records. Lots. Of. Records.

The records were his life insurance policy. In the event anything untoward happened to him, the few rogue Mulatese Tenebrae backing him up would have the means to go after Maximo Lavelle and use Kindred Law against the cocky male.

A hotel sat catty-corner from the coffee shop. He calculated the distance, gave himself a running start, and launched himself over to the hotel roof. He missed the edge and grabbed the rain gutter. It was not meant to take his heavy weight and noisily separated from the building. He swung his legs toward the building, flipped mid-air to land on the balcony, then scrambled up an iron post to disappear on the roof.

The gutter crashed to the pavement below.

Once he was secure, he observed the people below and hid in the shadows. They couldn't see him, but he saw everything. A maintenance man came out, but Siber wasn't worried about being caught and focused on Maximo from across the street. He took out his phone, a USB cord, and binoculars.

The technology for this pair of digital camera binoculars was state of the art. He hooked up the USB from his phone to the binoculars and started to record. Anything he observed would be recorded and backed up to his phone.

The bad part about it right now though? He was too far away to record audio.

He could see the shock on the baker's face, Maximo and the baker arguing, the baker pointing at the door, Maximo crossing his arms before lunging in full attack, and the baker trying to get away before Maximo broke his neck.

Siber silently watched as Maximo beheaded the male and shoved the severed head into the oven.

That didn't take long.

The blinds snapped shut, cutting off Siber's view. He'd seen enough though.

Quickly, he shoved the binoculars inside his vest and made his way back to the limo.

Remorse swept over him. There was no need for the baker to die.

A part of him wanted this servitude to be over; another part of him wanted to kill Maximo.

Siber had hoped to be seated on the Commission by now, and he'd be able to make a better life for those like him who could not fully shift into either humanoid or animal form.

The ones able to shift into human form wore contact lenses to hide the animal-like irises. He glanced down at his hand, turning it over. The black stripe descended from his arm all the way down and turned to end in the palm of his hand. He snorted. At least his claws were retractable, and the fur was light colored sable.

He needed time to think, and until then, he'd carry on.

Footsteps crunched over the small stones in the parking lot. Siber glanced down in the direction of the sound. Maximo's expression held a satisfied, smug grin, and Siber thought he was going to lose his lunch. He jumped down to the parking lot.

"Come on, Siber. I need to get cleaned up before my meeting, and I don't like to keep the merchandise waiting."

48

Chapter 6

Raquel's feet ached; she was tired, and she hadn't had breakfast or lunch. It was taking much longer than she expected to locate him. She knew the places he visited often and had decided to check all of them. Thank goodness the damn migraine was gone, or this little trip downtown would have been excruciating.

First, she checked Conroy's Bakery, but hadn't seen him. Next, she checked Adam's Antique store. Keith hadn't been there. So, she checked his usual shop, Retro Records; Keith wasn't there. Then, she headed west on Darby to the café; he wasn't there either. *Keith is around here somewhere.*

She tried calling twice on her way downtown, but the calls went directly into voicemail. *Where the hell is he?* He always picked up on the first ring.

Conroy's bakery. Surely he'd be there by now.

Conroy's was on the corner, and as she got closer, the door opened and Keith stepped out of the small red brick building with a white paper bag in hand. Hope bloomed in her chest. He had answers she needed. She drew in a deep breath and shouted, "Keith! Keith, wait up!"

He stopped cold on the bottom step. She literally felt the icy glare he sent her way. *What's gotten into him?*

"Oh thank God, I caught up with you!" She stopped in front of him, catching her breath. "Where have you been? I've been—I've been trying to get ahold of you."

He looked perplexed. "Me? Where have I been? Well, Miss Ditch and Run, I've been getting on with my life. You, on the other hand, I couldn't care less about. You've made it quite clear I was the wrong person for you!"

"Keith, I wanted to talk to you about why we didn't get married. When did we break up? Everything's so confusing!"

Surprise lit up his eyes before turning into heated embers.

She took a step back until she was backed up against a table on the sidewalk. He leaned in close to her. Being this close, she easily saw the bloodshot eyes; his breath smelled of cheap beer, and his once clean-shaven face now sported an unkempt beard.

He's really changed.

"You made your decision. You left *me* at the altar and high-tailed it out of here on a trip! You disappeared for four months! Most likely with your lover, Steffan Lavelle! You never called to cancel the wedding; you never acknowledged my emails. What exactly do you want me to say?"

Four months? No—what the hell? He sent me emails? My emails were empty. When? Raquel gawked at him. *Her... lover?* "Steffan is not my lover! What are you talking about?"

"Ohhhhhh, don't give me that! Ever since Genevieve met Roman, all you ever talked about was his brother Steffan. You commented on how he carried in the box of flowers for you, and he was so strong. You mentioned he was shirtless, and you had never seen soooo many muscles. After you came back from putting your flower arrangements together, you acted funny all night long. You kept shying away from me and said you didn't want to have sex that night because you 'were tired'."

He whipped around, heading away from her. But yelled back, "I got the final hint when you didn't show up at our wedding!"

"Keith! Wait! I don't understand! I can't remember!"

Keith knew things she didn't. He had to explain this all to her.

Desperately, she reached out again, clamping down hard enough that he stopped.

"Get off of me, bitch! I never want to see you again!"

He pivoted in such a way, he violently shook and shoved her hand off.

Ice-cold fear stabbed her heart as he shoved her hard enough to dislodge her hand on his bicep, losing her balance. She fell against a glass café table. The glass shattered as she pushed off the top to steady herself, and her arms went through the table. The glass fragments slashed her arms, and if she hadn't found her footing to regain balance and break her fall, her face would have been next. Strong arms wrapped around her middle and yanked her up. She found herself up against a rock, hard chest.

Who the heck... Keith? No. Not Keith. The aftershave was all wrong to be him.

She looked up into bright blue eyes. He was so close she could see her shocked reflection mirrored back at her.

"Steffan? What are you doing here?"

"Raquel, are you all right?"

His hot breath fluttered through her hair and against her ear. She shuddered as goose bumps rose, and her body was caught in a hot flash that started in her shoulders, raced down her back, and settled in her core. She swore her ovaries wept with joy.

The way he held onto her, with his arm was a steel band wrapped around her middle. It made her feel safe. This felt right to her. Familiar and she meld her body to his.

She frowned as she searched her memories.

Raquel's head started to throb the more she thought about the man holding her, until something popped.

Echoes of a memory assaulted her.

She had been cocooned in white sheets. Naked. Steffan had been naked. She distinctly remembered Steffan sitting by her bed, stroking her face, watching over her, and at some point, applying medicine on her back. He'd kissed her lips and another time, he kissed the side of her head when she laughed at a really bad joke. He'd taken care of her after she came back from Africa. His blue eyes were the first thing she saw when she woke up one sunny morning and he had rushed to the bed. But for some reason, he was blinking back unshed tears as he smiled and he seemed ecstatically happy.

The tension surrounding her temples eased, and the memory faded into nothing.

Oh my God! I slept with him?

Embarrassment suffused her cheeks.

Keith said, "So, this is Steffan Lavelle. I should have known, considering he and Roman look alike. It's obvious they're brothers. At least your brother showed up to the wedding. If anything, Roman could have had the common decency to tell you to back off of Raquel, but I guess she was with *you* on *our* wedding day."

Steffan steadied her on her feet.

Raquel heard someone say, "What the hell?" She observed Keith out of the corner of her eye. He hadn't said anything, and Steffan's lips hadn't moved at all.

God, I'm losing it.

51

Raquel winced at the pain, and he held onto her elbows so she wouldn't fall. Nothing else came to her. She dug her fingers into Steffan's sleeve and searched her memory, trying to remember if they'd slept together.

Steffan frowned and then blinked. The corner of his mouth lifted, and a quick flash of blue brightened before disappearing again.

He's amused. What the hell does he have to be amused at? I'm the one losing my mind. And his eyes keep changing color like a lava lamp. Unless its my migraine coming back for round two.

Keith stepped forward, and Steffan immediately maneuvered Raquel behind him, protecting her. *Did Steffan just growl? Sounded more like an animal.* She inadvertently placed her palm on Steffan's back and felt the awkward rumble vibrating against her palm and realized it had come from Steffan.

"I am. I should kill you for hurting her," Steffan replied, his tone glacial.

Raquel didn't want Steffan getting into a fight, so she stepped around him, putting herself between them. "Back off, Keith. Evidently, I must've had second thoughts about us. That's the only thing I can think of." This had to be the ballsiest thing she'd ever done.

"No, Raquel, you're just a two-timing whore." Keith shoved the white bag into Raquel's bloody arms. "You two lovers can have these. I've lost my appetite. And Raquel, you can go to hell for all I care. Steffan, *you* can have the little slut." Keith stormed off.

Raquel stared at Keith's retreating back.

What just happened?

A small gentle tug on her elbow turned her attention back to Steffan.

The sympathetic look he gave her was too painful to view. "Raquel, you need to come with me. I'll take you home. Toss the bag in the trash. You're getting blood on it."

What the hell is wrong with me?

He coaxed gently. "Please, *bébé*. Come on, let's go."

Chapter 7

Steffan tensed as a small crowd had begun to gather around them. The hairs on the back of his neck stood on end. Eyes on the street watched. Humans gawked in silence, and he sensed there was a Kindred about as he held Raquel. He desperately searched the crowd around him until he glanced across the street and identified a male Kindred standing on the doorstep of Retro Records. Steffan knew the male was a Beta and one he'd had recently interacted with.

Steffan reached out a mindlink, but the male denied him.

Stares locked in a silent battle.

Steffan needed to get Raquel off the street. Thank the Fates he had spotted her when he drove by on the motorcycle and found a space to park close by.

Fates, how much of her memory has been messed up because of me? I didn't wipe any of the guests for the wedding or Keith's memories. I just made it seem that she and Keith had broken up. And where the hell did she get the idea we slept together out of me taking care of her at the house?

The Beta hightailed it back inside, and Steffan led her back to his bike about a block away.

Not good. No doubt the male was tattling to his Alpha. If it got back to Roman, at least his big brother would put a stop to whatever lies had been spread. His celebrity status as the Beta to Alpha Roman Lavelle, Head of the Commission Council, made him recognizable. Especially in the state of Louisiana.

He ripped off the end of his shirt and wrapped her forearms with it. He took the helmet perched behind him and handed it to her. "Put it on. It might be a little big, but it'll protect you. I'll ride without one."

"Damn it to hell! Steffan, I'm not running from this."

"That's not what this is."

"Isn't it? I need to face reality. I have memories of things that aren't real and never happened and holes in others. I'm on the verge of losing my job!" Those sharp blues of hers shot to his gaze. "Steffan, do you have any idea what the hell happened to me?"

He tried not to flinch at her enquiry.

The word GUILTY flashed over and over like a neon sign in his brain.

Great. Now his Were-panther was enjoying his discomfort. *Sadist.*

"Let's get back to your apartment."

He straddled the bike and extended his hand to her.

Raquel looked at him, then at the makeshift bandages on her forearms, and then back at him.

He literally heard her mind shift into overdrive as she thought the situation through.

Is she aware she's broadcasting her thought into my mind? How is this possible?

Damn, he hadn't realized how much he'd missed her until now.

He wanted so badly to sweep her off her feet and put her on the bike with him, but then some human might think he was kidnapping her.

"Raquel, I know you have questions. If you come with me, I might be able to answer them." He held out the helmet to her and, out of the corner of his eye, observed people taking out their cell phones and recording. "Please, Raquel."

Raquel grabbed the helmet and quickly slid it over her head. The darkened visor shielded those gorgeous eyes, cutting off the connection. The only thing he sensed was his panther.

She straddled the bike behind him, and the moment her thighs clenched against his ass, his senses came alive. As she leaned forward, he felt the gentle weight of her full breasts pressed against his back, and when she scooted closer to get a better hold on him with her legs, his cock pressed painfully against his jeans, and he barely felt her grab the belt loops of his jeans.

Who would have ever thought he'd be turned on by a female behind him. He should be cupping her ass with his thighs.

She wiggled to get closer to him, and he imagined ripping off her jeans and fucking her on the seat of his bike. *Holy crap, I better stop thinking.*

He shook his head to clear his mind and took off down the street.

This should not feel so right. Raquel was human.

Hopefully, the news that I've been seen with Raquel in my arms in broad daylight won't travel further than Roman.

He parked the bike in a spot next to her white Jetta, and Raquel handed him the helmet to hang. He forced himself to calm his painful erection and got off the bike in time to see her stumble on the curb. He swooped her up into his arms before she did a face-plant on the sidewalk.

She gasped and grabbed his shoulder. He paused. Something was different about her. He thought it was his imagination back at the café, but she seemed... lighter, smaller.

Had she lost weight? I carried her up those stairs at her apartment ten and a half weeks ago. She'd been eating during the few months she was at Lavelle House. I'm sure she weighed a little more than she does now.

Her stomach rumbled loudly.

She's hungry.

He'd see to it she ate.

Steffan carried her up the steps to her apartment, willed the door open, and stepped through. He kicked the door shut and willed the lock into place. He had to fix her memories anyway; he might as well erase what he'd just done, too.

"Raquel, let's take care of those cuts, and you need to eat something." He placed her in one of the farmhouse style chairs at the kitchen table.

She looked up at him.

She snorted. "My stomach's been off lately. I've gotten a lot of migraines recently, and I always get nauseous. I'll be fine."

Guilt riddled him. "No, you're going to eat."

"I can take care of myself."

"I know you can, but getting a lot of migraines isn't normal. I think you should see someone about those. A doctor who specializes in head trauma. Maybe you should come back to the House."

"Steffan, I don't need to go anywhere."

Steffan rummaged through her freezer and pulled out a frozen dinner. He ripped the box open and popped it into the microwave to nuke it.

"You don't need to take care of me; I am fully capable of doing so. I am a nurse, remember? You don't need to tether yourself to me."

Teeeetherrrrr.

The syllables ricocheted around his brain like a Ping-Pong ball, and an image of Michelle's bound, broken, bloody body and her vacant death's stare floated in front of him. The vision of the black rope hanging from the rigging, soaked in her blood, pinned his feet to where he stood and his whole body froze with fear.

He tried to breathe, but the viselike grip around his throat threatened to take him to his knees. Anxiety clawed its way to the surface.

"Steffan?"

He clamped his eyes shut and tried to will his body to stop shaking.

"Um, Steffan? Are you all right?"

He didn't want Raquel to see him shift to his panther. He didn't need to add more to what he needed to repair, and once his panther understood that, the shifting immediately stopped.

Protect her.

I am.

He couldn't protect Michelle. But he was damn sure going to protect Raquel. Nothing was going to happen to her. If she got hurt or killed for what she knew, Steffan wouldn't be able to live with himself. He'd caused her enough pain, and if he only ran into her every once in a while, he'd accept that. He'd make sure she didn't remember anything about Were-shifters.

Gruffly, he said, "I'll get something to clean the cuts. Don't move. There may be small fragments of splintered glass embedded in your arm, and I don't want them going any deeper than they are."

"There's a First-Aid kit in my bathroom."

Shaking his head, he headed to her bathroom. He gathered her First Aid kit, a towel, a washcloth, and a basin of warm water to clean her bloody cuts. Willing the medicine cabinet open, he grabbed a small glass for washing debris out of the eye. Once his canines were elongated, he placed the cup underneath one tip, and the stimulus allowed the clear enzyme to flow freely. He'd have to wait and let it be exposed to the air until it turned milky white. If he didn't wait long enough, it would burn her.

Humans healed too slowly for his liking.

Raquel needed someone to care for her, and right now, he would gladly be her saving grace. *It's the least I can do.*

Steffan took the supplies back to the kitchen and got the heated dinner out of the microwave. He grabbed a fork and placed both in front of her.

She glanced up quizzically at him and continued patting her arms dry with a dishtowel. She had tried to get off as much blood as possible.

"You know there's another box in the freezer. You could eat with me."

He shook his head. "Nah, I'm good." He sat in the chair next to her and arranged the items on the table.

"You know what, Steffan? You're awfully quiet. A little *too* quiet, if you know what I mean."

"How so?"

Raquel uncovered her forearms. "For starters, I find it unusual that you just so happened to be in the right place, at the right time, and came to my rescue. I thought I saw you last week at the grocery store, but when I looked away and then glanced back, you were gone. How'd you know I'd be at the café?"

He frowned. "I didn't. I was driving by and saw you were in trouble, so I stopped to see if I could help. You and my sister-in-law are best friends. I thought the guy was harassing you."

"How'd you know where I lived? I never had you here before."

"When Roman and Genevieve started dating, as a precaution I ran a background check on her and her closest friends. I handle all of Roman's security needs. Since my other two brothers and I also run a real estate business, Roman, as head of the company, has garnered a few jealous enemies. We've had corporate espionage occur in the past that resulted in millions of dollars of lost revenue. I had to make sure you weren't hiding anything or working for someone and using your friendship with Genevieve as a ruse." The lie rolled of his tongue like honey.

She waited a hairsbreadth, and her cool stare never faltered. Quietly, she asked, "Do you have any idea why my memory is shot?"

How much of her memory returned?

"The look of shock on your face tells me you do know what happened to my memory. Secondly, why does Roman *need* security?"

Smart cookie.

"Ya think?"

Oh hell, did she hear me? I wonder if she suspects anything—

57

Raquel looked surprised. "Of *course* I suspect something—wait. Your lips didn't move. But I heard you plain as if you had said it! Ohhh God. I'm losing my mind!"

He frowned observing her. *How the hell did she—*

Abruptly, she jumped out of the chair, and he grabbed her wrists. He couldn't afford for her to panic. If she panicked, her mind would become like edged steel. It would take weeks for him to be able to safely sift through her memories. And he didn't have weeks; he had days.

"Raquel, calm down. Let me explain. You're not losing your mind."

She eased back down into the chair. Anxiety and fear radiated off her in undulating waves, and his Were-panther reacted.

Protect.

She'll need to know the truth—part of it at least.

"Steffan, do you know what the most frustrating thing about this whole scenario is?"

"What?"

"I have a sneaky suspicion *you're involved.*"

Her blue eyes darkened, and he flinched as he got the image of daggers flying into his chest.

Oh yeah, Raquel was pissed, and he knew what she was going to say next without reading her mind.

"How am I involved?" *Considering you're right.*

"I've dreamt about you lifting my body, transporting me in the back of a car I've never been in. I've seen you pop up in unexpected places like the grocery store. I saw you at work for the first two days after I returned from a safari. I keep seeing visions of us together in bed. I can remember all that clear as a bell, but I can't remember half of what I do for my job!

"Are you keeping an eye on me? How is Genevieve involved in all of this, because she pops up at work almost immediately after I screw something up, and considering she's married to your brother, I surmise your presence on the street back at the café was no coincidence. Tell me I'm wrong; I dare you!"

The female had fire; he'd give her credit. And her strong emotions stirred something within him. He didn't want to acknowledge the attraction he felt for her, but it was there. However, it would be best if she had no memory of Were-shifters or anything related to Kindred. She'd be safe, and in order to get her to calm down enough for him to erase her memory, he'd have to tell her the truth.

Quietly, he said, "You're right."

She stared at him.

"That's it? That's all you're going to say?"

"Let me finish. The day of your wedding, you and Genevieve were kidnapped. Roman, Cristoff, and I saved you both. You didn't hit your head on a rock, nor did you go on a safari. You hit your head during the rescue. You stayed at the house for a few months because it was easier to protect you."

Fates, he felt ill not telling her the whole truth. It was as though someone had punched him in the gut.

Raquel replied, "I was at the house for a few months?"

"Correct."

"Where did the pictures of the safari—and the large scar in the middle of my back—where'd those come from then?"

Fates, there's no way around it.

"You and Genevieve were around the Duprees. They are lion shifters."

Raquel's brows popped high. "Seriously? You're going with that?"

Steffan frowned. The smart-assed attitude wasn't what he expected. "Alpha Dupree gouged your back to mark you. Lion shifters either use their enzyme or claw a mark into their intended Mates."

Steffan didn't like the fact she had been marked either way, and he fought the building anger.

"Take off your top for me; I want to take a look at your back. You can leave the peach tank top on, but the white shirt needs to go. It's ruined anyway. I'll buy you another." Hell, he'd give her anything to make her feel better.

"Steffan, thank you, but why do you want to see my back? And that whole lie you just spun was unnecessary. There's no such thing as shifters. But if you want to see it, then fine."

She shrugged, took the thin see-through white blouse off, and leaned forward. The three-inch-wide scar had thickened, but the edges blended well into the healthy skin, and in the future, a plastic surgeon would be able to hide the scar better than the enzyme had. *I'll call Dr. Jeffrey and see if he knows any Kindred plastic surgeons at St. Joseph's.* The relief he felt quieted his panther, and the anger lifted. At least it wasn't going to bother her.

He gently traced over the rough scar, trailing down over her back and to her waist. He could feel the edges of the scar through the tank top that tucked into her jeans.

She shuddered, and he jerked his hand away.

"Sorry. Does it hurt?" Fates, he hadn't known a scar left by a Kindred would hurt, and he hadn't meant to cause her any pain. Man, he was racking up the points today and not in a good way either.

"Not really. It just feels weird. At times, it bothers me. I can't believe I was stupid enough to get out of the Jeep when I knew well enough that lions move in prides and there could be others around. They aren't lone animals like a cheetah is."

He paused as her words hit home. She honestly didn't believe him about a lion shifter doing this to her. No matter. Once her memory was rewired, it wouldn't matter anyway.

He moved back a little, and she turned to face him. "Thank you, Raquel."

She snorted and laughed. "You seem calmer all of a sudden. Since you're satisfied, you can go."

Damn female was infuriating. "Not until I help you with those gashes in your arm."

He grabbed a pair of tweezers from the First Aid kit and plucked out the shards of glass embedded in her forearms, dropping the fragments into the metal bowl. The delicate *plink* made him cringe inwardly each time he heard the glass hit the bottom of the bowl.

It might have been an accident, but had there not been other humans around, his fist would've connected with Keith's face. A memory of Michelle's blood ghosted in front of him. His inner panther slashed at his stomach, and the muscles contracted as if the scene was fresh. He stayed motionless until the sadness dissipated. The memory was uncomfortable, but he didn't want to let on how uncomfortable.

"Steffan, if the sight of blood bothers you so much, I can do this."

His hand halted in mid-air. *How'd she know if the sight of blood bothered me? I've killed humans, animals, other Kindred when it became necessary, and she thinks her blood bothers me? Only ghosts that my panther keeps reminding me of, bother me.*

"Excuse me?" She suddenly jerked her arm out of his grasp and regarded him questioningly. "What ghosts? Ya know, I could've sworn you said something."

She's been picking up my thoughts, and I haven't even tried to mindlink with her yet. How the hell—

"Sorry. I said I'm almost done."

He dropped the last few remaining shards along with the tweezers into the bowl. There were fifteen shards of glass, all the size of splinters.

"Go rinse your arms off and pat them dry in the sink. I'll put a salve on and wrap them for you."

Raquel rummaged through the First Aid kit, grabbing the Neosporin. "I can use this. It works well enough."

Not well enough for me. I want your skin healed... immediately. "There's a gel I carry with me at all times. That's what's in the cup here." He picked up the small glass, tilting it to the side so she would see what now looked like white gel.

She stared at him as if he had grown two heads.

He dipped a finger into the milky enzyme and felt it burn. He paused. This simple act of taking care of Raquel was more intimate to him. Steffan suppressed his thoughts on the intimacy of what he was doing and slathered the gel on her forearm.

"It's hot. Did you heat it?" She flinched and sucked in a hiss, pulling her arm away.

He'd forgotten how it reacted when it came into contact with human skin.

He applied the enzyme evenly. "No, *ma chérie*. The slight burn is killing off any bacteria so an infection doesn't set in." He took her other arm and applied a little, smoothing it out over petal-soft skin.

Her grateful sigh was music to his ears.

At least it's working.

Fates, he had forgotten how smooth her skin was. He loved how her muscles responded to his touch.

He hungered to see her reaction as he used the tip of his claw to stroke down the long column of her throat, press his body next to hers, listen to her soft sighs, and—

61

Raquel coughed and stuttered. "Um, n-no... it's fine. I wasn't expecting it to be so warm when first applied. Most creams are usually cool to the touch. This feels more like a lubricant, like massage oil. It's tingly." She swallowed awkwardly.

He continued to massage the enzyme into her skin and work over tense muscles. He heard her heart beating, her lungs filling with air every time she took a breath, and her scent enticed him.

A brief *flutter* brushed along his energy field at his temple. He couldn't explain it, but it reminded him of how cubs started initiating mindlinks with others. It confused him at first, considering he was the only Kindred in the room. He allowed the psychic connection to open between his mind and Raquel's.

He felt her, the blood flowing in her veins, and every time she inhaled, he sensed the air expanding her lungs and the contraction of her diaphragm. He felt her heart beating inside her chest and the undulation of her throat as she swallowed. Fates, he'd love to feel this closeness to a mate making love. The intensity of how he was able to *feel her so completely* shocked him, and for the first time since his mate died, he didn't feel so alone.

How the hell can she reach her mind out to me?

This was a bad idea. Her mind actually reached out to him, the edges of her consciousness barely pliable. Her scent unexpectedly bloomed for him.

His cell rang, causing the beautiful connection to snap and break like a frozen rubber band.

Raquel quickly grabbed her head, and he blinked away the sudden loss.

I forgot how much a mindlink hurt when it's shut down too quickly.

"Raquel, you okay?"

"Um... yeah. I feel like I got kicked in the head. I'm probably getting a migraine. Sorry."

Growling in frustration, he ripped the cell out of the holder on his belt—"What?"—and moved over to the counter, away from her arousing scent.

"Well, hello to you too. For a second, I thought I had called Roman by mistake." Cristoff laughed.

"No, you didn't. What do you want?"

"Have you found Raquel? Roman wanted me to check on you in case the entire pard was needed to help you search. I know how you tend to *lose* things."

Raquel moved out of her chair, and Steffan's tracking instinct took over. She rummaged in a cabinet for a glass and then got some orange juice out of the fridge.

"No, I found her. In fact, I was about to *fix something* when you called. You really have lousy timing." Damn, his voice sounded gruff, even to his ears. *Cool it, Steffan.* To make matters worse, his own skin felt like it was suffocating him. His panther obviously had an idea about what to do with Cristoff's interruption.

Raquel glanced at him as she drank. The air crackled with electricity, which shot straight to his cock. Those blue eyes of hers were going to be the death of him. Her lips pursed over the rim of the glass, and her neck muscles undulated as she swallowed. She brushed back a curly strand of hair, only for it to spring back into place.

Damn, her neck was gorgeous.

His gaze roamed down her neck and fell on the tops of her full breasts peeking out from the peach colored tank top, rising and falling with each breath she took, her nipples drawn into tight buds. Her bra didn't do a good job of *hiding* her nipples. God, he would love to suck one of those into his mouth and roll the nub around with his tongue.

Cristoff replied. "Hey, Roman wanted me to check up on you is all. He said you would understand. ... Steff? Did you hear what I said, or should I buy you a hearing aid for Christmas? ... Steff?"

Focus, damn it! "I understand. Don't worry about it." *Was it hot in here?*

Cristoff asked, "Will you be in the office tonight to sign for the sale of your house? I think we can close this puppy up in about a week or so after the Mating Ceremony."

"Yes. I should be back so I can close the deal."

"Good. And Steff?"

"What."

"If you don't show, I'll know you were banging her. I can hear that li'l sausage of yours between your legs sizzling with need. Don't forget: She's human. You might scare her." Cristoff roared with laughter.

63

Click.

Scare her. Human.

Those words echoed and left distaste on his soul. Who the hell was he kidding?

Raquel was a human; he'd have to remember that, and the small window of opportunity he had to fix her memory so she could go back to work was slowly closing.

He felt a sharp sting in his eyes, and a second later, he could see Raquel's aura glowing around her. His inner panther was enjoying the view.

She stopped cold.

Chapter 8

Weren't his eyes brown a second ago? Now, they're a shade of blue.

"RRRRRaquelll."

His voice had deepened, sounding like a purr.

The sound set off tiny flutters low in Raquel's belly then spread tingling warmth all over. Her thighs ached with the need to be touched, and her core thrummed alive.

The room felt like it was shrinking, so she sat back down in the chair. Steffan had suddenly become her lifeline—a knight in shining armor coming to her rescue.

He took a deep breath, and his shoulders and chest expanded. *Wow, he's really put together.*

The muscles under his shirt twitched, and his heated gaze roamed over her. Raquel found it hard to look away.

One word came to mind.

Predator.

And she was prey.

Images of him in a wooded area came to her, and she frowned. She'd only known him for a short while, yet there was this undeniable connection every time she looked at him. She thought she had slept with him in the past, but she couldn't remember. He was a damn fine piece of eye candy, that was for sure.

A thought occurred to her. Was it possible that maybe her soul knew him, like a past life or something? Gramma believed in it. It could be true, couldn't it?

Raquel's memories about him were fuzzy at best, but when she thought of him, she didn't get the usual headaches. He lived with Roman and Genevieve, and Gena never said anything bad about him.

She remembered him bending over the trunk of her car so he could lift a heavy box—*of what? Flowers... something, and he carried them for me.* He wore really tight jeans, and the muscles in his back flexed. All she could think about was licking and biting those thick muscles, and she secretly wondered how big the muscle that hung between his legs was.

He had been kind to her then. A memory bled through of how he thought she'd make a beautiful bride.

When was that? I'm so confused.

His blue eyes darkened, and she didn't dare look away. The intensity of his stare left her feeling naked. It was... hypnotic.

He sank to his knees between her own and gently cupped her face. The roughened palms brushed against her cheek, and he caressed her with his thumb, rubbing back and forth. A tremor started down her neck and into her shoulders.

Her heart thudded against her ribs. The heat from his hand seeped into her skin like a balm, calming the chaotic emotions she had held at bay. Keith, her trip to Africa—alone, her future at her job. Now, none of that mattered. A small part of her was afraid. Afraid to think about what she was doing, but to hell with it. Steffan was right here, right now.

Another flash of a memory of him helping her across a fallen tree and catching her in his strong arms. He had been there for her, just like he had been there for her when Keith shoved her today.

God, I wish I could remember us, if there was an us. There seemed to be an us, but damn it!

He leaned in, and everything disappeared. Except for the man before her.

Sharp, intense pain in the side of her head made her wince. She snapped her eyes shut and sucked air in through her teeth. A second later, the pain vanished.

He sighed slowly. "I'm sorry, *bébé*."

Raquel opened her eyes. "Sorry? For what?"

"The pain you have. I'd like to kiss it and make it better."

His smoldering eyes never left hers as he leaned closer to her. Strangely, her temples pinged with pain, but this lessened the closer he got.

The moment his lips pressed against hers, her eyes closed in submission, and she gave herself over to the chain reaction. No pain at all, and a part of her discerned she had found peace within the chaotic turmoil that had happened over the past few weeks.

Raquel welcomed the heat of his hand as it slid to the back of her neck, pulling her closer to him.

Basic instinct took hold, and she kissed him back, nipping his bottom lip. He moaned, and Raquel's lips parted, his tongue dancing a tango with hers. Fingers tangled in her hair, sending pinpricks of delicious pain racing along her scalp.

More. He feels so familiar. Like home.

Strange French words resonated from somewhere, and he abruptly pulled slightly away from her. His warmth gone, she opened her eyes and stared back at him. Confusion and curiosity shone in those blue eyes.

Had he said something? It sounded like him, but his mouth had been too busy to say anything.

Her swollen lips pulsed in time with her erratic heartbeat. She wanted more. He made her feel alive. She pulled him to her, and Steffan's tongue snaked out and licked the corner of her mouth. On instinct, she parted her lips, and his tongue dove into the depths of her mouth in a succession of mimicking thrusts.

Raquel scooted closer to him on the edge of the low seated chair and arched her hips against his.

Steffan's heavy hand slid down to the small of her back, fingers splayed while moving downward, and he pulled her closer to him. Using slight pressure, he ground his pelvis against her. The heavy cock hidden behind his jeans strained against her belly, begging for freedom. Damn, he was huge.

This was so wrong, yet her body knew what it wanted; him.

He immediately scooped her up into his arms and carried her down the hall to her bedroom. They were hard as steel. Her palm slid over the stubble on his cheek, up to the back of his neck, and held him closer while he devoured her mouth. He made her light-headed, and the next thing she felt was him lowering her onto her bed.

This was fire, and she was playing with it. Gramma always said, "Take care when one must dare to dance with the devil. You might burn." Dare she?

Fuck, she wanted to burn.

He jerked, breaking the connection and jostling Raquel in his arms.

Breathing hard, she didn't know what happened. "Steffan? Is something wrong?"

A sharp flash of light from his eyes blinded her momentarily, and in the next minute, he captured her lips. Only this time, the kiss conveyed an urgency, a desperation to have her, a claiming.

Steffan breathed, and she took his breath into herself. He controlled when and how she breathed; it was the oddest sensation. Time stood still, and she exhaled when he broke away, letting her breathe fresh air before reclaiming her mouth again.

Tongues danced. Breath mingled as one, and Raquel clawed into the dense muscle of his back and swallowed Steffan's throaty moan. His fingers returned the favor as he firmly squeezed her ass.

Raquel shuddered.

He tasted so damn good.

Her imagination ran wild. An image of a blue-eyed panther flashed in her mind, and the sleek, powerful cat stared into her soul.

The vision seemed so impossibly real, she opened her eyes and pulled back, heart racing, breath heavy and mingled with his.

Bright blue orbs stared back at her. He was breathing just as hard as she was.

Raquel moistened her lips and tasted something sweet.

Raquel whispered, "I need you." She nipped his lip, rubbing her nose against his. "Make me feel alive."

He froze. Panic crept across his features, and she immediately knew he was having second thoughts. The minute she asked him to make her feel alive he changed.

He cleared his throat. "Raquel," he croaked. "We need to stop. I... "

Quietly, Raquel murmured, "I need you. Sir." She placed her hand over his heart.

He pulled away, and she had to sit on the edge of the bed to keep him close to her.

A silent war raged on. His pupils narrowed, then he closed his eyes. Time stood still until the tension slowly ebbed from Steffan.

Whatever was going on inside his head, obviously, he had come to a decision. She should feel bad, shouldn't she? After all, she was the pathetic woman who was begging here.

He slowly took off his shirt. His breath was warm, his demeanor controlled. His voice was firm. "Raquel, take off my pants and touch me." He stood before her. "I can make you feel everything you want, but first, you will touch me."

Her hands had a mind of their own, memorizing every dip of rock-hard muscle on his chest and traveling over a well-chiseled stomach. His build was hardened muscle. A smattering of hair covered most of his torso and tickled the palms of her hands. The firm muscles twitched under Raquel's caress.

Raquel didn't hesitate and quickly popped the button on his jeans and tugged the zipper down, watching the teeth open on the front of his pants. The anticipation resembled what Christmas morning should look like. His cock bounced up to greet her.

Raquel licked her lips and leaned in.

He smelled so good, a combination of earth and man.

Thick fingers entwined in her hair, he pulled her head back, forcing her to look up at him. He drew her up to him and cupped her face, kissing her hard with desperate urgency. He pulled back, nuzzling his nose against hers, and commanded, "Suck me. Take me into that hot mouth of yours."

She didn't wait for an engraved invitation. She wrapped her lips around his cock, and her head bobbed up and down on his shaft, greedily sucking him. Her teeth grazed over the sensitive flesh, all the while her hand cupped and kneaded his balls. He growled, and his hands gripped her hair and pulled her off of him. She mewed in displeasure.

His voice had turned gruff. "Take off your clothes."

She licked her lips and smiled up at him. "Take my clothes off." The tip of her tongue rimmed around the mushroom head of his cock, teasing.

"If I do, there won't be anything left of them."

"Clothing is soooo overrated." She gave him a devilish grin.

He let go of her hair, grabbed the tank top and bra and, with both hands, ripped them open in the front.

Cold air assaulted her, and her nipples tightened. His arm wrapped around her, pulling upward so he could capture one of the nubs in his mouth. He suckled hard, nipping every so often. Flutters erupted in her stomach, and her core screamed to be filled. She arched into his mouth, and he suckled harder.

"Yesssssss."

He moaned—or was that a purring growl?

Hands worked at the button of her jeans, followed by the sound

69

of the material tearing down the front and between her legs until they were free.

He actually ripped my jeans!

He pressed her back down onto the mattress.

Raquel knew she was being reckless, but damn it to hell, she needed him. Her nails dug into his shoulders, and he let go of her nipple with a pop. His breathing was hard, his eyes focused on her. He nudged her legs open with his knee and positioned the swollen head of his cock at her entrance.

"Wait! There are condoms in my nightstand!"

He ripped the drawer out, dumped the contents onto the floor, and handed a condom to her. She took it from him, opened the wrapper with her teeth, then rolled the sheath over his heavy cock, which jerked in her hand.

He grabbed her hands in his and pinned them above her head. She cried out as he seated fully inside of her with one hard, satisfying thrust. The initial pain diminished, and she used her internal muscles to grip onto his cock.

Damn, he was bigger than she had anticipated. He was hot, and his cock jerked inside of her, but he refused to move.

She gasped, not out of pain, but with frustration that he wasn't moving his hips with her.

He breathed deeply against her neck as he asked, "Are you all right?"

In answer, she arched her hips toward him, and her core pulled on that rock-hard cock of his. "Never better."

He shuddered once, retreated, and then surged forward.

She gently nipped his neck, and he turned his head to hers, capturing her mouth and kissing her hard, pinning her head against the bed. His thick, heavy tongue mimicked his thrusts. He gained momentum, hitting that sweet spot. Tiny quivers began at the base of her spine until a full orgasm erupted. He fucked her mouth and filled her core.

Raquel smiled against his mouth, relishing the tingles firing along her nerve endings. She was aware of the intensely masculine sounds rumbling in his chest and escaping into the air, aware of the firm grip he had on her wrists, and aware of the man thrusting into her.

God, she had died and gone to heaven.

Not only did he possess impressive strength, but Raquel recognized a raw power rolling beneath his skin. She didn't know what it was, but there was a dangerous edge to him. Something her soul told her. But for some reason, she didn't fear him. He was a mystery to her, and he made her feel alive for the first time in a long, long spell.

He seized above her at the same time her orgasm hit her. He let go of her wrists to grip the blanket beneath her on either side of her head. Muscles in his arms twitched and shook from his own orgasm. She was floating. *This is what heaven must feel like.* He was magnificent, and on impulse, she dragged her nails down his chest and shoulder.

The sound Steffan made was more like a cat purring with its mouth open, startling Raquel.

Quickly, he pulled out, barely rested his weight on top of her and placed his fingers on both sides of her head.

"Raquel, you're amazing."

Steffan took a deep breath and opened his eyes, a definitive determination reflected in the brown orbs. *Brown?* This time, though, a ring of piercing blue circled his pupils.

"Your eyes... they changed."

Steffan stopped breathing all together for a second. "I want you to be aware of what you are asking of me. And of what I am."

She blinked. "I am. Now, are you going to answer me as to why your eyes change color?"

She licked the side of his neck and nipped at his collarbone.

"Raquel, I'm—oh, damn—I'm not human. I'm a Were-panther."

She smiled up at him. "You're funny." She giggled.

Surprise leapt into his brown eyes; she'd shocked him.

He drew in a hesitant breath, and his whole demeanor changed from satisfied man to one that was anxious.

"No, seriously. I am a Were-panther. I hold two forms: a human that can also change into a panther. My Kindred brethren have been hunted for thousands of years, and one of our laws states that if a human learns of us, the human must be either turned into what we are or killed. I don't want to see you killed, and despite what the law says, I don't think you need to be turned into a Were-panther. Your friendship with Genevieve means a lot to her and my Alpha's

71

happiness. Roman is the Alpha of the Lavelle pard, so I erased your memories and planted new ones in order to save your life. That is why your memory has holes in it.

"You had a real chance at going back to the human world. I erased your mind of the day you and Genevieve were kidnapped. Except... "

The intensity of those eyes made her drop her gaze to his chest. She wasn't so sure she wanted to hear the rest. The man was talking in circles, yet her mind was telling her the events had happened. The silence stemming from him irritated her.

"Except what?"

Why did men find it so hard to communicate what they wanted? Keith hardly ever did and now Steffan. Were most men stupid?

Steffan flinched as if she'd slapped him in the face. "I unintentionally erased a conversation about some of your medical training along with it, and according to Genevieve, you've been trying to remember what really happened to you."

Raquel stilled as soon as he mentioned her training. She'd had a hard enough time coming back to work, and here she thought it had been the lion's fault. Instead, Steffan was admitting to this.

Raquel sat up, and he pulled back to sit beside her. "H-how do you know this?"

"Genevieve said you have been having trouble at work. I'm sorry. I botched it. However, in order to fix what I did, I have to return your memories."

She frowned, unsure of what he was saying. *This isn't real. Can't be.*

Steffan growled, and his eyes flashed. He huffed. "Do you want to know why my eyes change color or not?"

"Um, ah, yes, I do. But you're not making any sense at all."

"Well, *bébé*, in order to do that, I need to unlock your memories."

She shook her head. *Am I hearing this right?*

The snarky smile did very little to ease her mind.

"And by the way, *you're projecting* your thoughts to me." He kept his mouth closed, yet in her mind heard him clear as a bell. "*I can hear you.*"

"*What the hell?*"

"I heard that, Raquel. I'm communicating with you through a telepathic mindlink."

She gasped. Was he telling her the truth? Was he really different than her?

Raquel stiffened her spine and looked directly into his eyes. "Then show me, but all I ask is, will this hurt?"

"A little. It depends how much bleeds back." Steffan sighed. "Do you want to know the truth or not?"

Raquel slowly nodded. She had to find out. It might hold all the answers to the missing periods of time and why she couldn't remember her job in the ED but she remembered other protocols in the hospital.

Searing pain ripped through her head. Her vision became snowy. Her chest felt like it was going to explode. She gasped, trying to breathe.

Steffan had wrapped her in his arms as a sonic boom ricocheted in her mind, and it was flooded with scenes she could have sworn never happened: getting ready for her wedding, the limo driver shot, blood splattered all over her pristine, white wedding gown, and Steffan nearly getting hit by a truck as he tried in vain to rescue her and Genevieve from the limo. The memories came out of nowhere.

Pressure grew worse, and ringing grew louder and louder until something popped. She screamed until the pain lessened, and the snowy haze cleared to reveal Steffan cautiously observing her.

She had been kidnapped with her friend Genevieve—on the day of her wedding. Steffan and Roman rescued both of them. "Oh. My. God!" *What the hell just happened?*

She gasped at a new image flooding her mind. The cell. She remembered. A madman held them prisoner. He wanted to kill her! *My back!* "It wasn't a trip to Africa I went on; a lion really did claw me. It was in the cell with me and Genevieve, and then... and then... why can't I remember?"

Steffan sighed in resignation. "Because, *bébé*, you hit your head against the cement wall of the cell and blacked out. But I can fill you in on it because I took care of you. Do you remember? Do you remember Were-panthers?" He gently caressed the side of her face. Only she pushed him away and covered herself with a pillow propped in front of her. "I'm so sorry."

Raquel scooted up the bed and clenched the pillow to her chest. *What the hell? I thought I was having a heart attack!*

"I'm sorry, *bébé*."

He lay on the bed on his side, leaning his weight on his one arm, legs curled. He didn't try to touch her again and kept his distance. Painful regret reflected back at her. "After Dupree was killed, I carried you and held you in the back of Cristoff's car the whole way home. Ascenza closed most of the wound on your back, using herbs to heal the skin. Genevieve stitched you up. I watched over you for months as you healed. When the time came, you agreed to have your memory erased. But I erased too much."

"You did *what*?"

"Do you remember?" He searched her face. "Search your memories. You saw Roman, Genevieve, and me shift into our alternate forms. I had no choice but to erase those memories."

The man must be nuts.

"Raquel, I am far from nuts."

He was talking in her mind, and every time he did that, her head felt like the stirrings of a migraine.

"Why? And how long does this headache last?" She clutched her head in agony. *I should just throw up on him. See how he likes it.*

"Damn it, bébé, your memories are there! Think!"

He growled, jumped off the bed, paced the room while mumbling until he stopped by her dresser with his back to her. He shook and hung his head before looking up at the ceiling. She threw a pillow at him, hitting him square between the shoulder blades. He whipped around.

She had a gloriously naked muscular man in her bedroom, one with whom she had just had the best sex with, and he was telling her things that weren't making sense.

She should be angry with him, but for some reason, with everything else muddling her life, he anchored her.

"Why, did you do this to me, Steffan?"

He grabbed his jeans off the floor and began putting them back on. "As I explained, it's our law. You're *human*. Other Were-shifters that have been around for centuries don't look kindly on humans mingling with those of the Kindred. Their first instinct is self-preservation, to kill in order to survive. I had to do something. Think back. You and me... out for a walk... getting fresh air."

Raquel thought hard. She stayed silent because of the onslaught of memories coming to her. "I remember a woman... short hair... yelling at you... at me... Something about calling the Commission members and..."

"It's for your safety. Our Commission would have killed you if I hadn't done as they ordered." His shoulders heaved in a heavy sigh. "I can break the telepathic link or you can shut me out, but I want to keep it open until I've finished fixing the problem."

"Yes, Steffan. You need to fix the problem because you caused the problem!"

When did everything in the cosmos go so, so wrong?

Chapter 9

Steffan thought for sure he could slip into a corner of Raquel's mind, fix the mistake by reweaving the fragments of her medical knowledge back together, and disappear from her life. Except he hadn't counted on his own body betraying him. All those months she'd spent at the house prior to him sending her back to her world had done something to him and it was something he was afraid to admit to himself.

He was a moth to her flame, and she warmed his cold heart.

The pained look on her face said it all. He'd fucked up.

Raquel's anger was like an acid burn aimed at him through the mindlink. It was rare to find a human who, once connected in a mindlink, could feel each other's reaction. But he sensed her, which meant she should also be able to sense *all* of him, panther included.

The anger drained away and, in its place—curiosity. "Do you honestly turn into a panther?" She paused, a firm resolve settled into place, and she squared her shoulders. "There's no way that can be real."

"Yes. And it's real. I know you're having a hard time understanding but—"

She snorted. "And to think with all this craziness in my life I picked someone that's delusional to have sex with."

Steffan fumed. "Why are you having such a hard time believing it's true?"

Why isn't she remembering any of my pard shifting into our alter egos? Is it possible it has something to do with the way she hit her head against the cement wall?

"Look, I know there are some things in life, like ghosts, demons, God, the devil, and unexplained occurrences, and in my own family, I have an aunt that can talk to the dead, but people turning into an animal that is double the size of a human—impossible."

Un-frickin-believable.

"I'm getting tired of this mumbo-jumbo about turning into

animals. Since you've established, you're going to wipe my mind, just do it." She swallowed hard. "And while you're at it, you can erase what we just did." She quickly grabbed her pants and got a clean white cotton t-shirt from the dresser drawer, intent on getting dressed. "If I'm going to move on, I'd rather not have a memory to haunt me at night."

Steffan hated this. She was too upset for him to do anything. She'd have to calm down before he attempted to wipe the memories again, and damn it, calming a pissed off female wasn't exactly his forte.

"Listen, Raquel, I can fix this."

"Honestly, I don't think you can."

Steffan's skin itched. Panther boy wasn't happy either.

He ignored the urge to shift and drew in a deep breath and released it slowly.

Softly, he said, "I'm sorry. Let me help you calm down so it won't be as painful. I'll go slower."

"No."

"I can go sl—"

"I said no. Hell no. What you just did by unlocking my memories was painful enough! And you want me to let you go back into my brain and rewire it so I forget things—again? NO! You messed up. I want your reassurance it won't happen again."

He didn't want resentment hanging between them. "I've done this a thousand times, and I will honor your request so you won't remember me in the way we just shared." *Even though I'll always remember how you responded to me.*

"If you've done this magic trick a thousand times, then why'd you mess up my life? I might—no, I *know* I'm losing my job because of you! What would I do for income?"

"If you had completely lost your job, your wages would've been compensated from the House of Lavelle. Now, let me fix it so you will be able to keep your job!"

Steffan hadn't meant to yell, but it got her attention.

"You're not going to drop this, are you."

"No. Will you please let me help you?"

Time stood still. The longer she waited, the less time he had to do this.

"Fine."

Thank the Fates she came to see reason. "Let me hold you."

She hesitated, but eventually, on her own, she allowed him hold her. He wrapped her in his embrace, and it took a moment for her to lean into him.

The mindlink had never been disconnected. When a link is open each participant was able to sense each other and yet he didn't sense her at all. For some strange reason, it baffled him as to why she hadn't closed it.

The mindlink was the most intimate act between Kindred, and the ability to see and feel each other's orgasm made it even more intimate. Normally after a climax, the link naturally shut down. With Raquel, she left it open, and it was just as intimate.

Her mind was unique. It was like seeing the past and present all in one shot. Those humans whose memories he had erased only ever showed him the past, and the resonating emotions riding the mindlink were always self-appreciating.

Not so with Raquel.

He prayed to the Fates her essence wouldn't leave an echo in his soul after she returned to her life. That wouldn't bode well for any future romantic relationships, should he move on to someone of his own kind.

He bit the inside of his cheek to keep his own emotions at bay and honed in on her memories in search of the right ones. He saw her as a young child, so cute, sitting on the front steps at a house. But she was sad. The little girl got up to peek in through the screen door and saw adults arguing. *They must be her parents.* The man shoved papers into the woman's hands, and Steffan read the letterhead through the little girl's eyes. They were getting a divorce. The child's emotions slammed into his gut, and he felt the rake of the panther's claws across his stomach. He wished he could reach out and console her, but he reminded himself these scenes were only memories, shadows forever imprinted on the soul. He couldn't change the outcome for her. It was too far into the past.

Steffan's heart ached for her.

In his mind, his panther raised its head.

Protect her.

Shut up. I am protecting her. She needs to go back to her human world, and I need to be with my pard.

78

A ghosted memory flickered before him. Raquel as a teenager beside her father's grave. Next, he saw her first boyfriend. The sharp stab of jealousy surprised him, but he quickly squashed his own emotions to concentrate on hers. He couldn't risk getting attached to her.

In another memory, she was older and standing at the foot of another grave. He didn't have to read the gravestone to know it was her mother's. Her pain was strong enough to elicit a painful response from his panther.

An image of his mother lying in her coffin at the funeral floated next to him.

Focus. I need to focus.

He forced himself to move past the rest of her teenage years, college, and the few boyfriends she had had, until he came to images of Keith. The ones pertaining to planning their wedding had to be around here.

Where the hell is it?

Something pulsed in.

She growled at him, and a second later, wall after wall formed around him, threatening to crush him. Her mind was protecting itself. *She's human. How the hell can she know how to shut me out and block me?*

Self-preservation took over, and he pushed back against the walls hard enough to shatter them to pieces.

Raquel screamed, and her stark fear cut through him like a razor. Immediately, he retreated from her mind, the urge to shift and protect was undeniable.

She shoved him away.

His bones broke apart, and he jumped back from her in time for a full panther mode to commence. She jumped back to the wall, eyes closed in a grimace, clutching her head in her hands as she slid down to the floor. She slowly slumped over as she lost consciousness, and the mindlink shut down.

Steffan blinked rapidly, clearing his sight. Things were brighter, more detailed. He looked down at his front paws, the claws flexing against the thick carpet pile on the floor.

Oh crap! What the hell happened?

He chuffed, pawed at the floor, and growled.

You just haaaad to make an appearance.

The only response from his panther was, *In pain; protect.*

What the fuck! I had everything under control.

Sitting on his haunches, his tail slashed from side to side.

Her physical pain had forced his Were-panther to react. Thus, forcing him to shift.

He sighed. *That didn't go well.*

Guilt wracked him. He'd pushed too hard. He'd have to take her back home and discuss this situation with Roman. He snorted. Yeah, the Alpha was going to skin him alive.

He nuzzled and sniffed her face. She didn't move.

Steffan irritably transformed back into his humanoid form and knelt alongside her. Reaching out, he smoothed the dirty-blonde curls from her face. So soft. So beautiful. Her breathing was shallow and even. Cocking his head to the side, he noted her heart beat languidly, immediately calming the beast within.

She'll be okay.

"Everything's going to be all right. I need to make this right. I promise."

There's no way he would risk taking her back to the house on his motorcycle. Not like this.

He retrieved his cell phone from his shredded pants and paused with a finger poised over Roman's number. *I better get Cristoff first. He's at the office, and it's only a few blocks away.*

He tapped the screen and waited for his brother to pick up.

Cristoff coughed. "What's up? I'm not done drawing up the papers. Are you *sure* you want to sell your home? I mean you're not even listing it at top dollar. If anything, you're going to lose money on this."

Steffan sighed. "I'm sure. But I'm not calling about that. I need a favor."

"Do tell. The only time you call me is when you *need* something. I'm waiting for you to ask me out on a date."

"Fuck you."

"Ummmmm, you're not my type. Hair's too short. What'chya need?"

Steffan glanced over at Raquel. She hadn't stirred. "I need to take Raquel back to the house, and I only have the bike with me."

"So? Do I look like a taxi service?"

Steffan growled. "No, but she's out cold. Thanks to me." He scrubbed a hand over his face.

"Again? She better *not* be bleeding this time. I bought a new car because I couldn't get the blood stains out of the upholstery the first time. If she's bleeding, you're going to buy me that Koenigsegg CCXR Trevita. It's only four point eight million."

"In your dreams. Just get to Raquel's apartment."

Cristoff chuckled on the other end of the line. "Well, it is in my dreams. A wet one."

Steffan hung up on Cristoff.

One of these days. Fates, I hope you're listening! I hope you've got a doozy of a comeuppance for Cristoff!

In the meantime, I hope to hell she has something I can wear.

Chapter 10

Gia smiled up at the huge warehouse. A zing of excitement coursed through her like a live wire. *This would work.*

A year ago, she spoke to her Sire about having her own business by selling foreign cars in Louisiana. She'd worked for Lavelle Brothers Realty for a long time and felt the need for a career change. That was also when he told her he wanted her to settle down and get mated. She didn't want to settle down. She was too young. A mating could wait. Right now, she wanted her own business, and when she declined Alpha Dupree's son, her Sire had given in and gave her the deed to this warehouse—with the stipulation the space was to be shared with Fievel.

Jerox told her he was a co-owner of this particular warehouse with Fievel, and Fievel had given the other half of the deed over to his brother Lars out of pity. Jerox told her he'd made it clear to them that she was the one running the show on her half of the property.

No big deal. His access was legally to the docks and half of the back of the warehouse. She promised her Sire she'd stay clear of the building when Lars had shipments coming, most likely illegal, and she didn't want to get caught up in it.

Gia would tolerate whatever business Lars had until she had enough of her own funding to buy the male out. It was a shame the Mulatese Tenebrae was unable to hide some of his markings in humanoid form, so he found others to do business for him. She'd have to talk to him about it. But on the upside, Fievel would need to clear it with her if he wanted to use the warehouse.

Gia turned away from the building and gazed longingly over the open water. The smell of the Gulf's salt water invigorated her muscles and tickled her nose. She grinned as her imagination played out what the future would bring. The cars would come into the dock and be stored in the warehouse until they were needed. A few dealerships in Louisiana had already agreed to work with her.

Voices filtering through an open window behind her brought her out of her musings. Curious, she glanced back at the building. No one was supposed to be here tonight.

Gia hurried up the concrete steps, carefully unlocked the steel door, and cautiously stepped through, onto the landing inside the door and stopped cold to view the massive interior. It was as big as two football fields end-to-end. Large shipping crates were piled on top of each other over to the right side, and other types of metal containers blocked most of what she saw.

But Gia's keen ears picked up the murmur of voices at the back section of the shipping containers. *A male? But who? The language sounds like Russian? He sounds familiar, but who?*

A second voice gave her pause. *Two males?* One of the deeds she'd worked on was for a property being bought from a deal Cristoff had drawn up for one of the Northern Commission members, the Northern Beta she'd spoken to on the phone recently. The male's thick Chicago accent was a dead giveaway.

He wanted to buy a home in the area to conduct business for the Northern Commission.

What's he doing here? Why is he in my building?

But that was impossible because Alpha Roman would have told the Commission members someone from the North was in town. According to Kindred Law, if a member from another Commission took up residency outside of their birth area, that member was to abide by the rulings of the current Commission Head Alpha and report to the Head Alpha because he was the local governing body. Roman hadn't signed the final deed yet so the male shouldn't be here *without* the Northern Alpha.

Roman said nothing about a Northerner being in either Bayou Cane or at the Port of Fourchon.

Gia descended the metal staircase with care. She didn't want to let anyone know she was there. She walked by the metal shipping containers, searching for the male who was speaking, and nothing turned up. The metal distorted the sound.

They must be farther back. Frowning, she followed the deep resonating voice.

She turned the corner of the large shipping crate, and a sharp, heavy sting exploded in her chest, knocking her off her feet, against a

83

metal container, and to the floor. She stared up at the metal trusses supporting the roof.

Searing pain in her chest and head clouded her vision, making it hard to breathe. She'd hit her head on the cement floor when she went down.

She gulped for air, and her hand felt over the left side of her chest, trying to ease the pain. Something warm and gelatinous was spreading over her chest. She lifted her hand in front of her face, and ice-cold fear enveloped her.

Blood. My blood!

She tried to look around to find out who her attacker was. It was difficult, considering how blurry and dark her vision was becoming.

"S-s-someone help me!" she croaked.

It hurt to breathe, and she tried to shift into her lioness to get away, but for some reason, the change wouldn't come. She started to lose her connection with her Were-lion, and the knowledge she would die soon strangled the words in her throat.

She inhaled as deep as she could and caught the scent of a male. Her fucking killer was standing over her.

A deep resonating voice asked, "Who is she?"

It *was* the male from the North. *Andros shot me*! A second later, her temples exploded with the sound of his voice. She screamed at the painful intrusion.

"She is the daughter of Jerox from the House of Kohlemte. Let her go. *Now.*"

Stavslaka! *Fates, I beg of you, don't let me die! My Sire has to know; my father needs to know about this*!

Stavslaka growled venomously. "I agreed you could use this facility, but I did *not* agree to you killing or maiming anyone. I will take care of her."

Andros bellowed. "Shit! No one was supposed to be here!"

Hot tears slid down her face once the intrusion left her mind. Her chest and head thumped in unison, and the lion inside of her began to recede in her mind. She barely felt the familiar effervescent warmth her lioness provided her. It was the first time she'd felt alone in her own skin. Cold. Very cold. Ice cold. The symbiotic connection between herself and the Were-lion was severing. The Fates were releasing her lion from her body.

She was dying.

She attempted to cry out for help, but no noise passed her lips. Sorrow engulfed her.

"*NO! NO-no-no-no-no! Don't go! Don't leave me!*"

Her world darkened with each strangled breath she took. The last thing she saw was the red glow of amber eyes peering at her from a silhouetted shadow before her mind plunged into darkness.

***

Stavslaka held his hand over her heart and stared into her hazel eyes. They hadn't glazed over into a cold death stare yet, but she was close—ohhhh so, so close. The female's heartbeat was barely detectable. Her chest barely rose with each struggling breath. The moment her eyes glossed over into unconsciousness, he closed them for her.

He hated to watch a Were-shifter's life drain away and couldn't bear to watch hers. Regret stabbed him. He liked Gia, had known her since birth.

Damn Andros! Now, he would need to contain this situation.

"If Jerox finds out I killed his favorite cub, I'm toast. He'll have me killed in front of my own pard. I might as well pick out a coffin!"

Stavslaka's anger surged, and he ground his molars as he listened to the male panic behind him. "She's not dead. At least not yet. And I don't think you'll need to worry about what Jerox is going to do."

"And why is—"

Stavslaka whipped out his .45 and fired a single shot into the male's forehead. The male dropped like a stone. "That's why. Consider *your* problem... solved." He growled, sliding the Glock back into the holster in the lining of his coat.

This was a mess. He sighed and briefly glanced up at the rafters in frustration, then pulled out his cell and tapped star five.

"This is Tabitha. You've reached the Kindred emergency hotline. This call is being recorded and will be reported to the local Commission. What's your emergency?"

He recognized the female's voice on the other end of the line. "This is Alpha Stavslaka. There's been a shooting down at the warehouses on the lower end of the docks. Send an ambulance. Discretion is advised."

He'd get rid of the Northern Beta's body himself.

The line got quiet before the female replied. "Sir, I've shut off the recording and erased the tape. You can speak freely. Is the survivor Kindred?"

"Yes, a female. Jerox Kohlemte's cub. Inform him his cub has been shot by a trespasser, but leave my name out of the equation. If he questions you, answer him and say it was an anonymous tip from a homeless person. I'll make my own acknowledgements to Jerox. Not you."

"Understood. An ambulance will be there shortly. Are there any other Were-shifters on the property needing care? What about the shooter?"

Stavslaka ground his molars. He hated being questioned but knew the female's supervisor was close by; otherwise, she wouldn't have asked the question.

"No one else is injured, and the shooter has been... taken care of."

"Understood, Alpha Stavslaka."

He hung up the phone, picked up the male's body, carried him over to a shipping container, and tossed him inside. Once the steel doors closed, he locked it. He'd have to wait to dispose of the body until the ambulance left with Gia. The mighty Mississippi would do nicely.

He levitated Gia's body, took her outside, and gently placed her on the ground. A small, strangled intake of air gave him hope. She was fighting to stay alive, and only time would tell if she survived.

He kneeled beside her and placed his hand over her forehead. He didn't sense her lioness, and her mind was dark. There was no way to erase what she'd seen. It might be better if he killed her now rather than face the consequences in case she regained consciousness. A quick, hard twist of her head would sever her spinal cord at the base of her skull and kill her instantly.

Sirens erupted, and he glanced up. Cops. Human cops and an ambulance trailed behind. Killing her would have to wait. If human cops were here, then a human must've called 9-1-1.

"What happened here?"

"I don't know. I found her like this. I think she was mugged."

Chapter 11

Ow... my head. What happened? Raquel squeezed her eyes shut and opened them to rapidly blink until her vision cleared. *Where the hell am I?*

She remembered him holding her, and then she sensed him inside her mind. She looked at her surroundings.

This. Is. Weird.

Raquel floated in mid-air, well, not entirely. Gold dust surrounded and completely covered her feet, and each time she moved, it reminded her of walking through sand at the beach. The floating sensation was discombobulating. When she took a step forward, the gold swirled around her legs, yet she couldn't detect her feet touching anything resembling ground.

Everything around Raquel was dark, except for the moving pictures on the wall. *Am I in a movie theater?* The pictures surrounded her like beacons of light. She turned toward one and watched the scene unfurl. It was her childhood.

What the hell? Where am I?

Something hard gripped her wrist. She looked down to see swirling gold dust permeate the air, and a man's fingers ensnared her delicate wrist in his. Then glanced up into piercing, glowing blue eyes and, despite the initial shock, a sense of calm encircled her once she recognized the man. *Steffan.*

"Raquel, don't touch anything." His voice was tinged with fright.

"Steffan, I don't understand."

"That makes *two* of us. You shouldn't be able to interact with me in here."

"Where are we?"

The frustrated sigh wasn't lost on her. "You really don't emjoy explaining anything to me; do you."

"We're inside your mind. These are your memories. Now stay

87

put and don't touch anything. You could harm yourself without knowing what you're doing."

"What do you mean, harm myself?"

"You're not a Dreamwalker, and you're not of Kindred blood, so if you touch anything in here, and you do not understand what you're doing, you could end up killing yourself unintentionally. I reiterate: *Don't touch anything!*" he barked.

"And how do you know what to do?"

"Centuries of practice," he stated flatly.

Pfffft. "Yeah and if you'd had centuries of practice, I wouldn't be in this mess!"

He let go of her wrist, and she pulled it close to her chest. Heeding his warning, Raquel followed close behind him but kept her distance.

"Explain this to me, please!"

He sighed. "The only thing I can think of is you have some sort of psychic ability. Your subconscious is tagging along on my power to influence your mind through the mindlink we are sharing. We're seeing this as *you want to see it* so your mind can make sense of it. Everyone is different. You're strong, and I can feel it resonating like a tuning rod. Do you feel anything?"

She waited.

"Steffan, I don't feel anything except like I'm floating in a snowglobe."

"It must be just me. I feel a low-level hum."

Trepidation warned her not to question him further.

Steffan walked away from her, the gold getting kicked up and floating around him. She looked down at her feet again and noticed the gold stuck to her like glue. Like it was a part of her.

She saw movement out of the corner of her eye and she observed an apparition trailing behind him. Raquel could see through the image. The woman's long brunette hair floated wildly behind her, and she had the saddest eyes Raquel had ever seen. The woman turned back to Raquel, smiled, reached for her, and motioned toward Steffan before she vanished.

Raquel blinked a few times, but the woman never reappeared, and Raquel racked her brain to figure out who she was and came up blank. No clue.

Images on the walls flickered. Her parents, school, and even Keith. Raquel saw what Steffan saw. If a memory intrigued him, he stopped, watched the image for a while, then moved on to the next picture. "What are you looking for?" He stood perfectly still, and the golden dust began creeping up his leg, threatening to consume him.

"I'm looking for memory lapses. Incomplete sequences of your memories."

A memory floated by. But the edges didn't look as solid as the others, and broken shards of reflective mirrors floated around on the one edge.

"This is it."

This is what? "I don't understand?"

The edges were blurred and frayed, like someone had brushed their hand through it, smudging the image of a painting not yet dry. The broken shards flickered with memory. Steffan gathered some of the fragments and pushed them closer to the edge.

"Steffan, what are you doing?"

She leaned closer and frowned, trying to remember if what she was seeing was real or not. It was the day she was supposed to have gotten married.

"This is the memory I need." He reached out and grabbed hold of the edge and started to use a loose thread to bind the fragments. Suddenly, the image was ripped out of his grasp by unseen hands.

"No Raquel, you need to stay calm! The more agitated you become; you're going to want to protect yourself. Stop!" He chased after it, growling, and bared large canines in his determination.

This whole thing was off. Something wasn't right. A man didn't have large teeth, nor did one have conversations with themselves in their own dream. That's what this was: a dream.

Raquel observed the unusual picture. When it flickered, it moved as if someone was turning it frame by frame, whereas the others were constantly moving. The wedding gown she wore had blood spattered all over the front of it. Then, she was shoved into the back of the limo where she held her best friend in her arms.

This isn't right! Why can't I remember?

She diverted her gaze downward to stare into the black abyss of her mind, the gold dust reached out of the darkness, swirling around her legs as she moved. Images flickered down below her, and she knew they were only memories. This made as much sense as a dream, yet she *knew* this was the truth.

Welcome to Wonderland, Raquel.

Raquel pivoted back to the unfurling scene.

Anxiety poured into her heart; blood pounded in her ears, and a newly realized sense of fear took root. This was going to be bad. She knew it. She had to protect herself.

"No! Not again!"

Raquel's arms shot out in front of her, warding off the impending doom. The gold dust immediately formed bricks and surrounded Steffan. He was the one doing *this* to her. He was making her see all of this. He was making her relive this. She wanted all of this stopped.

The gold bricks formed faster and faster, taller and taller, until she no longer saw Steffan's panicked face. The bricks began to wobble back and forth. "Raquel! What are you doing? Stop!"

If they fell, he'd be crushed! His fear was so sharp it cut through like a razor.

"I'm sorry, Steffan. I can't relive this! I have to stop this."

Raquel cried out for him as the gold dust and the images started to spin and close around both of them. The gold wall started to fall toward Steffan, and she heard a roar as everything exploded out of focus. Complete darkness surrounded her, and she screamed with every ounce of her being, thrusting herself back into consciousness accompanied by a raging headache.

Her vision blurred as soon as she opened her eyes, but she knew she was all right.

"Wait a minute. This is my bedroom. Where's the darkness, the pictures, the gold dust swirling around, and where did the dust come from?"

Something heavy and soothingly warm sat on her chest over her heart, a comfort to her. He moved his hand from over her heart and cupped her face. His thumb caressed her cheek. With each stroke, her vision cleared and locked onto Steffan's hauntingly beautiful blue gaze. He was perplexed.

She blinked at the clothes he wore. The clothes were definitely snug on him. They were Keith's. When had he gotten re-dressed? The man was a walking fashion disaster. Black dress pants and a bright blue t-shirt with a rooster on the front, straight out of the 80s.

It almost hurt to look at him.

"My clothes ripped apart when I shifted. I found this monstrosity in the back of your closet. You have a strong mind."

"How long was I out?"

"Long enough for my panther to force his way out. You were unconscious for a few minutes. Raquel, are you all right?"

She massaged the side of her head. Miraculously, the pain dulled considerably, leaving a faint headache. Cautiously sitting up, she wasn't nauseated.

"I think I am."

Once he took his hand away from her, his eyes went back to their original brown. Disheartened, pain etched his face.

"I thought you were going to *fix* my memory?"

He gaped at her.

"And by the way, who was the brunette trailing behind you? She looked at me and then pointed to you before she vanished. She didn't look real, and I've never seen her before."

Steffan paled considerably, and his lips compressed together. If Raquel didn't know any better, she would have guessed she'd blurted out something forbidden.

A ghost. The woman wasn't part of my memories; she was part of his, and I saw her. Thanks, Gramma for the psychic ability.

His spine stiffened, and he jumped to his feet and helped her up off the floor, mumbling what sounded like, "... take her to Roman." Abruptly, he turned away from her but not before she saw the pained look of mingled fear, confusion, anger, and hopelessness gracing his features. The man was an emotional lightning rod.

"Get dressed," he bit out. "My brother will be picking us up out front soon."

"If you need a car, mine's in the lot."

He shook his head and tossed her her clothes. "No. You've already been seen with me in public. It's better for your safety if we get a ride. I'll follow you back on my bike."

What the hell does that mean? "Seen? Why is it so bad you were seen with me?"

"I'm only taking precautions."

"Wait a minute. Did you turn into a panther? I thought I saw a large panther before I passed out."

91

He frowned but kept quiet. "Our ride will be here soon."

"And the woman?"

No response except a flash of pure iridescent blue in his eyes before fading back to the angry warm brown glare.

"Okay, the eye thing is freaky—but cool. How did you do that?"

He turned away from her slowly.

Fine. If he didn't want to talk about what she had seen and confirm she wasn't insane, so be it. She would at least be able to see Genevieve and talk to her about all of this nonsense of Were-shifters and her seeing too much. *This was ridiculous.*

He watched her as she got dressed. The heat of his stare bore into her. It was a little unnerving, considering the intimacy they had shared.

This whole thing is absurd!

She heard him clear his throat. *He couldn't have heard what I was thinking, could he?*

"Yes, I did. I can do other things as well. It's not important right now because you'll only be made to forget it." He beheld her with annoyance. "Let's get out of here."

She blustered. "Oh no, you're not going to make me forget anything. You've been in my head twice, and you messed it up the first time with my memory being full of holes. The only thing you've managed to do this time is give me the beginnings of a migraine, so stay out of my mind!" She followed him out of her apartment and down to the parking lot of her building. "It's a little disconcerting, knowing you can manipulate my mind." She crossed her arms over her chest. "Look, my car is over there. If you're in such a hurry to get back home—"

"I don't trust taking your car. It stays here. If any Kindred followed us here, it will look like you're at home. It buys us time to fix your memories. And by the way, I'm not manipulating you." He pointed down the road as a black Chevy Silverado pulled into the lot and parked next to the lamppost. "Our ride is here."

Damn him.

Steffan waved her over as he leaned on the open window of the door.

"I believe you remember my brother Cristoff." Steffan smirked at Cristoff. "You didn't bring the Beamer?"

"Ah, no. Not after last time." Cristoff waved to her. "Hey, Raquel. How's it goin', chérie?"

"I've been better."

Steffan growled.

Narella popped her gum. "Heyyyy, what about me?"

Steffan did an eyeroll. "And, of course, I'm sure you remember my sister, Narella." He mumbled, "No one ever forgets her."

Narella growled and punched him in the arm. "Hey!"

Raquel bit the side of her cheek while Steffan glared down at Narella. The retort made Raquel smile. Narella's head wobbled as if she was saying, "excuuuuuuse me" with all the attitude of a teenager.

You go, girl!

He opened the back door of the truck's cab, and she climbed inside, scooting over to the other side so Steffan could sit in the back with her. They waited as he loaded his motorcycle onto the truck bed.

Steffan slammed the door shut. "Thanks, Cris for the pick-up.

She smiled warmly.

"Don't worry, bro, I'll add this to the list of favors you owe me." Cristoff shot Steffan a cursory stare in the rear-view mirror. "Nice shirt, peckerhead. Oh, by the way, I called Roman ahead of time. He said he will meet you in his office. And Connor is waiting as well. Also, Alpha Bastiel and his family are visiting. I inadvertently interrupted a meeting when I called him."

The truck lurched forward and turned onto the on ramp for route 90.

Raquel didn't miss the amused smirk gracing Cristoff's reflection in the rear view mirror.

Steffan looked pale at first, then a crimson blush crept up the side of his neck, splashing across his cheeks. The air in the cab of the truck grew thick and heavy with tension. Steffan looked worried.

"Alpha? Who or what is an Alpha?" She couldn't help herself. She figured if her mind was going to be erased, she might as well know a lot instead of being the village idiot.

Steffan sighed and turned to her. "Roman. He is the head of our family. He is titled as the Alpha."

Narella gasped. "Aren't you worried if she hears too much, there'll be too much to wipe out from her memory? I mean, Roman said she shouldn't remember our family is a bunch of Were-panthers—"

"Narella!"

Seriously? Was everyone delusional? There's no such thing.

The poor girl bit the side of her lip and quickly gave Raquel a sheepish grin, mouthing an apology.

The dense trees of Bayou Cane thickened the farther down the road the truck went. Raquel had a sense of déjà vu.

"I was here... I think. I brought flowers here. Genevieve was going to help me put them together for my wedding. And... I can't remember if we did or didn't put them together."

She caught the worried glance Cristoff shot to Steffan, thanks to the rearview mirror, and pretended she hadn't noticed a thing.

Cristoff turned off the main road onto a long lane of the driveway and pulled into a spot in a four-car garage. A blond man, wearing a kilt and a white t-shirt, which strained over heavily corded muscles, waited in a lawn chair, drinking a beer, an ankle propped over his knee. The bright orange flip-flop dangling off of his foot completed an outstanding fashion statement.

The man smiled warmly at her as she got out of the back of the truck and raised his beer to her in greeting. His hair was pulled back and bound by a black leather tie. He seemed familiar. The kilt. The long blond hair, humorous stare, and the unusual footwear reminded her of...

Steffan stopped her. "This is Connor, by the way. You've, ah, met before."

Something popped, and another memory of Connor flipping pancakes at a massive stove and dancing to some retro '70s radio music came to mind.

Raquel sighed. "You—"

"Lass, 'tis guit ta see ye. If ye like, Genevieve was pickin' some flowers out back. Ye can join 'er, if ye wish." He pointed to the side in the direction of a flagstone path. "Follow that thar path around back. I need ta have a *word* with Steffan."

He gave her a devilish grin with a wink and a nod.

Looks like Steffan's in trouble. Good.

"Thanks. I think. I'll... ah, go and see how she's doing."

Raquel followed the path around the side of the garage and through the white wooden gate.

She left Steffan and Connor staring at each other. The air crackling with tension. Connor calmly downed his beer.

94

Chapter 12

Connor's presence in the garage was not the friendly, "hey, how are you" greeting, but the aggressive, "follow me, or I'll kick your ass" greeting.

Connor finished his beer, quietly rose from the lawn chair, and chucked the empty bottle into the recycling can by the garage door. The male crooked his finger twice for Steffan to follow him into the house. They stopped in the laundry room and Steffan quickly donned a plain blue cotton shirt.

"Ye brought the wee lass home. Roman is'nae goin' to like this." Connor smiled mischievously and clapped Steffan's shoulder. "I'll pick ou' a pine box fer ye. By the way, Bastiel and company are still here. Come. The Alpha waits."

Oh shit.

He had one job to do and had failed not once but twice. And since Cristoff had turned turncoat on him, Steffan would have to think of another way to keep Raquel safe before time ran out and her current memories became permanent.

The mahogany French doors of the office swung open and then closed behind them. Steffan viewed Bastiel from across the room and steeled his thoughts of Raquel. Her scent was all over him. He hoped the male wouldn't say anything.

Bastiel calmly sat in a leather chair in front of Roman's desk, quirking a brow at the intrusion. Steffan glanced from Bastiel to Roman. Roman's fingers were steepled in thought; his gold stare pivoted from Bastiel to him. If looks could kill, Roman was skinning him alive.

Steffan wished a black hole would open up and swallow him. No doubt this entire scenario with Raquel and the fear of one of the Commission members possibly finding out about her was a stage set for the detonation of a nuclear bomb.

Fates be damned. If anything happened to Raquel, it would be his fault. Just like it was his fault for not being able to save his mate's life.

The only saving grace here was that Raquel was with Genevieve in the garden on the other side of the house.

He needed a drink and headed over to the bar and picked up a bottle of Bacardi. The dense air in the room gave Steffan every warning to be cautious, and his skin itched and tingled.

Damn his panther.

A shot might help him keep his head together. Why bother mixing it with anything? He needed to dull his senses right about now.

Steffan gave a respectful nod to Bastiel. "Alpha Bastiel. May I pour you a drink?" If the male would at least have a drink with him, he wouldn't feel alone in this.

"No, *gracias*, señor. I will be leaving shortly. But since you're here... " The male leaned forward in his chair, curiosity evident on his face. "I'm wondering about the female. Is she your new Mate? Have you told anyone on the Commission?"

The Bacardi made it as far as Steffan's throat before he started choking, and it reappeared through his mouth and nose as he forcefully spewed the alcohol out. *Air... where was the air?* He coughed, swallowed, and coughed some more. *Fuck, that burns!* His eyes watered, and his throat burned. *His Mate... Oooh no.*

"Steff, we need to talk about Raquel."

He cringed at hearing his name. "You don't have to tell me anything I don't know. I know I fucked up, Roman."

"Bastiel, I do apologize for my brother. He's had a rough couple of centuries and hasn't decided to grow up yet."

Steffan turned to glare at Roman.

Bastiel tilted his head to the side and frowned, glancing quickly at Roman then back at him. "I'm sorry. I thought perhaps you'd lain Michelle's memory to rest and taken another female. At least I assumed this was the situation when you talked to Cristoff. I heard the whole conversation over the speaker. Perhaps I am in error, señor?"

Cristoff had me on speaker? Steffan shook his head. "Well, you're wrong." He coughed again to clear his throat. "She's human."

Bastiel frowned. Whatever the other Alpha was thinking, it

96

couldn't be anything good. By law, Bastiel had the right to challenge Roman for Raquel's death, force the issue of turning her, or demand to stay and watch Steffan turn her.

Steffan glanced over his shoulder at Roman. The Alpha sat there, his face resting on the palm of his right hand. Two fingers at his temple, the ring finger gliding over his lips in contemplation.

I seem to be digging my own grave right now.

Roman broke the awkward silence. "Steff has had to redo the memory wipe. He took too much info from the female the first time, so I sent him to *fix* the problem. But it seems my Beta ran into another problem, and I'm guessing that's why the female is here."

Roman and Steffan silently battled, glare against glare. Steffan prayed to the Fates that Bastiel would not make this harder and demand Raquel's immediate death. He'd messed up royally, and now Raquel would have to pay for his damn mistake. She was the innocent in all of this. Fates, he shouldn't have erased her memories in the first place.

Humans. Why did he always get in trouble with humans?

He poured himself another drink. A slight pressure began to build at his temples, and Steffan sensed Roman knocking to open a mindlink, and he wondered how long he could ignore the beckoning call. He hesitated before opening up a mindlink.

"Brother, stop drinking. We need to talk."

"Planning on handing me over to the Commission... again? She's not my Mate, but I don't want to see her killed."

Steffan turned around, facing the two Alphas in the room. "Bastiel, tell me... Your Mate was once human. Did the Commission ever threaten her life if you didn't turn her?"

Roman's eyes narrowed. *"Steffan, do not bring Bastiel into this. He's part of the Commission. He knows you were forced to change Michelle. Don't give him the upper hand. I'm warning you!"*

Steffan downed the liquor in one gulp and poured himself another. He contemplated the wolf sitting in the leather chair, wearing an exquisite two-piece charcoal gray suit. The male looked confused for a second, but then leveled his grey stare on Steffan.

"I know how this must look to you, Steffan, but I can assure you, I will not say one word to anyone on the Commission. That's Roman's place. This is *his* pard, not *my* pack. I *do* think, however, if the female is going to be residing within the House of Lavelle for an extended period, she should remain hidden or turned into a Halfling in order to *preserve* her life."

The wolf was smooth. He wondered if Bastiel had ever run into Little Red back in the old country. Steffan ground his molars together. "I think she would be best back in her human world." He suddenly felt queasy. Obviously, his panther had other ideas. He couldn't put Raquel through the change. He couldn't keep her, either. He had to let her go, despite his attraction to her.

Bastiel shook his head. "Just because you transform her, doesn't necessarily mean you *have to* take her as a Mate. You could remain the Tasheen, then pass her off, or she could live out her life without you. That is, once she's taught every thing she needs to know in order to survive."

The idea of Raquel going off without him was like a slap to the face, and anger bubbled up. Steffan dragged in a ragged, annoyed breath to keep him from shifting to his Were-panther.

"Wolves pass off to others; I don't. And I have no interest in taking a mate right now."

Steffan yanked the bottle of rum off the shelf and a heavy hand wrapped around his wrist. He looked into Connor's sad eyes.

The male spoke softly. "Lad. I consider ye ta be like a son from my loins. Ye were sober fer a week, and I ha' been proud of ye. Do'nae do this."

Roman cleared his throat. "Gentlemen, leave us. Bastiel, I thank you for coming over, and I will look into that problem of yours. I am sure your property could be expanded, and again, I apologize for *this* inconvenience."

Steffan didn't miss the daggered glare.

Property. Oh shit! I was supposed to survey Bastiel's properties to see if his store would clear with the city of Bayou Cane for an expansion. There's another job I forgot about.

Bastiel nodded. "Gracias, Señor Alpha Roman Lavelle for seeing me, although I believe you have more pressing matters on your hands." The male stood and came over to him. His teeth clenched tightly enough, Steffan saw the tips of his canines slide down. "Beta Steffan Lavelle, I will not say anything about the human female. Trust me. I give you my word. I do suggest you learn to curb your anger before it gets you into trouble with an Alpha not as forgiving as I."

The unspoken order to not offend Alpha Bastiel Cortez did not go unnoticed.

Trust him? Bastiel had been the one that blabbed to the Commission about Michelle still being human after they had a Mating Ceremony in the first place. He had been the reason why the Commission forced Roman's hand, who then forced Steffan to transform Michelle within one week.

Roman cleared his throat, and Steffan caught the moment his brother's pupils shifted into slits. "And Bastiel, for your sake, I suggest you not breathe a word of your knowledge of the human. I'd hate for your pack to be short a male."

After an intense moment, Bastiel nodded at Roman, then took his leave.

"Niiice. You played the Head Alpha card. Are you really going to kill Bastiel if he doesn't heed your warning?"

"I will. He might be a friend of mine, but no one messes with my pard. He's hurt you in the past, and I will not stand by if it happens again. I have your back."

That's a first.

"Connor, you can let go of my wrist now." Connor's firm grip tightened, and Steffan growled, shocking himself that he was being disrespectful to Connor.

"Let it go, lad, before I knock ye inta next week." The former Alpha's Scottish accent had thickened with anger. Too bad.

Steffan itched for a fight. The strenuous activity would be a welcome relief.

"Connor." Roman took the glass out of Steffan's hand. "I believe I will handle this one."

Connor gave a curt nod. "All right, Roman. I'm goin' t' look fer Alpha Bastiel's pups. I promised his Mate I'd help look fer 'em. They were playin' hide'n'go seek earlier. Those kids are around here somewhere." The male shifted into his panther, tearing through the shirt, and the kilt slipped down his waist and landed on the floor. Connor used his large paw to gather his kilt, picked it up in his mouth, and trotted out of Roman's office, leaving the torn shirt on the floor.

Steffan sank down in the leather chair Bastiel had vacated. Roman rubbed his hands together and sat back down in his chair behind the desk. The Alpha leaned forward, propping his elbows on his desk.

Whenever Roman was angry, furious, or all of the above, his whole demeanor became a silent, unreadable mask and more of the predator lurking beneath his skin. The male was unpredictable.

"Now that we're alone, brother, Cristoff filled me in on his thoughts about Raquel after the phone call. Why isn't the problem fixed?"

"She blocked me."

Roman's eyes narrowed. "How"—he loosened his tie—"is that even possible? When Raquel was here over ten weeks ago, I didn't sense she was a Sensitive. I was able to slip in and out of her mind with ease. Now you're telling me she blocked you?"

Steffan slowly nodded. Even he was stumped. Maybe it was his lust-filled mind, and he was having a hard time getting past it.

"Okay, let's start at the beginning. What happened?"

"Well, I found her on the sidewalk. Her ex-fiancé had shoved her against a glass table, and I took her back to her apartment. She seemed confused at Keith's reaction, and she had bleeding cuts on her arm. I used the enzyme to heal her cuts and—"

Roman's brows popped high. "You. Did. What?"

"I used—"

"I heard you the first time. You used *more* of the enzyme. Why on earth would you do that?"

He frowned. "I didn't want her to hurt any more than she already had; that's why I did it. Look, I didn't mark her or anything."

Roman growled. "Steff, you may not have marked her, but if enough of your enzyme gets into her bloodstream, it most certainly will. I understand you don't want her suffering. The enzyme can heal, yes, but it can also produce changes in the body. You took an unnecessary, uncalculated risk. It was bad enough you used the enzyme on her back. Her back was a large wound; the glass table were small cuts. Those weren't anywhere *near* being life threatening."

"I thought since Michelle had healed really quickly when I applied it to her skin after her brush burn when we went hiking, I saw no harm in treating Raquel's injuries. And it worked."

Roman gaped. Wow, he'd shocked his older brother.

Steffan quickly assured Roman. "Raquel's fine. No harm done. She's healed, although I need help fixing her memory so she doesn't remember."

Roman glanced at his watch. "I can't help you. She's imprinted on you. You do realize you only have three days to fix all of this, and in three days my Mating Ceremony will take place? All of the Commission and their clans will be here! Is she with Genevieve?"

"Yes. And yes."

"Fix this. Immediately." Roman's eyes quickly turned to gold. "And by the way, do *not* give her any more of your enzyme."

Three days. Steffan glanced out the window at the setting sun. Unease consumed him. If he couldn't undo it, then he'd be the one to transform her, and thus, save her life. He really didn't want to force Raquel into changing into a Halfling.

The laws sucked in all of this.

The laws... Unless...

"Mine Alpha. I hereby make a formal request to be the proxy for Raquel to amend the laws governing the mandate to change a human into a Halfling or for the human to be killed if they acquire knowledge of our kind. Let Raquel's life be spared, and even though she and I are not mated, I will invoke the right to see her moved to a neutral territory and take full guardianship over her while she still draws breath. I will hand over my title and responsibilities as your Beta to our sibling, Cristoff."

Silence.

Steffan waited. The difference between this request and the one he'd made for Michelle was that he was willing to be Raquel's Guardian and give up his ties to the pard. He'd have to dig into his own financial stockpile to provide for the both of them and pass on his title of Beta to Cristoff. He would not be allowed to return to the pard until Raquel died, and his title would remain with Cristoff. At least she wouldn't be forced to become a Were-panther, and he wouldn't have to see her killed. The only downside, he and Raquel would be limited to travel only within all neutral territories.

A thudding interrupted his thoughts. Was that his heart pounding? No. It was two. His and Roman's, only the Alpha's rhythm was slower than his.

He remained motionless as his brother leaned back in his chair, shock registering in his brother's golden glare.

This had to be the first time in four hundred years he'd managed to shock Roman, not once, but twice.

101

This was a hard slap in the face, not only to Roman but to the Lavelle pard as a whole. This request was going to be risky. It meant he was cutting himself off from the pard—for her.

"Pleeeease." He tried to keep from sounding desperate.

In all the time he'd been a Beta, he'd never played the "Guardianship card", not even for Michelle.

Steffan drew in a deep breath as he waited for a response. For some reason, it felt right. Betas had more of a choice, and if Raquel should ever ask for him to change her into a Halfling, then they both could return. Otherwise, he'd return after she died from natural causes.

Steffan remained motionless until he heard Roman walk around the desk and place a heavy hand on top of his head. The warmth spread over the back of his head.

"I hear your plea, but no."

"No?" Immediate anger replaced Steffan's shock. He jumped to his feet and squared off with his brother. The sharp piercing pain of his eyes transforming into his panther's was met by Roman's own golden stare. Claws burst out of the tips of his fingers. He'd fight Roman if he had to.

"I will try again to persuade the others, but you will have to heed what the Commission says. It's a vote, and since I will be presenting this, I cannot vote. But you should know this type of request will require the other Commissions from all over the country to be involved in this. We are not isolated from other Commissions."

Steffan's hope sank. This was a slim to not a hope in hell chance. Wow. Great odds.

"Steff, you are my brother, and I would do anything for you, even though you are sometimes a pain in the ass."

Steffan was firm. "I don't want another female hurt because of me."

"I know. Now sheath your claws or go out into the bayou, get some air, and run off your anger. Raquel is under my roof and under my protection. She's safe."

Steffan nodded. "Thank you, Roman."

"Steffan, I have one question."

"Which is?"

"Are you throwing your life away for this human female because you're fond of her or because our worlds are intertwined, and her life as she knows it is over? I want to know your reasoning. If I'm sticking my neck out for *her* and *you*, then I have every right to know."

Steffan swallowed hard and set the glass back down on the desk. He hadn't given it much thought. "I don't want her hurt any more so than she has been already. Our kind has taken her life away. I do find her attractive, Roman, but I'm keeping in mind she's human. I went down that road once before and look where it got me."

Roman nodded once. "Here's some food for thought. Just because you went down that road before, doesn't mean you can't travel the same road using a different vehicle. By Kindred Law, I had to make you aware of the laws you broke and that the kill order from the Commission would've been carried out by someone else; however, you turned Michelle into a Halfling."

Steffan frowned. "Roman, what are you saying?"

"Nothing that doesn't need to be said. Just use your head this time. I'd hate to be put in the same position again. Understand?"

Steffan's claws retracted, and he drew in a ragged breath. He felt like he was teetering on the edge of a cliff.

"Understood, Mine Alpha."

Chapter 13

Steffan slowly climbed the steps to the attic, glancing at the familiar surroundings. The thick, stale, dusty air tickled his nose. Old steamer trunks sat like coffins off to the side. He smiled as he thought back to when they were young cubs and how he had locked Cristoff in the massive gray trunk while they played hide and seek. Well, it was Cristoff's fault for hiding in there.

He ducked underneath a bicycle hanging from the rafters and sat down on a torn up red velvet high wingback chair. The chair used to be in his bedroom, and whenever he became frustrated, he would rake his claws over the upholstery. His mother was pissed and had one of the staff place it up here.

He tugged on the end of a sheet, exposing a black steamer trunk. With a thought, the latch automatically flipped open. He remembered learning how to move objects at the age of four and relished the idea of scaring the crap out of his first human friend, John Williamson. John had thought his house was haunted. Now, telekinesis was second nature.

He willed the lid open and pulled out a small box, now stained yellow with age. He opened it and carefully pulled apart the old tissue paper, revealing one of the ugliest pieces of pottery he had ever made.

Lifting it out of its confines, he held the three and a half century old vase up in the dim light. The lip of the vase was distorted, one side higher than the other and he had painted it half blue and half red. The handles on either side didn't match their shape.

"Mother, how you ever liked it, I'll never know."

"I liked it because you made it."

He stilled. "*Bonjour, Mère.*" He replaced the pottery back in its container and glanced at the mirror next to him.

"Son, if you remove the rest of the sheet from the glass, you'll be able to see me."

He willed the rest of the sheet off the gilded mirror. He had forgotten how massive the thing was. After his mother's death, his Sire had placed it up here. One year later, still having a hard time dealing with his mother's death, he went up to the attic, and she appeared to him. It had only been once since her death fifteen years ago.

The surface shimmered with an iridescent blue light, and Janeé Lavelle's massive panther form appeared before him.

She hung her head and blinked before glancing back at him. His heart ached. It'd been so long since he'd seen his mother in her panther form, he had almost forgotten how shiny her pelt had been and how the sound of her voice brought him peace.

Steffan stretched out his hand at the same time she stretched out a paw and placed it on the glass. There was only the sensation of cold glass beneath his palm.

He didn't feel her.

A fresh wave of sorrow engulfed him.

"It's been a long time. I know. It's all right, son."

Fates, he missed talking to her. "You're dead."

She snorted. *"Obviously."*

"Okay, how is it you are here? I mean, I'm happy to see you, but... "

"I requested the Fates spare me from going over to the other side. I've watched over my children in life and in death and have made myself known when I want to. The dead use mirrors, surfaces of water, and any reflective object to view the living. Which, at times, can be quite interesting—if you know what I mean." She paused. *"You have an interesting hobby doing Shibari. Now, let's get back to you. What troubles you?"*

Steffan felt the heat radiate off his face. He never wanted his mother to know about his sex life.

"Mère, what do you know?"

"Honestly, Steffan, I'm your mother. I know about you hiding your courtship with Michelle from your Sire. I know you still eat chocolate covered cashews in bed when you're stressed out. You hate underwear. And I know you are having a hard time moving on."

He shook his head. Not having a hard time moving on, more like afraid to. Kindred died around him. People died around him too.

Steffan took a deep breath. "In a nutshell, I messed up clearing out memories from a human's mind. It turns out she is a Sensitive. Her name is Raquel, and she's in the garden with her best friend Genevieve. Genevieve is Roman's First Mate. That's how I met her."

"Yes, I know about Genevieve, and I approve of her. Your Mate, Michelle, was a human was she not?"

"Yes."

"I'm sorry for your loss, my son. The Commission had no right to have her killed."

Steffan's chest ached from the bullet Janeé had just delivered. "I thought Roman would have notified the Commission that Michelle had been transformed, but he didn't!"

His mother's green stare bore into his. Normally, he should feel pressure build at his temples from someone trying to initiate a mindlink, but none came. He had to remind himself his mother was a ghost.

"Son, I've been watching you beat yourself up time and time again for not being home to protect your Mate. You've blamed Roman for keeping you away from the house, and you are not to blame either. Unfortunately, there are those on the Commission who think the same way Maximo did and would never have accepted Michelle, despite you turning the female."

Unshed tears burned Steffan's eyes.

"Mother, I can't live with myself if another human dies because of me."

Steffan pulled his hand away from the glass.

"Then make the right choice." Janeé's image shimmered. *"I don't care if the female you choose is of Kindred blood or human. I only want you to be happy. But know this: having a human for a Mate is not going to be easy, and neutral territories can only protect her as long as the two of you remain within the borders. So make the right choice. Don't be an idiot."*

"Mom, are you trapped?"

He hadn't really thought about the possibility she might be trapped on this plane of existence when she chose to remain behind to watch over the pard. But it was a possibility.

Janeé turned back to him. Her giggle eased some of the tension between his shoulder blades.

"No, I am not. I can pass to the other side when I want. For the

moment, I will remain in the in-between. If I decide to pass on, you will be the first to know; Roman will be the second."

"Why Roman second?"

"Because I have not contacted him since my death. You are the only one of my children that know about me."

"Does anyone else know you're here?"

"Yes. A few. Like I said, I choose when I want to be heard from. It is very taxing on my energy to let anyone see me or know I'm around. By the way, I'm sorry for breaking that ugly watercolor art you had hanging in the hall. I didn't like the artist."

Steffan chortled. "That was you? It fell to the floor, and the frame busted."

"If a ghost is strong enough, we can manipulate objects. But it takes a lot of energy and sometimes requires me to withhold viewing your plane of existence for a day or two. I let the frame fall and break. I didn't like Daleena in life, and her personality has only gotten worse over the course of time. I grow weary. As I said, it takes a lot of energy to communicate with the living."

She disappeared, and the only reflection in the mirror was him sitting in the tattered chair.

The silence embraced Steffan, and he welcomed it.

Steffan thought about the laws. Everything was outlined in there. What to do if a human found out, what to do if captured by humans, how to escape, how to play dead or kill in order to be free, how much erasing of memories should be done, anything having to do with business, everything.

He couldn't have Raquel end up on the run the rest of her life, despite any neutral territory providing a safe haven. Raquel needed to go back.

Sadness enveloped Steffan.

It would seem any hope he had was shot down one way or another, and when his Sire was alive, Steffan had been afraid to dream.

Raquel had given him hope, but if the Commission had his former Mate killed, like his mother had said, then any human female he ventured to have a relationship with was doomed.

Fates, why have you cursed me thus?

Steffan quietly shed the tears he had been holding back and hung his head. At least, in the attic, no one was around.

107

***

Janeé hung back from the front of the mirror, tail whipping from side to side; her heart bled for her son. He was a grown man and heartache was part of growing pains. She knew he couldn't see her because she wasn't directly at the mirror's edge. She thought about Steffan's First Mate and once the female had passed onto this plane of existance she had a brief conversation.

Michelle was worried and it took some time to assure the female that everything was going to be alright before she passed on.

The Fates will take care of him.

Chapter 14

Connor kept his nose to the ground. *Whar the devil did that kid go?* He wasn't too keen on having to find the lad. The wee lad was slipperier than a greased up pig at a county fair. He loved playing hide and seek, but this li'l runt was givin' him a run for his money.

Cats generally didn't like dogs, and the stench of wolves was worse. So much for helpin' Alpha Bastiel and his Mate, Maria, look for their missing pup.

He chuffed as a new scent tickled his nose. *Finally! The runt's gone out to the garden. Ohhhh shit. Raquel and Genevieve are there! Damn it.* He could'nae just romp over there; she'd die of fright as soon as she laid eyes on a panther. He'd have to shift and get dressed.

He galloped to the kitchen window and tapped on the glass with a pointed claw. His beautiful Mate glanced in his direction, rolled her pretty pale blue eyes, came over, and opened the sash. *"Hello, lass. Tis a beautiful eve. Care ta go fer a run?"*

Ascenza huffed, sending the loose white strand of her hair fluttering away from her face. "Connor, you old male. You're still trying to flirt your way back into bed with me? I thought you were going to patrol the bayou tonight."

Her soft French accent sent a shiver racing along his back as if she'd caressed him. Aye, he'd mate her all over again. He shifted back to human form, naked as the day he was born and leaned against the open window frame. "O'course, my Queen. Fer ye, I'd never give up. I will love ye till I draw my last breath."

"Connor."

"Can ye hand me a kilt?" He beamed a smile at her and waggled his brows. She rolled her eyes then smiled back. Thank the Fates she was his.

Confusion sparkled in her eyes. "Why do you need your kilt?"

"Because Bastiel and Maria's pup has been playing hide'n'go seek with Narella and me, and I've been searchin' fer 'em. The lad's in the garden with Alpha Genevieve and her friend Raquel, and if my nose is right, he's in wolf form, not human."

Ascenza blanched.

Uh-huh, thought tha'd get yer attention.

"Raquel's here? Oh my... "

"Now lass, don'nae get yer knickers in a knot. Roman and Steffan be takin' care of everythin'. Nae t' worry."

"You don't think Steffan holds any affection for the female... do you?"

"Perhaps. I think she be a guit match fer the whelp."

"Connor."

He held his hands up in surrender. "Although that's nae fer me ta say."

She abruptly headed into the laundry room. Damn, the sight of that derriere as she walked away from him made his mouth water. She returned and tossed him his kilt through the open window.

"See anything you like, *monsieur*?"

"Aye, I do lass, and I'd do more if I had time right now." He winked at her.

Connor wrapped the tartan around his waist, flashing his Mate a few times and making her blush. When he came to their bed tonight, he'd have to pick some of the roses in the garden to give her. They were the same shade as her blush. He was eternally grateful to the Fates for putting her in his life.

He hurried to the back of the house and stood by the lilac bush. He observed Genevieve and Raquel sitting on a bench talking. Every once in a while, Narella's dog would fetch a toy or stick for them to throw, and the Were-wolf chewed on a bone a few feet away from the females.

Guit. Now, how ta git the lad's arse over 'ere and nae freak out the human female?

Connor whistled and smooched to get the pup's attention. The wolf glanced at Connor once before going back to his chew toy and took it over to Raquel, laying it at her feet. Raquel threw the bone, and the lad ran after it.

"Boy, come 'ere!"

The pup ignored him. *So much for a mindlink.*

Connor chuckled to himself as he listened in on their conversation.

110

"Genevieve, this whole thing is crazy!" Raquel exclaimed.

He understood all too well how his world seemed different from hers. But wait till she met a vampire. That's a whole other ballgame.

"Raquel, just think about what you saw. It is real, and I'm afraid, until things can get settled with what you know, you'll be living here."

That's it, lass. Don'nae need ta tell her she could be killed.

He didn't want to intrude on them. He sensed Raquel's tension, and even his inner panther wanted to brush up against her leg to comfort the wee lass. Hopefully, she'd be able to find some sort of peace, and they could keep her hidden here. Bastiel was a good male, and so was his Mate, Maria. They would'nae dare go against Roman and the House of Lavelle.

Connor sighed. The Were-wolf pup laid down and rolled in the mud. *Maria's gonna have a fit. Glad he's nae my young'un.*

Connor stepped out of the bushes. Genevieve smiled, and he smiled at her, nodded his head discreetly to give her respect and smiled at Raquel. He rubbed his hands together. He wanted to pick up the muddy pup but didn't want to risk the pup turning into a three-year-old boy.

"Hello, Connor."

"Raquel. Genevieve. I see you've been keepin' the wee lads busy playin'." He motioned in the direction of the dog and the Were-wolf, lying on their bellies with their tongues hanging down to the ground as both panted in exhaustion.

"I think I tired them out." Raquel smiled. "Is everything all right with Steffan? He didn't come back out from his meeting with Roman."

"Aye, lass. Everythin' be fine. I came ta get Bastiel's son—pup. I meant pup. They would like ta go home, and he mentioned getting' ice cream on the way before a store closes an'—"

Raquel's gaze shot past him, and her face completely drained of color.

"Lass?" *Wha' th' feck's gotten inta her?* Connor pivoted to the Were-wolf. *Oooohhhhhh, feck me! The whelp shifted!*

"Is Daddy gettin' ice cream, cause I's want rainbow sprinkles on top of mine, last time I's wasn't allowed, and I only gots one scoop, but it wasn't enough so I's hope this time I can have so'more. I like black cherry, but sometimes they's don't gots it, then I's have to pick somethin' else." The boy took a huge breath. "Daddy said it was going to be too much sugar, and I—"

Feck. Time ta get the chatterbox outta here.

"Hey, yous said a bad word. You said 'fuck'. I'm tellin' my daddy. He's gonna spank yous good, but don't worry, he might not. I don't really know if he would spank yous 'cuz you're bigger than he is, and I don't know—"

Raquel's brows popped, and Genevieve bit her lip, obviously trying really, really hard not to laugh.

Connor opened a mindlink to Genevieve. "*Ye got this? Please, in the name o'the Fates, tell me ye can explain the shifting-naked-kid ta her?*"

The First Mate only nodded quickly while she snorted a laugh.

He said to the still chattering three-year-old, "Time ta go with your parents and get some ice cream."

Connor picked up the muddy, scrawny little Were-wolf in his arms. As they left, he felt the boy wave over his shoulder. *Fates can the pup talk!*

"Thanks for playin' wif me." He turned to Connor. "I likes Alpha Lavelle's mate. She's nice. And pretty. I likes it when the human threw the toys, but I didn't understand at first what she did that for till the dog showed me how to plays with them. Humans are funny."

"I can imagine, laddie." Connor tried not to laugh. Shifters played more like humans than pets.

"I guess the human is pretty too. But she smells funny. Didn't her momma lick the human right for a bath? Sometimes, I miss my armpits."

Connor's burst of laughter made the child smile. "Nae, laddie. Humans don'nae lick their young. They use tubs fer washin'. As ye should."

"My momma licks me when I's am in my wolf and gives me a bath when I's in this form. I didn't know how humans washed up. I hope I's didn't scare her."

Thank the Fates the lad did'nae tell her she stank.

"The lass will get over it."

Chapter 15

Raquel numbly waved back at the child in Connor's arms until he turned and vanished around the corner of the house.

Is this real? What just happened?

"Raquel? Look at me."

Raquel turned toward Gena. Her best friend saw what she saw, right? "I'm not losing it, am I, Gena?"

Gena's green eyes shone bright with concern and embarrassment. She reached across and covered Raquel's hand with hers.

"No, you're not losing your mind. Far from it." Genevieve shook her head. "Believe me when I tell you this: I was as shocked as you were when Roman first shifted in front of me. It took some time getting used to it, and I'm sure you'll get used to it."

Raquel regarded Genevieve. Was it possible her friend, her BFF, was one of them? "Have you... Are you... " She looked Genevieve over from head to toe. Same height, same build, same color hair, only healthier, and her green eyes held a happy, content gleam. When her friend smiled, there was nothing out of the ordinary.

Gena's thumb caressed the back of Raquel's hand in her grip. Genevieve didn't feel any different to her except her usually icy cold hands were warm. Otherwise, Gena was the same.

"Yes, I'm one of them. Roman changed me. He took me as a Mate and Marked me." She lowered the collar on her top, and Raquel saw the intricate swirling design of blue and black lines.

"I thought you'd finally had some ink done. It's not?"

"No. According to Roman, Were-shifters secrete an enzyme. If given too much, the enzyme can kill. If given in small amounts, it reacts with the surrounding skin to look like a type of tattoo. The blue and black shows everyone I belong to the Lavelle pard or family. The darkness of the blue indicates I am First Mate to the Alpha." Genevieve smiled at her. "Once he marked me, he had to change me.

113

It's in their laws. I would have been killed otherwise. Roman is a Were-panther, as are his brothers and sister. There are others too—a whole community hiding in plain sight of humans but kept separate."

Raquel quietly listened to Genevieve, digesting the information. Genevieve would have been killed if she hadn't been changed.

Which was the same reason Steffan had brought her here.

Fear spread through Raquel like wildfire, and she found it hard to breathe.

"Take it easy. You're safe here."

"Take it easy? Genevieve, if it's in their law to kill humans, why haven't I been killed yet? You're my friend; what am I supposed to do?" She jumped up with the intention to hurry back inside the house. Someone might see her and kill her.

A firm hand gripped her wrist, and she spun to face Genevieve. Her heart lodged in her throat, and she gasped for air.

"Raquel, calm down. As I said, you're safe here."

She quickly glanced down at Genevieve's hand on her wrist and let her emotions dwell on the connection. She mentally reached out for any kind of impression, but to her surprise Gena blocked her intrusion.

Raquel swallowed and slowly dared to look into her friend's eyes. She saw the darkened shadows haunting her gaze. "Roman and I will protect you. You have nothing to fear while you are here. Trust me."

"How will you protect me?"

"I don't know, but I know if Roman can keep his entire pard safe, then he can keep you safe, too"

Raquel still saw the shadows in Gena's eyes, but her friend was blindly relying on Roman.

I knew it. Who needs a telepathic link when all I need to do is physically touch someone.

"I think I need to have a chat with Steffan," Raquel bit out and yanked her arm free. "Have fun at work tonight."

As she hurried past the roses, she swallowed the lump in her throat. *This is all Steffan's fault. I wouldn't be here if it hadn't been for him. Where is he?*

She headed inside the house from a side entrance and entered a mudroom. The hallway led out to the rest of the house and was decorated in a 1950's style of contemporary art deco of black, white, and beige mosaic tile flooring with walls painted a soft ivory. Doors lined the hallway. She listened for voices but didn't hear any and began opening each and every door in her search for Steffan. She reached the end of the hallway and was about to open the last door.

"Can I help you find something?"

Raquel spun around and faced one of the maids. The young girl startled her, and she waited for her heart to catch up with her. "I'm looking for Steffan. He came in earlier with Connor. Perhaps you could save me some time and tell me where he is."

"Well, the Beta is upstairs in his room. But if you'd like to wait in the formal sitting room, I can go get him."

Raquel held her hand up. "Don't bother. I'll go to him. Which way is it?" She hadn't meant to snap at the maid; she was just irritated.

"It's the fifth room on the left side of the hall."

Raquel forced a grateful smile and headed toward the stairs. The plush red carpet of the upstairs hallway cushioned her feet as she approached Steffan's door. She raised her hand to knock on the door but, instead, turned the knob and barged in.

Steffan paused, his head barely poked through the neck hole of the shirt, and his abs rippled before he yanked it off and tossed it into the hamper.

Her mouth went dry, and her traitorous core clenched. Damn, he was a fine specimen of a man. Except he really wasn't a man.

Steffan's stare felt more like a caress as he slowly looked her over from head to toe. There was something different, though. There was hesitation, uncertainty, and a whole bunch of mixed up emotions.

Raquel blinked, and her temples eased.

"Were you reading my mind? I thought I... felt you."

"Your mind reached out to me. It awes me that you can mentally reach out to me with your mind, and you're not Kindred. I take it you want something? I was only changing."

Yeah, you... naked.

His eyes narrowed, and she mentally slapped herself for forgetting he could hear her thoughts.

"I was having a most wonderful conversation with Genevieve up until she mentioned that you might have to kill me!"

An irritated sigh was answer enough. Those light brown-turned-blue eyes were grim.

I was right. He was going to kill me.

A second later, he vanished. The door slammed behind her, and she pivoted to the door and found him behind her. She gaped.

"Wait! You were just over, I mean, how the hell did you get from the other side of the room to the door? I didn't move!" She pointed back and forth from where she had seen him to where he stood now. "You're not human."

"No shit. I was born a Were-panther. We've been through this. I take it you're finally comprehending it? My concern for you, however, is your comprehension of any of it, because I'm wondering how much *more* I will need to erase from your inquisitive mind."

Damn, she was tempted to punch him. "From the looks of things, you're going to have to rewrite history! I saw a puppy turn into a kid. Genevieve showed me her tattoo... Mating Mark... whatever it is... and you crossed a room at the speed of light! None of this should be happening, yet it is, and when I touch things around here, I get the most unusual impressions. I see animals, people, ghosts... "

Steffan frowned. "Wait. What do you mean, you're getting impressions? What kind of impressions?"

"Ohhh no. You first! Show me that you're a panther. According to my memories—and they are scrambled at best, thanks to you— most of the people I have seen can turn into some sort of panther. I have yet to see you change. I want to see some kind of physical evidence that you and the rest of your family aren't escapees from some psychiatric hospital!" She paused. "If you do that, then I will tell you the kind of impressions I can see."

Honestly, she really didn't want to admit what she could do. Growing up, Gramma had been taunted for the psychometry gigs she did for people, and Raquel was made fun of at school. Those emotional barbs never went away.

Frustration marred his features. "I crossed the room like anyone else and—"

He was not getting out of this so easily. Raquel took a bold step forward, locking her gaze with his and crossing her arms over her chest. He towered over her. He had to be at least six feet two inches, maybe four, considering she was five feet eight inches. His eyes flashed bright blue, and the hairs on the back of her neck stood on end. There was something dangerous lurking in those eyes.

116

"Your slip is showing, Steffan. Your eyes change colors, and you move so fast, it can only mean one thing!"

His pecs flexed, and his shoulders seemed bigger. Her fingers itched to run down the corded muscle of his chest and abs in front of her, but to keep from doing so, she held her arms tight, and her nails dug into the muscle of her arms.

"You're not human! I just found out there's a strong possibility I might be killed, so either way, show me!"

***

"You want to see what I am? You shall!"

Steffan's anger quickly boiled to such a point that his skin itched with a vengeance. He let the change come to him but purposely slowed down the transformation so she would see, and he prayed she would finally understand what he was. This was going to be as painful as passing a kidney stone.

Fur poked through the skin, and bones broke apart all over his body. He roared through the pain as his arms and legs broke, and the fragments reknitted together. Muscles ripped, creating a brief moment of agony until they repaired themselves, forming the much larger muscles of the panther. His pants shredded to pieces to accommodate the much larger framework of his cat.

Thank the Fates, it was over with. That's the last time he would ever shift slowly. He waited for the haze of pain to subside before lifting his head; his sides billowed with each breath as he tried to calm his breathing.

He stood on all four paws, stretched, and dug his claws into the thick carpet. He felt his hackles raise and settle, and he shook out the rest of the tension on a sigh.

Freedom. This is what pure heaven felt like.

Raquel stood frozen to where she stood and gawked the whole time. The mental microscope he was certain she was studying him under made him damned uncomfortable.

He had expected her to faint, but she hadn't. The only thing she started to do was he detected a slight tremor, and when he started to move to the side so he could sit, she jumped a foot backward against the wall.

This is what you wanted to see, so take me in. Take in all of me.

117

I'm a killer, a predator, a being that is part human and part animal. This. Is. Me."

Raquel's eyes were huge, and the next second, she slammed the mindlink closed.

Damn it!

Embarrassment flushed her cheeks once she realized what she had done. Her hand combed nervously through her hair, sliding down her neck with a slight quiver of uncertainty, then she held her fingertips in front of her plump lips. He was fairly certain she was suppressing a startled scream. The slight trembling in her hands and her eyes bright with fright were a dead giveaway.

Minutes ticked by.

She quickly re-crossed her arms in front of her, holding herself. "So that's what you look like." Her voice shook, but he heard the courage underlying the question.

He tested the telepathic link but retreated when Raquel grabbed the side of her head. The beanbag chair in the corner beckoned him, and he flopped down on it and rested his head on his front leg. His tail swished with agitation.

Why hadn't Raquel blocked him earlier? What kind of Sensitive was she? Did she hear spirits, see ghosts?

She slowly crossed over to him and tentatively laid a hand on his head. He chuffed, and she yanked her hand back. *Oh for the love of the Fates...* He head-bumped her hand. It had been a long time since anyone had stroked his head.

Her hand skated over his head and back. Eventually, as she became sure of herself, the strokes became braver and steadier.

The corner of her mouth relaxed into a lopsided smile.

"You're very soft. I suppose you can't talk like this."

Steffan's fur rippled, and he reformed on the beanbag, sweaty and naked, and his cock was erect as he breathed heavily to ease the discomfort of changing from one form to another.

"Actually, I *could* communicate with you; however, your mind shut me out. And if you're wondering why I'm not wearing any clothes, it's because they don't magically form when I do."

Raquel blushed, kneeled next to him, and tucked a stray curl behind her ear. Something was bugging her. The smile faded not only from her lips but her eyes.

118

"Steffan?" She spoke so softly that, had it not been for his supernatural hearing, he never would have heard her. "Will I be killed?"

He wished he could change everything and protect her. A part of him wished he had been born a human.

"Don't worry. Roman will figure something out, and I am determined to keep you safe. I was about to get changed to head to a Commission meeting tonight."

Raquel's gaze darkened. "Don't worry? Really? This is my life you're talking about. Please don't patronize me."

Her pupils dilated as she slowly took him in.

He sat there naked and let her look her fill.

"What about if I want to stay here? I-I mean... it's safe for me here. Genevieve said as much. I'd like to stay with you."

He blinked back his surprise. *She wanted to stay? With him?*

Could he dare to hope to have a life again?

He swallowed hard. He didn't want to force her hand and transform her into a Halfling. She'd hate him for the rest of her natural life.

"Not possible. I'd have to force the change on you. I'm not going to do that. Don't you think it would be best to go back to your apartment, go back to work, and maybe plan a future with someone? If you stayed here and remained human, you'd be killed within a week. I'd have to turn you. Tonight's meeting is so you don't have to be changed and to be permitted to retain the knowledge of our existence."

His panther didn't like the idea of her going back, and Steffan felt the razor edge of claws slice across his abs. The muscles contracted. He had no choice. He wanted her to live and there was only one way he knew of, to do that. But he had to get past those barriers she'd erected in her mind.

Time to change tactics.

"You made a deal with me." He inched closer to her.

She licked her bottom lip, moistening it. "I did?" Uncertainty etched in her expression.

Steffan nodded. Getting onto his hands and knees, he locked gazes with her. "You did. Tell me about the impressions you've been getting?"

Her head tilted to the side as if she was trying to guess what he'd say. Embarrassment flooded her beautiful heart shaped face. It didn't take a genius to realize this was one of those sensitive subjects she found hard to talk about.

A haunted shadow crept over her, and her gaze became unfocused. *Something in her past gave her that ghost, but I need answers.*

He leaned in, nipping her bottom lip.

Raquel jerked back to reality and focused on him. "Tell me, *bébé.*" He slid his nose up the side of her cheek and huskily whispered in her ear. "It's all right. Whatever it is, remember I'm not exactly a typical human being." He licked the shell of her ear out of pure curiosity.

She gasped. "When I was little, I could touch an object or a person and get these... um... impressions."

He ran the side of his nose down her cheek and brushed his lips gently over her lips, quickly kissing the bottom lip. "Go on," he murmured. His lips trailed ever so lightly down over her chin to her neck. Her scent was amazing.

Her breath hitched, and she grabbed his arms. He stopped and planted a tender kiss at the base of her throat. He mentally pushed. The link was pliable, but he couldn't penetrate all the way through and complete the link.

"You're making this difficult for me to think."

He chuckled. "I know. Continue, please."

"I see visions of sorts if I touch an object. Usually of something that's happened in the past. They're only flashes of images. But for a long time, I didn't have these visions. If I touch a person, I can read them the same way."

"I see."

"I hit my head when I fell out of a tree when I was younger and lost the ability."

He thought for a second. Psychometry. *The head injury she sustained in the cell might have enabled her to embrace the ability again. Which means it will get stronger with time, and time for her to stay alive is crucial.*

He suckled and nipped at her lips. Protect her, keep her alive, let her go, keep her close; he was so confused.

Steffan froze and pulled slightly away, barely noticing how she nipped his lower lip in return. Her eyes popped open, and he stared into her face.

Eyes perfectly spaced apart, lips that were soft and plump from biting them. He remembered how soft and giving they had been when he kissed her, and a jolt of realization went straight to his cock. He was naked. She had far too many clothes on.

His deliberate attempt to distract her had backfired on him.

"Steffan?" Her whispered voice was husky. Sexy.

He cleared his throat, praying he wasn't purring. "Yeah"

"You're naked. And I'm not."

"Then take your clothes off."

He reached for the hem of her shirt.

A loud, rapid knock on his door threatened to split the wood, and Steffan growled at the intrusion. He willed the door open, and Roman stepped through, eyeing Raquel and then him. Raquel turned three shades of pink and quickly got up from the floor, made a mad dash for the bathroom, and slammed the door shut.

Steffan met Roman's disapproving glare. "What the hell are you doing here?"

Talk about getting caught with my pants down.

Roman's brow furrowed, and golden eyes bored into Steffan's.

"I'm here because *we* have a problem, and it concerns *her*. Looks like I interrupted the two of you from doing the horizontal cha-cha." He pointed to the closed bathroom door.

Steffan let out a menacing growl. "I don't think it's any of your business who I am with. Raquel's mind is more pliable when I have her mind *and* body occupied; it's easier to slip in."

"I thought you respected my Mate's friendship with Raquel, and here you are, trying to get into her pants?"

Steffan vehemently shook his head. His brother had no fucking clue how hard this was for him. He needed to see Raquel safe, and by the damn Fates, he was most certainly going to do just that! Even if it meant giving up some one, he found attractive in order to save her life.

Roman stalked to Steffan, his gait clear he meant business. "Listen. I don't *care* if you want to pity-fuck her or just get both of your rocks off. That's not why I'm here. You need to *listen* to me. Take Raquel and get the hell out of this house! Pronto."

Anger, frustration, and confusion rolled off Roman. This was so unlike him.

"Why?"

Roman clenched his teeth, and the frustration hit Steffan square in the chest. "Stavslaka informed Jerox his cub Gia had been shot at the warehouse. He found Gia alone, lying in a pool of blood. I got the call a few minutes ago from Jerox. He and his First Mate went to the hospital to be with Gia. So guess what? The Commission meeting at his estate has been moved—"

Steffan frowned. "That means—"

"Will you let me finish? To *here*. Every single Alpha in the US is coming *here*. Tonight. Genevieve is going in to work tonight, so she'll miss it."

The sharp urge to protect Raquel rushed over Steffan as if he'd been doused with a hose. "And you want Raquel to go too."

"I know for *you*, English is a second language to sex, but pay attention." Roman nodded and shoved a set of navy blue scrubs into his hands. "Give these to her. Tell her she needs to go to work tonight. I'll call and talk to her boss. I'll let them know she's coming to look after Gia. They can think she has a temporary job as a visiting nurse for the time being. I want you to *talk* with Dr. Greer in ICU, find out how Gia is doing, and *come back* in time to sit in on the rest of the meeting. The less Raquel knows the better."

Steffan pursed his lips together before retorting, "You do realize that I'm running out of time to clear out what she knows about us, and you interrupting me didn't help matters much?"

"Steff, you don't need to remind me, and this meeting is important. Remember when you placed a motion on the table?"

"Yeah. But you said the Commission voted no."

What's he getting at? I'm not mated anymore, and I still have some time to adjust Raquel's memories.

"I got an email from Alpha Talon. Apparently he is having a similar situation in the Western Commission, and it actually is *he* who is putting this notion back on the table. This type of request will impact *all* Commissions." Roman started to leave but abruptly turned back to him. "And do me a favor. Get dressed. That pea-sized creamless cannoli is scaring me. No wonder Raquel ran from the room. You have twenty minutes before anyone gets to the house."

Roman closed the door behind him. Steffan looked down at his deflated cock. "It's not a cannoli." *Okay Fates. And the reason I wasn't an only cub is because...*

Out of the corner of his eye, Steffan caught the flicker of a distant star in the night sky. It didn't surprise him that at least one of the Fates was likely amused.

Chapter 16

Raquel placed the medical supplies on the shelf and dragged in a deep breath. The familiarity of the sterile room soothed her scattered nerves.

So far so good. No hiccups tonight. Considering I've only been with Gia all evening and from what I've been told, Gia was going to be my only patient.

Dr. Jeffrey hadn't looked too pleased at first when she and Steffan popped into his office. After all, it'd been only forty-eight hours since she'd taken her leave of absence.

Raquel took out a pair of nitrile gloves and put them on. The thin film stretched over her hands. It sort of reminded her of Steffan's skin stretching over his bones before ripping apart to reform as a panther. His face had lifted up to hers, and when her eyes locked with the massive cat's piercing blue orbs, reality took a nosedive.

It had been real: the eyes, the sharp protruding canines, the jet-black fur, the claws gripping the carpet, were all real.

"How are you holding up?" Penny smiled.

Raquel jumped back against the shelf, clutching her chest. "Oh my God, Penny, are you trying to kill me?"

Penny scoffed. "Sorry. I didn't mean to scare you."

Raquel shrugged. "I'm doing a lot better. I will admit I was scared to come back to work, after being sent home earlier and the look on Dr. Jeffrey's face when I walked through his office door with Steffan was priceless."

Penny patted Raquel on the back. "Well, I'm glad he allowed you to come back. But I'm surprised to see you on my floor tonight. It's been awhile since you pulled a shift in ICU. How long will you be here?"

Raquel smiled at Penny. "Dr. Jeffrey put me up here, and I have one patient to tend to. He said if I didn't kill anyone he'd welcome me back to the ED. I don't know what he said to Dr. Greer, but the man's been watching me like a hawk."

Penny shrugged. "Don't worry. You'll be back in the ED in no time." Penny grabbed a stack of gowns. "See you at break."

Raquel took of the glove and tossed it in the trash and locked the supply cabinet. Turning around, she spied Henry, one of the security guards, leaning against the wall, sipping from a blue travel mug while he talked to someone on his headset. Raquel couldn't help but stare at him, and when his gaze locked with hers, he jutted his chin to acknowledge her presence, smiled, and resumed his conversation as if she wasn't there.

Actually, this was the fourth time Raquel had run into Henry on this floor. She turned back to the spot he occupied and... *He's gone?*

Raquel whipped her head around, searching for the security guard. It was bad enough her friends had been checking up on her, now security was too?

Then she remembered what Steffan had said before he left. *"Roman has a few people watching over you to make sure you're safe. Don't be alarmed."*

She didn't like knowing others were watching her. Her anxiety spiked, and she sucked in a breath and held it for a count of ten before releasing it slowly.

"I'm human, that's why; oh Raquel, calm down, things will go back to normal."

Dr. Greer sidled up to her and leaned down next to her ear. "You know, if you walk by the psych ward while you're talking to yourself, they might think you belong there." He grinned, straightening. "You're taking great care of Gia, by the way. Her family will be pleased." He handed her the iPad before going off in the opposite direction.

Raquel tapped the edge of the device against her hand. This was normal, everyday stuff. It felt really good to have something familiar to do.

Raquel's smile stretched from ear to ear as she headed past the check-in counter at the nurse's station. The overhead lights in the hall had been dimmed on purpose to simulate evening to keep in time with circadian rhythms. It aided in better healing responses.

She looked down the hall the closer she got to her destination and was surprised to see Steffan standing inside Gia's room consoling a man with long golden blond hair. He should've left over an hour ago.

125

That might be the father of the girl.

Steffan's eyes darted in her direction the closer she got.

The blond haired man turned to her, and her heart went out to him. His pupils glowed red through the amber.

She stopped cold. He hadn't been in the room earlier.

Is he like Steffan?

Gruffly, he choked through a sob, but then the red faded from his eyes, leaving behind only amber-gold irises.

"Jerox, she knows about us."

He's a Were-shifter, like Steffan.

The blond haired man sighed. "I'm sorry. I'm a bit out of sorts."

British?

A beautiful woman came into the room and glided into his arms. She too, had been crying. She said to Raquel, "Don't let our baby die." There was a flash of gold in her eyes, and inconsolable pain was etched across the woman's face. Her husband held the woman close, tucking her next to his body.

"We are doing all we can, and the doctors are taking extra measures to make sure your daughter is not in any pain. Right now, your daughter is stable. But she's lost a lot of blood. Time will tell."

Steffan cleared his throat. "Jerox, why don't you and your Mate go get something to eat. I'll stay here until you get back."

Jerox tugged at his Mate's arm and led her down the hall. Henry had turned the corner, and Raquel was shocked as the security guard dipped his head and kept it lowered until they both had passed.

Raquel waited until the couple had gone. "Steffan, what are you doing here?

Henry passed by.

"Henry, return to doing your job. Let me handle this." Steffan leaned in closer to Raquel after the guard walked past. "I'm here investigating Gia's shooting. Let's be careful. Henry's of a different Pride, but he still shows respect to Jerox and his female. They're Alphas; Henry's an Omega. They know you're human, and with how emotional Jerox is right now, I'd rather not have to fight him off if he goes ballistic due to his anxiety over his daughter."

"Steffan, did you ask Henry to keep an eye on me?"

Steffan frowned. "No. Roman did."

Raquel snorted. "Look, how long will you be here? I have a

break in fifteen minutes. We could get ourselves a bite to eat in the cafeteria. I wanted to say thank you for letting me go back to work earlier, but you left Dr. Jeffrey's office so fast I thought you'd disappeared into thin air, and he shuffled me up here in ICU."

"Roman called Dr. Jeffrey and explained some things to him. I was there for moral support. I know how hard—"

A strangled gasp erupted from Gia, and an alarm sounded.

Steffan panicked and went to Gia's bedside and helplessly looked at all the machines Gia was hooked up to. "What's wrong with her?"

Raquel glanced at each machine. "According to the stats, she's getting the right amount of oxygen, but why the hell are the alarms going off?" Her hands followed over the tubing. "There's no kink in the line. Do shifters require more than a human?"

"She might. The relationship with the animal side is a symbiotic one. If the human side is damaged, then her lioness might be breathing for her, and a lion's lung capacity is triple a human's. Not only is the human side healing, so is her lioness. That's why we look like we're gasping for air every time we shift back from the animal form." He placed a hand on the bedrail.

She didn't like the look of uncertain fear etched into his features.

She adjusted the buttons on the respirator to allow a higher concentration of oxygen to flow through the tube and adjusted the bed from a forty-five-degree angle to sixty, to assist respirations and improve air exchange. She glimpsed at the monitor. The levels were still reading normal even with the increased flow.

Someone down the hall yelled out, "Marco?"

Raquel replied, "Polo."

Steffan quirked a brow. "Marco Polo?"

"If an alarm is turned off before the lead nurse has a chance to get out of his chair, he calls out *Marco*. I replied Polo because I was letting him know I've taken care of things. If Gia had crashed, I would've hit a panic button to bring every available nurse to this room."

She tucked Gia's hand under the sheet and straightened it around her shoulders.

She turned to face him. He had this awkward gleam in his eye. "Something wrong?"

Steffan blinked and quickly averted his gaze elsewhere. Anywhere but at her. "No, I—" He cleared his throat. "You're very gentle. Thank you for taking care of my friend. And I wanted to know if you wouldn't mind doing me a favor."

She crossed her arms over her chest. "What is it?"

"When your shift is over, stay here. I'll pick you and Genevieve up from work." He went over to the other side of the bed. He cupped either side of Gia's head and closed his eyes, his brows drawn in concentration, lips pursed tightly together.

"What are you doing?"

Steffan sighed. "I've been trying to mindlink with Gia's lioness. If I can reach Gia, hopefully she'll wake up sooner. Then I can find out what really went down. Jerox doesn't believe this was a mugging. And quite frankly, neither do I. A Beta from the Northern Commission was found in a metal shipping container not too far from the dock. The container got caught on a ledge under the water. He'd been shot between the eyes." He paused. "Whoever did this to Gia is still out there. I want to know *why* Gia was shot. I keep getting this feeling of curiosity and then stark fear from her but... damn it!" He growled in frustration. "I lost the image!"

Steffan shook his head and pushed away from the bed. He paced, hands clenched into fists. When he relaxed and finally stood still, Raquel noticed the long claws at the end of his fingers.

He looked at her, and the claws turned back into regular, human-looking, manicured nails.

"Sorry. I'm frustrated. I hate seeing any female hurt, and I worry about your association to me and how much you know about my species. Besides, knowing someone tried to kill Gia makes me realize I don't know what I'd do if something happened to you."

He's worried about me. Raquel's heart ached for him. This weirdness was wearing off. She was getting used to the idea of different types of humanoid beings living on earth.

He sighed and closed his eyes and, this time, reached out to touch Gia's head. After a few minutes, Steffan crossed his arms over his chest.

"Anything?"

"No. I found her lioness. She is also unconscious."

"I don't understand. I thought your... *panther*... was a part of you?"

128

"Not entirely. In the physical sense, the shifter can transform whole or partially, but not in the emotional sense. My panther has his own thoughts and feelings, which he can relay to me or be a stubborn jerk and not communicate at all. The animal side communicates with images and emotions directly, or if he's pissed with me, I can feel his claws raking across my abdomen.

"The panther helps to initiate telepathic links with other Kindred or read the minds of humans. That is to say, if my brother was here, he and I could have an entire conversation without speaking audibly, and to you, it would look like we were standing around, doing nothing but staring at each other. While he and I have an open telepathic link, our panthers can communicate with each other. It's faster for us. That is why it is the preferred method of communication between Kindred.

"But this isn't normal. I should be able to get through to her lioness even if Gia is unconscious. Gia is a Dreamwalker. So when she initially lost consciousness, her mind would still be active enough to record her surroundings and make a mental log of all of it. The fact I can't connect with her is aggravating."

"I see." Raquel chewed her lip for a moment and laid her hand on Gia's shoulder. The palm of her hand tingled unevenly. Gia might not be able to communicate with them, but maybe on a psychic level she could reach Gia. It was worth a shot. "Maybe I could try?"

"How are you going to try? You're not even one of us," he snapped.

She jerked her head to him.

"I know you're frustrated about your friend, but there's no reason to take it out on me! I'm not like you; but as I explained to you, I get images from people by touching them or holding onto something they have held. Emotions get imprinted into objects. How do you think objects become cursed in the first place? They weren't cursed when they were made. Energy had to be put into that object *to* curse it.

"I could try with Gia. I feel *something* emanating from her. It's very faint though."

He looked from her to Gia. The muscle in his jaw ticked. She knew he was frustrated, and from where she stood, he didn't believe her. His hand reached out and carefully brushed back a stray hair and tucked it behind Gia's ear.

129

Raquel was a little unsettled at how attentive he was toward Gia.

There could be the possibility that Steffan and Gia had been involved with each other. After all, they both were Wer-shifters. What if this brought them closer together? Negative emotions rose up from out of nowhere, and abruptly she left the room.

Raquel made it half way down the hall when a hand gripped her wrist, spun her around, and she found herself pinned against his chest. His arms were like steel.

"Let me go!" She wriggled and pushed against him, but he kept his arms locked around her. Frustrated, she attempted to stare him down. A sparkle of blue appeared in his irises, mixing with the light brown. A second later, the color receded.

Damn him; he's amused!

Steffan studied her face. A lopsided smile teased the corner of his lip. "*Bébé*, you have a lot of fire in you. I find that very attractive."

"I see your panther is keeping tabs on me."

"It's his way of making sure he doesn't need to force his way out and protect me. He sensed my anger and frustration. Look, I'm sorry. I shouldn't have snapped like I did. I have a lot of things on my mind."

He soothingly rubbed her back, and her jealousy receded to the point she had to ask the question burning in the back of her mind.

"What is she to you?"

"Nothing more than a close family friend who works as a secretary in the office at Lavelle Brothers Realty. I've known Gia for seventy-five years. Kindred can live thousands of years."

"Thousands? How old are you?"

"I'll be four hundred and two in June. Do you really believe you can help me by touching her?"

"I think when I hit my head, it unlocked something within me. Something reached out to me a moment ago when I touched Gia back in the room. I saw water and a building, but then it disappeared. It's only flashes of images. When I was a kid, I used to read people. However, I'm not sure if I can control it to gather enough information for you. It's been a long time since I last tried to read a person... or a Were-shifter in this case."

God, I hope I'm not making a fool of myself.

Steffan suddenly released her and took her hand, guiding her back to the room.

"I have an idea. If you touch Gia, I might be able to magnify and connect your mind with hers, and both of us will be able to see what happened. A three-way mindlink, so to speak. I remember your mind reached out to me before you knew what you were doing. I'm pretty sure all three of us working together can help you stabilize those images."

She relaxed a little but didn't know what to say about all of this. Would it work? Raquel had never tried anything like this before and hesitated to answer him.

Raquel gave an uneasy sigh.

"Steffan, I don't know if I can; and how is Gia going to help? You— I can connect with. I still am not sure how but I can."

"Once you and I connect, I'll project us into Gia's mind. Gia is a Dreamwalker. I couldn't reach her by myself but together I hope we can."

This whole crazy notion might work.

"Trust me, Raquel."

She nodded and went over to the bedside, laying her hands-on Gia's shoulder and arm.

Time seemed to stand still.

The energy expanded and grew, but Raquel only saw darkness behind her closed eyelids. She heard the monitors and the rhythmic sound of the oxygen pumping into Gia's lungs. The sterile scent of the room filled her nostrils as she breathed deeply to steady her mind.

"Steffan, I'm not getting any pictures. I—"

"I'm going to hold on to you. Keep trying."

He stepped up behind her and wrapped his arms around her waist. His body vibrated with an intense, calming heat. She was a little shocked at first that she understood what Steffan was saying about the Were-shifters and their symbiotic relationship with their inner animal. She sensed the panther within Steffan. Funny, she had not noticed it before. The moment Steffan pressed his body against hers, his presence and the vibration of his panther became magnified, and images flooded her mind.

She winced when the panther sent her an image of a white rose.

"Does it hurt?" His warm breath tickled the hairs on her neck.

"Not really. But it is uncomfortable. I don't know how long I can do this. This isn't as easy as I thought it would be."

His head leaned against hers, and he rested his chin lightly on her shoulder. "It'll be a quick trip, and I don't know if you will be able to see me or not once we're inside her mind."

"Am I safe?"

"Yes. Nothing can harm you in there. Everything you see happened in her past. Not the present."

"Will it look the same as when you and I were inside my mind?"

"No. Your brain echoed back to you, and it put together something you would recognize; a theater. You're going inside Gia's mind with my help, so her mind is going to reflect what's familiar to her. If she dies while we're in there, it's going to be a really short trip because her mind will lock us out, but we will feel her spirit leave her body."

"How do you know this?"

"It's happened to me once or twice. Kind of creepy, if you ask me. Please, focus."

Raquel's mind went blank, and an opaque-like scene slowly appeared and sharpened before her. The docks.

This was so different from when she simply held something in her hand. The color was astounding!

Raquel watched a plastic bag float on the breeze, but she couldn't feel the wind. Seagulls overhead looked like they cawed, but she heard no sound. She saw everything as normal yet experienced no sensations except being keenly aware of the heat from Steffan's body behind her.

"Raquel."

She whipped around to look at Steffan, but he wasn't there. She glanced down at her hands, only she could see right through them. She looked around again. "Steffan? Where are you?"

"Raquel, please focus. This isn't easy to do. I'm in your mind, but generally a person's mind can only absorb so much. You'll be seeing things through Gia's eyes. If you were a Dreamwalker like her, you could follow her. I can guide you."

A moment later, Raquel felt her body being pulled in the direction of the warehouse. "I have this need to go inside."

Steffan's voice echoed in her mind. "Go with it. These are only memories. You and I are nothing but shadows to her and inconsequential."

The silence was almost deafening. Thank goodness at least she could watch the visuals.

Once inside the warehouse, Raquel noted that Gia was trying to look over the shipping containers into the far right back corner.

Something had drawn Gia's attention to that corner but what?

She cautiously walked forward, and Raquel sensed the trepidation that grew with each step, and her skin tingled.

"Steffan, something's wrong. My skin on my arms and neck tingle like I have a bad rash."

She heard him chuckle.

"What's so funny?"

"I find it funny that since you're connected with Gia's mind, you're sensing how her lioness felt. That's how the inner animal communicates with us. Gia wanted to shift."

"Oh."

She continued to walk down a metal staircase, onto the cement floor and around a metal shipping container. Suddenly, Raquel felt a heavy, burning, sting impact her chest, and Gia's body lurched back into the metal container and fell to the floor.

Raquel felt the separation of her mind from Gia's, and a second later she knelt beside Gia's body.

"Steffan, I'm no longer linked to Gia. But I'm kneeling beside her. What's going on?"

"Can you see me?"

"No and for some reason I'm stuck kneeling low."

Raquel sensed Steffan's confusion.

"I think since Gia is a Dreamwalker, her lioness is giving you the ability to see through her eyes. Lions walk on all fours, so your body is going to adjust. Tell me what you do see."

"Well, I don't see a lion, that's for sure." Raquel looked around. "On the far end are men and women, some with children, aligning a wall in the back. Some are crying. Steffan? Are you seeing this?"

"Yeah, I am. Do you see anything else? Look back at Gia."

Raquel forced herself to glance up—at a smoking gun.

Steffan dryly exclaimed. "So she wasn't shot as part of a mugging as previously reported."

Raquel shuddered as she heard Steffan snarl. There was nothing anyone could do in this moment. This was the past.

Another man came over and closed Gia's eyes then whipped around to shoot the man with the smoking gun.

"Steffan, do you know them?"

Gruffly, he spat out on a hiss, "Yeesssss. I do. I know both of them."

Raquel's heart raced and pounded against her ribs. She shook in fear. An audible growl erupted behind her, and she sensed Steffan had stepped away from her back.

Immediately, the warehouse disappeared, and Raquel gasped for air as the reality of what had happened fully sank in.

She blinked, clearing her vision to stare at the monitors regulating Gia's heart rate and breathing. The monitor showed Gia's heart rate had slowed, and as Raquel observed Gia's face, she noticed how peaceful she seemed lying there whereas before, her face was etched with pain.

Bereft, knowing the fear and the pain Gia had gone through, and with Steffan now pacing the room, the chill and loneliness were overwhelming.

Raquel wrapped her arms around her middle. "Steffan? Did that really just happen?"

"Yes. I'm surprised her lioness showed you as much as she did and let you know what it's like when the animal wants to come out. My skin is tingling right now, and I have to force my panther to hold back. It's reacting to my anger."

He stood there, wringing his hands, the tips of his canines dropping into place. He kept his eyes closed. "You will stay here at the hospital until I come for you. I need to get back to the house and tell Roman. Don't leave the hospital under any circumstances!"

"You said you recognized the man with the gun. Who was he?"

She reached out to him, and he flinched. *I've caused him pain.*

Steffan's cold stare made her shudder.

"I think it would be best if you didn't know. I didn't mean to pull away. I don't want you to touch me right now in case our minds connect and you figure out who the shooter is. But stay here at the hospital."

He ran out of the room, pausing momentarily by Dr. Greer's side in the doorway. They stared at each other before Steffan made a beeline down the hall to elevator.

I'm so different from them.

Dr. Greer quirked a brow and came over to the computer.

"Her vitals are stable for now," Raquel mumbled.

"Good." He clicked on the mouse and another screen popped up. "And judging by these new stats, things are looking up. I want another course of antibiotics for that bullet wound."

"Yes, sir. Of course. Mind if I ask you something?"

Dr. Greer's fingers flew over the keyboard as he made a notation on Gia's digital chart. "What is it?"

"Are you... I mean... how did Steffan... "

Dr. Greer grinned and pointed to his temple and tapped the side of his head with his index finger. "Steffan must care something for you for him to ask me to keep a watchful eye on you. Your male sent me a message through the mindlink. I'm not an Alpha or a Beta, but I respect Steffan. I'll see you later."

Dr. Greer left, and Raquel saw Henry nod his head slightly to the doc then turn his back to her in the door.

He was standing guard.

Chapter 17

Maximo quietly glanced at the females in the lineup of shifters he and Lars had smuggled into the United States. Most of the group were typical blue-collar workers: merchants, bakers, and some had experience in the textile industry.

The males openly glared back but none said a word to him. All of them had sacrificed a lot to be here. Each Kindred had a different reason, whether it was wanting a new life or they had been outcasts for breaking the law and were hunted; it did not matter. Fear, relief, hope, and uncertainty permeated the air like cheap perfume.

If someone made a fuss about the conditions they were in, then Maximo would make the choice of whether the male or female was sent back immediately, or died.

Maximo eyed the prostitutes, wanting someone... *special* for the evening. A certain female to take his mind off of Stavslaka's idiocy. Fates be damned; why the hell had Stavslaka taken the Northern Beta to the warehouse. At least Stavslaka had enough brains to move everyone to the 115-foot yacht parked at the end of Port of Fourchon and clean up his mess.

Trafficking Kindred into the US was lucrative. The money flowed freely between buyers and remained untraceable, and Maximo pocketed most of it.

Unfortunately, it also made Lars' wallet fat too.

Maximo hated having to deal with the Mulatese Tenebrae, but a deal was a deal. Fievel and Lars would help Maximo achieve the status of reigning ruler once all the current Commission members were disposed of. At least he wouldn't have to kill every Were-shifter. Only those that opposed him.

A scraping noise to Maximo's left brought his attention into focus. He stared at Lars.

Lars had gathered a small box into his arms. Gray claws instead of humanoid nails extended from the tips by half an inch. His skin was tarnished brown from the fine lynx fur covering it. The male's younger brother Fievel's coloring was much lighter. Lars always joked the inkwell had gone dry and that's why Fievel's fur was lighter even when he shifted.

Lars handed the box to Maximo.

The hazel eyes of Lars' lynx collided with Maximo's panther.

The Were-panther bristled underneath Maximo's skin, pulling it taut. He itched to kill the bastard. Unfortunately, Maximo needed the Mulatese Tenebrae's connections with other mixed bloods to operate under the radar of not just the Southern Commission, but also the Northern, the Southeastern, and the Western Commissions.

Maximo willed his Were-panther to settle down and tore his gaze away to walk down the line and hand out envelopes to each of the Kindred.

"The envelopes contain your new identities. Along with those comes your silence about witnessing the shooting and your silence about how you came to America. If you reveal any of this information about me or the shooting, your life will be forfeit and the whereabouts of the rest of your families will be made known to the appropriate entities."

Most of them nodded, but a few remained silent and pulled out the paperwork to review.

"There is a bus outside waiting to drop you off at your new Alpha's home. Those of you who didn't receive packets must remain here."

The remaining fourteen individuals and the five prostitutes gathered around Maximo. He motioned to Alpha Stavslaka to join him. "This is Alpha Stavslaka. He will be seeing to your needs. What you do in this country is up to you, but you will need to report to him." Maximo hooked a hand around a brunette's arm. "You're staying, my dear."

Stavslaka laid a hand on Maximo's. "If you take her, I want her returned. *Alive*."

"Don't worry." Lars smiled, baring long canines. "He will. Won't you, Max. Otherwise, your payments could potentially... stop."

Fates, he hated Lars. The Mulatese Tenebrae male had him by the balls.

The small protruding whiskers on Lars' face twitched, and Maximo growled.

Stavslaka sighed. "As much as I would like to see the two of you go at it, I am needed elsewhere." He waved to the two bodyguards standing in the shadows of the room, and they marched the rest of the females out.

The muscle in Maximo's face ticked. "She will come back alive."

"Good choice."

Maximo snarled. "When I'm done with her. Although, Stavslaka, I'd like to know what the hell was going on when you killed the Beta. Kunigund Maldonado is not going to be pleased. You shot and killed the male within the Southern Commission's territory. There'll be repercussions. I know it. Crossing Kuni is a death sentence."

"I've already texted the male. He thinks, like I told Alpha Jerox, it was a mugging, and I killed the human. So, neither party will come snooping. I wish things hadn't gone down like they did. Gia could've been dealt with in other ways."

"Well, Alpha Maldonado will be here in Louisiana within the hour. There's a Commission meeting tonight."

"Yes. I know, and it's one I'm going to miss after being so *distraught* over such a senseless loss."

"Did Gia survive?"

Stavslaka nodded curtly. "Yes, but she's in a coma, and according to Jerox, they can't sense her lioness. Her Sire is trying to make the decision to pull her off life support, but her mother is refusing. Since Gia is the firstborn from his First Mate, she has every right to keep her cub alive."

Maximo felt uneasy. "What about your spy at the hospital? Any word?"

Stavslaka pulled out his phone and texted someone. Maximo's patience grew thin.

Stavslaka replied after a few minutes. "It would seem Steffan and a human have been doing some mindlinking. I don't know how a human is capable of such a thing, but if I know Steffan, he'll be able to decipher whatever Gia saw. Should I have my man kill her?"

"No. It would raise too much suspicion this close to her shooting."

"Soooo... "

Maximo sighed. "We wait. There is a possibility Gia might not have seen anything. According to you, she came around the corner; the Northern Beta shot Gia at close range, and she collapsed. She wouldn't have had time to see you. And I would rather not deal with Jerox right now. He's not to be killed just yet."

Stavslaka grinned. "As you wish."

Chapter 18

Steffan's brain still reeled about connecting Raquel's and Gia's minds together. Unfortunately, he had to wait until the meeting was over to relay everything to Roman.

Steffan took a deep breath, hoping to calm his racing heart, and plopped down in the chair next to Roman. Fates, he was so late.

Steffan opened himself up to the mindlink from Roman. *"About time you showed up."*

He sensed the silent, curious inquisitions from each of the Alphas around the conference table. He didn't dare meet any of their gazes head on.

"Your Beta is interrupting tonight's meeting. I think he owes us a reason why. Once those doors close, no one is to be let in." Alpha Kunigund sat back in his chair, the pale gray smoke from the cigar trailing silently upward.

He kept his eyes lowered for a minute before glancing up and focusing his attention on Roman.

"My Beta was checking in on Jerox's cub, Gia. We are helping with the investigation. I believe that's all I am going to say about the issue. Any other questions you can direct toward Jerox. Now, let's continue shall we."

Alpha Kunigund jutted his fingers holding the cigar as a silent directive he agreed with continuing.

Roman returned his formal obeisance with a slight nod and Steffan leaned back in the chair.

"Some of you thought Steffan was resurrecting his petition for this meeting tonight. He is not, but someone else has run into the same issue, and I'm hearing from other pards and clans there have been instances. I'm in agreement that the issue needs to addressed again. The Alpha is remaining anonymous, as is his right. His young wishes to marry... "

Steffan never heard the rest of what Roman was saying. He was too wrapped up in the events at the hospital. Raquel's mind had been so easy to mindlink with, it scared him.

Pressure built at his temples.

"Lad? Ev'ry thing all right? Ye look as if ye'r gonna commit murder, or are ye constipated?"

Steffan glanced around the table before replying. *"To a point, things are fine. But I need to speak with you and Roman. I found out what happened to Gia. Have I missed anything important?"*

Connor's brow rose sharply above cobalt blue eyes, and he sat heavily back in the chair. *"Nae' really, laddie. Only a pissin' contest between Marc and Daleena. Although I think Daleena secretly had a pair of balls strapped on."*

Steffan snorted at the mental cartoon Connor sent him and brought the current ongoing conversation between Talon, a Were-eagle from the Western Commission, and Kunigund Maldanado, of the Northern Commission to a stand-still.

Shit. Steffan wanted to disappear. Of all times for a Northern Alpha to show up and visit, this wasn't the best. Even though it was a requirement for the other commissions to send their Head Alphas to a meeting with a proposal such as was on the table, most of the time they didn't show up. He prayed the house staff had cleaned his room thoroughly so Raquel's scent wouldn't be detected in the house.

"Connor? Did Ascenza have the staff clean... everything?"

"Aye. Now pull yer head out o' yer arse, shut yer mindlink off, and shut yer yap."

Steffan sighed in relief but immediately tensed when someone started to painfully rummage inside his head. With a growl, he slammed the open channel of the mindlink closed, but not before he caught Alpha Kunigund's brows furrowed at the abrupt disconnect. The male's eyes grew stormy.

Ahhhh, shit!

"Roman, I think since your Beta mated a human and turned her, *he* is the reason you initially petitioned for humans to remain... breathing while knowing about our kind. You, Alpha Lavelle, took a human, marked her, and then turned her. Perhaps we need to be educated on this new adventure your pard and others are partaking in, because I still can remember a time when I was locked up in some laboratory after being rescued from some circus in the early 1900's. This notion is dangerous.

141

"A real mate is one who is worthy enough to see things through and be supportive, and it's easier if they were born a Kindred. Halflings take a long time to accept our ways, our laws.

"I'll put up an example. Roman, you have two Halflings in your employ. We all know when you found them on the streets of London, they were feral. Their Tasheen had abandoned them. Yet it's been two hundred years, and they still hide behind your pard like cowards."

Roman growled, getting everyone's attention. "I don't see your point. Those two Halflings were found at the height of vampire slayings, killing of werewolves, and the like. They're scared shitless. And furthermore—"

Steffan saw the anger flashing in Alpha Kunigund's eyes.

"Humans shouldn't be trusted with our information. Period!

"And I was also informed today that my Beta, Andros, was killed by a human. It took three years to find a good Beta and get him voted into position. My cousin was mugged, apparently, and Stavslaka saw to it the piece of trash was taken care of. I see Stavslaka is not here, therefore, I can't formally thank him. So forgive me if I seem short tempered."

Bullshit.

Kunigund casually leaned to the side in his chair.

The other Alphas started to argue.

Roman stood up, silencing the room, and leaned in on the table, claws extended. "Let me be the first to extend my condolences to your pard. I know how much Andros meant to you. Your cousin will be mourned. However, if you are going to criticize my Beta's choice in mate, you will address me. I brought this petition to the table on behalf of another Alpha, not Steffan. It is no secret what happened to my sister-in-law, Michelle Lavelle. She loved him for what he is and fully accepted our ways. My First Mate, Genevieve, made the same sacrifice by giving up her own humanity. Should by chance Steffan take another human as mate then I fully expect them to follow Kindred Law.

"It is because of others who've taken on humans as mates that this petition exists. Too many have left their family homes to take up residence within the safety of neutral territories. Humans no longer hunt us in fear. They no longer hold onto superstitions like they used to over a century ago. I'm not saying we should advertise our existence, but there should be some allowances for those who have found happiness, and not force the issue of them transforming their intendeds into Halflings or having to kill them."

Alpha Tomasina interrupted the arguing. "We all understand the issue. But is it really necessary? I would like to propose an Addendum to this petition."

Roman's glare narrowed. "Like what?"

"Humans that are going to be mated, or are mated to a Kindred won't be killed. Humans that are co-workers and have learned of our kind should be killed or have their memories wiped. They might not hunt us with pick-axes and torches like they did back in the seventeenth century, but some of us remember, and I, for one, have nightmares about it.

"Roman, this is about protecting our species as a whole. I don't want to see us go lax in our decision and end up as some scientist's lab experiment or at time of death, displayed like dinosaurs in the Smithsonian Museum."

Steffan folded his fingers together and placed his hands on the table. He barely listened to his brother and Tomasina drone on and on about the consequences. The Addendum made sense. There really was no reason for humans he interacted with at the real estate office to know about his panther. They came in, he helped them look at houses for sale or rent, and helped them get the right kind of mortgage.

He wished the law had been in place when he started courting Michelle. He wouldn't have had to hide from anyone.

Hiding.

Raquel was still at the hospital. He had to hide her there in order to protect her. He knew the other Were-shifters in the hospital would keep an eye on her. But his panther started to stir and push against his skin. The edge of the fur made his skin tingle.

The intensity this urge to protect Raquel surprised him. She was a smart female. It was a blessing she could see things by touching objects, and she astounded him when she stood up to him. She was a strong female for sure, and he hoped this meeting would be over soon. He'd talk to Connor and Roman and then go pick Raquel up from work.

He glanced at the other Alphas and Betas around the table while Roman sat down in his leather chair. There were a few males nodding in agreement. Obviously he had been too wrapped up in his own thoughts to notice what had been agreed upon. Did they agree with Roman? Or were they agreeing with Kunigund?

Daleena stood up and addressed everyone. "I will never take a human as a Mate, nor will I accept one into my fold. But I do have a question for *your* Beta, Alpha Lavelle."

A hush settled upon the room.

Steffan opened a mindlink to his brother and Connor. "*What the hell is going on here? Why is it all of a sudden, I'm the center of attention?*"

"*Well, laddie, ye did take a human as a First Mate and were forced to change her.*"

"*So was Roman!*"

Roman sighed through the link. "*Calm down, Steff. Let's hear her out.*"

She took out her phone, scrolled through it, and then tossed it to Roman.

"As you can see from the picture I received, your Beta has other interests in humans. Michelle wasn't the only one."

Roman's face drained of color and froze once he viewed the picture on the screen. He shot an accusatory glare at Steffan. The Alpha was too calm for Steffan's liking. In other words, Roman was beyond pissed. Roman shoved the phone into Steffan's hands.

"*Steffan. I thought you took care of Raquel?*" Roman's golden glare hit him. "*Like I said before, I don't give a damn who you fuck with. But this doesn't look good to others here!*"

Steffan looked at the image. Someone had taken a photo of him embracing Raquel while he amplified her visions for her. But this picture of them looked *way* more intimate than it was.

A menacing growl of frustration rumbled in his chest. For Fates' sakes! Raquel was at the hospital with a stalker watching her. No doubt whoever it was intended to kill her. Damn it to hell!

He shot a furious glare to Daleena; her cool demeanor only angered him more. "If you all need to know what transpired, I will tell you. I was using my ability to mindlink to magnify Raquel's Sensitive ability. She can do psychometry, and I wanted to find out what happened to Gia. That is all that was going on between us. And before you ask, yes, she knows about Kindred, but not for long. I'm going to erase what she knows about our kind." He threw the phone at Daleena and abruptly stood, toppling the chair onto its side. "Alpha Roman, I need to speak with you in private. I—"

Fuck propriety!

Steffan hastily headed up to his room. It wasn't his most graceful exit from the meeting, but his panther urged him to get out of there. He was suffocating.

***

Kunigund snatched up the phone from in front of Daleena. This was getting out of control.

Roman squared his shoulders, giving an air of being in control. "Thank you, Daleena, but I knew about this situation already, and it's being taken care of."

Kunigund's focus shifted from the phone to Roman and back to the phone. "So if I can sum everything up, Steffan used his mindlink to help his girlfriend here talk to Gia. I get it. But she's a human. The less she knows, the better."

Roman viewed Jerox's empty seat with a sigh. "She was mugged down at the docks. The situation has been dealt with, and we are all waiting for her to wake up soon. If she doesn't, then Jerox and his First Mate will need to make a decision regarding her welfare."

Kunigund boldly commented, "Such a nice way of describing having to pull the plug on someone, Alpha Lavelle. But if she was down at the docks, as was my Beta, then perhaps we can take some comfort in the knowledge that the human has been disposed of. At least that is what was relayed to me by Alpha Stavslaka. He seemed to think it was a human. Anyway, I digress. The proposal needs to be voted upon."

Roman shifted his gaze from one Alpha to another. Out of the twenty-four Commission Alpha seats, four remained empty, and Jerox's and Stavslaka's were empty as well tonight. If the vote was yea, then all the Commissions in the US would need to send out a decree letting all Kindred know of the new Law.

"All those in favor, raise your hand."

Roman's heart sank at seeing only six Alphas raise a hand.

"I take it everyone else is opposed then."

Daleena answered for the group. "Yes, we are. Now, if you'll excuse me, I have some unfinished business to attend to." She rose, nodded at the others as she passed by them, and closed the door behind her.

Roman sat back down in his chair. "Then this meeting is adjourned, and I will send out a notification email claiming the proposal has been vetoed, and Kindred in neutral territories will need to keep their human mates in said territory. Thank you all for coming."

The noise of the chairs scraping across the wooden floor echoed as the Alphas and Betas left. The question of what to do with Raquel was becoming paramount. Steffan had run out of time, and it gutted Roman to tell Genevieve her best friend would have to be killed since he knew Steffan would not force Raquel to change into a Halfling.

He glanced at Connor. "Go and find Steffan. We need to talk."

***

Steffan willed the door closed behind him, stripped, and quickly shifted. Once his paws dropped to the floor, he stretched and tested his grip in the plush rug for traction. He couldn't wait for this evening to be over. He should have gone out into the dense forest of Bayou Cane; however, he really needed to speak with Roman. At least with shifting, there was a type of release that appeased the Were-panther.

What was going to happen now? How was he ever going to feel contentment that Raquel was safe? Could he transform Raquel? No. He wasn't going to force her into something she didn't want. It pained him to think how she would reject him if the deed was forced upon her. He'd seen that same look on a few of his friends who had become Tasheens. He was not going to go through with it. Look at how his Mate turned out—dead and on display.

Pain ricocheted around his heart. The photo of him and Raquel on Daleena's phone was burned into his brain, and his fur bristled. The entire Commission knew about Raquel. The photo was damaging enough and proof he hadn't erased her mind.

I looked damn cozy pressed up against Raquel like that. Fates, do I have any time left that I can erase her memories? Now that the others think I—

146

A delicate knock on the door startled him from his thoughts. He willed it open, and Daleena stepped through. *What the hell? She followed me to my room?*

He snarled at her, forcing a mindlink to her.

"You fuckin' bitch!"

She folded her hands in front of her. "I have an offer for you. I can forgive you for your outburst *if* you will be my First Mate. You can never be an Alpha over the cheetahs since you are a panther, but you will be given the respect you deserve as my First Mate. In regards to young, I'll take on a cheetah as Second Mate. I don't want young from you. They would be considered outcasts, and even though we are two felines, it would be unknown if they could shift or not."

He snarled at the imagery her words brought on. *"Get. Out. I never want to be an Alpha! I knew it was a mistake to have any sexual contact with you, but at the time, you were very convincing. I should have never tarnished Michelle's memory like I did!"*

He reared up, ready to pounce, and she slipped out of her dress, while simultaneously shifting into her cheetah form, and raked her claws across his muzzle. He had no real desire to fight her. He only wanted to be alone. His sides billowed with every breath as he stood his ground.

"I said, get out."

He didn't know if it was anger, pain, or plain stupidity that caused him to challenge an Alpha.

"You still grieve, and I sympathize, but heed my warning. Humans are nothing but trouble. You deserve better, and I can give you everything you've dreamed of. Think about it. I can wait. And the female you were holding? Let her go. For her own safety."

Daleena grabbed her dress, shifted back to her human form, and put it on a little more slowly than he liked. She was taunting him, sashaying her hips back and forth until the dress settled. Daleena backed out of his room, and he willed the door shut and locked it.

A First Mate to her? I'd rather sleep in a bed of leeches.

He shuddered at the end of his transformation and pulled himself off the floor to pace the room. He'd never been this confused. Sweat peppered his skin, and he drove a hand through his thick hair. He wanted to rip it out he was so frustrated.

A heavy knock on his door brought Steffan out of his train of thought.

"Look, I don't want to be your Mate!" He tore the door open.

Connor smiled. "Well, 'tis guit ta know. Ye are'nae my type. Lad, let's chat."

This isn't my night.

Chapter 19

Maximo wiped the fried chicken grease off his chin with the napkin and tossed the bones into the trashcan next to the garage. The female he had been with barely satisfied him, and he'd made sure to return her to Stavslaka.

Movement from the corner of his eye forced him to partially shift his face. *I'm playing with fire by being here. I shouldn't have come.* He sniffed the air and moved to the opposite side of the driveway, placing himself downwind. It was a steep gamble, standing this close to his own home, but he needed to see how many members had come out.

Mentally he ticked off the number of Alphas and Betas. He'd been told this evening's meeting was important, so it was guaranteed all of the Betas would be here, or at least the ones still alive. He wasn't disappointed.

Maximo was about to leave when he noticed Alpha St. Claire quickly descending the cement steps of the front of the house. Her gait firm as she stomped to her car. The air carried her scent to him and along with it, he detected a hint of Steffan's. She'd been in his room or in close proximity to his brat. She'd always had aspirations about his son in the past. If he remembered right, Steffan and Daleena had slept together in the first month after his mate's death.

Humans will never make good mates for shifters! The Fates must've frozen over the Netherworld.

An idea took root and blossomed in the back of his mind. *If Steffan formally mated Daleena, it would put him out of the way. With him living with her, Roman wouldn't have a Beta to take his place. I could kill Steffan off a lot sooner. Cristoff would have to be voted into the seat by the pard, and that could take years. However, I should be back by then to retake my place before that happens.*

The idea was risky.

He followed her to her car.

Keys jangled and dropped to the macadam beside her silver

149

Crossfire. Daleena bent over to retrieve them, but he swiped them up, closing his fingers in a tight grasp.

Confusion marred her features, and her nostrils flared. She recognized his scent. Her brows shot up in surprise. *Oh yes. You know who I am.*

Daleena opened her mouth to scream, but Maximo slammed the palm of his hand over her mouth and dragged her to the bushes. She struggled against him.

"Calm down, female."

She kicked at him and wriggled in his arms.

His voice thickened with the combination of his own voice and his panther's. The sound usually put fear into humans, but to another Were-shifter, it was more than a threat. It held the promise of death. "I said, calm down, and stop fighting me. I have a proposition, and it concerns you and my second son, Steffan."

Maximo shoved her down to the ground but maintained his grip on her wrist, painfully twisting it behind her, holding her in place.

She gasped. "You're alive? What the hell! How can you be alive? Let me go!"

He relished her fear. "You're going to help me, or rather, you're going to help yourself."

"With what?"

"I know you want Steffan as your First Mate. I have always had plans for you and him. Since, technically speaking, I'm dead, you're going to draw up the necessary paperwork for a Mating Contract. Have *it* pre-date my death by one month. Then I will have Roman deliver his sibling to you."

Daleena stopped struggling, and in a show of good faith, Maximo forced himself to let go of her wrist. She stayed on the ground, elegantly curling her legs to the side. Distrust shone brightly in her light brown eyes. He knew she was contemplating how she could get away from him, but that would be a mistake. She would know her cheetah was no match for him. She might be able to outrun him, but she lacked the strength of his panther.

"My dear, if you value your life, I'd suggest you not shift right now while we are negotiating. It's rude."

Her nostrils flared. "Why in the name of the Fates should I help you? You're alive; why not take your seat on the Commission?"

"If you don't help me, I will see to it your imports accidentally go elsewhere. I know how much you value your fragrance and cosmetic lines. It really would be a shame if you were no longer able to acquire the proper ingredients." His smile showed fully extended canines.

She shook her head. "You wouldn't dare!"

He yanked her arm upward forcing a yelp out of her.

"I'm going to let you go and you're going to listen. Otherwise I will kill you and take my offer elsewhere. What'll be?"

She quickly sucked in air and nodded her compliance. He let go of her wrist and she sat up on the ground massaging the circulation back into her hand.

"Good. Now, do you want Steffan... or not?"

"Why are you doing this?"

"There has been a great injustice done to some of our Kindred, and I am merely an instrument to set a wrong to right. Most of the Commission is corrupt." He forced the lie out and smiled serenely to put her more at ease.

"If you are wondering *why* I couldn't accomplish this while alive, I'm only trying to find out the list of members that are corrupt and deal with them. I'm sure you noticed the deaths of several Alphas and Betas recently, have you not?"

Daleena's face took on a reflective expression, and a short time later, she refocused on him. He folded his hands in front of him. Inside, his panther clawed, and his belly flexed. His panther urged him to hurry up.

Her head tilted to the side. "I have. Do you know who has done this?"

He shrugged. "No. But I'm close." He paused to gauge her response, and when there was none, he said, "Very close."

She stood up, and he kept his distance. It would do no good if she sensed his lie.

Her stare narrowed. "Steffan's heart is with his dead Mate. I'd be competing for it. It's not going to matter."

"With a Mating Contract in place, he has no choice. Especially when his signed name will appear at the bottom next to yours and mine."

She frowned. "How the hell are you going to do that?"

151

Maximo started to walk away. "Leave it to me, my dear. Meet me in town in the old ice factory. I'll have everything ready for you in a few days. Oh and ah, you're not going mention to anyone that I'm alive either. The consquences would be... dire."

Chapter 20

Steffan swiped a pair of jeans off the floor and quickly put them on. The heat of Roman's and Connor's stares burned into his skin. He didn't have to open a mindlink to them. That damn picture said it all, and they wanted answers.

"Well, thanks for at least letting me get dressed."

Roman stated flatly, "I was trying to figure out where to shove my foot first."

"I can explain."

"Lad, this'd better be guit."

Steffan turned around to face Roman. His brother leaned against the wall, arms crossed over his chest, canines lowered, and gold eyes staring back at him. One finger tapped up and down on the sleeve of his forearm. He pushed off the wall, getting up in Steffan's face.

"Let me get this straight: We have a meeting to vote to keep humans alive who are potential mates or are already mated, and I find out via *Snapchat* from another Alpha's phone you haven't erased Raquel's memory and sent her back to live a normal human life. Is there any time remaining to erase her memories? Do you have any idea whatsoever what you've done? Tell you what, brother; let me answer both questions for you: There is no time, and no, you don't!"

"What do you want me to do? Are you going to order her death?"

Roman took a step back. "I might have to," he responded softly. "The other Alphas are going to expect that, and if I don't deliver, it could mean war on the House of Lavelle!"

Connor piped up quickly, "Roman, you'll have to contend with ye mate then. Those two are thicker'n mud. Alpha Genevieve would 'ave yer hide." He took a breath before addressing Steffan. "Lad, I believed ye back there at the meetin' as to what was really goin' on in the picture. Ye said ye had word 'bout Gia. What is it?"

Steffan glanced from Roman's golden glower to Connor's

inquisitive cobalt blue eyes. At least Connor provided him with a chance to explain.

"I went to the hospital to see if I could push a mindlink through to Gia. I figured her lioness would still be able to communicate with me even while Gia was unconscious. However, her lioness was close to death and remained in a coma-like state. She wouldn't acknowledge me or communicate with me. Then Raquel volunteered to try."

The confused frowns on both of their faces was almost comical.

"Lad? Wha' d'ye mean?"

"If Raquel touches something Gia has used, or in this case Raquel laid her hands on Gia, she can see what happened to Gia. I took a chance and figured I'd magnify what she saw. But in order for me to do that, I had to press myself against her. Honestly, that's all it was. I know I'm not a Dreamwalker like you, but I didn't want to pass this opportunity up. You weren't available at the time."

"So noted. Now, what happened to Gia?"

"A male from a Northern Commission shot her. I didn't recognize him, but there were females and a few families lined up outside a shipping container. Gia's mind shut down the moment she was shot, but her lioness allowed us to see what she saw. Her lioness projected herself outside of Gia's body and kept watching things for a period of time before she too lost consciousness. If I'm not mistaken, I believe Stavslaka has been using the docks to bring in undocumented Were-shifters."

Roman sighed. "It makes sense now. The Northerner was Andros. He had been voted into a Beta position after Kunigund lost his brother. He was here to scope out a place for his daughter Cara to live—or so he says. I suspect he had other types of business dealings to deal with and used it as an excuse for his own cover. The question is *why* was he down at the docks and inside the warehouse? He had no reason to be. If he was looking for a residential area for Cara to be in, then the docks aren't it."

"It doesn't make sense." Steffan fidgeted with the hem of his shirt. "And the only one who can answer such a question is Stavslaka."

The room grew quiet.

"Lemme go 'ave a word with Stavslaka."

Roman shook his head. "No, Connor. I'll do it."

"Aye. Ye could. But I call dibs on Stavslaka. He'n' I go way back, an' I know how ta get information out o' him. Besides, ye'r gettin' mated, and Steffan has the problem of figuring out how ta best help Raquel. Otherwise, Roman, yer nuts are crushed. And actually, I have an idea... take Raquel to the Matin'."

"What?" Roman and Steffan simultaneously exclaimed.

Steffan thought someone had punched him in the gut.

"Nae, seriously, take the lass t' the Matin' Ceremony."

"Connor, I don't think—"

"See, there ye go, thinkin' again. Listen. It'll be guit. Ye can keep an eye on her, and once the others see Raquel is a decent human, they'll leave her alone. Afterward, ye can deliver the female to a neutral territory."

Roman said, "No human has ever witnessed one of our Ceremonies, and I won't allow her to be seated next to a predator. We can hide her here at the house, or Steff, I can set her up financially for a time until she is able to get back onto her feet. Unless she's going to be your Mate."

Steffan felt nauseous. *Take her to the Ceremony? Was Connor nuts?*

"She's not my Mate! There's no way I'd be stupid enough to mate another female."

"Errrr, perhaps ye be swingin' ta the other side?"

"NO!"

Connor chuckled. "Just checkin'."

Roman rolled his eyes. "If you two are through, there's still the problem of Raquel's memory. It's past time to fully erase what she knows. I'm sure while she's at work and Genevieve is there as well, no harm will come to her."

The hairs on the back of Steffan's neck stood on end. Daleena might try and harm Raquel. "I need to get back to the hospital. I told her not to leave until I came and picked her and Alpha Genevieve up at seven, and it's almost sunrise."

Connor nodded and left.

Roman placed his hand on Steffan's shoulder. "We'll figure something out."

Steffan shrugged it off and pulled a t-shirt over his head, grabbed his keys to the blue Camaro, and hightailed it down to the garage.

155

Chapter 21

Ascenza smiled slowly over the brim of the cup she cradled in her hands. The delicate white and gold teacup had been an anniversary present from her Mate. *Hundred and seventy-fifth, I think.* She found the heady aroma of the chai tea calming after the hectic late night Commission meeting. Once everyone left, the household fell blissfully silent.

The silence after a busy evening was an affirmation that things went well. At least there was no bloodshed at this one. She glanced at the digital clock on the microwave. Correction. Five in the morning. The meeting had gone on longer than expected, and she wanted to make sure all of the Commission members had been well taken care of.

She had enough time to enjoy her tea and then start breakfast for the pard.

The slam of the front door echoed through the house.

Well, almost.

Connor walked into the kitchen and sat down heavily in the chair next to her with a sigh. He grabbed a sheet of loose paper she had been using to make her shopping list and folded it over and over. His large, calloused fingers creasing the paper into angles. She sat silently silently sipping her tea, observing her mate. Her gaze roamed over his profile. The softness of his long, loose hair beckoned for her to thread her fingers through. She reached out and lovingly smoothed back a long wave, the end turning up and wrapping around her finger.

His lips were tightly thin. The rim of the cup perched at the edge of her lips. *He's not himself.*

"Origami?"

He smiled but continued folding the paper.

Something must've occurred at the meeting. He's too quiet.

"Aye, lass. Origami. I have ta talk wit' ye. An' I don'nae know where ta start."

156

Ascenza frowned and gently sat the cup on the saucer. This must be serious.

Connor set the elegant swan in front of her. Taking her hand, he kissed the back of it and then folded hers within his. He stared at their joined hands. She loved the rough feel of his palm, but he was too quiet to her liking.

"Something's wrong, *no*?"

"Depends. Steffan told me what happened to Jerox's cub Gia. Poor lass. Jerox an' his sons are out fer blood, I can imagine. But that's nae what be on my mind."

Connor took a deep breath and squeezed her hand. He held it in a death grip.

"Connor, you're scaring me. What's wrong?"

"Thar be nae way ta say this, so... um... Stavslaka found Gia shot. Tha' we already know. But Steffan found ou' the shooter was'o'the Northern Commission, an' somehow Stavslaka is involved. Roman had an earlier discussion with Alpha Maldonado. He'd sent his Beta down 'ere to buy a house. For some reason, Kunigund Maldonaldo's Beta ended up at the docks, and they figured the same Kindred tha'shot Gia killed him."

Her mate stilled and his even stare expressed anger, resentment, pure hatred to the point she saw his pupils turn to slits. The way he glanced at her sent chills down her spine.

"Who was the Northern Beta?"

"Kuznetsov. Andros Kuznetsov."

Dread blanketed her. Blessed be the Fates! There's no way the male had come for her. Her past was over. Kuznetsov. The bastard had kidnapped her over a century ago and sold her for an evening to Stavslaka. After "it" was over, she'd begged Stavslaka to help her escape from Andros. He refused until she agreed to introduce him to her grandpère: a male with no identity, a male with ill-gotten riches, a male not to double-cross, and someone Ascenza had not had contact with since she had taken Connor as a Mate and turned her back on her pard.

Grandpère had the connections Stavslaka wanted to utilize.

She didn't care. She only wanted to go back into the safety of Connor's arms. She had been separated from Connor for over a century, and she'd done whatever it took to get back to him. That day she placed a call to her grandpère and vowed never to reach out to him again. She wanted no parts of her bloodline. With Connor she had found freedom.

The only way for her to truly escape from Kuznetsov's clutches had been for Stavslaka to *buy* her from him, and while she was at Stavslaka's home, she'd met Maximo Lavelle.

Ascenza swallowed the bile threatening to suffocate her. She suddenly lost the desire for her tea. A nice glass of wine would be better—or several glasses perhaps?

She closed her eyes and felt Connor's hand squeeze hers.

"Why is Stavslaka involved? Half of our lives were on hold because of him! Are you sure Andros is dead?"

"I'm positive." Connor yanked her into his lap. The heavy palm of his hand rubbed firmly over her back. He knew how to calm her down. "I know. But I'm eternally grateful ta him fer helpin' me find ye, *a'bhanrigh agam.*"

He was placating her. Whenever he called her, "my queen" he didn't want to talk about the past. Even now, she reached out with a telepathic mindlink, and he shut her out.

Ascenza shuddered as the unpleasant memories began to surface. This wasn't the time nor the place to discuss the past.

She left his lap and took the teacup and saucer and placed them in the sink. She turned to face him, leaning against the counter. "I heard someone run down the stairs."

Connor nodded, crossing his ankle over his knee. "Steffan be on his way ta the hospital ta pick up Raquel and Genevieve. I'm sure Dr. Jeffrey will keep them safe, but a picture of Steffan and Raquel pressed t'gether like they'd been superglued be makin' its rounds on... um... some picture site. Almost *all* o'the Commission Council has seen it. I'm sure tongues'll be waggin' ta the ones that *weren't* here. Steffan thinks the snapper-happy Kindred are still at the hospital."

Ascenza chortled. Raquel was human, but Steffan hadn't shown any interest in someone since his Mate was murdered. Now he'd taken a shine to Raquel. *Good. It's about time he starts to live again, instead of sinking into a bottle of alcohol.*

Connor's cobalt-blues flashed. She knew that look he threw her. She didn't want to think of the past anymore, and Connor had a way of bringing her mind back to the present.

"Lass, I think ye and I need ta go fer a run. So why don'nae ye strip down and come with me." His smile widened. "I can... I mean... it'll make ye feel betterrrrrrrr." Waggling his brows.

That devilish purrrrr set off butterflies in her stomach. He always knew how to get to her, even after two hundred and fifty years.

Ascenza's skin tingled. Her panthress was definitely on board for a chance to run at the break of dawn and be with her Mate. Her pure white fur was too noticeable during the full light of day. At least at dawn, dusk, and during a Blood Moon, she could "ghost" through the area virtually unseen.

Connor rose from his chair, slipped off his kilt, and kicked off his bright orange flip-flops. "Strip."

"Yes, sir, Sir Bryce."

Connor growled and made grabby-hands at her.

She squealed and giggled, and made a run for the back kitchen door, shifted, and roared at the break of dawn. She didn't care about her clothes, never had. All she cared about was being with the male she loved.

Chapter 22

Maximo impatiently waited by the side of the old cabin. He perused the old beat up shack. It looked as bad as he felt. The cedar roof sagged in the middle. Time had waged war on it, and eventually, without proper care, the structure would collapse.

His life resembled the structure. The difference though, he'd rise to greatness, just as he should have from the beginning, and he wouldn't have had to go through all this trouble. His father, Silas, was an idiot. The European Commissions had maintained their monarchies to this day. One would think his Sire would have been smart enough to place the Lavelle pard in the same predicament, but no.

"It's *his* fault I have to set things right. So far, the pieces are falling into place. Three Alphas have died unexpectedly, and in a short time, I should be ready to take on my son."

The sound of leaves crunching echoed in the distance. Maximo stood perfectly still, inhaling the air, trying to pick up the scent of whoever was traipsing on his property. He scanned the dense coverage of the treetops. Siber and one of his followers stood guard, ready to pounce should this meeting go wrong.

The footfalls got louder, and he forced a pleasant smile and tapped the cardboard tube against his leg.

Showtime.

Maximo mentally double-checked the partial shift, taking meticulous care to ensure he didn't look like himself. The wind picked up, and a long annoying length of hair flitted up to his chin, swiping over his nose. Why people liked to have long hair was beyond his comprehension. Hopefully, this meeting wouldn't last too long. He moved to the right and made sure to be downwind from his opponent.

"Tom! Hello. It's good to see you." *Tom is a simple male, so this should be easy.*

160

Tom scratched his head. "I came when I got the call. What's this about?"

Maximo grinned tightly. "Well, it would seem Maximo Lavelle entrusted me with some paperwork pertaining to a purchase you had invested in while he was still alive. I do need to apologize though. I was cleaning my desk out and noticed this stuck to the back of the drawer." Maximo waved the tube, back and forth, in front of him. "I believe these documents are the offer you made to purchase land near and around the lake west of the Lavelle property."

Tom's whole face lit up with excitement. "I thought Sir Maximo had forgotten."

Thank the Fates I didn't.

"No, he didn't. Plenty of fish too. Maximo told me his good employee loved to fish. All I need from you is your signature. Maximo had signed the deed already, but because he's been dead for some time, I will need another signature from the current Alpha Lavelle."

Tom's expression fell. "Master Lavelle and his First Mate will be away for a few days."

Maximo chewed his bottom lip. *Good. With the whelp out of the way, this will be easier than I thought.* "Well, son, this whole deal is time sensitive. If you want to forfeit building your cabin next to the lake, I'll understand."

"No, sir. What can I do?"

"Is there currently a Beta in the pard? He could sign as proxy for the Alpha. It would be legal until Alpha Roman can sign on the line for his signature. Like I said, Maximo Lavelle already signed the papers when he was alive, so they're good to go."

Tom's face brightened.

"Here's the packet of papers. Make sure your Beta signs the proxy line, and then I can hand over the rest of the deed to the land. I'm afraid I will have to hold onto it until you do so. Meet me back here in an hour."

Tom took the tube and rushed back to the house.

Maximo leaned back against the tree and waited. Time went quickly, and forty-five minutes later, Tom rushed back, his face bursting with a grin.

"I didn't think he would sign it. I caught him running out the door. He said he was on his way to the hospital. Not sure why, but here."

He shoved the tube back into Maximo's hands. Max uncapped the end and pulled out the papers. He flattened them against his knee. Sure enough, all three necessary signatures were in order. The top sheet was the transaction paper for Tom. The second and third sheets stuck fast to the top paper making it look and feel like heavy stock paper. The second and third ones were the Mating Contract he had discussed with Daleena.

The female had done a good job drawing up a contract that supposedly existed before he died. One for his records and one for Daleena's.

"Tom, did Beta Lavelle notice anything different about the papers he was signing?"

"Um, no. He glanced at them and quickly read through the top. Once he saw the word DEED on all three papers, he signed them without question. Frankly, sir, I think he was in too much of a hurry."

Good. The less focused my son is, the better.

Maximo easily peeled off the top document and handed it to Tom. "Here you are. This is your copy. I need to keep the other copies for legal purposes. You understand." Maximo forced a grin. "Thanks for your help."

"Thank ya, sir!" Tom headed off in the direction of the lake.

Maximo encircled the tube with his hands, wringing them around the circumference, as he watched Tom scamper off. Scamper was the wrong word for it. Hell, the male actually skipped and jumped like a female, he was so excited.

He glanced at the papers before rolling them back up. Everything was in order. Only thing needed was to slip Alpha Roman the signed Mating Contract. That was the only snag to his plan. *I'm sure Daleena can handle that one.* Giving away the land to Tom was a very small price to pay.

A heavy thud behind him and the familiar frustrated growl set Maximo on edge.

"What are you doing? I thought this was supposed to be where you got intel from one of your former lackeys and how you were going to finish gaining the trust of the other full-bloods."

Maximo slid the papers into the tube. Damn the Mulatese Tenebrae!

"Siber, how I do things is none of your concern. You really should have some patience. Coming back from the dead takes time."

162

Maximo started to walk away, but Kajong stepped in front of him, blocking his escape. The male had the audacity to meet his gaze. "I think you're stalling. Kill the rest of the Alphas, along with the Betas, and get back to the living. You pretending to be dead is a lost cause."

Maximo glared at Kajong. "Siber, I believe your new recruit needs some training. Do be of good mind and do it."

Kajong replied. "Siber asked you a question. I would have thought full blooded Kindred would at least have *some* common courtesy."

"And I would have thought low-life dogs such as you would know their place."

Maximo jumped to the side to avoid the right hook and laughed as the bark exploded off the tree behind him. Kajong howled in pain and body slammed into Maximo. Maximo braced his feet and twisted so he bared his claws before driving them deep into Kajong's upper chest.

The second his claws pierced Kajong's chest he wrapped his hand arpund the beating heart. The look of absolute terror on Kajong's face was pure joy to watch. Maximo squeezed it in the palm of his hand, and his claws sliced through the thick walls of the heart. Kajong gasped a few times before going limp against him, and Maximo tossed the dead Mulatese Tenebrae aside.

He took out a handkerchief and wiped the blood from his hands and observed Siber.

Thick, corded muscles twitched in Siber's forearms, and the male's stormy glare might have singed his fur had he given a fuck. Siber wanted to kill him, but then the chance to be back on the Commission would vanish for all Mulatese Tenebrae.

Maximo smiled. "Do you have something to say?" He finished wiping the blood off and toosed the handkerchief down onto the body.

Flashes of green and amber sparks glittered at Maximo.

"I didn't think so. Anyway, keep your cell on. Things are starting to heat up, and so far, everything is going according to plan."

***

Siber rushed to his fallen comrade and cradled the male's head in his lap. Rage engulfed him, but there was nothing that could be done; at least right now.

He popped the safety on the armband, and the makeshift bow opened, the arrow directed to and lined up with Maximo's back.

Siber's heart raced, and his finger itched to kill the bastard.

"Siber, put your toy away, unless you don't want to keep our little agreement. Your brethren Mulatese Tenebrae won't stand a chance of gaining any leverage for equality."

Maximo continued on his path, shifted, and took to the trees, leaving Siber alone.

Pop-whoosh-clank.

Once the arm-bow retracted back against his arm, Siber lowered his arm and glanced down into Kajong's lifeless eyes.

Siber swallowed hard and gently closed his friend's eyelids.

He knew once he agreed to help Maximo, there'd be consequences. But not like this.

I better keep my eyes open.

Chapter 23

Raquel closed her locker with a satisfied sigh. She grabbed her purse and slung it over her shoulder and ran a hand through her hair. At least she was working even though she had been told due to her circumstances that had occurred in the ED, she was allowed to tend to Gia.

And she was informed "you'll be watched."

Fine. Whatever. It was a slice of normalcy to me. At least my stint up here in ICU will get reported back to Dr. Jeffrey and hopefully that will change his mind.

It was a little unnerving having Dr. Greer watch over her like he did, and he made excuses to come into Gia's room when Raquel knew he had already entered things into the chart. He helped her change the tubing on the machine and had gone out of his way to hold a conversation with her.

"Something wrong?"

Raquel turned around to face Genevieve. "No. It's just all confusing."

"Do you have any plans?"

Raquel held the door open for Genevieve as they exited into the hall. "Not today. I have to stay glued to Steffan though, remember?"

She tried to withhold the sarcasm from her voice but grimaced as it still came through loud and clear, even to her ears.

"I know, but it won't be for much longer."

"What did you have in mind?"

Genevieve's smile broadened. "Let's go out to eat. Relax. I'm sure Steffan wouldn't mind."

"What won't I mind?"

Raquel startled. *Does he ever make a sound when he walks? Maybe I should buy him a little bell.*

Genevieve snorted a laugh while Steffan frowned.

They both read my mind. Oops. Raquel felt the heat in her face. She needed to remember to curb her thoughts around Steffan.

165

Genevieve said while laughing, "We didn't read your mind. You projected to us loud and clear."

"What do you mean I *projected*?"

Steffan looked like he wanted to say something but Genevieve interrupted him.

"Roman said you had a psychic gift; so to speak. My guess is with using it, you're starting to be able project thoughts and you're not being selective enough to who hears them and therefore any Kindred within a short distance of you can pick up on the thread of thought."

Raquel frowned. "So I need to learn to stop it."

"Can someone please tell me, what won't I mind?" Steffan's brow popped.

Raquel turned to him. "Genevieve wants to go out to eat tonight."

"We can't. Someone took our picture together when you and I were trying to get inside Gia's memories, and now everyone on the Commission *knows* about us. If we go out, you'll be killed on the spot, and Roman and I will be ordered to a tribunal for not killing you."

Genevieve sobered. "I thought with everything going on, a change of scenery would be nice. A picture of the two of you? That's not good."

Steffan replied flatly, "Let me think on it. Are you two females ready to head home? 'Cause I think we should get out of here. There's no telling who is going to come after Raquel."

He abruptly turned and hurried down the hall.

Genevieve cleared her throat. "Raquel, we better follow him."

Raquel frowned. Steffan's sudden change in attitude baffled her. "He sounded bitter."

Genevieve chewed her lip then muttered under her breath, "On second thought: Going out to a public restaurant might not be a good choice right now."

"Gena, I'm sick and tired of all the secrecy, all the damn bullshit—"

"Raquel, it's not bullshit. Roman and his pard have gone to great lengths to keep you alive. Up until recently, humans were killed if they found out about Kindred. We'll figure something out. But I'll schmooze Roman. He'll see to it we can go out. I know what it's like to be cooped up." Genevieve grabbed Raquel's arm and walked through the automatic doors to the curb outside.

Steffan waited impatiently, leaning against the car with his arms crossed over his chest. The frown on his face spoke volumes. "Is something wrong? And why does Genevieve have a triumphant smile on her face?"

"Raquel would like to go out somewhere. You shot down going to a restaurant, so how about Sanctuary of Desire? It's a neutral territory where both humans and Kindred go."

"No."

"Steffan, seriously? You're saying 'no' to your Alpha?"

Genevieve's sweet smile didn't fool Raquel, and when Raquel shot Steffan a quick glance, his eyes flashed blue, and the pupils constricted to slits. Ohhh man, he was pissed Genevieve had played the Alpha card.

Raquel's chest tightened, and she gripped the purse strap tighter. "Since you have a problem with going there, you can stay home."

Steffan immediately whipped around to face Raquel.

"You're not going to Sanctuary. Get in the car."

That tenor of his voice was much lower. Gena's brows rose in shock, and she quickly got in the back seat, and Raquel got in the front passenger seat and slammed the door.

He looked around and hurried to get into the driver's side, slamming the door shut and shaking the entire car.

"Why?"

"You're really not in a position to question me. For starters, you've only been allowed to come back and take care of Gia. I'm sure security has it on tape of you and Genevieve leaving tonight in my car. Who knows, the picture of all three of us leaving the hospital might end up on Snapchat too. If Roman wants to take Genevieve to the club, then they can go; you can't."

"I need to do something. Steffan, I'll stick to you like glue. I'll be by your side the whole time and you can tie me—"

Raquel let go if what she was going to say next. Instead, her attention diverted to the fact Steffan looked up, murmuring something, and the muscle in his cheek ticked twice.

Was he praying? He was.

He scrubbed his hand through his hair and placed it back on the steering wheel. Dread shone his gaze, and she quickly glanced back at Genevieve, who only shrugged.

Steffan said, "First of all, I had to get you out of the house quickly. I didn't want you dying at the house. Secondly, We don't know Gia's full story; we saw only the things she saw clearly. If I were a Dreamwalker, I would have the ability to stay in Gia's mind because, even unconscious, the mind may still *register* sounds, and I would have been able to ascertain who the other male was and hunt him down. There's a difference between being able to read minds and being a Dreamwalker. The only one in our pard that can do that is Roman. There will be hell to pay when Jerox finds out who is behind his daughter's attempted murder. So, until things calm down with Gia, the answer is no."

His voice had come out sharp and loud enough to make Raquel jump. *He's really having an issue with going to the club.*

Genevieve calmly replied. "Roman can keep an eye on Raquel if you aren't going to go to Sanctuary."

Steffan gripped the steering wheel so hard his knuckles blanched.

Unbelievable.

The car jerked forward into traffic.

Raquel grabbed onto the oh-crap-hang-on-for-dear-life handle above her head and kept silent the whole way back to the house.

168

Chapter 24

As soon as Raquel and Genevieve got home, they practically sprinted up the stairs. He could almost feel the heat from Raquel's anger the way she glared at him.

The whole damn night he tried focusing on work: perused security tapes, and made himself busy with prepping a sale of a bed and breakfast. When he came down for a meal, he noticed Raquel had stayed in her room, but nothing took his mind off keeping Raquel safe now that everyone knew about her.

In his own emails he had Kindred threatening to kill her if they saw her and one of them wanted to know where he had hidden her.

Fat chance in hell he'd let anything hurt her.

Steffan waited at the foot of the stairs, resting his arm on the bannister at the bottom step. She wanted to go out. *I could take her to Sanctuary myself.*

As soon as he thought it, his heart hammered inside his chest. He had trouble breathing, and his palms started to sweat. His skin crawled with anxiety and he felt the fur start to sprout on his forarms and the back of his neck.

He should've known better.

He'd tried going in the past and ended up in a full blown anxiety attack over just getting inches within the door. He's had centuries of practice with rope bondage and his desire died to practice the day his mate died.

He knew he was afraid. Afriad to explore with a new submissive. He'd had no intention of marring his Mate's memory by using random available females to play. Not to mention, his panther hadn't wanted to be with anyone.

He'd had nightmares about the ropes coming to life and cause serious harm to who ever he placed in his dream and he would wake cold, clamy from the sweat pouring out of him and it took him a few minutes to realize he was in his bed.

He drew in a calming breath. It did very little to calm his inner panther.

No way in hell was going to allow Roman to safeguard Raquel. The mere thought of Raquel being at the club, under Roman's protection, made not only him but his inner Were-panther nauseous.

Part of it had to do with an old law granting any Alpha the right to take more than one mate, not that Roman had any aspirations toward Raquel, but still, the thought made Steffan uncomfortable.

Steffan laid his forehead down on his arm and closed his eyes as Genevieve relayed the plans for tonight through the mindlink to Roman.

He really wished the Aphas had kept him out of the loop on that.

"Sanctuary of Desire," he murmured.

It wasn't that he didn't want to take Raquel. He'd had no desire and no reason to *return* to Sanctuary *at all*. It was as if a part of him had died along with Michelle.

Until recently.

Raquel.

Steffan kept picturing Raquel when he'd brought her home after rescuing her and Genevieve from Dupree. Steffan had placed her on the bed in the guest bedroom, her blonde hair fanned out on the pillow. Her hair was the softest thing he had ever touched. It had been a balm to him to watch her in slumber, knowing she was safe. Alive.

And for the first time since his Mate's untimely death, Steffan's panther had stirred.

Over the months while Raquel's body healed, he'd learned how she breathed in her sleep, how her heart sounded in slumber, how she talked in her sleep; he knew everything.

He admired Raquel's strength. Not just him, his Were-panther did too. His inner cat woke whenever she was near, making his skin tingle. He longed for her to touch him.

But was he strong enough to go back to the club with another female, another human, and not have someone try and kill her, considering Daleena had just shown all the Commissions that he was nuzzling up to a *human*?

He growled. Their differences stuck out like a huge red banner.

"Steff?"

Startled from his thoughts, Steffan jerked his head up, to stare directly into Roman's gold eyes. His brother casually toyed with the Cuban cigar he held, rolling it lightly in his fingers. The thin stream of blue-gray smoke rose to the ceiling. No doubt Roman's panther sensed Steffan's unease. Those eyes stared him down, but there was something else in them, and he couldn't put his finger on it.

Out of respect, he lowered his gaze to Roman's chin for a split second.

"Did you— Is there something you need?"

Roman drew long and hard on the end of the cigar and expelled the smoke through his nose. It slowly rose and swirled in the air. "I found it interesting my Mate told me about going to Sanctuary of Desire. Then she mentioned Raquel's name and said she was going with us. The question is: Are you?"

Steffan shifted his gaze over Roman's shoulder to the large grandfather clock sitting by its lonesome on the other side of the room. The heavy brass pendulum swung from side to side, the tick-tock cadence echoing his heartbeat.

"Steffan, as far as the Commission knows, you entered into a relationship with the human Raquel a week ago. I lied to them to cool their jets. Some have already called for her death."

"Yeah, I'm aware of that. I've gotten more than one email to prove it."

Roman shook his head and shifted his weight from one foot to the other. "Then this won't come as a shock to you either. There's been a kill contract placed out on her now. I just received the email. You have no choice. In order to save her life, you'll have to transform her."

"I know," Steffan grumbled, gritting his teeth.

"You've run out of time. Don't force me to do something I know will cause you to hate me for the rest of your life." Roman paused but quietly stated, "If I have to—"

"Mine Alpha, are you going to kill her?"

Steffan's heart pounded, and the back of his arms started to tingle. He'd liked Raquel since he first met her. He wanted to continue protecting her, knowing full well Raquel's life hung in the balance. It would seem his panther had the same idea, and the skin over his back drew tight.

A resigned sigh escaped Roman. "No. You've suffered enough. However, the Commission can't find her here as she is."

"I know this, Mine Alpha."

Carroll, one of the house staff, came up to them and patiently waited.

Roman glanced at his watch. "It's early. I don't have anyone scheduled to meet with me today, Carroll."

"I beg your pardon, sir, but Alpha Daleena St. Claire is here to see you and Beta Steffan. I had her wait in the library, and I locked your office door."

Roman glowered and placed the cigar in the holster of the white marble ashtray next to the stairs.

"Very well. Steff, let's go see what the female wants."

That's not a good sign.

Steffan followed Roman to the library outside of his office. Daleena stood when they entered, and the smile she gave Steffan made him falter. *She's up to something.* The mere sight of her made him unusually nauseated.

"Alpha Daleena. This is a little early to be doing business, is it not? The meeting was only a day ago. I've requested not to be disturbed until late afternoon for any business. Since you are here, state your business."

Daleena slightly bowed her head before making eye contact with Roman.

"Head Alpha Roman, I am here on a more *formal* matter."

The small hairs on the back of Steffan's neck rose. The female was a conniving bitch. First a photo taken of him and Raquel together, then Daleena going up to his room, and now she was here?

"Proceed," Roman said.

Daleena uncapped the end of a cardboard tube and slid out the contents. The parchment settled on the library table, and he unfurled it, smoothing his hands over the document.

The two-tone color and the acrid, musty smell of the thing told Steffan the parchment hadn't seen the light of day in a long time.

But why is she showing this to us?

Daleena's Were-cheetah flashed in her hazel-green orbs. "A solicitor brought this to my attention."

"For what?" Roman murmured.

Roman read the parchment, cautiously lifted his head to stare Daleena down before slowly sitting in a leather chair. A vein ticked on the side of his neck. His right hand shimmered for an instant before settling. Roman's poker face betrayed almost no discernable emotion, but Steffan sensed his growing unease and tension the second his brother laid eyes on the paper.

What did Roman find so infuriating that he fought the shift into his panther? Obviously, Daleena had challenged him for something. Sickening dread settled in the pit of his stomach.

"Mine Alpha?"

A sharp pain in his temples and Steffan opened the rushed mindlink Roman had sent.

"Steffan, you will keep yourself calm no matter what. Is that understood?"

Steffan bit the side of his cheek and steeled himself. Whatever it was must be disastrous.

Roman stared at Daleena. "Steffan, this"—he drew the word out very slowly— "is a Mating Contract... for you and Daleena."

Not disastrous. Cataclysmic.

"What the hell—in the name of the Fates—do you *mean*, it's a Mating Contract for Daleena and me?"

Steffan snatched up the parchment and read it. When he got down to the bottom, he deliberately held it up to his nose to smell the dried ink. *The signature has been forged*! Hers and Maximo's, his Sire, had been there for some time, but it was most definitely Maximo's scent. Steffan's scent was missing! *Impossible*! Another shifter's scent wouldn't last five years! This smelled a few days old. Steffan glanced through the contract. This was made to look real.

"How is this my signature? It's been copied! My Sire *never* had me sign something like this! You fucking bitch!"

Roman moved so fast, Steffan never saw him move to his side. He grabbed Steffan's elbow to stop him from throttling the wench.

"Steffan, back down. Now. I will handle this. I told you to remain calm." Roman turned to Daleena, the tips of his canines protruding. *"Where* did you get the Mating Contract, and *how* did you get Steffan's signature? The date you signed is one year before our Sire's death, but even I can tell the ink on my Beta's signature isn't completely dry; therefore, it is recent. Not to mention, he took a mate two years after Maximo's death, and you never came forward with this!"

Daleena smiled and blushed. "I went to Maximo and bartered a contract. At first, he wouldn't give me one until I promised ten percent of the fragrance line I had going at the time. He wrote up the contract, and we signed it. I don't remember when Steffan signed it. I wasn't there, but Steffan did, and now you must honor it!"

"I told you before"—Steffan leaned close to her face, teeth tightly clenched—"I will *never* take you as a mate, and *this* means nothing to me!"

Roman jerked him back, but Steffan's claws ripped through the contract, letting the shreds of the paper fall to the floor. He wanted to leave, but knew he couldn't. His skin hurt so badly with the need to shift into his panther, tears came to his eyes. He had never been so angry, so stunned, and so blindsided. He shrugged off Roman, stepped away from both of them, and made his way to the bar on the opposite wall, keeping his ears perked on the heated conversation behind him.

His hand shook as he reached for the decanter of cognac. How did this happen? The only thing he'd signed recently was Tom's deed. All he had cared about at the time was getting to Raquel. With his name on the contract, Daleena could kill Raquel herself! How could he have been so blind? His signature meant he wanted the contract to go through.

There was only one way to save this and save Raquel.

Steffan growled and threw the glass decanter against the wall, halting the argument between Daleena and Alpha Roman. He turned to face them both. A surge of power exploded through Steffan's body, fur sprouted all over him, and the clothes he wore ripped off his body. He had to kill her! The panther's muscles twitched, and Steffan zeroed in on Daleena.

Daleena took a step back, fear emanating from her like the musky perfume she wore. Roman took a step toward Steffan.

"Steffan! Stop! Control yourself!"

Roman's voice cut through the red haze. Steffan froze, tail erratically twitching back and forth. He reached out with his mind, opening a mindlink between Alpha Roman and Alpha Daleena.

"Mine Alpha, I have been tricked under false pretenses. I signed a document as proxy for you earlier. It was a simple deed to a parcel of land near the lake. I did not, nor would I ever sign a Mating Contract with Daleena."

Daleena's shrill voice rose. "The contract states we are mated! It's legal and binding! Roman, I'm sure your solicitor has another copy of it."

Roman scoffed. "I'm sure he doesn't. When our Sire died, I received all the papers Maximo had been working on—past and present. The Mating Contract for you and my brother was *not* among other contracts, and I will be *damned* if you think for one minute you can come in here and blackmail my brother in front of me."

"He's *mine*." Daleena snarled.

"I will never be yours, bitch."

Steffan slammed the mindlink closed. He stalked toward her, claws gripping the carpet, and fantasized about tearing into her.

"Steffan, I forbid you killing her here."

"Mine Alpha, I have every right—"

"I said I will handle this. You are not to kill her." Roman's outstretched hand motioned to Daleena then the door. "I believe it's time for you to leave. I suggest you leave my brother alone. And *do not* bother going to the rest of the Commission with this charade, or I will kill you on the grounds you tried to blackmail me and a member of my pard. Is that clear?"

Steffan jerked and clawed the rug to keep from launching and taking Daleena down in one blow.

Daleena shot her glare from Steffan to Roman and back to Steffan. Her voice dripped with venom. "Perfectly."

She hissed, and the enzyme flew from her mouth, hitting Steffan's fur. She hastily spun on her heel, retreated from the office, and in seconds, the front door opened, then slammed shut.

Steffan's fur and skin sizzled where the enzyme had landed.

Chapter 25

Roman observed Steffan from out of the corner of his eye. His brother was more than ready to kill Daleena, which was why he'd stepped in and made the threat himself. His father was dead. He knew right away something was off with the contract. Could she hold Steffan to it? Absolutely. But he wasn't going to let her have the chance.

Daleena had balls. If Steffan had honored the contract, as a living Beta, if Roman died, according to the law, Cristoff would need to be voted in to become the new Alpha of the House of Lavelle. It quite possibly could take up to a year to be voted in. Until then, all property, financials, and businesses under the House of Lavelle would be in limbo until Cristoff took the position.

No fucking way was that going to happen. And for once, Roman had never been so grateful to be the Head Alpha of the Commission. He didn't have to call on the entire Commission to veto that contract.

Roman waited while his brother shifted back to his human form then tossed him the blanket from the chaise lounge.

"Well, that was mildly stimulating."

"I can't believe she had the audacity to try and corner me like that!"

"Next time someone shows you papers to sign—*don't*. Skip the proxy line and say you can't. Now I'm going to have to double check Tom's paperwork. He's a simple Were-panther, and I will not stand by and have any of my staff hoodwinked."

"Noted. And what about the land Tom thinks he owns?"

"The male can have it. I know which part of the lake he wanted to build his home on. It's beautiful there. By the way, you owe me a new glass decanter. The one you broke, FYI, has been in the pard for a few centuries."

Steffan gave him a middle finger salute, and Roman laughed.

"Now, back to this business Genevieve mentioned about going to the club. Are you going?"

Steffan's shoulders sagged, and his whole demeanor became unreadable. Roman tried opening up a mindlink, but Steff shut it down.

It pained him to know that Steffan, a once sought-after master rigger who taught how to properly use rope safely, now shied away from his craft. This was going to be hard for his little brother. Hopefully, Raquel would be able to help him in some way.

"I don't know," Steffan muttered.

"Brother, I know you miss certain aspects of it, but if it brings back too many memories for you, I will keep Raquel safe."

Disbelief emanated from Steffan, and Roman prepared for the backlash.

"How are you going to do that when you and your mate are playing?"

Roman shrugged. "The club is neutral territory and the safest place for her. It's named *Sanctuary* for a reason. Raquel can wear a collar. I'll also have one of the bouncers keep an eye on her, and while my mate and I play, the bouncer can keep her company and provide anything she needs. Besides, we won't be playing all night. Just an hour or two, and because she will be wearing a Lavelle collar, no Kindred will bother her. She'll be safe."

***

"Roman, Daleena's goons also go to Sanctuary, and after what happened here, I'd rather Raquel stayed here. She's safer."

Roman crossed his arms over his chest, and his gaze narrowed. He just stared at Steffan and chewed on the corner of his lip.

"What?"

Roman sighed. "If I didn't know any better, I'd say you had a thing for her."

Steffan guffawed. "Think what you want. I don't see how Genevieve's best friend needs to be killed for knowing about our kind. Raquel should be allowed to live."

There was no way in hell Steffan was going to admit anything to Roman with regard to Raquel.

Roman nodded with a tilt of his head.

"Roman, I fail to see how this all translates to you thinking I have *a thing* for Raquel."

A tapping sound got Steffan's attention, and he and Roman faced the large mirror above the bar. The surface shimmered with a green aura, and Janeé appeared in her panther form, tail twitching in amusement.

"Hello, Mother. What brings you here?"

Roman's eyes bugged out, and Steffan nudged his brother.

Steffan whispered. "I forgot to mention to you, Mom's been hanging out."

"Eh, yeah, I see that." Roman coughed, sniffed, and did a quick wipe under his nose as Steffan caught the scent of unshed tears. He smiled up at the mirror.

"Roman. Steffan. I see you two are actually having a conversation for once. I just happened to be peering into the library when I caught sight of Daleena. Dreadful little bitch. I can't believe she gave you those papers."

"Yes, well, it's taken care of, Mother."

Janeé's eyes narrowed. *"What of the human?"*

Silence permeated the room.

She sighed. *"My son. If she remains human, her life will always be in danger. Do not underestimate Daleena."*

Steffan grimaced. "I'm not underestimating her. Anyway, what's your opinion on letting Raquel go out?"

Janeé's tail thumped against the glass of the mirror.

"If you want to keep her alive, stay home. Do your hobby in the playroom you two have set up in the east wing of the house."

Steffan glanced at Roman the same time he glanced at him.

Mom knew about the playroom? Oh my Fates! Steffan felt like puking. His face felt really hot. Fates, was he blushing?

Roman stuttered. "Y-you watch us in the playroom with our mates? Tied down? The cat-o-nine tails, whips, hot wax, you watch?" His mouth opened and closed, but nothing more came out.

The idea of their mother watching them with their mates...

Janeé jerked her head up. *"Of course not! Don't be crass. I go to another mirror when I see you enter the room. Good grief, boys! If I were alive, I'd be washing out your mouths with soap."*

"Yes, ma'am."

Steffan snickered.

"That goes for you too, youngling."

Steffan sobered. "Yes ma'am. Of course. It's just been a while since I heard Roman... well... be submissive to anyone." He held in a laugh, but ended up snorting.

Janeé rolled her eyes. *"I might be dead, but I still hear things and see things. Keep Raquel here. I grow tired. Should you need any more of my opinions, you know how to summon me."*

Janeé vanished, and Steffan shot Roman a quick glance before his brother punched him in the arm.

"Ooow, what's that for?" Steffan laughed.

"For you being a pain in the ass."

Chapter 26

"Raquel."

Her head snapped around at the sound of Steffan's voice. He crossed the room to stand next to her and willed the bedroom door closed. The moment the door shut, the quiet of the room became deafening.

Steffan searched her expression. A plethora of emotions crisscrossed his face like wildfire.

"Roman and I both think its best you stay here."

Usually, after a long night at work, she easily slept during the day. Not this time. In anticipation and to ease the restlessness, she had showered, shaved, and prepared herself for a night at Sanctuary.

"Excuse me?"

"You're staying here, at the house."

"Steffan, I'm beginning to feel like a caged animal. I was watched when I first went back to work, I was watched here, I was watched over in ICU... I thought it was settled; I am going out."

"It's not safe for you, and if anything happened... Well, I'd rather not lose you."

Raquel huffed. "First, you whisk me off to the hospital because of some Alpha/Beta bonding meeting going on here and tell me not to leave the hospital. Then, when we get back here, I can't leave—again. Make up your mind! You're doing nothing but confusing me, and I feel like everything is out of control. I need... "

The corner of his mouth barely lifted, but she caught it. Steffan squared his shoulders, and his voice deepened. "I know what you want, what you need, but we are staying here. I have an idea. Come with me. I'll show you."

His roughened fingertips trailed up her spine, and he rested the palm of his hand on the base of her neck. The center of her core fluttered, and the hypnotic pull of his stare brought a sense of quiet to her mind.

"Where are we going?"

Steffan drew in a deep breath. "A playroom."

"You have a playroom here?"

Steffan answered a little too quickly. "Yes. In the east wing of the house."

Raquel waited for him to go on, but he didn't. He only stared down at her, barely breathing, and his hesitation about the playroom piqued her curiosity.

"How come you never mentioned it before? Did you move your rope bondage class here?"

His nostrils flared slightly, but she got no other reaction to her enquiry.

"For practical purposes, I left Sanctuary after Michelle's death. I haven't played or taught classes since I left. I only conduct business there as necessary. However, if it was safe enough for you and I to be seen together, then I'd take you out." He hesitated before continuing. "Do you trust me to bring peace to your mind and your soul? I've kept you safe thus far. I know you feel like a caged animal. Let me bring some calm and control back into your life."

Raquel stared into his blue eyes. The pupils constricted to slits before the irises changed back to the normal brown. Steffan released her neck and moved away from her.

"If this is what you truly want, answer me with a yes or no.

With his physical distance, her mind began to spin out of what little control she had.

Without hesitation, she said, "Yes."

The second her answer flew out of her mouth, it dawned on her what she was about to do, and her body responded on its own to his voice.

"House rules of Sanctuary also apply the second you cross the door's threshold. Follow me."

She kept close—no more than a foot was between them—and stopped only long enough for him to place his hand on a biometric screen. A wall quickly slid aside to reveal a dark wooden door. It automatically opened, and he ushered her through. Once inside, the door slid closed.

Raquel squinted in the dark. "Any chance there are lights in here?"

"One moment."

Candelabras against the walls leapt to life, and an eight-foot mirror, anchored on an angle between the ceiling and the wall, helped to illuminate the room. Raquel's breath caught in her throat. Not what she expected.

The warm glow cast light on the floggers, whips, chains, dildos, and feathers neatly displayed around on the dark, red velvet walls, and ropes neatly bound together hung on a rack.

Holy crap, that's a lot of rope.

"Sir..."

He took the red rope off the rack and turned to her. Excitement zipped up her spine.

Steffan's warm hand encased her wrists, his thumb caressing the skin over a small, prominent vein. He drew the end of the buckled loop of rope slowly up from her elbow on one side, over her hand, and with an equal feather-light touch, down the other.

"Clear your mind. Focus on the sensation of the rope gliding over your skin. Lose the clothes. Eyes up and forward to the black metal ring on the wall. I want to see your emotions in them."

Raquel pulled her hands down to her side and took a step back. She reached around to the side of her corset, undid the brass hook and eyes, and let the garment fall softly to the floor. She drew in a deep breath as her breasts fell freely from the confining contraption. The air conditioning kicked on, and her nipples puckered.

Raquel waited silently. He walked behind her and then reached around her waist to run a palm over her stomach, pulling her back against the soft fabric of his shirt. His rough hand glided upward to cup her left breast. She gave in to the warmth, arching against his touch, and his thumb flicked back and forth over her nipple. Then, taking the tip between his fingers, he tugged... hard, eliciting a moan from her.

God, she loved it.

Steffan murmured against her ear, his hot breath tickling her ear and neck, sending chills racing down her arm. "Lose the thong and keep the heels on." He slowly tugged on her nipple and on the last word drew the sound out; pulling the nipple between his fingers before letting go.

She dragged in a ragged breath, and her core wept.

"I doubt you'll use a safe word, but it's the normal green, yellow, red. Do you understand? Answer yes or no."

He dragged the silky rope between her breasts.

"Y-esss," she gasped.

"Yes; what?"

"Yes Sir."

He withdrew his hand and slowly unwound the red rope, letting it fall to the floor in a puddle. He drew the end over her arms, teased her nipples, and slowly dragged the length over her neck.

Steffan soothed her to help her relax. There was a great deal of trust embodied in this art, and she knew she had to give herself over completely to clear her mind.

He hummed softly as he worked the rest of the sixty-foot rope around her body into a corset at her middle with a trinity knot between her breasts. Steffan pulled her arms in front of her. The nylon rope slid sensuously around her arms with a tug every once in a while, which caused goosebumps, and she shuddered. *A dragonfly design.*

"How do you feel? Any numbness or tingling?" He used two fingers to check every inch he had tied. She knew he was gauging the color of her skin, discerning if he had cut off the blood flow. If he didn't like how it felt to him, he'd loosen it slightly and redo the knot.

"No, Sir. It's fine."

Steffan scooped her up over his shoulder and laid her down on the bed, bent her knee, and tied her ankle to her thigh. Once he was satisfied, he bound the other leg and checked the ligatures.

He placed a vibrator through the knot between her hands, turned it on, and lowered her arms.

The vibrator pulsed and buzzed.

She held her breath, not sure if it was on low or high. It was whisper quiet... or had the blood pounding in her ears taken over as the anticipation escalated? Her core clenched at the first strike against her clit. She couldn't arch into the pulse and fought against the building orgasm.

Raquel's breathing became erratic, and Steffan eased the pressure slightly—but only for a moment—before guiding her arms down until the vibrator hit home.

Sweat broke out all over her body.

183

"Hold it for as long as you can."

Steffan lowered and raised her arms in sequence. The vibrator hit her clit harder each time, then the pressure eased.

She mewled a complaint, and he took a dildo he had on the side, turned it on, and inserted the tip into her, dragging it in and out, rubbing from her clit back down inside of her.

Raquel squeaked, "Sir?" then gasped as the torture continued. God, she didn't know how much longer she could hold out.

"I want to see you in your full glory. Eyes wide, nostrils flaring with each breath, and every single one of your muscles tensed and coiled as your release overwhelms you, and you feel the vibration running its course through the rope."

If that's what he wants, I'll be there in no time.

He pressed firmly on her clit, and fireworks set off in her mind. Her body shook against the rope.

The last wave of her orgasm crested, and he removed the dildo, and raised her arms and attached them with another rope to the rigging above her. A claw shot out of the tip of his finger, and she held her breath until the tip made contact with her skin. She yielded to the pressure of the initial sting of his claw as he traced down her inner arm and down over her breast, before the claw retracted. He firmly squeezed and kneaded her breast once.

Steffan stood back and stared at her, satisfaction written all over his face.

Raquel panted through the receding waves of the orgasm. Her pussy was wide open for his view, and like a kid in a candy store, he sank three fingers into her, filling her. He fucked her with his hand. The heel struck against her drenched pussy, the shock building pressure in her core.

The back of her head pressed hard into the pillow as she arched her neck, and Raquel thought for sure she would get off, but he stopped and pulled out to lick his fingers. Slowly. On cue, her core clenched with demand, and she panted hard, wanting completion.

God, she had been so ready to go over the edge. Panting hard, she shot her gaze to him.

He smiled devilishly back at her, his long tongue visually teasing her as he licked his fingers.

"Tastes like honey."

184

It was so hard to think right then. All she could do was watch him.

Steffan took off his shirt and pants, and she wasn't shocked he hadn't worn anything underneath. His cock stood straight out, the tip glistening with a pearl of fluid, and she mewled. The muscles in her legs twitched but were unable to do much more because of the ropes that bound her. She wanted to wrap her legs around his waist and ride out that bad boy.

He crawled up onto the bed and lowered himself between her legs. He didn't penetrate her but rubbed slightly against her tender groin.

Silk. He felt like sensuous silk.

Raquel closed her eyes, and he stopped. A deep resonating sound echoed in her head.

"*Open your eyes. Look at me... let me connect with you.*"

Raquel quickly opened her eyes and stared directly into deep hypnotic blue eyes.

"Permission to speak, Sir."

"Granted."

"Sometimes it's hard to tell if that's you or your panther talking to me."

His stare never wavered, and he pressed his hips toward her. She sucked in a breath.

"It's me. Always me. The panther only communicates to me, but he's aware of you. The only way he can communicate with you is when our minds are joined as one in a mindlink. It's through that symbiotic state I can project my thoughts to you via a mindlink and can read your mind... or any human's mind. If I was completely human, I couldn't do it."

He leaned down taking in her nipple, suckling and nipping the sensitive bud with his teeth. He dragged an elongated canine from one breast over to the other and lavished attention to the other breast. She moaned and his bulbous head penetrated her. She sucked in air as he slid into; filling her.

Damn he was huge and he slowly pounded into her, her core clenching around him as another orgasm hit her. He built momentum but ever careful to draw out the sensation. He plunged into her deeper and deeper until his whole body shook and he roared out his completion.

He kissed her lips with the softest intensity.

His gentleness moved her in a way, tears burned the corners of her eyes until she openly cried. She'd never felt closer to anyone before until Steffan had connected her mind with his.

Immediately, his hand shot to the skin on top of her foot, and he pulled out of her and sat up and started to untie and unwind the nylon rope from her legs and sliced through the rest of it with his claws, freeing her. Raquel found herself pressed against his steel body. His arms held her tightly, giving her the support she desperately needed.

This was so embarrassing. *Why am I crying like this?*

His firm hand stroked over her hair.

"I'm guessing, *bébé*, you bottled up your emotions and shoved them deep down inside of you. Sorry, but I read your mind. The rope has its own power of influence and can bring hidden emotions bubbling up to the surface. You've been dealing with a lot since I came into your life."

Steffan held her as she cried. On instinct, she breathed in the rich manly smell unique to him, and it helped to center her.

He turned her over onto her back, tucked the sheet around them and spooned against her side.

She focused on the smooth muscle in his arm, which flexed as he moved. His touch eased from firm to feather light as he stroked and rubbed his hand over her hip and up her back.

"Go to sleep. I'll wake you in a little while."

He was still hard and she felt his cock twitch against her backside.

"What about your needs?"

"Right now, that's not important."

He continued to gently massage her back and neck

She was so relaxed, he tucked her in beside him; his arm became her pillow.

***

Gently, he blew out a breath he hadn't realized he'd been holding, and she startled, barely cracking open an eye, before settling against him.

He hadn't meant to disturb her, but the impact of her release felt like a noose around his neck had been sliced off.

For two years, he'd remembered the tangled mess he'd found his Mate in, and ever since then, he'd been afraid of using the ropes on someone. He blamed himself, fearing that somehow his specialty had killed Michelle.

And now, Raquel had cast a spell, dissolving the fear.

Steffan perused her sleeping form. Her lashes were feathered against her cheeks, and her hair spilled over his arm in a waterfall of curly softness. The dull ache he'd carried in his chest for some time now eased. His eyelids were barely closed, and he noticed the mirror on the opposite wall shimmered briefly with a green glow.

"*Mère?*"

"*Be at peace. Let the Fates take care of you. Sleep.*"

A second later he plummeted into a deep, restful sleep.

Chapter 27

Connor stayed within the shadows of the club. From this vantage point he had a side view of Stavslaka at the bar; talking to someone on his cellphone. He wished the male would turn towards him. It would make reading the bastards lips easier.

Come on ye bastard. Who ye talkin' to?

As if by a miracle, Stavslaka leaned on his right arm, thus forcing his body in the direction Connor wanted.

Thank ye Fates. Ahhh lemme see. Somethin' 'bout a shipment of live goods.

Stavslaka hung up the phone and motioned the bartender to refill his glass.

Connor fumed. He hadn't read what the *live goods* were since the bastard turned away from him. His guess was good as any. Trafficking.

Connor downed the ice-cold Pepsi and took out his anger on the few remaining ice cubes, crunching and chewing them to chards.

He surveyed the bouncers near the bar and the exit. Hopefully, they would stay put.

Connor shoved away from the wall and headed straight for his target. He made it to within three feet when a heavy hand landed on his shoulder.

He looked up into a Were-bear's deadly stare.

"Lad, ye'r wrinklin' my shirt. Get yer mitt off me."

"I don't think you have an appointment."

"I 'ave business with the male."

"Simon, let Connor through."

Stavslaka motioned for Connor to sit next to him.

Connor knocked off the bear's hold on his shoulder, straightened his clothes, and took the seat offered to him. "Alpha Stavslaka, thanks fer yer time."

"And to what do I owe this unexpected pleasure?"

"I'll get t' the point. I don'nae like ye or yer business of shufflin' Kindred around like a deck o' cards and distributin' 'em anywhere ye like, all in the name of profit. These are lives ye be playin' with. Ye an' I both know who Andros was and his connection to ye."

"I really don't care what you think. Business is business. There's money to be made."

"So be smart in answerin' me this: Ye say when ye came across Gia, she'd been mugged."

"Correct." Stavslaka rolled his eyes and sipped on a glass of water.

"What did the bastard look like?"

Stavslaka shrugged. "I have no idea. All I know is, she had been shot."

"Aye, that's the story we've all 'eard."

Connor didn't miss the flash of red sparkling around Stavslaka's pupils or the white knuckles of his fist.

"It's the truth."

"Oh now, I'm nae arguin' that. But tell me, how is it, Alpha Maldonado's Beta was killed and in the same location?" Connor smiled. "No one knew the male was in the territory."

Stavslaka turned on the barstool to face Connor. "I have no idea. I was supposed to meet with the male around eleven o'clock. I was purchasing a vehicle from him. He never showed up. I waited after the ambulance took Gia to the hospital."

"What time did ye find Gia?"

"About nine thirty."

And he says the beta never showed up.

"I suspect ye had somethin' t' do with both of their li'l *accidental* shootings."

Stavslaka abruptly stood and started to take his leave. "Go fuck yourself, Connor. You're nothing but an old senile Alpha male with no pard who has nothing better to do than to stand around and accuse others just because your noble heart won't let you enjoy the spoils of your Sire's trade. I think that Scottish/Viking blood of yours has frozen over."

Connor grabbed Stavslaka by the front of the throat and slammed the male back against the bar.

Simon rushed forward, and Connor growled low at him. "I'd back off, if I were you."

The male halted, looking at Stavslaka.

"Stand down, Simon. I'm sure Connor and I are only having a misunderstanding. Now, Connor, admit it. Daddy dearest traded in slavery and reaped the wealth from the Vikings. If memory serves me right, your dear ole mum was a slave."

Connor applied more pressure to the male's throat. Killing the male would be a means to an end. Especially with how corrupt Stavslaka was. The bastard had caused enough grief for his family. The only good thing the male had ever done was bring Ascenza back to him.

"My mum was a Noble female an' so was my Sire!"

The male's face started to turn red from the amount of pressure Connor maintained on his throat, cutting the blood flow to the damned Were-fox's brain.

An electrical zap hit his stomach, followed by an even more painful blow to the lower back. Connor growled as he sank to his knees in pain. The shock loosened his hold. When he glanced up, Stavslaka stood over him with a cattle prod in hand, and Viktor and Simon were ready for a fight. Viktor's hawk-like stare watched every move Connor made. Simon grabbed one arm, and Viktor grabbed the other.

He should've known the bastard kept something up his sleeve.

Connor was in so much pain, all he could do was formulate a mindlink.

"Fecking bastard! I know ye had somethin' t' do with both! Ye'd be lying if ye said ye did'nae!"

Stavslaka leaned down next to Connor's face. "I think it would be wise if you left. And don't come back. Or I might let Viktor here and a few others take you out back. Think about it. Oh, and while you're thinking on your actions, just remember: You've only had Ascenza back in your life for seventeen years. I'd hate to see that come to an end."

An inhuman warning growl erupted behind Connor, and the unmistakable menacing hiss put a bit of starch in Connor's britches. He relaxed. *"'Bout damn time ye showed up."*

"Alpha Stavslaka, are you actually threatening a member of my pard in front of me? I'd suggest that Viktor and Simon take their hand's off of Connor. You'll remain breathing."

Roman hoisted Connor off the ground. "Connor, you were not to talk to him by yourself. I pretty much heard everything. Including the threat."

Stavslaka coolly smiled at Roman. "A misunderstanding then. I have my business to run, and this little activity is causing a scene."

A misunderstandin', me arse. "Roman, he knows who shot Gia."

"I assure you, Mine Alpha Roman, that I am just as perplexed as you are. Now, if you'll both excuse me... please."

Roman tilted his head, permitting for Stavslaka to take his leave.

Once the Were-fox and his guards were out of the way, Connor frowned and viewed Roman. It wasn't like him to back down. "Lad, ye know what happened. Were ye able to read his mind or nae?"

Roman nodded. "He never sensed me inside of his mind. Although there were other things I would have liked to peek at, once I saw you shocked with the cattle prod, I figured you'd need me more. I have enough information."

"Aye. If ye don'nae mind, I'm, goin' t' head home. I don'nae like Stavslaka threatenin' my Mate. I will'nae lose her again."

"If something does happen, let me know. And don't do anything on your own. You're part of my pard. Go ahead, Connor."

"Uhhhh, where's Genevieve?"

"She's secure in my private suite. I asked her to wait until I come for her."

"See ye back at home."

191

Chapter 28

A noise jostled Raquel awake from a wonderful dream. Yawning, she stretched, rubbed her eyes, and cracked an eyelid to glance at the candles, their light illuminating the room.

A pained whimper sounded from a darkened corner. She frowned. Had the dog come into the room and now needed to go out?

Nothing, except for Steffan quietly snoring beside her.

She swung her legs over the side of the bed and headed into the bathroom. On her way out, she grabbed a hand towel and listened.

A low, resonating, haunting, inhuman whimper gave rise to goosebumps erupting on her arms.

"Steffan?"

Raquel frowned and quickly crawled back onto the bed. Steffan's face was scrunched in pain, so much so a tear glistened on his cheek.

"Steffan, wake up." She jostled his shoulder. "You're having a bad dream."

Softly, he sobbed, "Michelle, my love, why'd you leave?"

He leaned into Raquel's hand, curling his body around her knee.

Raquel froze as an electrical current radiated through her. The images of Steffan and Michelle, together in bed assaulted her, and waves upon waves of pain flowed from Steffan, hitting Raquel like a tsunami. It felt as though the woman was a part of him. A part of his soul.

Raquel jerked her hand off Steffan's shoulder, pulled it to her chest, and silently cried.

Damn this curse she had! Why'd she pick up on an image like that!

All this time he had been taking care of her, and now she was competing with a ghost.

She didn't want to wake him, and she couldn't face the truth of what she'd inadvertently discovered.

192

She gathered her things and headed into the bathroom to take a hot shower and get dressed. Thankfully, Steffan had mentioned about bringing a change of clothes.

How could I be this stupid? I'm so different from them. How could I have any type of relationship with Steffan?

Raquel was still not completely dry when she pulled on her clothes. She put her hand on the door, feeling for a latch or a hidden lever and sighed when she found none. She looked back at Steffan's sleeping form. He seemed more peaceful, but it did nothing to displace the hurt she felt.

This whole mess started because of her, because she's human. They had all said she would have to die if her mind wasn't erased. Or her other choice was to be turned into one of them.

She glanced at her reflection in the mirror. What would she look like as a Were-panther? And did she have the courage to give up her life, her family, and be turned? She saw her family at reunions and weddings and funerals. If the Kindred killed her, how was her death going to be explained? On the other hand, why did she have to be turned? Her way of thinking was she's a woman, she has her own wants and needs and she shouldn't have to lower her standards and do what *a man tells her to do*. There didn't seem to be a way that she and Steffan could have a relationship; was there?

She turned back to the door and studied it for a way out. Steffan had opened it with it his mind.

Softly, she murmured, "God, I wish I could get out of here without waking him."

She pushed on the door one last time. She heard a click, and the heavy door swung open.

* * * *

Janeé watched as Raquel exited the playroom. Her tail swished behind her.

She didn't want Raquel to know she'd heard everything the female thought, but the dead, could do a lot of things the living couldn't do.

It was a coincidence Raquel pushed on the door the same time Janeé willed it open. Janeé let out a sigh and laid down, making sure she stayed back from the edge of the mirror and watched her son sleep. Should he glance at the mirror, he wouldn't see his mother.

Janeé was eternally grateful to Raquel for bringing him his inner peace, but perhaps the human was right to wonder about the situation as a whole.

Chapter 29

Daleena casually crossed her arms in front of her chest and pretended to listen to the boorish male beside her. Why she hadn't bothered to pick a better submissive was beyond her. Perhaps it had been a mistake, but then—

Hello, what do we have here?

She shooed her disappointing submissive aside. "Leave me."

"Mistress?"

Alpha Roman and that piece of crap he called his First Mate walked out from the back room of Sanctuary, and the satisfaction on both their faces was so palpable one could cut the air with a knife. Roman's eyes shot to the rich gold glare of his panther once he glanced Daleena's way.

Feeling threatened, are we?

Roman hooked a protective arm around Genevieve and ushered her toward the locker room.

Daleena forced herself to look elsewhere. Anywhere. Roman was only a reminder of what she couldn't have. Steffan.

"Mistress St. Claire. You don't look like you're enjoying yourself. A drink perhaps?"

"Be gone. I am in no mood for company this night."

"As you wish, Mistress." The vampire vanished into thin air.

Daleena locked gazes with Stavslaka and sent him a mindlink across the bar. "I need your help."

"Do tell? But I'm occupied this evening. Find another play toy. Yours usually wind up broken."

"Now you know why I always request a vampire; they're already broken."

"What is it that you want?"

"I want what belongs to me: Steffan!"

Stavslaka's mouth twitched in amusement, and his eyes sparkled with mischief. "In that case, how can I be service?"

195

Daleena smiled. "Do you still deal in the trade of humans?"

"Always. So long as you understand I require a ten percent down payment and a twenty percent disposal fee."

She hooked her arm around his and gently pulled to get him to walk with her. "Let's cut a deal."

Chapter 30

Genevieve entered the guest bedroom with steaming mugs of coffee in each hand. Raquel stopped her pacing and gratefully accepted the warm mug, wrapping both hands around the cup. The rich aroma lifted her spirits enough to make her smile.

She thought Steffan had been as attracted to her as she was to him. They'd had sex, outstanding sex, but she wished she'd never heard him talk in his sleep.

A cold dose of reality chilled her to the bone.

"How could I be so stupid?"

"Raquel, calm down and tell me what happened."

"What happened? What happened is Steffan is only using me. I thought he cared. Tonight, it felt really good being tied up by him, and it was everything I wanted. My mind just zoned out into subspace, and I was aware of nothing else, except him, the rope binding me, and his touch. I was able to put my *trust* in him until he called out for Michelle in his sleep. I'm competing with a ghost." Raquel wearily sat on the settee. "I'm the only human around here, and I'm starting to feel like I'm a disease or something, being cooped up in this house."

Genevieve snorted her coffee before falling into a coughing fit.

"Try not to die from drowning in coffee. I don't need to add killing my best friend to my bucket list."

"I'm sorry, Raquel. You're too funny. But men do stupid things. Ever since I've been here, I've never known Steffan to relax around me either. Has it occurred to you that he was able to finally relax to the point his mind was able to think things through, that he might have been dreaming about his former Mate, telling her goodbye in his way?"

"Gena, I touched him and all these images of Steffan and Michelle fucking each other invaded my mind. How much of a goodbye is that? It's not." Raquel's lips pursed over the rim of the cup.

"Okay then, how about his mind was sorting through his own emotions about you? Or Steffan might have been caught in a memory from the past. Something in the room possibly triggered it; you don't know. The mind is a strange place. According to Roman, his little brother hasn't been with anyone since Michelle died. You're the first female Steffan has shown an interest in. *And* played with."

"I am?" Dare she let hope bloom?

Genevieve smiled. "Yes. I think Steffan is afraid to love someone again for fear of losing them. Michelle's death was grisly. Roman confided in me that, for a time, he had worried about Steffan until you entered the picture. Steffan seemed to change. At least I've seen an improvement in his demeanor."

Gena's reasoning was plausible. Nevertheless, Raquel knew what she had seen when her damn psychic gift connected with Steffan. The love, the look of devotion on the woman's face as she stared up at him had cut like a knife. Raquel knew Steffan had been happy in the dream.

Do I make him happy?

Raquel lowered the empty cup to cradle it within the palms of her hands and closed her eyes. The image of Steffan and Michelle remained fresh in her mind's eye.

Steffan made Raquel feel alive. He'd cared for her when she cut her arms on the broken glass, he'd kept her safe, but it was time she faced the truth.

She was a human trying to survive amongst the Kindred, and her life would always be in danger. He kept her hidden to protect her. She couldn't live like that.

"Genevieve, I appreciate all you and Roman have done, and I've learned to accept the situation as it is, but I think it's time I head home."

Genevieve shook her head. "It's not safe. Besides, you said you'd be here for my Mating Ceremony."

"I guess, but what am I supposed to do here? Am I allowed to sit among the guests? Penny and Nancy are going to be jealous when they hear you got married and you didn't even invite them."

Genevieve smiled awkwardly. "Well, from my understanding, you won't be able to sit and watch with everyone else, but you'll be able to see the whole thing from the house. You'll be in the attic on the fourth floor. It's far enough away no Kindred will be able to sense your aura through all the electrical wiring and normal sounds of the household. Plus, they won't scent you either. It's too far of a distance for anyone to detect."

Raquel rolled her eyes upward. *Why does that not surprise me?*

Quick and succinct scratching at the bedroom door made them both turn toward the door. The knob turned, and Narella peered around the edge. "Hey, what's up?"

A little dog bolted into the room and jumped up on the bed. He barked and rolled over, exposing his belly for a good rub. Raquel reached out and stroked the soft fur. Narella smiled, glancing between Genevieve and Raquel.

"I was starting to explain about the Mating Ceremony. Ascenza has been doing most of the work since I don't know what is involved."

Narella beamed. "The magic of the Fates blesses the Mating. If the Fates are displeased with the choice of Mate, when the drum is struck during the presentation of the elements, they will not allow their elemental power to be used for the Blessing. It's magic in its purest form. That's it in a nutshell. If there's no magic, the ceremony will continue but everyone will know it wasn't Blessed by the Fates."

Raquel barely listened in on the rest of the conversation about the Mating Ceremony. It was hard to swallow. She sat back against the headboard and placed her mug on the nightstand. God, she never really realized how different Gena had become until now.

Gena fits in around here; I don't. I'm different.

Raquel wished a hole would open up and swallow her.

***

Steffan rested the palm of his hand on the mouse, clicking through screen after screen, sifting through hours of security footage of the five vacant properties Roman owned. A few weeks ago, he thought he'd caught someone breaking into the cabin in the woods, but when he went to out to check on it, things were as they should be. Quiet.

At least the footage gave him a much-needed distraction from the ice-cold shoulder Raquel had presented. Something had upset her enough to make her leave the bed.

He hated waking up alone in the playroom. After his shower, he knocked on the mirror and when Mom showed her face, she told him she hadn't seen anything but mentioned Raquel had gone back to the room she stayed in.

The act didn't sit well with Steffan. Raquel might not want to talk to him, but she would speak with Genevieve. He thanked the Fates when Genevieve replied to his text.

Steffan perused the monitor for the upper hallway of the house. The door was still closed.

Cristoff had barged into Steffan's office only once, looking for his keys, or so he said. "You're hiding from the female. She's gotten to you. I'm going to New York. Wanna come?"

He declined the offer but almost hated to admit Cristoff's assessment was true. Raquel *had* needled her way under his skin. And now thoughts of her were intruding on the very task he was using to distract himself with. Clearly, his plan wasn't working.

He chewed his lip, and the screen flickered in front of him, his hand hovering over the mouse as he tried to push thoughts of Raquel to the background.

"Lad, ye'r back early."

Steffan nearly jumped out of his skin and sat back in the chair.

Connor chuckled. "Jumpy, are we?"

Steffan grumbled.

"Aye, now who rained on yer parade?"

"No one. I didn't go to the club with Roman. Raquel and I stayed here, but I think I fucked up."

"Ye did'nae scare her off. Yet. The lass be upstairs havin' a gossip session with Narella and Alpha Genevieve."

Steffan groaned, continuing to flip through the screens of the properties. He knew what the topic of discussion was: him.

"I hope not."

"Then ye mind if I ask ye something?"

"What?"

"Ye thinkin' 'bout 'er as a possible Mate?"

Steffan yanked his hand off the mouse as if it had burned him and stared into Connor's hopeful blue eyes. Connor didn't press; he'd simply asked. As old as Connor was, though, Steffan knew the male was picking his brain. He sensed the slight ruffle of emotions. The male was sneaky.

"Um, I really hadn't thought about taking another Mate, Connor."

"Well then, who would ye be mating? Daleena? Nae. That female will ne'er do. Ahh, how 'bout a panthress perhaps?"

What's with him? "Connor, I never said I was mating anyone."

"Lad, ye're thickheaded. Ye'r missin' the point."

"Why are you trying to play matchmaker?"

Connor faked a stunned, not-so-innocent look before he started laughing.

"You're senile, Connor. I think the centuries have finally caught up with you. I'll let Ascenza know you're ready to live out the rest of your life in your panther form."

Connor sighed. "The point, lad, is I think ye'r blind and are nae seein' the female that's right under yer nose. Michelle be gone, not forgotten. The lass lives on in yer memory, but ye'r a young, virile male. Ye should be having cubs of yer own."

"Michelle was killed under the law."

"Ye assume she was."

"Two Mulatese Tenebraes killed her. They had to have been for hire. The same thing is going to happen to Raquel."

"Ye waited too long t' transform the lass. A Halfling's physical strength grows with age." Connor took a deep breath. "I know ye have a thing fer Raquel. How deep? That's t' be seen, and the fact the lass is upstairs and has'nae run fer the hills screaming about what a lunatic ye are says a lot."

Steffan stared at him, thinking.

Raquel provided him with a lifeline.

Connor clapped him on the shoulder and made for the office door.

"I take it the Sirely advice is over."

"Aye. Ye need someone else t' do the thinkin' at times. Yer head is full of the *what-ifs*. I see it. I'm goin' t' go for a run in the bayou t' clear my mind. Yer mind needs a guit clearin'. Quit bein' surly. Those images of Michelle need to go. I'm nae sayin' completely forget her." Connor shuddered and then shifted before leaving Steffan alone.

Surly? I'm not sulking here.

Steffan shook his head, glanced back at the security footage of the main house, and moved the camera to the garage. His heart sank, and he had to blink a few times to make sure he was seeing things right.

Raquel used a coat hanger and slid the wire between the glass and the door. With a twist and a yank, in less than thirty seconds, she popped the driver's door to *his* silver Porsche open. She tossed a duffle bag over onto the passenger seat and plunked herself down into the seat.

Raquel was supposed to be upstairs with Alpha Genevieve and his sister. *Instead, she's stealing my car.*

Steffan urgently reached out with his mind—*"Genevieve! I thought Raquel was with you and Narella?"*—and high-tailed it out of his office and down the back staircase to the kitchen.

The Alpha's reply sliced through him. *"She was but slipped by me when I took a shower. She's adamant she wants to go back to her apartment."*

He cut the mindlink off and almost ripped the French door off its hinges, scaring the crap out of Mirabel who was starting up lunch. A heavy, pelting rain bore down on him, and in the distance, getting smaller and smaller, was the glow of his car's tail lights as Raquel turned the corner at the old servant's house.

Steffan gritted his teeth— "Oh no, you don't"— shifted, ripping through his clothes, and took off after her. Sharp claws dug deep into the muddy earth, tearing into the terrain as he cut across the side of the property. He was going to reach her before she had the chance to get to the main road.

Chapter 31

Damn, this rain is coming down heavy. The intensity of it pounded against the metal on the roof only added to her disquiet, and navigation from the house was treacherous. To think someone actually built a plantation style mansion out in the middle of the bayou with at least twenty miles between the house and civilization.

It'd be about thirty minutes until she reached the main road.

All Raquel wanted to do was get to her apartment and call Genevieve to let her know she'd arrived safely. Gena had argued with her about leaving, but this whole world of theirs was too much.

She had a lot of *heavy thinkin'* to do, as her Gramma would say.

Raquel glanced down long enough to turn the radio on, but when she looked up, an enormous panther darted out from the tree line and stopped dead in front of her. The force of the bright blue glowing spheres pegged Raquel, and for a split second, her temples ached.

"Steffan, no!"

"Raquel! Stop!"

She slammed on the brakes, and the car slid sideways. She turned and counterturned the steering wheel as she tried to correct her trajectory. "Ohhh God!"

Her whole body jerked hard against the seatbelt on the rough ride, but she managed to get control of the car until the front tires blew out and the car skidded to a halt, and a tree branch crashed through the passenger side window, stopping inches from her face.

"Oh my God, Steffan!"

Breathing hard, she pulled on the lever to open the door, but it wouldn't budge. She was stuck.

"Help me!"

She pounded her fists on the door to get it to budge when the door suddenly peeled back like a can opener, rolling back the lid on a can, and Steffan tossed the mangled mess a few feet away. Raquel glanced up and blinked. Blue glowing orbs pierced through the rain. His shoulders and chest heaved with each labored breath.

"I ought to take you over my knee and spank you for not only stealing my car but for also risking both our lives."

He trembled as he used his claws to slice through the seatbelt as if it were nothing more than paper and plucked her from the car. He sat her on the hood of the car and palpated all over her body, testing her limbs. His hands gently examined her head and neck, and the whole time, she focused on the rivulets of rain sluicing over his body.

"Fates, you scared the daylights out of me."

Raquel stared up into anxious bright blue eyes.

"Steffan, I'm all right."

She was sore but nothing was broken.

Here I am, sitting on the hood of a Porsche, in the pouring rain, with a naked man checking me out.

She snorted.

He cocked a brow and stopped checking her body for injuries. The confusion written all over his face. "What's so funny? Hold on a second. You *stole* my car, and now I'll have to get a tow truck out here because the car's totaled. I'm trying to see if you're seriously injured, and you find this *funny*?"

"I wasn't going too fast, but what the hell did you think you were doing, jumping out at me like you did? I could've killed you!"

Raquel shoved him, hopped down, and retrieved the duffel bag from the seat. She spun on her heel and collided with a wall of muscle. He gripped her elbows, holding her steady.

"I thought you were told you couldn't leave until after the week is over."

His pupils dilated, and the side of her head throbbed.

Raquel swallowed and forced herself to look elsewhere. The throbbing got worse. "I take it your kitty is on high alert. Is that why you're trying to read my mind?"

The ache miraculously ceased.

His brows furrowed, eyes narrowing. "Eh-yeah, I would say so. He does his own thing when he can't get the information from me. You scared me."

An unusual, feather light sensation caressed the side of her neck. Goosebumps rose down her right shoulder and over her arm.

Was tha—?

"Yes, that was my Were-panther reaching out. He's only making sure you're all right. And no, I didn't read your mind... it was written all over your face." His eyes darted to her throat.

He was so close to her, the heat from his body enveloping her.

The slight chill of the rain no longer mattered.

"Blocking others was something I learned to do when I was little. If I didn't, then I'd get overwhelmed and anxious." She paused. "You said your panther was making sure I'm all right. But what about you?"

Confusion graced his features. "I've chased after you for a while, nearly *killing* myself in the process, to cut you off! I'm more concerned about stopping you from leaving. In another half a mile *you* would've crossed the property line! And guess what, it would've been open season for you. Roman has gotten emails wanting your death; I've gotten emails to hand you over to the Commission so you could be killed."

Raquel sighed. "Look, I really don't know what your game plan is, but let me go. I don't belong in your world. I don't fit in, and I've no idea what you want from me."

Blue eyes flashed. "Your *life* would've ended. Alpha Tavia has been watching our borders ever since she saw you the first time." He paused. "She's the reason why your memory was erased in the first place, and I know now I did it in haste and messed it up!" He sucked in air. "I don't want to lose you!"

"Lose me?" Raquel's voice quivered. "You're still in love with Michelle, and I can't compete with a ghost."

There, she said it. She felt like she was on the verge of breaking down in front of him, not to mention feeling like the biggest fool there was on this side of the Mississippi.

His hand slid up to her neck, and he pulled her close. His breath mixed with hers as he simply leaned his forehead against hers. He stayed quiet, and then the cool rain started to pelt her skin.

"Steffan, can we get out of the rain? We should head back to the house. I—"

The way he kissed her stole her breath and any coherent thought she might have had, fizzled from her mind.

Owning. Conquering. Tongues tangling, each kiss became

urgent, and his tongue mimicked what was now on her mind as it thrust in and out of her mouth. Her body leaned against him, seeking his warmth. He held her tight, pulling her up against his hard chest. Raquel's fingers had a mind of their own, and she dug into his flesh before sliding her arms around his neck, and he moaned into her mouth.

A jolt of pure adrenaline fired her blood. He pulled her closer and deepened the connection. Something ruffled inside her mind, and she saw an image of running free along with petals falling out of the sky.

A rumble from deep in his chest vibrated against her body, and her core clenched. She shuddered in his arms.

Steffan immediately broke the kiss, his breath coming hard. "You're cold, and I will not have you walking back to the house in sheets of rain. We'll wait it out. Come. There's a cave nearby. Here. Hold this."

"A cave? We're going to a cave?"

He shoved the duffel bag back into her hands and picked her up, carrying her farther into the bayou.

"I can walk, you know."

"Hold on tight."

He started to run at a break-neck speed—*okay, maybe not*—and she clung to his neck for dear life.

The rain felt more like ice as it pelted Raquel's exposed skin. And she barely saw anything between the torrential downpour and the top speed Steffan ran. She buried her face in the crook of his neck.

He suddenly stopped and his chest rose and fell sharply as he tried to cacth his breath. It took her a moment to realize the rain no longer pelted her. He dropped her legs down to the rocky ground. She looked around. The only light, barely visible, came from the mouth of the cave.

He gave her space, but she knew he intently watched every move she made.

"Nice cave. I like the way you decorated it." Raquel hooked her thumb at the fire ring of rocks and the neatly stacked woodpile in the corner.

"We'll stay here until the rain stops. Honestly, I don't feel like running naked in the rain with you in my arms, and you'll fall off of me if you ride on my back in my panther form. Not from slickness but from the speed. I won't risk you falling and getting hurt."

The penetrating lull of his voice had deepened. She turned to face him and froze. His pupils were huge, swallowing the glowing blue irises. It was hard to look away from him. A tremor rippled up her back.

I'm the mouse. She quivered, realizing for an instant that she was prey.

He blinked, and the spell instantly broke.

He moved to her side immediately. "Take off your clothes. You're soaked through and through, and I will not be responsible for you getting sick. Plus, I need to know if you have bruising from the car accident."

Slowly, she licked her lips; he tracked her tongue. Damn, he made it hard to think. "Um, actually, you are responsible if I do get sick. How am I supposed to keep warm? I don't have any matches to light a fire."

Steffan held up a finger and walked to the back of the cave, disappearing into the darkness. A few seconds later, he came back and handed her a blanket then proceeded to take a second blanket and place it on the floor of the cave.

Raquel laughed. "You have blankets in a cave. Do you come here often?"

"No, *bébé.* There are a lot more blankets in the back of the cave, but they were placed here for Genevieve's comfort. Most of the honeymoon for Roman and Genevieve will be in panther form in this cave. Ascenza comes out here sometimes as well. Mostly whenever she's pissed at Connor for something."

"And if you hadn't made me crash your car, we wouldn't be here."

He loomed over her, his hand caressing the side of her face. "The car is replaceable. You are not. Take off your clothes, or I will take them off for you." She leaned into the palm of his hand.

The way he said *or I will take them off for you* was low and controlled, with a hint of the possibility of punishment should she refuse. Or was she subconsciously longing for him to punish her? Not only was it communicated in the way he spoke, but also in his body language. He took a deep breath; well-defined muscular shoulders flexed, and... he waited for her.

207

Raquel's lips tingled with the desire to feel the pressure of his lips against hers. Her core tightened as heat suffused her veins.

His nostrils flared.

He knew. Damn it, he *knew* how he affected her. Damn her libido.

Steffan crowded her. But she didn't mind. His hand slipped down the column of her throat, and he took her mouth again. This time, Raquel sensed his urgency. A raw fever took hold of her, and she gave in.

The sound of tearing clothing woke her from the trance, but instead of pushing him away, she helped him rip off the rest of her clothes.

A moan escaped her, and a razor-sharp sting in her bottom lip made her pull back.

Steffan's canines had elongated, and his intense blue eyes stared into hers. A haze cooled the stare to the point his eyes began returning to the warm brown. Slowly, he started to pull away from her.

Dear God, he was having second thoughts about them.

Raquel swallowed hard. She whispered between her erratic breaths, "Steffan, you have me so confused." She lowered her head until her forehead touched his chest. Wearily, she said, "I don't know what you want."

Fingertips pushed her chin up, forcing her to look at him.

"I'm not pushing you away. I want you."

"But what about Michelle? I saw it in your eyes. You pulled away from me and... "

God, she couldn't live through being called another woman's name.

Breathily, he said, "You're human, just like Michelle was. *That* is what's on my mind. Your humanity. I do have dreams about Michelle, but she's dead. She'll always be a part of me, but I've moved on. If I hadn't, I would not be here with you right now, this minute. Why did you bring up Michelle?"

She chewed her lip. "You, ah... you said, 'I love you, Michelle,' in your sleep."

Shock graced his features. "Is that why you left the house?"

She nodded. A part of her was ashamed she'd run from him, but a larger part was hurt. She couldn't compete with a ghost, and since

208

going on this wild ride, she didn't have the energy to hang on. She wanted him to love her as much as he loved Michelle. Was that so much to ask for?

Determination replaced his shock, and right before her eyes, his stature seemed bigger, shoulders firmer, and his chest widened with each breath. The aura of a resolute decision he'd made beckoned to her, and her core bloomed.

"Then let me show you how much I want you."

A predatory shadow darkened Steffan's features.

In one swift motion, before she said anything, he picked her up by her thighs and wrapped her legs around his waist, he managed to pin her up against the cold, rough rock wall. Raquel's heart pounded as his nails dug into her rear, his arm provided somewhat a barrier between her back and the stone wall. He took her wrists in one hand and pinned them high above her head. He planted his lips on hers.

The kiss was raw, primal, and ignited an instant need to be with him in the most sensual way. The rough wall disappeared from her senses, and all she knew was him.

He broke the kiss, stealing a glance before the hand palming her rear adjusted her hips, and he slid home in one easy movement, rolling and grinding into her.

On a gasp, he captured her lips, breathing into her mouth. He stole her breath, and with each rhythmic stroke of his cock pounding into her core, she was completely at his mercy.

Her body was keenly aware of his, and she found it thrilling how easy it was to submit to him. She trusted him. He controlled how she breathed; making sure every so often to break the kiss, allowing her to draw in the cool, moist air of the cave before consuming her mouth again.

Steffan's hips thrust harder against her, and she mewled around his tongue.

All she cared about was crawling inside his skin.

Her mind opened to him, and she was hyperaware not only of how her body ached for release, but feeling that pressure within him as well. He was holding back his own release.

"*I know you can hear me. I can sense our minds have joined. Right now, there is only you. I need you.*" His cock pumped slowly in and out of her. Teasing her with each thrust. "*You will never steal another car again.*" His tongue tangled with hers. "*You will keep yourself safe by staying with the pard. Is that clear?*"

She sensed the unexpressed determination with each thrust as he kept taking her to the edge of her climax before retreating. The man was a tease. He knew each time she was ready to go over that blissful cliff only to stop.

His cock twitched inside of her, drawing out a moan of protest from Raquel.

His lips fused to hers. "*Answer me with your mind. Focus. If you don't, or if you take too long, I'll break the connection and have my own release, and you won't feel 'us' climaxing together. You'll only feel your own. With our minds joined like this, we can feel each other's orgasm, and it is so much more intense than you could ever imagine. I want us to experience that, and it will prove my feelings for you.*"

"I—" She tried to answer him, but he reclaimed her mouth. This whole communicating with the mind was really cool, but damn it, he was dragging out this orgasm.

"*I'm waiting. Use your mind to answer me.*"

The dull ache in her temples started to subside. He was retreating from her mind; it was growing quiet and made her feel alone.

Raquel didn't like the growing silence and barely felt him now. "*Yes.*"

"*Yes, what? What are you forgetting?*"

"*Yes, Sir. I will stay with your pard until its safe.*"

"*And... are you going to steal from me again?*"

"*No. I won't steal anything from you ever again.*"

He deepened his kiss. "*Tell me what you want.*"

"*I want us to climax together, Sir. But only if you want us to.*"

His answer was to release her lips long enough for her to drag in cool air before he again devoured her mouth, and those hips of his fucked her hard enough so all she knew, all she felt was them. Together. Body and soul, aching to reach a euphoric release as one.

She arched upward on the last roll of her climax, hitting the jagged edges of the stone wall with her shoulder. It grounded her back to reality.

He moved her to the blanket on the ground, laid her out, and turned on his side, hooked her leg over his hips, and entered her again with the same raw hunger as before.

He licked her neck, the sandpaper-like sensation soothed before the dull bite on the column of her neck set off her climax and his. She climaxed hard around him, milking his seed, and a full array of starbursts lit up her vision.

A roar surrounded her, and she couldn't tell if it was her screaming out his name or if it was him. With her mind linked to his, she felt the intensity of the sound rip right out of her with a force so hard, her whole body seized alongside his.

It wasn't until everything was quiet except for their combined heavy breathing that she dared to try and move.

Wow. So this is what Jell-O feels like.

Steffan chuckled and released her neck and gazed down at her. He kissed the tip of her nose, then spooned beside her. She loved how he kept her warm with his body.

He laid the palm of his hand gently between the swell of her breasts, and she noticed he had retreated from her mind, shutting the connection down.

This time, though, she didn't feel abandoned.

"Our hearts beat simultaneously." He whispered the next words to himself, but thought she heard him say, "I've never had that happen before."

What did that mean?

Raquel's breathing slowed to an even rhythm. She slowly closed her eyes, and the weight of his hand on her chest was a comfort since the connection of his mind was gone from her. She was content to lie next to him and fall asleep.

"You warm enough, *bébé?*"

She peered up at him. "Yes. Why? You're a heater, remember?"

The warmth expressed in his chuckle made her smile. He pulled her closer, and instantly his attention refocused on the entrance of the cave. She quickly followed his gaze and frowned, not seeing anything out of the ordinary.

"Something wrong?"

He shook his head. "No. It has stopped raining, so when you're ready, we can head back to the house. I assume you have a set of dry clothes in that duffel bag you had."

Back to reality. Ugh, he had lousy timing.

She sat up with a grunt.

211

His thick fingers traced over the length of the scar with such gentle tenderness that it sent goose bumps racing along her spine.

"Are you in pain from the wall? There are a few scrapes on your shoulder. I thought I did better with my arm behind your back; I guess I didn't."

"Sore is all. It doesn't hurt."

His fingers traced over her shoulder blade. Oddly, in some spots his touch was feather light and soothing. In other areas, the only thing she felt was the slight pressure from his fingertips tracing the outline of her scar and nothing more. Gentle and firm were his movements, slowly moving his hands up her back, over her neck, and then he tilted her head to the side. His fingers stopped over her pulse point. He pulled himself up to sit behind her.

Raquel couldn't discern what he was doing.

He didn't say anything, and she stole a quick glance back at him. From the forlorn, shadowed look crossing his features, he was deep in thought.

"Penny for your thoughts?"

Abruptly, Steffan stood, startling Raquel. He held out a hand to her and helped her up.

"Nothing. We should get going."

She tried to discern what he was thinking but got nothing and he seemed distant.

"Are you having regrets about what we did?"

He glanced down at her. "I regret nothing we did. I want to be with you. But while I was tracing over your back, I noted movement outside of the cave. I can't detect a scent of what or who it might be. I'd feel better if we went back to the house."

She quickly glanced at the mouth of the cave and didn't see anything. She returned her attention back to Steffan.

He shifted so quickly into his panther form she hesitated to make any sudden movements. Steffan retrieved her bag and dropped it at her feet. He sat back on his haunches and glanced from her to the bag and back to her.

Silently, Raquel got dressed in dry, clean clothes and went to put on the shoes she thought she had packed. *There aren't any. Crap.* She didn't have dry shoes, so she tugged on her wet canvas sneakers and followed Steffan out of the cave.

She heard him chuff so she stopped. He'd moved behind her and nudged his massive head between her knees, forcing them apart, and stood up. Raquel slid past his shoulders and onto his back. He was about as tall as a Great Dane. She shouldered the duffel bag and gripped fistfuls of fur in her hands to keep from falling off.

"You could have said something about what you were going to do, you know."

The mindlink opened up from him.

"*I know. But this was more fun to give you a kitty-back ride. Hold on tightly.*"

Raquel laughed.

Chapter 32

Raquel awoke from having slept most of the day; she fantasized about sleeping the rest of the evening too considering how her body ached. Steffan wore her out. But tonight, Genevieve and Roman were having a Mating Ceremony.

She was happy for her best friend and knew Gena was fervently joyful Raquel would be able to witness the event, even though Raquel had to remain hidden. Being the only human in the house really sucked right now.

Steffan came up with the idea she would be safe in the highest point of the house—the attic. Not the most cheerful of places to be. Right away she noted the temperature changed. It was hotter than the rest of the house considering the cooling system had been running all day. Raquel followed Steffan through the attic door and up eight steps.

Lucky her. Not.

The audible sigh she released had him momentarily glancing in her direction, but he said nothing while he uncovered a high wingback chair next to a window. Heavy dust swirled in the light cast from a single lightbulb in the dead center of the room. It didn't do much to chase the dark shadows away.

She glanced up. There were other lights in the ceiling, but he only flipped one switch.

She reached over to the other switches, flipped them on, and in a second flat, the lever flipped down with unseen fingers.

"Leave the other lights off. If you turn more of them on, someone on the ground level will know someone's up here and animal instincts will kick in. Kindred in the past have been hunted by humans so a light on will call attention, and whoever discovers you will kill you. Some of the Commission will be attending. Others attending are Kindred civilians and family. On the bright side, you'll have an aerial view of the Mating Ceremony taking place in the garden."

"So this is where I'm going to *hide*, during my best friend's wedding. Can a fan be turned on? It's an oven up here."

He motioned for her to sit and moved a large six-foot gilded mirror closer to the window.

"Is it really necessary for me to be up here? I'd be a little more comfortable in your room. I thought Cristoff could wire in a live-feed so I could at least watch."

Steffan stopped maneuvering the large mirror, remorse etched all over his face.

"He could, but my room is too close to the main floor. It's on the side of the garden and on the second floor. Other Were-shifters will be mingling in the foyer prior to the Mating Ceremony. They'll detect your scent. That's why you're up on the fourth floor and away from everyone. Just don't get too close to the window. You'll block the mirror and the reflection of the moon's glow will highlight you. The mirror will provide some type of camouflage for you. If a Were-hawk glances this way, the mirror will reflect the moonlight and project a ghostly image on the window. The only thing you need to do is sit still. I'll open the vents so the area will cool down for you."

"Thank you." Raquel nodded. "So I'm going to be up here... alone."

"Ehhhh... not entirely. And it's also the other reason I brought you up here."

Steffan knocked on the glass of the mirror with his knuckles, and Raquel frowned. He seemed nervous about something.

"My mother will keep you company."

Her eyes darted to the attic stairwell, half expecting to see a woman's head bobbing as she ascended the stairs.

"Then where is she? No one's said a word about your mother since I got here. I was under the impression she was dead."

"She is. But due to the violent nature of her death, her spirit has stayed behind. You can communicate through this mirror." He paused as the mirror's surface began to shimmer and glow. It did not take long for the shape in front of Raquel to take the form of a large panther with green sparkling eyes which resembled emerald gems. "Mom? This is Raquel. Raquel... this is my mother, the former Alpha Janeé Lavelle."

All the air rushed out of Raquel's lungs at once, and a second later, her butt planted in the cushion of the red chair beneath her. Dust swirled around her, causing her to cough. She'd seen some pretty weird stuff since coming here, and now a panther ghost made her day.

"H-How? I mean—"

"*Bonjour, Raquel. I will keep you company, but Steffan needs to go and prepare for the ceremony. Steffan, leave us.*"

His gaze bounced back and forth from her to his mother in the mirror; hesitating.

The panther in the mirror rolled her eyes before saying, "*Good grief. Get going. She'll be perfectly fine. Now go before I ask the Fates to zap your butt into moving.*"

Steffan practically jumped as a spark rushed from the mirror and zapped him in the side. He rubbed it and left Raquel with a simple nod.

"*Well, my dear, I've seen some good things about you. For a human, that is.*"

Perplexed, Raquel shook her head. "I don't understand this. How did you become trapped inside a mirror?"

"*I'll give you the condensed version. When I died, I made the choice to stick around to watch over my pard, and since this mirror was hanging where I died a violent death, it became a portal for my soul to enter. But I'm not trapped. I reside within the Veil. I am on both sides of the Veil; neither crossing over nor residing on your plane of existence. I see everything through all the mirrors of the house and hear conversations. That is how I know about you.*"

"So you're not some lost, condemned soul?"

Janeé giggled. "*No. I can depart this plane of existence anytime I wish.*"

"If you can leave anytime you wish, why haven't you?"

The panther's head tilted to the side, but she remained quiet, lost in thought.

"*I have my reasons for staying.*" Janeé paused. "*Well, you know about me, tell me what you are doing with my son. I must admit, when Steffan told me you were human, I was shocked he would take on another human. Kindred don't look kindly on humans; yet here you are.*"

Raquel bit her lip. The panther almost sounded disgusted she was here.

"In a nutshell, Steffan has been trying to erase my memories ever since he helped Roman rescue Genevieve and me from Dupree's dungeon. He thought it worked, but it didn't, so here I am."

The room grew quiet.

The intensity of Janeé's stare caused Raquel's heart to pound. Her temples ached from the sudden pressure enveloping her head, and the weight on her chest made it hard to breathe.

Raquel ground her molars from the pain and surprised herself as she growled, "Get *out* of my head!" Her nails dug into the armrests for support.

The tension eased immediately.

Once Raquel's vision cleared, the panther stared back at her. "I take it you were not expecting me to be able to sense you invading my mind without asking me."

"I apologize. I didn't know you were what my kind call a Sensitive. That explains why you were in pain. Normally, had you been a human without psychic ability, you never would have known I was sifting through your memories. In the future, I will ask. It also explains why Steffan wanted you in here during the ceremony. Kindred are able to detect any Sensitive provided the human is close proximity to them. The normal magnetic fields from the electrical wiring, the vents for the AC, and the insulation between the floors will mask you. You're far enough away being on the fourth floor of an attic that your psychic gift can't give you away."

Raquel sat back heavily in the chair. "I thought the dead couldn't open mindlinks like you just did." Raquel rubbed her temples.

"You'd be surprised what the dead can do to the living. I will keep out of your head unless I sense you hiding something from me. Deal?"

Let's change the subject. "Tell me about Steffan. Every time I think I'm getting close to him, he pushes me away."

The panther shrugged and laid down, tail switching back and forth. *"My second-born has always been difficult. Part of it is the expectations of holding the status of a Beta. They are second-in-command to the Alpha. Should anything happen to an Alpha, all those duties plus the Beta's duties will fall on Steffan's shoulders until Cristoff takes the Beta's role. The Mate of a Beta not only holds the familial duty of bearing cubs, they also need to be an equal partner in*

217

sharing the Beta duties for securing the pard. A human cannot perform any of those duties because it puts the pard at risk of exposing them, and it makes them weak within the pard's communal mindlink.

"Steffan is aware of this. His First Mate was a human but gave up her humanity, just like Genevieve did, in order to be fully with the pard. You, my dear, are a human. Steffan surely can't expect you to perform such duties while in human form. From what I've witnessed in the mirrors and listening in on conversations, it's too late to erase your memories of our kind. If you move into a neutral territory so you can survive, Steffan will be ripped from your life. He won't be allowed to have any contact with you. It's for your safety. You will be financially taken care of—Roman will see to the funding—but any contact with Kindred will cease."

Was it going to be that complicated?

"Raquel, if you think he would leave his station as a Beta, you're wrong. That, too, is complicated. Even though the duties would fall to Cristoff, because Steffan is not dead yet, Cristoff cannot transition into the role of an Alpha if something happened to Roman. Roman's life is always going to be in danger."

Janeé's pregnant pause only cemented Raquel's thoughts. She was nothing more than a human. That point had been driven into her ever since she met Steffan.

"Perhaps if you are going to remain in the company of the pard, you should transform into one of us. It would be easier for everyone."

Raquel ran a hand through her hair. *To be changed into one of them.* She honestly didn't think it was necessary. Her friend Genevieve had changed into one of them, and she seemed happy. But for her? She'd be giving up everything. And if it was against their law to be around humans, then she wouldn't be able to be with her side of the family. She'd have to stop going to family functions.

"I take it you don't want Steffan and I together."

"On the contrary. I'd be happy with any female so long as my son is happy, but I think you need to ask yourself: Will it work out? Many Kindred shifters won't accept you as a human, and the House of Lavelle sustains a prestigious reputation. Your humanity affects everyone, not just Steffan. I may not be able to smell your scent, but I do sense hesitation within you. I take it Steffan hasn't demanded that you change."

Raquel blinked and shook her head. *Demanded?*

"In addition, how long before resentment forms between you two and the panther that dwells under the surface begins to lash out? Do not forget the panther also has needs. Our races were created around the same time. If the panther's needs aren't met, over time, Steffan might lose control of the panther. He could potentially kill you. Maximo's great-great grandsire lost the ability to control his panther, and the panther trapped the human side inside. The male died in panther form, malnourished and sickly. I'm not saying this will happen, but the Were-panther is still a wild animal. I think you should fully understand what all this really means."

The knot in Raquel's stomach tightened.

Janeé blinked casually.

"This isn't easy."

"I know. It's not meant to be, and truth be told, I'm more concerned for your wellbeing. I was a human centuries ago, and I know what you're feeling. The only difference is that this form was forced upon me by Maximo Lavelle. You have freedom of choice in today's age. I never resented my children, only Maximo. And if you're curious, my cubs are considered full bloods. I'm a Halfling, and should you decide to be with him and he turns you, you'll be considered a Halfling too."

The sound of a heavy drums resonated through the air, vibrating the windowpane.

"The ceremony starts. Let me tell you what is happening. The Guards strike the ceremonial drums to call upon the Fates to bless the Ceremony. If there is no Blessing, you won't see the magic, but the ceremony will continue, and the Kindred will accept the mating couple. It's quite a light show as I remember it."

Raquel viewed the garden below. Tiki torches lined the outer edge of a large ring of sand, and small white lights intertwined through the bushes cast a romantic glow. It was hauntingly beautiful. Two eight-foot drums sat off to the side, away from the circular sandpit, and were struck by two Were-shifters. One looked like a tiger, and the other was a rhino, both only partially shifted. The lower half of their bodies was the waist and legs of men.

The strike held weight to it as their bodies leaned into the drums while the cadence that followed grew softer. *Thunk. Da-da-da-dum-*

thunk. Da-da-da-dum-thunk. Over and over in a hypnotic rhythm, and soon Raquel's heart pounded in time with the drum.

There was something primal about the drums as Steffan and three other Were-shifters came out from underneath an awning from the house. The men had partially shifted into three black panthers and one lion and followed a narrow path lit with white candles. Their strides synchronized to the point they moved as one. Raquel smiled as she recognized immediately which one Steffan. *I guess the panthers don't look alike.*

***

He felt her.

She was watching.

He wanted desperately to turn around and look up and double check she was seated far enough away from the window but could still see, but he dared not give away her location. Steffan and the others' upper torsos would be partially in their animal forms, except for Roman and Genevieve. The Bride and Groom would perform the ceremony in their humanoid forms.

Steffan managed to overhear a hushed conversation between a Beta and his Alpha discussing the possibility 'a human might be here'. It gave him pause, but he had already instructed the staff should anyone ask about Raquel, they were to deny any knowledge.

Damn Snapchat. He prayed the Fates would reveal who took that picture.

The drumbeat pulsated through the air, and Steffan led the males up to a stone altar, each one reaching out a hand atop one another over the limestone, and moving in a circle around the altar once before each one walked four paces outward, forming the four main points of a compass. The eastern point was left open for the Alpha and his intended First Mate to enter the ceremony circle.

Steffan took on the Guardsman role and called out, "Ah-ya!" and turned back to face the altar. The fine, cool, gritty sand covered his bare feet and licked up around the soft, black muslin pants. The other three Guardsmen were dressed alike. No shirts, only a leather sash holding a ceremonial sword strapped across their partially shifted backs.

Steffan, Cristoff, Connor, and Jerox all faced into each other. Traditionally, the Guardsmen kept watch of the opposite direction in case of attack.

Jerox stood at the northern point. Connor took the position in the east slightly off center to allow the Alpha and his Mate through and then move to the eastern point. Cristoff was in the position considered the south, and Steffan stood in his position to the west. Since Steffan was in the position of what was considered the west, he guarded and would kill anyone threatening to attack coming from the east.

Steffan and the Guardsmen slowly bowed their heads in unison to show respect at the appearance of Roman and Genevieve. The couple stepped off the porch in sync, her hand secured in the crook of his arm. The white filigree lace gown matched the scrollwork design of her Mating Mark. Normally, the female was presented naked. Roman had allowed Genevieve to change that, and they had also added something called a Unity candle, which sat next to the wooden bowl on the altar.

Steffan prayed the Fates agreed with Roman's decision to take Genevieve as his First Mate.

He was envious of the way Genevieve looked up at Roman. Steffan saw the warmth, the desire, and on some level felt the love radiating toward Roman. It was a sensation Steffan had always hoped for.

Once the Alphas were settled in their position at the altar, Connor took his stance in the eastern point, completing the four corners.

Steffan breathed slowly to clear his mind but kept thinking about Raquel. She amazed and scared him at the same time. She calmed him and his Were-panther at the same time. The time they spent in the cave perplexed him. He'd never experienced the unique oneness felt with their mate during an orgasm and here Raquel exceeded it. He'd sensed every fiber of her being during the climax, and to an extent, it bothered him that he'd fallen for Raquel. It puzzled him, yet deep inside his heart, Raquel held him together. She'd proved she was a strong female.

Steffan's temples throbbed, and he relaxed and heard Connor say, *"Lad, I be glad ye got yer rocks off, but stop thinkin' 'bout dippin' yer schmeckle inside Raquel's lady box. I don'nae want t' be goin' through this whole Ceremony with havin' ta listenin' in on yer*

221

thoughts of Raquel's body. An' thank the Fates ye had the sense ta have the public placed further back in the yard. Yer playin' with fire if any one hears yer thoughts. They might go an' look fer' her."

And then there was silence in Steffan's head. *Thanks for the visual. I need my mind bleached and scrubbed now.* He swallowed and quickly glanced around. No one was moving out of their seats.

The drum continued its beat as Jerox scooped up some sand and placed it in the wooden bowl on the altar. "The Earth is our Mother and giver of life; she will bless this union for the earth touches everything."

Connor stepped up to the altar. He cupped his hands over the center of his chest before swooshing them outward. A blast of air and blue light pushed the bowl to the Unity candle, spilling some sand onto the altar. "With thy Breath o'the Fates, this union will be blessed. They will be joined as one, live as one, breathe as one. No Kindred will put this Mating asunder under penalty o'death in accordance with Kindred Law."

Connor repeated the sweeping hand gesture, and a gust of wind picked up the edge of the veil hanging down Alpha Genevieve's back and it regally resettled around her. Roman smiled at her, and her eyes sparkled. Connor pushed the air toward Roman and Genevieve, and on cue, they breathed deeply the air brought from the Fates.

At Genevieve's sharp intake of breath, Steffan and the Guardsmen drew their swords and took a stance to protect the couple until Steffan realized Genevieve wasn't expecting the force of the gust of wind. Roman was also affected but tried hard not to flinch.

Steffan swallowed. His Mating Ceremony hadn't gone as well, and he and Michelle hadn't had the experience of taking in the breath of the Fates. He had been disappointed. Rumor had it, the Breath of the Fates was akin to breathing in lava; it was hot and consuming. The Breath made Roman and Genevieve one. Both wore a sheen of sweat across their forehead which had nothing to do with the weather.

The Fates had given their Blessing. Thank the Fates.

A ripple of shock coursed through the gathered guests. Steffan smiled at Roman and the other Guardsmen. Now no one would be allowed to condone the Mating or put it down for the rest of their lives. To do so would bring a curse from the Fates on the offending party's bloodline.

The ceremonial drum slowed after Connor stepped backwards to his position and knelt on one knee to the couple in the inner circle.

Cristoff stepped forward, uncapped a bottle he had been reverently holding and poured it into the bowl, mixing with the sand. "The water symbolizes the Tears of the Fates. As water replenishes the earth to bring things anew, so shall the union between Roman and Genevieve be renewed. Genevieve and Roman, hold out your hands over the bowl and kneel."

Cristoff took the sword out of its sleeve and drew it slowly across Roman's and Genevieve's palm. Steffan didn't miss her small flinch.

He took their hands and clasped them together, squeezing drops of blood into the water. A white light began to pulsate from inside the bowl, gathering in strength,

Steffan inwardly smiled. Genevieve would kick Cristoff's ass for the pain she felt. Roman leaned in and whispered something into her ear, and her green eyes sparkled. Steffan bit the inside of his cheek to keep from smirking.

Once Cristoff backed away and knelt on the ground, Steffan came forward.

The elements in the bowl called to him. He sensed the incompletion of the elements and he did not hesitate to wave his hands over the small taper candles. They popped to life with flame.

"The flame represents the purity of the life force, the purity of the journey between male and female. You both have agreed to be a Mate to each other, and Alpha Roman has decreed there will not be any other Mates except Genevieve Thompson."

He motioned for Roman and Genevieve to each take a candle and light the center pillar. Normally Steffan would have made a ball of fire appear in his paws, but the addition of the Unity candle was a nice change.

Steffan cupped the flame on the Unity candle, and the flame jumped into the wooden bowl. Swirling flames engulfed the sand, the blood, and the water to the point Steffan had to control the funnel. Roman and Genevieve stuck both their hands dead center into the fire and sparks flew out, straight up into the air.

Steffan looked up. High above the altar were the two auras of panthers, intertwined in blue and white light as one being.

223

It was the most magnificent thing Steffan had seen. The fact that everyone could see the physical form of both Alphas as well as their Kindred forms was proof to everyone the Fates had blessed the union. This was one of the few times anyone saw their animal side without the aid of a mirror.

A roar erupted, and the ground shook. The auras faded back into each of their owners and Roman's black muslin tunic ripped off his shoulders. The muscles rippled as he quickly shifted, and the ghost shadow of the panther was seen no more. Genevieve roared, and her gown tore away from her frame as she also shifted to her majestic panthress.

Steffan held his breath as he watched Roman and Genevieve circle around each other, sizing one another up. How she chose to submit was up to her, but the female had to submit. The female's options were either to let the male mount her in front of everyone, change back to her human form and wait until Roman would do so, or simply bare her belly to her Mate.

Steffan caught Connor's worrisome glance, and he looked at Jerox. Jerox raised a closed fist, giving the signal to wait.

Snarls and hisses from both drew hushed murmurs from the guests.

Come on, come on, come on.

Genevieve roared and crouched down as if she would pounce in an attack; instead, she rolled onto her back, exposing her belly to Roman. Roman gripped Genevieve's throat and shoulder in his jaws, and she went limp.

Steffan inwardly sighed, and he heard the approval of the Lavelle relatives. At least the pard accepted the gesture. A quick glance into the crowd told Steffan there were still a few that wouldn't accept Genevieve.

Roman let go of Genevieve's neck and walked to the altar, shifting back into human form, and raised his right hand. The drums immediately stopped.

"My pard. Brothers and sisters of the Kindred. Behold my First Mate, Alpha Genevieve Lavelle. She is with me; I am with her. No one has the right to question or put asunder our Mating. I know some of you have mixed feelings about my First Mate, but you will treat her with the same respect you do me. We thank you for your time and for participating in tonight's service. My mate and I will be unavailable for the rest of the evening. Thank you for coming."

Roman shifted, roared, and nudged Genevieve toward the dense tree line at the edge of the garden.

Steffan watched his brother and sister-in-law disappear into the thicket, no doubt heading to the cave.

The guests started to disperse, and Steffan stared at the altar. The fire never consumed the wood of the bowl. Only the contents. As it should be. Had the bowl burned, the old wives' tale of a doomed mating would echo among the Kindred.

Funny how he never thought of it before.

He turned his gaze to the attic window. He saw only the reflection of the full moon against the glass.

Raquel was watching behind the glass. He sensed it.

Connor coughed, pulling Steffan's attention away from the fourth-floor window. "Lad, ye're wool gatherin'. Thinkin' 'bout Michelle?"

"No, not this time."

Cristoff poked Steffan in the stomach with the tip of the sword. Sharp pain forced a growl out of him. "Well, at least you haven't turned to stone. If you're thinking about what I think you're thinking, I approve. 'Course, then again, I always think about females and a good romp in the sack." Cristoff chuckled.

Steffan shoved the blade aside and bypassed his younger brother. The sandpit could wait to be dismantled. He wanted to get to Raquel.

Chapter 33

Raquel's palm rested on the doorjamb of the attic. The uneasy sensation hadn't gone away the more she observed the ceremony. In fact, it had increased to the point of making her sick to her stomach.

The Ceremony was simple and beautiful, but the whole time, Janeé kept talking about the importance of the symbolism of the elements during the Mating Ceremony and the major differences between their species.

The encounter left her feeling raw.

Gradually, she turned and headed down the hall, but decided to stop and study Steffan's family portrait. Roman sat in a gilded chair, his brothers behind his left shoulder, Steffan closest to Roman and then Cristoff to the left of Steffan. Narella was off to Roman's right side. There was a woman standing between Steffan and Narella, and Steffan's arm draped around the woman; hand resting on her right shoulder.

She recognized the woman. She was the ghost-like figure within Raquel's mind.

That's Michelle. He seems so happy. What can I offer him?

The longer she regarded the portrait, the more a vibe rippled off of it. Raquel's curiosity got the best of her, and she slowly lifted her hand toward the woman's face. She glanced down at the corner of the portrait for the signature: ML. Raquel's hand stilled on the dry textured surface of the oil painting.

Images flowed into her mind. A flash of bare breasts, a playful smile, and a paintbrush held between her teeth flickered like a damn neon sign, and Raquel jerked her hand back to stop the images from flowing. The painting held Michelle's emotions. She had been nude while she painted the picture, and she had done so from her memory.

God, I wish this curse had never come back!

Raquel's resigned sigh filled the silence of the hallway. *This isn't going to work.*

226

Strong hands enveloped her waist, pulling her back against a hard body. Lips pressed firmly to the right side of her neck, and a soft purr reached her ears. She smiled half-heartedly, but her heart ached for something she knew she could never have.

"So what did you think about the ceremony? Before you answer, I want you to know that Genevieve requested for Roman not take her on the altar. She didn't want you to feel... odd."

She tried to turn, but Steffan trapped her in front of him. The bulge in his muslin pants pressed against her backside, and he swayed gently from side to side, her body responding to his.

"I figured as much. Your mother was quite... forthcoming with her information on the Mating. When was this picture done?"

He stilled behind her. "Michelle was still a human then. She painted it the day I moved her in here. She spent a lot of time hiding out in the bedroom prior to her change."

"She's beautiful."

"As are you. I don't like you comparing yourself to the dead."

"I'm not."

He turned her to face him, his brows turned down, creamy caramel brown eyes full of unspoken questions, but instead of asking her what she was thinking, he remained quiet. She thought he'd intrude and braced herself for a mindlink to open up between them, only none came.

"Steff, the ceremony was beautiful."

Perhaps if she got him to focus on something else besides her, she could focus on asking him about going home. It was for the best. The longer she was here, the more dangerous it became for her.

I'm not sure I want to be changed into a Halfling.

Steffan relaxed his shoulders, and his features smoothed out evenly.

Raquel forced a smile.

Steffan cocked a brow. "You're very quiet. Did my mother say something to offend you?"

A nervous giggle erupted from Raquel, and Steffan jerked slightly.

This wasn't going to be easy, and her nerves were getting the best of her.

"No, no, your mother was fine. I just... uh... you said I could go back to my apartment after the wedding. I think it's safe enough to say its time."

"It's only safe provided your memories are erased. It's past that point, so no." His arms dropped to his side. "The only other choice is for me to turn you."

"Steffan, please. I need some time to think about *all* of this. Your family, the Commission, the fact that our differences would likely stand in the way of us being truly happy. Then there's the fact that you're still in love with Michelle. I saw you making love to her when you were dreaming about her. I can't compete with a ghost, and I don't believe I want to be turned like Genevieve has been."

The way his eyes flashed warned her to tread lightly.

"Your wife is deceased, but I know you still have feelings for her. And I know when someone has lost a loved one, it can take time to heal. I believe you've only just begun to heal from that emotional wound. I don't want to a rebound mate for you."

"*Bébé*, I have feelings for you too. Michelle has been on the other side of the veil for three and a half years now. Her soul is at peace. I need you."

"But are your feelings strong enough to keep me safe as a human? You might demand, as your mother put it, to turn me into a Halfling. I want o stay as I am; human."

He remained silent, took a step back with one hand shoved into a pocket of his pants and frowned a couple of times before strangling out, "My mother did say something."

"No, Steffan. I don't want to rush into whatever we have right now when, essentially, we are both on the rebound. We've had great sex a couple of times, but you and I aren't really communicating. If you and I connected again during sex, would Michelle be in your thoughts? I felt her spirit when we were together. I mean, you called her name in your sleep."

He recoiled. "You think this is all rebound?"

She shrugged. "I don't—"

He whipped around to walk away, stopped, and came back to Raquel. His nostrils flared when he breathed and the tips of his canines elongated. Raquel stared into the most exquisite blue-gray eyes. He was furious.

She had to stand her ground on this.

228

"Listen to me and listen well, Raquel Dulcati. When a *male* decides to *take* a mate, *of choice*, he's given it a lot of thought. I did a lot of thinking about Michelle and had to wait a few years until my Sire died in order to take her as my First Mate—"

"See, you just did it."

"—an unwanted mating isn't pretty to watch. I've seen enough of those to last a lifetime. I chose you because—" Steffan frowned. "Did what?"

I knew I was right. "You're speaking to me about Michelle instead of defending *us* and making our relationship work. I'm a human. You're shifter. I'm not changing anything for nobody. I've accepted the fact that she was in your life prior to me, but I'm not sure I want to be turned just so I can keep on breathing and I can't hide forever under this roof. That's not living. I'm sorry, but I'm going home. Tonight. I think we need the space, and you need to think about... *us*."

"I chose you because I'm in love with you. You can't go."

"Watch me. You say you love me, but everyone has given me the impression it would be safer for me to return to my life when the Ceremony was over. Well, it's over. Have one of your security guys watch me from an unmarked van across from my apartment. I don't know, but I'm going. Just lie to everyone about me knowing about Were-shifters and such! Tell them you erased my memory. I'm sorry, Steffan, but I can't do this anymore!"

She stormed past him until she broke out into a full run. Tears streamed down her face. She quickly glanced back at him, then continued to the guest room she'd been given.

Raquel slammed the door, locked it behind her, and leaned heavily against it. She'd have to wait until everyone left. The house was full of shifters. She had to be careful if she wanted to get out alive.

Her phone vibrated in her pocket, and when she viewed the screen, relief washed over her at Genevieve's enquiring text, and the next second, her cell went off.

"Genevieve, I thought you were with Roman? Why are you calling me?"

"Is everything all right? Roman and I just got a mindlink from Steffan. His kid brother isn't too happy right now and left the house

229

in a full-on rage. Steffan's panicking. It was loud enough to interrupt Roman's... ah... let's just say we didn't get to finish because of the interruption."

"Genevieve, please. I need to go. I can't stay here any longer."

"Roman wanted me to call you as soon as Steffan reached out to both of us. He's going after Steffan to talk some sense into him. Or kill him, I think."

Raquel sniffled back the tears. A part of her knew this had to end, but why did it have to hurt so much.

"I'm sorry, Gena. It's for the best. You and Roman have each other. Since I can work now, I'm going to look for a new job in another city, away from all of this."

"Raquel, don't go—"

"I need to."

She hung up on Genevieve's protest and headed over to the window to view the garage and the lawn. The last of the guests pulled away from the edge of the lawn, and she sighed with relief.

Coast was clear.

She observed her surroundings as she made her way out of the quiet house to the garage. She pulled up short. Her Jetta sat next to a tricked-out, bright pink Porsche, complete with eyelashes on the headlights.

She yanked on the door to her Jetta and dropped down into the bucket seat, pulled the sun visor down, and caught the spare keys in her hand. Then wiped away a tear.

Chapter 34

Raquel felt drained. It had been two days since she had left Steffan and had barely slept. Her mind kept going over whether or not she'd made a mistake and had to remind herself it was for the best. Besides, Steffan hadn't checked up on her or if he had someone watching, her from a distance, she didn't know about it.

She flopped down on the couch in her apartment, stared up at the ceiling, and watched as reflected car lights meandered from the window to the edge of the doorway, then to the hall, and disappeared into the darkness.

She'd stay the night. In the morning, she'd pack a few things and head to her aunt's house in Kentucky. Maybe put in an application for a job at the local hospital. Make a new start for herself.

She had no ties here in New Orleans other than work, a few friends, and Steffan.

Her chest ached, and tears flowed quietly out of the corners of her eyes.

A quiet thud grabbed Raquel's attention, and her heart throbbed with fear. It was coming from her second bedroom. Or was it her noisy neighbors having sex again? Their bed always banged against the wall. She waited a few seconds... and nothing.

"I'm losing it."

She grabbed the remote and channel surfed until *Vikings* on the History channel popped up. She turned the volume down and punched and shaped her pillow a few times, making herself comfy. She tossed a blue blanket over herself and buried her nose in its warmth.

It smelled like Steffan.

This isn't going to work.

Flinging the cover off, she started to sit up, and a hand slammed down over her nose and mouth, pushing her down onto the couch. She screamed and kicked at her assailant, and in an instant, a second person zip-tied her wrists together and bound her legs at the ankles.

Panic rose, and she breathed deeply, angrily looking up into glowing lavender eyes.

Not human! Oh God! They're going to kill me! She screamed as loud as she could, the hand pressed firmly down onto her mouth blocking most of the sound.

"Shhhh, female. Be still. It will all be over in a few minutes. The drug takes time to work, but soon you'll fall asleep."

I'm drugged? But how? I was at the house, then here. I haven't had anything to drink or eat.

She blinked rapidly at her darkening vision, and she thought she tasted something sweet on her tongue. She had tried biting the gloved hand. There was a chemical on the glove.

***

Titus eased his hand off the female once her body calmed and her eyes closed. She was a pretty little thing, and he had no clue what his employer wanted with a small, human female. But it wasn't his biz. Just so long as he got paid upon delivery.

He glanced over at Kam. "You ready?"

Kam gave a curt nod. "Yeah." He reached out with his mind to Daleena. The female had decided to wait in the van in the parking lot while he and Titus did the dirty work. *"Package obtained. Once we are down, I expect full payment. Otherwise, we let the human female go and you'll have to deal with the consequences, yourself."*

Titus hoisted the female over his shoulder and followed Kam down the flight of stairs to the darkened parking lot. The van was parked in the shadow of the building.

Daleena got out of the van and came over to him. "Is she dead? The female is no good to me dead."

Kam replied, "No she isn't. The effects of the poison will wear off in a few hours and she's going to have one hell of a headache. Now pay up."

Daleena handed over a black duffel bag to Kam. He rummaged through it before giving the thumbs-up to Titus. All was well, and the money was all there. Titus placed the human female in the back of the van then joined Kam in the shadows while Daleena took off, driving the van.

Titus hi-fived Kam. "That has got to be the easiest money we ever made, and we didn't have to kill anyone."

"I was worried she wasn't going to go for the twenty thousand dollars."

"And what are you two jabber-heads taking about?" Siber had quietly joined them in the shadows of the building. "What twenty thousand?"

Titus shouldered the duffel bag. "Kam and I were paid for the retrieval of a human female."

The speculation on Siber's face was nothing new to Titus.

Siber asked, "By whom?"

Kam and Titus looked at each other. Titus hadn't said anything to Siber, and he knew Kam hadn't either. They shouldn't have to.

"Siber, it was business. Nothing else."

Siber glared but coolly replied, "I'm afraid it is my business. You see, I've been trying for a little more than a century to get us to hold a seat on the Commission, and I'm wondering if you two meatheads didn't go and fuck it up! Who was the human female you abducted, and who paid you?"

Kam hissed. "Alpha Daleena St. Claire wanted the bitch out of the way. She plans on mating with Steffan.

"I. See."

Titus got in Siber's face. "I think all this shit about getting a seat on the Commission is just crap! It ain't never gonna happen, and the sooner you realize that, the better. Besides, Siber, the money we get as mercs is good, and we can get what we want."

Siber ground his molars together. "It matters to me and to some of the shifters. Maximo is—"

"Yo, dude, wake up and smell your ass! Maximo is using you. Let me ask you one thing: Even if we get on that Commission council, what then?"

"What do you mean? Our brothers and sisters wouldn't be persecuted anymore. They won't be used as thugs for hire, and they could have better opportunities, all because of us having a seat on the Commission."

"Nah, that ain't it. You see, we will still have the same problem that the Fates themselves cursed us with."

"And that would be—"

Titus replied coolly, "We still won't be able to shift into an animal form; therefore, our kind won't be accepted among society due to our genetics." He hissed.

Titus followed Kam out of the parking lot. Kam glanced back once and shrugged at Siber.

Chapter 35

Steffan punctured his claws into a branch of the cypress tree hanging over the water. He marked it and lay down, lungs gasping for air to the point his ribs hurt every time he inhaled. By the Fates, that felt good. Two whole days of doing nothing but staying in his panther form and running and exploring the bayou and the wilderness preserve next to the Lavelle lands was what he'd needed after Raquel rejected him.

His heart slowed, and once he breathed normally, he lowered his head down onto his paws, snuffling a few times with agitation. This was not at all how he'd planned his night.

The Fates must really hate me to hand me a life like this. My First Mate was killed; another human female comes into my life, and just when I think I'm getting somewhere and can move on—BAM— the Fates end up saying, "Fuck you for loving a human."

He closed his eyes and let the sounds of the night permeate his mind.

There was something about the way the water lapped against the shoreline of the river when something disturbed the surface and caused the ripples to expand outward. The wind caressed his fur, easing the pain away. Almost like Mother Nature herself knew how much he hurt.

Where did I go wrong?

In the past, females practically clawed their way to the pard to solicit his time in a hopeful mating because of his Beta status. Then he met Michelle, and after her death, most females no longer bothered because of how he had tainted his status with a human.

Had he compared Raquel to Michelle?

No. Yes? Possibly.

A low chuff and vibrating quip erupted out of the noise of the birds, and a rabbit took off in a hurry. Steffan held his breath, reached out with his mind, and easily connected with Roman. Steffan wasn't sure if he should be annoyed, leap for joy, or run for cover.

The water lapped around Roman's twelve-foot panther form, breaching the current until he crossed to Steffan's side and stood on dry land. Roman shook all over, and droplets flew everywhere. He looked up at Steffan.

"I knew I'd find you here."

Steffan chortled. *"Mind if I ask how?"*

"Well, you left a trail of debris from the house all the way here. I've been circling to make sure you were safe and already killed one Mulatese Tenebrae that was trailing you. Now what the hell was that outburst through the mindlink? And Genevieve is empathic, so she picked right up on it as if you'd tagged her too. You interrupted the beginning of our honeymoon, so not only am I concerned about you, but I am also pissed that I am out here, in the middle of Bayou Cane, and my Mate is elsewhere. And just so you know, I purposely waited thirty hours before going after you; otherwise I would have killed you. At least it gave me time to cool off and Genevieve helped to alleviate the tension."

He shuddered. *"I really don't want to hear about your wedding night in the cave, but since you're out here, I have something to ask you."*

Roman blinked rapidly before his eyes narrowed slightly. *"This had better be good, li'l brother."* He gave a quick, forceful huff, and steam flared out of his nostrils.

Steffan drew in a deep breath.

"I know I've been a pain to you, but I want to know if you think I've compared Raquel to Michelle."

There. He said it, and Roman was going to answer him one way or the other.

Roman hissed, ears flattened against his skull. *"You interrupted us to ask me that? Seriously? All right, since it's so dire that you know what I really think about all of this, I will tell you. Yes, you've been a pain in my ass since I found out you had the hots for a human. I've been generous in protecting you. In regards to your comparison of Michelle and Raquel, I'm going to say yes."*

Steffan jerked and abruptly stood up on the branch, then jumped down to stand beside Roman, tail twitching from side to side. He reared to strike out, but a second later, Roman tackled him, taking him down into the watery depths of the river.

He floundered as he shifted back to human form and sharp

236

canines gripped his neck. His body went lax as Roman dragged him up onto dry land and dropped him there at the water's edge. Steffan coughed until the water in his lungs emptied on the ground. He rested face-down against the cool muddy ground, the scent of earth, decaying leaves and moss surrounding him. He heard the Alpha's heavy breathing next to him.

"Wh-what the hell did you do that for?" He raised his head and coughed, dragging air into his burning lungs.

Roman shifted and shrugged his shoulders. "You needed to cool off. You asked me to tell you the truth, and I did. You're clinging to Michelle's ghost instead of moving on. I understand your fears, but your fear is what's keeping you from letting go. When I worried 'bout you the most I took a peek inside your thoughts—"

"You did what?!"

"Shut up and listen. I know how you found Michelle's body. I know you feared stepping back into your role as a Master Rigger at Sanctuary. I know you're attracted to Raquel, and I am well aware that you think Raquel is going to end up dead. Look, Raquel is alive, and everyone at the house knows how you feel about her. The problem lies with you. Stop denying it."

"I'm not denying it. I know the anxiety and post-traumatic stress Michelle's death has caused. But I've moved on. When she said I was comparing her and Michelle, she bottled up her emotions and I felt her shut me out. She's afraid of me, and I don't want her fear. And I won't force our way of living upon her. I want more time with her, but not if she's afraid."

"Steff, worry not. I think she's more worried about not being the type of female you need. Think outside your imaginary box for a minute. You *are* a Beta to me. You *need* a strong female by your side who will *assist you*, give you *cubs*, and *support your purpose* with the real estate business and the security of the House of Lavelle and *not cower* from friends you have in both the human and shifter world. But it is an undeniable fact: *She will have to be turned, in order to undertake a relationship with her.* I hope you are aware of this. From what I gather, from the shadowed thoughts you tried to hide from me, you are thinking about Raquel as a Mate. Am I right?"

Steffan hesitated. "Yes." He wasn't sure he wanted to know Roman's reaction. "What am I to do?"

237

Steffan felt the weight of Roman's stare. The Alpha remained quiet for a few moments as if he were judging Steffan's question.

"Tell her how you feel inside; make her understand what you are willing to go through. But I hope you are not going to go into neutral territory to live. The pard won't accept you back as a Beta if you do that. So that's not an option. How does your panther react to her?"

"He's calm around her."

"Then your furry beast has already made up his mind about her and accepts her. So, my advice, take things slow, but let her know upfront how you feel. Raquel has no choice in refusing to be turned into a Halfling. It is a subject that will need to be addressed sooner or later. I will do all in my power to protect you both until you can convince her."

"And if she doesn't want to be turned? What then?"

Roman remained quiet and started to walk away from him. "Let's cross that bridge if we come to it. Now, if you don't mind, I'm going back to my Mate. If you need any more counseling, call Connor. Not me. I'll kick your ass if you do."

Steffan heard Roman shift back into his panther and leave by diving into the fast moving current and popping up to swim across the river to the other side.

He sighed and tossed a few rocks into the water. His brother's voice rang loud and clear but the unspoken part was since Roman didn't want to kill Raquel out of respect for Steffan; Steffan knew his brother would force the change on Raquel and Roman would be her Tasheen.

Steffan's hand gripped the rock in his hand until it broke apart.

Hell would have to freeze over before he'd let that happen.

Chapter 36

Muffled voices penetrated through the dull, pounding ache in Raquel's head. Weakly, she forced them open. Everything was blurry, and she blinked rapidly to clear her vision. Her head throbbed as she lifted it, and the room started to spin as soon as she sat up. Something soft lay at her fingertips, and she gripped it hard to anchor herself.

"She's awake," someone softly said nearby.

Raquel's gaze darted to a woman who had spoken and focused until the woman's features became crystal clear. Almond shaped, jet-black pupils filled the space of the iris, stared intently back at Raquel. *Not human, shifter.*

"Where am I?"

A glass of water suddenly appeared in front of her.

"Drink this. It'll help to flush whatever drug you were given out of your system. You have a name, honey?"

"Raquel." Slowly, Raquel leaned against the wall and drank the cool refreshing water. "What's going on? Last thing I can remember is lying on my couch and a hand came down over my nose and mouth."

"Well, honey, I heard an Alpha female of the St. Claire clan had you brought here. She wanted you out of the way. My name's Kia, and like you, we were all brought here for one reason or another. Although, I must say,"—Kia chortled— "you're the first human to be brought into our group."

"Where's *here*? What group?"

"My guess is we're down at the docks. I heard a tanker's horn blow a few days ago."

The docks? That's where Gia was shot.

Kia never answered the last part of her question. But she did look familiar to Raquel. *Where have I seen her before?* She observed the other woman who sat and stared at her with almond shaped eyes. *She's familiar too.*

239

A revelation came to mind as a remnant of the image she had seen when Steffan helped with the mindlink at the hospital. *Gia. These are the women lined up in the warehouse. I saw them right before Gia's vision gave out.*

The door at the other end of the room swung open with a loud, metallic groan, and two men walked inside. Raquel's heart leapt into her throat, strangling her. The one didn't look like a human or a Were-shifter.

Cold calculating cat eyes shimmered in the low lighting, and Raquel shrank against the wall. Small nimble fingers gently gripped her shoulder.

Kia whispered in her ear. "Take it easy. Your kind don't hold value among the Kindred."

Was that supposed to be comforting?

A gravelly voice echoed in the room. "Kia, I need you and the girls to line up in the hall. Leave the human here."

Kia and the other eleven women quickly filed out the door. The door closed, and Raquel realized how alone she was.

Except for the Kindred in the room. He gave her the creeps. His ears were pointed with black hair on the ridge; the nose was wider than a human's, and Raquel couldn't tell if he had a tan or if fur covered his face and extremeties. The gleam in the hazel eyes was foreboding. Raquel stood, and for once, she had to look down at a man, thing, whatever he was.

He smirked.

"I'm surprised Daleena brought you to me, and what's more surprising, I heard you were involved with the Lavelle Beta, Steffan. And you're alive."

"What are you going to do with me? Steffan doesn't want me. I won't tell a soul about the Kindred. You can trust me and let me go. Please? I have a job and—"

"Yes, I know about your job at St. Joseph's Hospital. Letting you go isn't an option, and selling you for profit isn't an option either."

"Sell me? You mean you traffick these women?"

"It's business, female. Sit tight, and I'll make up my mind as to what to do with you."

He left, and the heavy clank on the other side of the metal door indicated she was locked in.

She scooted back on the mattress and pulled her knees up to her chest, resting her arms and head on top of them. The center of her back tingled oddly until it itched. She scratched at it until the itch disappeared, only for it to annoy her a few seconds later. Raquel dug her nails into where she could reach her back and scratched ferociously.

What the hell was back there?

She looked around and found a mirror over a sink. She got up, moved closer to the mirror, and lifted the hem of her shirt in the back. Something black peeked out at her from the edge, so she hiked her shirt up even more.

"What the hell is that?"

She couldn't see; the lighting sucked in this place. In frustration, she hoisted up her shirt and froze. The scar she had from where the lion mauled her had shrunk considerably in size, and a faint, barely discernible curlicue black and blue design covered a lot of the scar tissue, trailed between her shoulder blades, down her spine, and stopped near her waist.

Another small part of the design started to appear and get darker.

Raquel frowned. It wasn't there yesterday.

Glancing at her back in the mirror, the flowing design of the black and blue curlicues reminded her of Genevieve's Mating Mark.

Stunned, she lowered her shirt and sat back down on the mattress.

I bear Steffan's Mating Mark.

Chapter 37

Steffan kept calling Raquel for an hour, and all of the calls had gone directly to voicemail. He must've left ten messages by now. Why wasn't she picking up the phone?

I'll try one more time.

The way he'd left things between them was like a dagger to his gut. He sighed on the beep. "Hey, Raquel. Um... it's Steffan, again. Although you probably could guess. I take it you're still pissed. It explains *why* you're not picking up the phone, *ma chérie*. I need to talk to you, and I... ah... I wanted to apologize. Ya know, for... uh... making you think... so... ah... call me back? We really should talk."

He sighed and slipped his phone into the back pocket of his jeans. Loneliness wrapped its ugly fingers around him. He hadn't meant to hurt her. This was absurd.

Damn the Fates! This is entirely their fault!

Narella waltzed down the hallway, drinking from a can of Pepsi with Rags the dog prancing alongside her. She stopped in front of him and smiled, batting her eyelashes.

"Can I help you, *ma petite belle?*"

"Did you get ahold of Raquel?"

"Not yet. She's probably at work or went out to see a movie with one of her friends from work."

Her mischievous smile broadened. "Or *maybe* you scared her away. She is human, after all. Anyhooooo... can I have forty bucks?"

Like I forgot she was human.

"For what, might I ask?"

"I need gas in my Porsche."

"You really need to get a job." Steffan pulled out two twenties and held them up between his fingers. She quickly grabbed the bills and shoved them into her jeans pocket.

"You going on a date tonight? You have lip gloss and make-up on."

242

Her face paled. "Yes, I am." She feigned a smile.

"So does this flavor of the month have a name?"

"I'm seeing James tonight."

"James from the Gianti pard?" Steffan prayed it was that male so Narella would be spared the heartache he had suffered in the past.

"James Sweitzer, from the Pizza Palace on Marion Street. He's human."

Damn it!

"A human? Seriously?"

Shock exploded in her expression. "You're not going to give me a lecture, are you? I already endured one from Ascenza and Cristoff, and Connor handed me a box of condoms."

Oh. My. Fates! Okay, condoms? TMI. Then again, he shouldn't be the one to lecture anyone on dating preferences. "Don't let Roman find out. And you're not fucking anybody!"

"Steffan!"

"You're sixteen, and you do not need to get pregnant or settle down yet. And if you do get pregnant, there'll be hell to pay from me, and I'm sure Roman isn't ready to be an uncle. Roman will yell, and will hunt down this human James, so let me stress this again: You. Are. Not. Fucking. Anyone."

Narella's cheeks flushed crimson, and tears edged the corners of her eyes. She blinked them back.

Great. Just frickin' peachy. I'm certainly racking up the asshole points today.

Rags nipped at Steffan's feet and growled.

He quickly sighed and managed to get control of his anger. "I'm sorry."

"You didn't need to be a dick and take out your anger on me. You're the one that falls for humans, not me. And for your information, I plan on going to college first, and waiting a long time before seeing someone seriously. Not to mention... "

A cloud of heavy malaise settled around Steffan. Narella's angry tirade sounded distant and funneled. His skin itched and tingled from the heat erupting over the surface, and for a split second, time stopped. The tiny hairs on the back of his neck stood out. Nausea rolled in the pit of his stomach, and sweat poured off him. Steffan slowly drew in a long breath and released it. His temples pounded in

243

sync with the pulsating ringing in the ears. He fell against the wall and dug his claws into the drywall, trying to keep his balance.

"Oh my Fates, Steffan, what's wrong? You're pale. Here, breathe, sit on the floor, put your head between your knees and take deep breaths."

He heard Narella, but there was someone else.

"*Steffan—help!*"

He jerked his head to the side to pinpoint the sound. It was in a mindlink but distant, and it didn't sound like anyone in the pardhouse.

Who the h—

"Steffan, what's wrong?"

Narella's voice was edged with fear, and Steffan forced himself to breathe.

His lids snapped open. Narella's face paled.

"You look as if you're going to shift and tear my throat out. I didn't think I pissed you off when I said I was going on a date with a human."

"No, no, no. That's not it. I thought I heard something."

"What did you hear?"

He swallowed hard and shook his head. "I-I don't know. All of a sudden, I feel sick and in danger for some reason." He reined in his fur and kept breathing until the cloud passed.

Steffan frowned at Narella. One of her brows rose sharply, and her demeanor changed to curiosity. "Did you say something just now via mindlink? 'Cause I heard a female, or it sounded like a female." *It sounded like Raquel, but that's impossible.*

"No. Why?"

"Did you hear anything through the mindlink? You had to have heard it too. It was too loud not to, and I don't think they blocked anyone out."

"Ah... no. I believe your imagination from your lack of sex and your job are affecting your mind. I think you're losin' it. I didn't hear anyone except you."

Her confusion mirrored his.

A few minutes of silence passed, and Narella shrugged and wandered away with mutt in tow. Steffan waited.

Nothing. He reached out with his mind in the general direction he thought it came from but met empty space.

He rushed downstairs, keeping his mind open, but his thoughts returned to Raquel over and over again. The more he thought of her, the more his anxiety spiked. He really should go and see her.

Steffan passed Connor on the way to the kitchen. The aroma of hot coco wafted from the mug he carried.

"I think I'm going to go by Raquel's apartment."

Connor gave him an incoherent response. All Steffan deciphered was, "Aye... have fun."

Chapter 38

Steffan jumped out of his Camaro and ran up the flight of the stairs to Raquel's apartment. His heart pounded in his throat. This was a gutsy move, but one way or another, he'd convince Raquel they were meant to be together.

He didn't give a shit about his position in the House of Lavelle. All he cared about was a future with Raquel.

The gray metal door loomed in front of him, and he forced himself to calm down. If he busted the door down like he wanted to, most likely, he'd scare her to death.

Steffan lifted his hand and rapped on the door.

"Raquel, it's me; let me in."

Steffan casually glanced around. Her car was in its space, so that meant she was probably home.

He knocked again and waited.

This was taking too long. If she'd wanted him to leave, she would have yelled at him through the door.

Steffan placed his hand over the locking mechanism, willed the bolt to disengage along with the knob, and walked in. It was dark, and no sound reached him. Something wasn't right. Even if she was in her bedroom, from this distance, he would be able to hear her breathing.

Steffan willed the lights on and stilled. Raquel's apartment had been trashed, and it looked like she gave a good fight.

There was a faint metallic smell in the living room, and a stab of fear struck him like a bolt of lightning.

Blood.

Steffan yanked the blanket off the floor. He eyed the droplets of blood, then glanced around. There should have been some evidence of someone else here—*unless*... He inhaled deeply and only his scent and her scent were detectable.

"Ohhhh Fates... NO!"

He ran to the bedroom, and all the while, his inner panther

wanted out. Raquel wasn't there, and the scent of blood triggered memories of bloody rigging, a mangled body and this time it wasn't Michelle he pictured. Raquel had taken Michelle's place, and he was imagining Raquel's broken body.

The lights came on, and he held his breath. The room was intact. Not a thing out of place. Raquel wasn't lying in a pool of her own blood like he had imagined. "Fates Raquel... "

A noise from the living room broke through Steffan's focus. "Where the hell are you?" a female's voice yelled out from the entryway of the apartment.

"Raquel?" It sounded like a pair of heels walking on the wooden floors.

Sudden relief flooded his senses, and he ran out to greet her, only as soon as he stepped into the hall, he stopped cold, and the hair on the back of his neck rose.

He hissed. "Daleena, what the hell are you doing here?"

A cold, wicked grin spread across her face. The tips of her canines protruded, and her amber eyes flashed. "I've come to give you one more chance. I want you to be my First Mate. Come with me, and we can be together."

"Do you have a hearing problem? I said no. I honestly don't know how to spell it out for you. Maybe if I spoke in Swahili or another French dialect instead of simple plain English and French, you might get the message."

Daleena growled, and in seconds, she had him shoved up against the wall, her fingers wrapped around his throat. The sudden move stunned him, and his skin itched. He let his fur come out in a partial shift. Her claws dug into his fur.

"First of all, Beta Lavelle, you don't ever speak to me like that. Secondly, I would have thought with Michelle and your human bitch out of the way, you'd see the light."

"Get your hands off me. I don't want to hurt you."

"Oh you won't hurt me, and do you know why?"

Steffan growled low, grabbed her wrist at his throat, and twisted it to break her hold, but she raked her claws across his stomach. He shoved her hard, and Daleena fell back against the end of the sofa, grabbing it to steady herself.

"How *daaaaare* you!"

Daleena lunged, claws fully extended and aimed for his face. This time, he caught her wrists and swung her around, locking her arms crisscrossed in front of her. He forced himself to calmly hold her there.

It would be so easy for him to dislocate her shoulders from this angle, but he would never hurt a female. That was his Sire, not him.

Damn, this was wasting time! He had to stop this and go find Raquel.

"I think it would be wise if you cease and desist with this notion of me taking you as a mate, and stop coming after me."

"Why do you always go after humans? Huh?" She whined. "They're weaker than us; they don't live as long, and for some Fate-awful reason, you like screwing them! Well, you won't have *that* female ever again!"

He froze. "What do you mean?" He swung her around to face him and pinned her arms behind her. Her body slammed up against his.

Daleena laughed and ground her hips against his.

Steffan knocked her legs out from under her and took her down to the floor.

"Why, Steffan, if I'd known you like it rough, I would certainly have obliged." She toyed with him.

"Shut up! What did you mean: I won't have her again? Tell me! *Tell. Me!*" he roared.

Daleena's smile sent a chill down to his bones. "Your mind has been so fixated on humans, I made sure to get rid of your *precious* Raquel."

He tightened his grip on her arms, and Daleena cried out.

He hissed, and enzyme flew out, hitting her in the face as he spoke. "If any harm comes to Raquel, I will hold you responsible and come after you myself. Where is she?"

She recoiled at the pain. The female would heal soon enough.

"I had her delivered to one of Alpha Stavslaka's trafficking rings. By now your human is probably dead from spreading her legs for some Kindred."

Steffan literally saw red and shifted completely into his Were-panther. He let go of Daleena's arms, and she rolled onto her stomach to get away from him. His paws pressed down on the middle of her back. She shifted into her cheetah, but Steffan maintained his hold on her. He outweighed her easily, and he fully intended to crush her beneath him.

The rage overwhelmed him, and he wanted to kill her slowly.

"Lad, I have an oatmeal raisin cookie fer ye if ye let 'er go. Don'nae kill her. We'll need her later."

Steffan lifted his head to the doorway. Connor stood there, munching on a cookie, and held out one for him. The absurdity took him by surprise, but it did the trick.

A calming stillness settled around him, but he refused to let up on his hold. Daleena's body went limp beneath him, and his rage immediately dissipated.

Oh Fates, what have I done?

He backed away from her and shifted back to his humanoid form. He stared at her. Daleena wasn't moving. He looked up at Connor in the doorway.

Steffan started to shake violently. Daleena didn't budge from where she lay. "Did I... "

He had never killed a female before, and bile hastily rose in the back of his throat. The anger and rage he had been feeling vanished, and in its place, unadulterated fear took root and crept up his spine.

Connor closed the door and went over to the still female, placed his fingers below Daleena's nose, and waited, while he shoved and chewed the rest of the cookie in his mouth.

Fates, let her be all right, Fates, let her be all right. Fates, please...

"Nae, Steffan. She's breathin'. I sense her cheetah. She's only out cold. Here. Eat this."

Connor glanced back at him, the unspoken question of what the hell happened shone brightly in his blue orbs, and he handed him the oatmeal raisin cookie.

Steffan couldn't bear Connor's daggered glare.

He swung his focus to Daleena. Her body slowly shifted to her humanoid form. Normally, a shift would have brought her around.

Steffan checked her pulse—slow, but strong. His shoulders slumped, easing the tension.

"Connor, I need to find Raquel. Daleena did away with her." He tossed the cookie onto the coffee table.

249

Connor's eyes narrowed. "Did away how?

The clipped edge in Connor's voice lingered like nails on a chalkboard.

"She sold Raquel to Stavslaka."

Steffan turned back to Connor in time to see Connor's demeanor turn downright deadly. The male's canines lengthened on a hiss, and Steffan didn't know why Connor was as angry as was. Steffan had only seen it one time before, and he shuddered.

"Let's get goin' then. I'll call Cristoff since Roman is unavailable, an' I'll join ye. Ye'r nae alone in this. As far as I'm concerned, Raquel is yer female. I don'nae give shit if she's human. Any idea where she might be?"

Only one place came to Steffan's mind.

"Gia was shot down at the docks. She saw something. Stavslaka does a lot of business down there and Daleena's make-up ships into the docks in the same place. That's where she'll be."

"Ye sure?"

"Positive. I can feel it in my soul," Steffan hissed. "If one Kindred touches Raquel—"

Connor's eyes turned stormy. "Noted lad, an' since Stavslaka's involved, I want his arse. Ye focus on getting' Raquel out."

250

Chapter 39

Steffan, Connor, and Cristoff made their way through the claustrophobic subterranean maze built underneath the main warehouse. The only sound he detected was their combined breathing and the pounding of their hearts. He hated being confined in a small area. He couldn't shift comfortably, and even if he could, maneuverability was limited. On the bright side, it became even ground. The other Kindred would feel *exactly the same* and resist the urge to shift.

He drew in a breath through his mouth. Stavslaka's scent kept getting stronger. *That male's down here, somewhere.*

He glanced briefly at Connor. The male's hand gripped the .45, claws extended in the other. Cristoff's claws were already fully extended, and no sound was uttered, nor did they open a mindlink. Hand signals were used instead, the plan to extricate Raquel now in motion.

Cristoff lifted the bar on the metal door, and they snuck inside. Voices drifted from the other end of the hall.

Close. So close.

"Lad, ye feel that?"

Steffan opened his senses, and briefly closed his eyes. His ears detected more than one voice; all females, but each tone was the wrong pitch to identify her as Raquel.

"Raquel's not in there. Only the same group of females I saw in Gia's mind, one guard, and Stavslaka is in there too." Steffan met Cristoff's amber gaze. "You and Connor free the females by any possible means."

"Where are you headed? There's no coffee machine here."

"Remind me to kick your butt later. I'm going after Raquel. She's down here; I can feel it."

Cristoff's eyes narrowed. "You mean you have a hunch."

"No. I feel her; I can't explain it."

"You... ah... didn't happen to mate her and she bear's your Mating Mark by any chance, did'ja?"

Steffan pulled up short, glaring at his little brother, then noticed Connor's curious stare.

Cristoff has lost his mind. I'd never put her life at risk. "Get the females. I'll meet you both topside."

Steffan ran down the metal staircase, going deeper into the belly of the earth. He had to hand it to whoever dug out these tunnels; they'd done a tremendous job, considering this was well below the Gulf of Mexico. That was a lot of concrete and steel. No wonder Stavslaka's *business* thrived.

The hairs on the back of his neck rose. Someone was coming.

He jumped twenty-five feet, straight up, bracing his hands and feet against the wall, holding his breath. The small ledge of metal trim provided a great foothold, and he flattened himself against the ceiling. Below, four guards turned the corner and passed underneath him undetected.

That was close.

He released his hold and fell to the floor in a crouch.

Where the hell are they keeping her?

Closing his eyes, he reached out again with his senses. This time, his panther refused to astral project to another area. Instead, the furball changed his heartbeat. Slowed it down, forcing him to focus on the unusual cadence.

This was no ordinary heartbeat. It was Raquel's. For once, his inner panther had given him something useful.

He stopped short of an intersection in the hall. His heart still beating in the humanoid rhythm. He started to turn left, and his heart rate rapidly went back to the quicker rate that was typical for a Were-shifter.

Okay, wrong direction. So which—

The Were-panther inside used him like a compass.

Steffan turned to go down the right hallway, and the rate remained the same until he went straight ahead and the cadence decreased to a human's heart rate.

He paused, closing his eyes to think. He should not be able to hone in on Raquel like this. He frowned.

There was only one-way he would be able to zero in on Raquel and that—

Oh Fates!

His skin tightened, and he remembered the cuts on Raquel's arms after going through the table, the scar on her back, and how, in both instances, he had used his enzyme to heal her. There's no possible way he had given her too much of the enzyme.

His stomach roiled. *It's not possible! There's no way I Marked her! I was careful! Oh, fuck no! If I did, I've signed her death warrant!*

Raquel's face appeared in his mind, and then he heard her voice. *"Help me!"*

He popped his eyes open, took off running, adrenaline fueling his muscles, and literally followed the sound of the heart beating inside his mind. He didn't have time to dwell on the consequences now. He had to get Raquel back and get her to safety.

A Mulatese Tenebrae turned the corner, took out his knife, and slashed at Steffan. Steffan grabbed his wrist and forced the blade into the male's chest, effectively slicing him from sternum to throat before breaking his neck. The Mulatese Tenebrae fell where he stood.

He looked down, breathing hard from the exertion. An overwhelming sense of determination enveloped him. "I'm coming, Raquel. I'm coming. Hold on."

A blue metal door opened, and another Mulatese Tenebrae came out. Steffan punched him in the jaw, sending the male back into the room. Steffan leapt on top of him, only to get thrown off, and he crashed against some filing cabinets.

A female screamed.

Raquel!

The fear in her scream ignited his resolve into a fast moving fire. Steffan pushed through the pain and let agility take over. The determined look on the male's face did little to persuade Steffan.

Steffan reached for the male's jacket, and something sharp sliced over the top of his hand, and he yanked it back. Blood dripped from the open wound. His other hand shot out for the male's throat. He dug his claws into both sides of the male's Adam's apple and shoved him up against the wall.

The male gasped, trying to shake him off.

No matter. This fucktard will be dead soon.

Steffan dislocated his jaw, opened wide, extended his canines,

253

and faster than a cobra strike, he crushed the male's windpipe in his jaws. The body of the Mulatese Tenebrae jerked in his hold, and the sound of blood gurgling out of his mouth brought on a small victorious joy. The animal side of him relished the kill. He ripped out the male's throat and spat it out on top of the dead Mulatese Tenebrae.

Raquel sobbed out of fear. "S-Steffan... what the hell did you do?"

Oh God—Raquel! He spat the blood to the floor.

Her eyes spoke volumes: confusion, anger, fear, relief, fatigue, all rolled together. She kept darting her gaze from him to the dead male on the floor.

Steffan's heart ached with the realization of what he had to do. There was no way around the problem, and the problem was him and his species.

She was right. She needed to go back. *I won't force her to change into a Halfling. Fuck the law.*

In one swift move, he stood in front of Raquel, placed his hands on either side of her head. Raquel stared up into his eyes. His eyes stung from shifting to his Were-panther as he forced his way into her mind.

Fates, I'm so sorry.

"Raquel, I'm sorry, but my life is too dangerous for you, and I'm not going to force you into this life. You have to go back to your world. I'm going to erase your memory and will be careful of your knowledge."

"Steffan, please... "

Steffan didn't give her a chance to explain and quickly invaded her mind. Her fear turned to anger.

She clawed at his hands with dull, human nails, breaking his skin, and shrank toward the floor to get away from him. He'd gladly take the pain. She kicked at him.

He choked back a sob of his own, smelling his own tears as they ran down his face and dripped onto her neck.

She lurched and twisted beneath him. Her face turned bright red, and her pain-filled grimace etched into his brain.

He had to get her home, get her to safety and away from him. This was the only way and he risked her being in a vegetative state or end up having seizures for the rest of her life, but he didn't want to see her killed.

He wasn't going to force her to change but if he completely erased things about him and the Kindred from her mind was the only way, then he was going to sacrifice himself.

Time ticked by. He felt older than he was. Every single muscle hurt from overstraining, and he sensed the sorrow from his Werepanther.

Slowly, her body relaxed and fell against him. His legs gave out, and he collapsed to the floor with her in his arms.

She didn't move. He gulped on a sob. *Fates, let her live a normal life; please, I beg of you!* He waited for any signs of convulsing from seizures and tried to sense any damage he might've done. There wasn't any, and his mindlink remained until he was satisfied.

She breathed slowly in her forced slumber. Her cheeks were stained red from the exertion of fighting him, and tears glistened on the ends of her lashes. Her lips were plump from crying.

Fates, he was never going to forget her.

He'd tracked her. With his mind. There was only one way to do that: She had to bear his Mark.

Fates, let me be wrong about this.

He took her wrist and glanced at each of her arms—no marking. He eased her into a sitting position and leaned her upper torso against one arm, lifting the hem of her shirt up to her shoulders; and froze. His pulse pounded in his ears. The telltale black and blue coloring of the Lavelle Mating Mark trailed between her shoulder blades and down to just above her waist.

Oh Fates, no.

Gingerly, he traced over the Mark before he pulled her shirt down and cradled her to his chest. *No. Fates, why did you do this to me? To her?*

He quietly sobbed as he clutched her in reverence. She was a First Mate to him. He could push the issue and force her to be changed. But Fates, she would grow to hate him. And he had to let her go in order for her to stay alive.

It was the right thing.

No matter what happens, Roman will see to it she has the

255

financial stability and safety, and I will leave the area for however long she remains alive. Roman can funnel a portion of my pay from the pard treasury to her. She can live out her life.

Steffan gathered her in his arms and carried her unconscious form all the way up the stairs, and with each heavy step, a piece of him died, and by the time he reached the outside of the warehouse, he felt nothing.

Chapter 40

Connor ripped the metal door off its hinges and stepped inside. Cristoff flanked him. "Well, Stavslaka. I see ye'r hav'n a party an' ye did'nae invite me. I'm hurt."

Stavslaka simply smiled smugly before flicking his gaze to one of his bouncers. The Mulatese Tenebrae started for them, but Connor fired his gun, and the male dropped like a stone.

"Lad, take care of the females. I need ta have a chat with this male."

Stavslaka swallowed, and Cristoff nodded.

Cristoff charmingly smiled and motioned toward the door with a slight bow. "Ladies, this way, if you please."

The females' gratitude shone brightly in their eyes, and they whispered their thanks. There was a sense of satisfaction as the females took their time, each spitting on the dead Mulatese Tenebrae as she passed the body.

It struck a chord with him, and for a second, he remembered how Ascenza's face shone with that same brightness once she had been freed. A knot formed in his throat, and he swallowed hard at the memory. It had taken him a long time to find his Mate after she had been abducted.

And Stavslaka had been the key to getting Ascenza back. Connor's menacing growl caused Stavslaka to take a step back. He remained quiet, although Connor sensed the male's fox hiding his essence, or at least trying to.

A small human woman stopped in front of him, and Connor forced himself not to shift and beat the ever-lovin' bloody shit out of Alpha Stavslaka. Her eyes glistened with unshed tears.

"Can you help me go home? I-I want to go home." She started to sob, wrapping her arms around herself in an effort to bring herself some small measure of comfort. "*Please!*"

Connor's anger rose another notch, and his skin felt like shrink-wrap. He forced a mindlink with Stavslaka. *"Ye mothafeckin,' piece o' shit, mixin' it up with humans!"*

"Go with my friend. His name is Cristoff. He'll see to it ye'r taken home."

The female nodded her thanks and followed the other females out the door. Cristoff turned back to Connor and raised his brows.

"Leave, Cristoff. I'll catch up."

Connor heard the metal door clang shut behind him.

"Well, it's just me and you, old man."

"Aye, and where shall we begin? Ye'r still traffickin' females, I see." Connor cracked his knuckles and took a step toward Alpha Stavslaka.

Stavslaka's glare narrowed. "You should know by now that I'll do anything for a quick buck."

"Don'nae fantasize 'bout shifting into that fox of yers. Ye would'nae last three seconds against my panther."

The cold, calculating smile that graced Stavslaka's face nearly froze Connor's blood.

"How about I call for Reciprocal Immunity since what I am about to reveal falls under the Law of Amnesty."

He's feckin' jokin'.

"Did you hear me, old man? Perhaps you finally need a hearing aid."

"Nae, ye bastard, I heard ye plenty. But it does'nae mean I have ta agree with ye. An' dependin' on wha'ye say, I may'nae kill ye."

Stavslaka glared at Connor. "The Immunity guarantees my life."

Connor nodded. "Aye, fer now. But I have noooooo pard, so we shall see."

"You have no pard, but you have been operating under Alpha Roman Lavelle." Stavslaka's cold eyes drifted over Connor before he forced a smile. "The information I have will remain with me; therefore, I am requesting you take me into custody. If I remember right, the Lavelle pard still holds the keys to the cells underneath the house. You know the ones I'm referring to... the ones Maximo had built."

Stavslaka held out both of his wrists, exposing the underside to Connor.

"I suggest ye walk on yer own out ta the car. Ye might live longer, an' I'll forget ye requested asylum."

Connor shoved Stavslaka out the door, and once they were topside, he took a look at Steffan putting Raquel in the back seat of the car. The lad stood and closed the door. His cold, dead gaze pierced Connor. *Ahhh, nae, lad, ye did'nae.*

Connor remembered that look. He'd seen it over the centuries on the faces of males who had given up their mates or from those that had lost their mates to death. Only in this case, it was Steffan who'd died.

Chapter 41

Steffan numbly stood in the foyer of Lavelle House. He gripped the heavy wooden post at the base of the stairs, and his nails dug into an old scratch on the wood molding. He memorized each of the paintings on the wall while contemplating what his next move would be.

Leaving Raquel at her apartment was the hardest thing Steffan had ever done.

He'd carried her to her room, pulled the blanket over her body, and lain next to her. He cried, silently, the whole time he was in Raquel's bed. He wanted to remember how the curve of her body fit next to his, and while lying there, he thought of all the things he would miss out on by not being in her life.

Through her bedroom window he saw the sun peak over a set of buildings, and the sky turned from midnight black to majestic reds, oranges, and pinks. Steffan stayed the day with her, in bed, watching her for the last time. His mind kept willing her to continue to sleep.

He eventually got the nerve to get up from her bed and kissed his mate's cheek before saying goodbye.

He was never going to see his mate again.

Do I stay in Bayou Cane, or leave for fifty years and go back to France? I can't stay in the States.

"Monsieur?"

He turned to Ascenza but immediately looked down at the floor. He hated the pitiful expression on her face.

"What is it, Ascenza?"

"*Pardonnez l'intrusion,* it's good to see you home. Roman wanted to see you when you got home. He and Genevieve have returned early from their honeymoon. He got a call from Connor regarding something. I think pard business has taken a front row seat for now. I'm headed to bed, but I can tell him you'll see him on the morrow, if you wish. *Oui?*"

"No. I'll go to him now. Where's the Alpha at this time of night?"

260

"Very well. Alpha Roman is upstairs in his bedroom. *Bonne nuit, monsieur.*"

"*Bonne nuit.*"

Steffan sucked in a deep breath and headed to Roman's bedroom. He knocked, and the door immediately opened with his older brother's slightly hairy frame filling the doorway.

"I see you're shifting. Can you put some pants on, or do you always greet people with your little hose in the breeze?"

Roman gripped Steffan's shoulder and pushed him away from the door, closed it behind him, and then Roman crossed his arms over his chest.

"Connor returned two days ago. Where the hell have you been? You didn't answer your cell, and no one has seen you at any of the properties."

Two days? I hadn't thought I was with her that long.

"I took Raquel home."

"I see, but why isn't she here? It's too late to wipe her memory, and she now has a target on her back. Steff, she's human."

Steffan's skin started to crawl under the scrutiny. Best to get this over with.

"You won't have to worry about her anymore. I erased her memory of everything that pertains to me and what she's seen."

Roman's double take was almost comical. "How is that possible? You botched it the first time; what makes you think you did it right this time? Hopefully, she won't end up a vegetable. Damn it, Steffan! You're reckless."

"I know she's fine, because, while I was inside her mind sewing threads of memory together, she kept putting walls up to protect herself. Her mind is a lot stronger than any human I've encountered. That psychic ability of hers acts as a safety cushion and one I had to step over a few times." He paused and quietly continued. "No seizures."

His next words were gonna hurt.

"I will be leaving the area. I'm not sure where I'll go or where I'll stay. I might go back to France. Who knows? But, with what I erased, she can't ever see me. It might trigger a reversal of what I've done, and she'd start remembering things. I can't chance it."

Steffan could have heard a pin drop.

"I see. You will need to be here for meetings concerning the Commission."

261

"I'll do it by proxy. No one will see me for at least fifty years or so. By then, Raquel will be old or dead from old age."

Roman's stance changed from casual conversation to Alpha. "I don't accept these terms."

Steffan guffawed. "Weeeelllll, you're going to have to. And one more thing, while I'm gone, I'm charging you with Raquel's safety."

"Why? If you're leaving the area, she won't be needing a baby sitter."

"She bears my Mark on her back. She's my Mate, and I refuse to change her into a Halfling. That's why I'm leaving Louisiana. She's safe; unless someone on the Commission oversteps the Laws, then I'll be back with a vengeance." He pinned Roman with a hard stare.

Steffan's chest ached, and his inner panther sent him a visual of how it disagreed with his thinking. It pained both of them to leave.

"She bears your Mark? What the hell, Steff? You're going to regret this. There might be another way."

"How— how is there another way? The Commission vetoed the notion of a human remaining human. I know she doesn't want to be changed. If they find out I have a human mate, she's dead. Just like Michelle, and I can't endure living through the pain again." He choked on a sob. "It almost killed me the first time. Promise me you will see to her safety, and tell the Commission I said they can go fuck themselves and that I left because of them. Please, Roman. Give me your vow you'll protect Raquel."

Roman sighed, the muscles in his cheeks working as the Alpha ground his molars.

"I give you my word. Stay safe and call me if you need anything. I'll see to Raquel, and the secret that she is your Mate will remain with only me. Even Genevieve will never know. You said the Mark is on her back. If someone ever sees it, sees the coloring, I'll think of something should it come to be questioned as to why a human bears the Mark from the House of Lavelle. Maybe something along the lines that Raquel loved Genevieve's tattoo so much she got one of her own to cover the scar on her back."

Steffan nodded. "I owe you. I'm going to pack a bag and head out to my old house in the morning before I leave. I have some things I need to get from there, and then I'll head by the tree overlooking the property. I want to take a last look at the property before I go."

262

Chapter 42

Raquel hurriedly brushed her teeth for the third time within thirty minutes. She still had a weird furry taste, like she'd licked a carpet for hours. She had been up since noon, couldn't fall back to sleep, and decided to head in to work early.

It didn't make sense, and despite not sleeping through the entire day like she normally did before going in for third shift, she felt rested. Except, there was this haunting impression she'd slept with a man, only she woke up alone. Once she thought she heard someone sobbing.

The pillow next to hers had been soaked with what could only be tears. She glanced into the mirror. Her eyes were normal, not bloodshot. So, who cried on the pillow next to hers?

She finished in the bathroom and grabbed her name badge. An unexpected wave of emotions and images flooded her vision. "What the hell?"

She threw out her hand to keep from stumbling and gasped at the images flooding her mind.

A man with soft brown eyes appeared in front of her as solid as could be. She reached out a hand to the familiar apparition only to have it disappear. She tucked her hand to her chest.

"I know him."

Her back itched like crazy, and she hiked up her scrub top to see if she was breaking out in a rash. She twisted to view her back in the mirror. A tattoo with curlicues of navy and black lines was evident between her shoulders and down to just above her waist.

When the hell did I get a tattoo? It-it's almost like Genevieve's...

Something popped in the back of her mind, and she grabbed her head. Genevieve, a wedding, Roman, a cave in which she had sex with... with... *Steffan*!

Raquel remembered all of it.

"Steffan came to rescue me. Oh my God! He let me go."

In her heart, she wanted him. The emotion of losing him forced her into action. She grabbed her keys, left her apartment, and almost ran over her neighbor as she sped out of the parking lot.

Thankfully, there weren't any speed traps en route. Raquel had the pedal of her little Jetta pegged practically to the floor the whole way to the house.

I remember! He tried to take it away, but I remember! I know he'll have to turn me into Halfling.

Raquel slammed on the brakes and skidded to a halt under the portico. One of the staff nearly jumped out of her skin as Raquel tossed her the keys.

"Sorry! You can move the car if you need to, but I have to find Steffan!"

Raquel burst through the front doors and ran from room to room. She heard a man talking and followed the sound. "Steffan? You here?"

Raquel skidded to a stop and saw Connor and Roman in the midst of a meeting. Roman's mouth opened to say something, and confusion graced Connor's face.

"Ooops, sorry." Raquel nervously laughed. "Have either one of you seen Steffan? I *have to* speak with him."

Roman's brow curiously popped up. He casually flicked the ashes from his cigar into an ashtray. "Um... Raquel. What are you doing here?"

"I just told you."

"Yes, I'm aware, but you shouldn't be here. At all. I was under the impression your memory had been wiped."

"Well... ah... it had been or at least it was until I touched my name badge for work."

"Yer name badge, lass?"

Raquel nodded excitedly.

Roman scrubbed his hand down his face. "Connor, Raquel has a psychometric ability. She can see what happened in the past by touching something. Touching her name badge most likely unlocked her memories. Steffan wasn't careful enough and should've remembered."

Connor's face lit up. "Well then, can ye come out back t' the corner o' the property? There's a pile o' shit that doesn't seem t' belong t' anyone. Perhaps ye can—"

264

"Connor!" Roman shook his head. "I'm sorry, Raquel, but Steffan went to his old house. He's planning on leaving the area." He glanced at the clock on his desk.

"Leaving? Why?"

"To keep you safe."

Raquel laughed. "Me? To keep me safe? I fail to see how running away solves anything."

Roman cleared his throat. "Steff isn't running. If he leaves the area, no one on the Commission will go after you to kill you. They will be told your memory was wiped, and you can live out your life. It's *because* of the human's short life span, they will let you live. Once you die, Steffan can come back here. Our life span is anywhere from a few hundred to a few thousand years, depending on species."

She didn't care how Roman sugar coated it—running was running. "I need to find him."

"If you want to catch up with him, I know he'll be going out to a tree on the edge of the property. I was supposed to hand him documents he will need to have on him considering he's disappearing for half a century. I'll take you, if you'd like."

Raquel smiled. "Yes! Please!"

Roman gave Connor a sideways glance.

"Well now, lass... Roman. If ye'll 'scuse me, I'd like t' go back and make a sandwich to take down to our 'guest'."

Roman ushered Raquel out of the office and into a car. He drove out as far as he could before pulling over to the side of the road and parked on the shoulder. Raquel tilted her head toward him.

"Why'd you stop?"

"This is as far as we can go by car. The rest is on foot."

The second he led her down the trail, the heavens opened up, and Mother Nature let loose.

"Again? I swear I get caught in more rainstorms than ducks!"

Roman chuckled. "This way."

Chapter 43

In the time it took to walk from the car to the tree, the rain turned into a light drizzle. Cold mud sucked against Raquel's shoes, but the humidity clung in the air making this trek doable. Her wet shirt didn't bother her. She viewed Roman's back and followed him into the dense growth of the bayou.

"How much farther?"

Roman stopped and pointed to a tree dripping with moss. Steffan sat at the base of the tree, knees bent, his wrists resting on top, and hands folded over one another. He looked like a drowned rat—hair slicked down, wet clothes plastered to his body, rain dripping off the tip of his nose.

Steffan stared vacantly out over the bank of the rapidly rising river. The muddy water threatened to breach the edge and swallow everything around it.

Roman quietly leaned down to her ear. "This tree is ancient and sacred to our pard. That's why he's here. It is a meeting place for any Lavelle. This land, this part of Bayou Cane is a beacon to our blood, and my brothers often come here when troubled. I know Steff is worried whether or not he's doing the right thing by leaving. From the way he looks, he's communing with the spirit of one of our ancestors for guidance."

"Does he know we're here?"

"It's hard to tell. At this distance, he's blocking any knocking I've done at his mindlink door to let him know you are here."

Raquel chewed the corner of her lip.

Am I making a mistake? How's Steffan going to react to me being here, let alone digest the knowledge I can remember every detail of being with him?

"I know you love him. I can see it. Go to him. But Raquel, if you want to be with him, you must embrace being changed. Remember that. If you don't, Steffan will leave, and I'll be entrusted with your safety until you die. You're his mate. That Mating Mark on your back tells everyone that you are part of my pard."

Raquel acknowledged Roman with a nod, and her heart caught in her throat.

I want the relationship, but to be transformed? Raquel swallowed and smiled as she thought about what it would be like to be like Steffan.

He hasn't noticed me yet. God, what to do?

Raquel drew in a calming breath. Damn, he was breathtaking.

She knew she wanted to be in his arms.

He rose to his feet and took a step but pulled up short once it registered that she stood not too far away from him. Soft brown eyes flashed blue, and unusual warmth spread to every fiber of her being.

Nervously, she smiled at him. "Hi."

"Raquel?" Those piercing blue eyes turned back to the softest brown. "What are you doing here? Wait... exactly *why* and *how* are you here?"

Roman cleared his throat. "Steff, it's all right. I escorted her here, and given the fact you failed miserably at erasing her mind, your Mate should be with you. Since my presence is no longer required, I'll let you two have a chat."

Roman's eyes flashed at Steffan, and Raquel got the sense some communication had occurred between them when Steffan gave his brother a curt nod.

Steffan leapt across the water and crouched when he landed. The distance was over twelve feet. She nervously laughed. He was amazing.

He stood, and Raquel eased closer to him.

"I had to find you. Why are you leaving?"

He took her hand and pulled her closer to a nearby tree. Raquel quickly glanced up once she noticed there was enough foliage to provide some shelter from the now misting rain.

"I was leaving to save you. But I'm surprised to see you here. Is it true? You remember?"

"Yes."

"And how does that make you feel?"

She tilted her head, gave him a sly smile. "Honestly, I don't know. I mean, I'm glad I remember, but some of it is a little fuzzy.

His brown eyes shimmered with blue flecks, radiating hope. It was something she also felt. "I prayed to the Fates to spare your mind. I couldn't live with myself if you hadn't been able to remember the main parts of your life."

She cleared her throat. "Roman said I was your Mate."

He cupped her cheek and lightly caressed it with the callused pad of his thumb. "You are. When I healed the wound on your back, I might have released too much of the enzyme, and I ended up Marking you. But it hadn't shown up til recently."

Steffan traced down her arm and looked down, lifted her hand up, and studied her forearm.

Raquel's gaze followed his, unsure of what he was looking at. "What's wrong?"

He traced over a thin black line up one arm. "I think, in a few hours, your forearms will be covered with a 'tattoo sleeve' from the enzyme. That gel I used in your kitchen was my enzyme. It appears I've Marked you—not once, but twice. A rarity in my species."

His gaze flicked to hers, and the intensity of his resolve burned in those blue orbs. "I love you, Raquel. But I vowed never to force my Mate to change into a Halfling again. I'm not forcing you into something I know you don't want."

The pitter-patter of the rain through the leaves broke the silence.

"You should go. This is hard enough as it is. I'm sorry. Our Laws are never going to change; I know that now, and I have to let you go. I was leaving to keep you *alive*. I lost one mate, and I couldn't go on living if I lost you too." Despair coated every word. "Fates, I was foolish to think I could have a slice of happiness!"

He turned away from her.

No. He can't leave me. If we're going to be together, I need to make a choice. There's only one choice to make.

Raquel drew in a deep breath and captured his wrist in her hand, forcing him to look back at her.

"I'm here because I *want* to be with you," she said tersely.

"Raquel, you don't know what you are saying... "

"Yes, I do."

She couldn't read him, but in a sense she knew he was afraid.

"The only way we can truly be together is if I turn you."

"Then do it. Let me bear both of your Marks with pride as your true First Mate. I love you, Steffan."

"Are you absolutely sure?" His sullen gaze, filled with hope.

"God, yes. Make me yours. I love you, Steff."

"You have no idea how long I've wanted to hear those words come out of your mouth."

Steffan sliced through Raquel's clothes with his claws. The rain patted her skin in an even rhythm as he laid her down at the base of the tree. She pushed at his rain-soaked shirt and ripped it off with the rest of his clothes before lying on top of her, shielding her from the rain. The cold, wet ground provided a stark contrast to the muggy air, grounding her.

She wanted him, to be with him, and was willing to give up everything for him. He kissed her hard. His body radiated heat, and his tongue beckoned her with an urgency she no longer wanted to ignore.

She inhaled deeply and wrapped her legs around his waist. A naughty smile spread on his face as he pushed the head of his cock into her heat, and her nails dug into his back. He moaned and kissed her again. She arched to accommodate his length and mewled as he took her. God, she loved him.

She noticed that he took his time and drew out the sensation. His hips eagerly thrust against her, and at the brink of going over the cliff into an orgasm, he suddenly pulled away and cooler air rushed over her bare breasts. A tiny, gentle pulse echoed in her mind. A mindlink had opened between them, and suddenly, she felt not only her body as it blossomed for him, but she was also aware of his body. Thrust for thrust, she knew what Steffen felt as he languidly made love to her. It was magic and so much more.

She opened her eyes on the brink of a powerful orgasm in time to see Steffan's canines elongate right before he struck her neck hard and fast, sinking into the bones in her spine. With their minds connected like they were, she was every bit aware of what he sought. He sank deeper into her spinal column but stopped right before he hit the main nerve. She knew his enzyme was being absorbed into her marrow and flowing into her spinal fluid. It was like getting hit by lightning, the pain blinding her momentarily.

She involuntarily bucked beneath him.

"I know this hurts. It will be over soon."

She gulped in air and tried not to cry out. She didn't want to look

269

weak in front of her mate, and she heard him chuckle once she thought it.

"*My First Mate, my love, you will never be weak in my eyes.*"

The pain lessoned, and she moved her hips in sync with his as the pain turned into a pleasurable pulse. He quickened his pace, and she cried out as the orgasm erupted within her core.

He let go of her neck and kissed her lips gently.

She sensed him: truly sensed how his heart swelled with pride, swelled with happiness at becoming her Tasheen or whatever that was, and how much he loved her. It was so beautiful, she cried at how happy she was.

"You didn't finish. I want to feel your orgasm inside of me."

"Ooohhh, don't worry, I plan to. But for the next hour or so, I'm going to drag out your pleasure."

"I feel strange, Steffan. Like I'm drunk."

Steffan thrust into her bringing a pleasurable gasp from her.

"Your body is reprogramming itself. Soon you'll really know what it's like to change into a panthress. A word of caution though."

"What's that."

"Don't close off your mindlink to me once you've shifted. I'll need to be able to coach you through shifting back to a humanoid form."

His eyes twinkled, and he kissed her hard before pulling out of her, and she saw him shift into his panther form. The mindlink remained open, and her temples pulsed. "*Raquel. Shift like I had. Your back will be the first of the bones to break apart, and the rest of the body follows. I'm here. The first couple dozens of times it hurts like a bitch, but your body becomes used to it. Your panthress is a lot stronger and will allow your body to heal. Shift, now.*"

She rolled over onto her hands and knees. Her back arched, and the first intense pain hit her so hard she thought she was going to pass out. He kept his word and guided her as her body reknitted itself back together into a much larger, much stronger Were-panther. By the end of her painful transformation into a Halfling, she was exhausted and fought to keep her eyes open.

She looked around with new eyes. Things were brighter, and as she observed Steffan, she was well aware of an aura surrounding him pulsating around his body.

"You should be able to really see me now. Can you see my essence?"

"If by your essence you mean the blue surrounding you pulsating, then yes. It's beautiful."

"Bébé, every Were-shifter has one. You look tired."

"I am. And hungry."

Steffan pranced over to her, nuzzled her neck, and rubbed along the side of body until his tail encircled hers. *"Let's go home. There's fresh meat at the house. I'll teach you another time how to hunt off the hoof. But after we eat, I want to thoroughly enjoy that body of yours; my Mate."*

Chapter 44

"Alpha Stavslaka." Connor pulled a chair over from the wall and straddled it in front of the cell. "Let's talk."

He eased down into it with his arms sitting on the back of the chair, glaring at the male behind the century old bars. He knew better than to take his eyes off the bastard. He wanted to kill the male with his bare hands. The bastard caused nothing but pain to those that were around him. The male's only redeeming quality was that he had helped him get his Mate back seventeen years ago.

The cocky male quirked a brow at Connor, and Connor tossed the sandwich through the bars of the cell. Stavslaka caught the sandwich and sat down on the bench inside the cell.

"And what shall we talk about? Hmmm?" Stavslaka smiled. "You and I have no business to attend to."

Connor leaned forward.

Connor stared at Stavslaka through the bars, and his inner Were-panther itched to get out. He scratched over his forearm, hoping to appease the beast.

"How 'bout the topic o'the current sex traffickin', the drugs, guns, et cetera, et cetera, and why all o' the sudden there is heightened activity with the Mulatese Tenebrae. It seems, where there's death; yer there. That be for starters. And if ye think ye'll be threatenin' my Mate again, I'm goin' t' kill ye. 'Tis my right under the law, ye know." He smiled.

Stavslaka took a bite of the sandwich, chewed slowly, and swallowed before wiping his mouth with the back of his hand.

"The only thing I'm going to say is that the Mulatese Tenebrae have made an alliance with someone powerful enough to help their cause. They've been bound to hiding in secrecy for eons. It's time they were given their due. My brother died because he was a Mulatese Tenebrae."

"Aye. I agree, but there are other ways ta be doin' it though. Killin' Alphas and Betas is ne'er goin' t' get the job done."

"Oh but that's where you are wrong. A lot of the Alpha's and Betas have a few hundred years on 'em. They think like thay're back in the old country. They're diseased. If something is diseased, it should be excised."

Connor's glare narrowed. "Whoever's doin' the killin' is a six-pack short of a case."

"On the contrary. I believe Alpha Lavelle's plan is going splendidly."

Connor did a double take. *The male was 'nae serious, was he?*

"Roman?" Connor yelled and, on a growl, said, "He's *nae* behind the killin's! Ye'r a liar!"

Stavslaka shook his head. "No, you idiot. Maximo Lavelle."

The floor suddenly felt like it had dropped out from underneath him. It had been something he suspected but every night when he patrolled the surrounding property for proof of life to bring to Roman and the Commission; he found none.

"Ye mean the bastard is alive? But 'ow can that be? I saw his body burnt t' a crisp."

"Oh, he's alive all right. Let's just say I have *a lot* of information. That's why I am requesting Reciprocal Immunity."

Connor sprang from the chair, launched himself at the metal door of the cell, and ripped it off its hinges. He growled, canines quickly protruding, and he reached for Stavslaka's neck, slamming him up against the wall.

The male clawed at his hand, but Connor didn't care. He squeezed tight and forced his way into the male's mind through a mindlink.

"Ye feckin' Were-fox! Why? Why now?"

"Things should go back to a monarchy of the clans, not this democracy shit that Silas Lavelle wanted here in the States! The days are numbered, and when every Alpha and Beta have been eradicated, Maximo will rise and put to rights what should have been established in the first place! Now take your fucking claws out of my neck!"

Conner shook Stavslaka, his head banging against the cement wall.

"Ye'r an Alpha as well. Ye think ye'll be alive after all this? Think again. If this is Maximo's plan from the beginnin', then ye'r as guit as dead too!"

Stavslaka gripped Connor's wrist, trying to dislodge him. "Maximo has plans for those that pledge to him. There are others helping him as well. Get your filthy hands off of me!"

"Where. Is. He?"

"I don't know," Stavslaka spat out.

"What's goin' t' happen t' Roman?"

"That bastard is as good as dead."

Nae on my watch, he's nae! Connor's claws punched through the neck muscles, and he twisted hard with a roar and tossed the body to the opposite wall. Connor dove after the body, letting his rage erupt, and for once, he wasn't going to stop it as he shredded Stavslaka's body with his claws, ripping the male's arms out of the sockets. When the acrid scent of blood finally penetrated the haze of rage, he stopped.

Connor heavily sank to the floor next to Stavslaka's body. He stared at the blood covering his hands and sucked in huge amounts of air. "Ye will ne'er hurt anyone e'er again."

So, that be the plan. Kill Alphas and Betas, and put Mulatese Tenebrae on the Commission.

He glanced at the shock gracing Stavslaka's features. It was frozen in death upon his face.

Maximo was alive. No one can know.

"This stays with me, fer now. I'll have ta do some diggin' on my own. There's only one way t' do that."

Connor pulled out a cell phone from the small pocket Ascenza had sown into his kilt. Fates, he was blessed with a guit female. But before he called his Mate, he'd better call Roman.

"Hello?"

"Aye, yes, Roman. Sorry ta trouble ye, but I'd like ta buy Sanctuary of Desire."

If ye wanna find a rat, ye gotta dig. Hopefully, what I find will yield the info on others supportin' Maximo.

THE END

About the Author

Miranda Montrose lives with her husband, daughter and the cat, Prince Vladimir, who is aptly named, in southeastern Pennsylvania. To her, family is everything and has a goal of expressing just that very sentiment through everything she writes. She always had a wild imagination, from little on up and is only now expressing herself through her writing.

Miranda works in a busy dental office full time and manages a busy household when she isn't writing.

If you have questions or would like to contact her, she can be reached at mirandamontrose@outlook.com or visit her website http://www.mirandamontrose.com or follow her on Twitter @MirandaMontrose and facebook.com/miranda.montrose.52

Made in the USA
Middletown, DE
16 June 2020